Jilted

RACHAEL JOHNS

Jilted

Refreshed version of *JILTED,* revised by Harlequin HQN

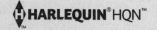
HARLEQUIN® HQN™

ISBN-13: 978-0-373-77936-9

JILTED

This is the revised text of the work, which was first published by Harlequin Enterprises (Australia) Pty. Ltd. in 2012.

Printed in U.S.A.

HARLEQUIN®
www.Harlequin.com

For Granny and (in memory of) Grandpa—
a real-life heroine and hero!

Acknowledgments

My *hugest* thanks to Haylee Kerans and the team at Harlequin Australia for seeing something special in *Jilted* and deciding to publish it—you made my dream into a reality. And also to Aden Rolfe, editor extraordinaire, who seems to know what I mean and how to say it even better than I do.

To *all* my writing buddies who are not only colleagues but also good friends. The following people especially, who read and critiqued *Jilted* way before it was polished: Bec Sampson, Cathryn Hein, Jackie Ashenden, Melissa Smith and Joanne Dannon.

To non-writing but equally awesome friends Peta Sattler and Penny Bruce—you both rock. Thanks for loving *Jilted* too.

This book has already been published in Australia, but I owe its publication in the United States partly to fabulous book reviewer Christi Snow from *Smitten with Reading* who read and reviewed *Jilted* when it first came out and then emailed the team at Harlequin US to say her fellow Americans had to have the chance to read it. Thank you, Christi, for going above and beyond the role of a book reviewer. I will be forever grateful.

Also to my agent, Helen Breitweiser, who came on board after receiving *Jilted* at an Australian Romance Writers conference. Helen read the manuscript on the plane home to America and cried so much the flight attendant asked if she was okay. Ever since then she's been in my corner, and I thank her immensely for that.

And lastly, thanks to my long-suffering family: to Mum, Craig and the boylets! You gave me the precious gift of time...time to write, time to edit, time to dream. Without your support, my writing would not be possible and I *love* you for it.

Glossary of Terms

Arvo—Slang for *afternoon*.

CWA—Acronym for Country Women's Association; a group of rural women who get together to improve life for women, children and families in rural Australia. Known for their fabulous baking and craft skills.

Dag—A teasing term for someone who is not cool; also the term used for the bits of manure that stick to the long wool around a sheep's bottom.

Dill—Slang for *idiot*.

Dizzy-whizzy—When an adult spins a child around by their arms.

Larrikin—The life of the party; someone who is always having fun, a bit rowdy. Usually a young person.

Metho—Shortened term for menthylated spirits; a cleaning product.

P-plates—Holders of a provisional driver's license (driver's permit) must display small squares with a *P* on their windshields and back windows to identify them as new drivers.

Ridgy-didge—Slang for something genuine, the real deal.

Road-train—Semi-trailer truck with two or three trailers.

TAB—Acronym for Totalizator Agency Board; a Betting Shop.

Ute—Shortened version of *utility vehicle* used by farmers; similar to a pickup truck.

Yabby—Small freshwater crayfish, sometimes found in dams on farms.

The Co-op, Hope Junction,
Western Australia—Saturday, 9:30 a.m.

Today. It's true. Well, I don't know, I guess she'll be tak-ing the bus from Perth. Although being a celebrity and all, maybe she's chartered her own jet. She has got a nerve, I couldn't agree more.

   Oh, hi, Mrs. Willet. Just the apples this morning? Yes, I was just chatting about it with Linda. I'm surprised the news isn't front page of today's West, *I thought* she *would have rated higher than the premier opening a regional hospital. You're absolutely right, it's because it's* here. *Small town, back-of-beyond. Oh jeez, but if they knew the truth, if they only knew what she left behind. She was always a bit of a snob at school, none of us could believe it when they started going out. And then when, well, you know...*

   Me? I would have sold my soul to marry him. We all would've. Phwoar...speak of the gorgeous devil.

About Coffee Time, Hope Junction,
Western Australia—Saturday, 9:45 a.m.

The usual, thanks, Sherry, but make it extra strong today. My nerves need it. Oh, you haven't heard? A jet plane apparently. Chartered. You know, I'm not one to listen to gossip but she's bringing her own pilot. A toy-boy, barely over twenty but buff as they come. Or so I'm told. You ask me, he'd have to be pretty damn alluring to hold a candle to our Flynn. Most Saturdays, you say? Well, he'll no doubt be a little flustered this morning. Maybe give him a free slice of your fabulous chocolate cake, and your ear. You're still single, aren't you, dear?

*Outside the post office, Hope Junction,
Western Australia—Saturday, 10:00 a.m.*

Sorry, can't stop to chat, I have to get back to the café. I'm expecting Flynn—he grabs the paper at the Co-op and then comes for a late breakfast. A lot of the foot-ballers do, I feed them up good before the game. Do you think he'll still come? You're right, he might be keeping a low profile. Maybe won't even play today... He's not one to dwell on the past but Mom always says that's a front. Men, they're not as strong as us, you know, they don't get over that sort of knock easily. I bet he still thinks about her. Hard not to when her smug face is on the telly every night. Ouch, what'd ya do that for?
   Oh, hi, Flynn.

*Hairlicious, Hope Junction,
Western Australia—Saturday, 10:10 a.m.*

Sure, I heard about it yesterday, people tell hairdress-ers things, you know. You'd be amazed; sometimes it's a real chore. Yeah, I did her hair once. Between you and me, it's quite thin and flyaway. They must have good hairdressers and makeup artists at Channel Nine. Me neither, I always thought she was a bit skinny, anorexic even. Too worried about her image, I suppose.

She'll not have it easy around here, though. There's not a person within two hundred kilometers who doesn't like Flynn. You are so right, there's probably not a girl anywhere who wouldn't like him. And she won't do well with the blokes, either. They're not as shallow as those city guys. Just because her legs never end and you could wrap your fingers round her waist, won't mean a thing to them. They'll not go near her. Boys from the bush look out for their mates.

What's that, Emma? Is he really? Ten-fifteen. Well, well, well...

CHAPTER ONE

WHEN FLYNN QUARTERMAINE drove into town, he couldn't get a newspaper or pick up his mail without being stopped by someone or other on the main street. He'd lived in the small farming community of Hope Junction—southeast of Perth and affectionately known to locals as Hope—every one of his twenty-nine years. He knew everyone and they knew him. And he was famous. Aside from his legendary streak across the oval on Grand Final day ten years ago, he was the last baby born in the local hospital, having just slipped out before the maternity ward was closed and everyone had to travel farther afield.

What was most embarrassing to Flynn was that people still talked about this. Whenever someone new came to town, or a long-lost relative was passing through, the first thing the introducer would say was, "Meet Flynn, he was the last baby born in our hospital." Nothing about the fact he ran one of the biggest farms in the district. Nothing about almost doubling his family's income by introducing South African Meat Merinos (or SAMMs for short) to their flock. Nothing about how other local farmers followed suit. But then, perhaps he should be grateful people didn't mention other things.

There were some things no guy liked to be reminded about.

Today, however, there wasn't a single mention of

babies. And instead of flocking when they saw him coming, people quickly turned away. It was odd. Flynn picked up some supplies for his mother and drove back out to the family property, keen to return and get onto the football oval, run around with his mates and shake this sense of unease.

The feeling started to dissipate as soon as he turned his ute into Black Stump—the 5,000-acre property that had been in his family for four generations. As corny as it might sound, he loved the place. He'd been raised on the massive homestead, with board games round the fire in winter and fun in the dams—when they had water—in summer. He belonged to this land and it had a way of calming him like no person ever could. Well, not anymore.

But the moment he walked through his mom's kitchen door, the strangeness returned. His heart kicked up a notch and he knew he hadn't been imagining the weirdness in town. In fact, he sensed Saturday was about to get a lot more than strange.

Flynn's grandmother sat at the family's big oak table knitting another tea cozy to be sold at the CWA craft stall. Karina, his mother, hovered at the stove stirring something that smelled a lot like her famous crisis-time minestrone. It was her contribution whenever the townsfolk got together to provide for volunteers in an emergency. And his teenage sister, Lucy, had her iPod around her neck and one foot on the table, painting her toenails a ghastly shade of purple, which no doubt had some ridiculous name like Flashbulb Fuchsia. They were deep in conversation. Or had been, anyway. He could tell, because the moment he stepped inside, the room went eerily silent and they all feigned over-the-top attention to their various tasks. Exactly like every shop he'd stepped into that morning. *What the hell was going on?*

Flynn stomped to the fridge, retrieved an ice-cold can of Coke, cracked it open and turned to face them all.

"Okay. Out with it. Have I grown an extra head or what?" He ran a hand through his blond, freshly cut hair. Even Emma, his hairdresser, had been strangely quiet. She hadn't tried to con him into enhancing his tips as she usually did.

"No need for sarcasm, love."

He tossed a reproachful glare at his mom and, for one terrible second, wondered if someone had come good on their promise to enter him in Australia's much-loved *Farmer Wants a Wife* show. Friends and family had been threatening for years: *You're almost thirty, Flynn.* As if being thirty meant he should suddenly hang up his single cap and find himself a wife, a four-wheel drive and a white picket fence.

He wouldn't do it, though. No matter how good the PR would be for the town, there was no way in hell he was pimping himself in such a manner. Unlike some people he knew, he didn't see the appeal of publicity and bright lights.

Still eyeing him warily, Karina dumped the wooden spoon in the pot, wiped her hands on her apron and sighed. "Well, I suppose if anyone has to tell you, it might as well be me. Sit down, Flynn."

Sit down? He looked long and hard at the three women scattered around the traditional farm kitchen. People only ever said sit down when it was bad news. When someone had been killed or given months to live. But they were all breathing—even Granny, who'd just celebrated eighty years, was healthy and vibrant—and he'd already lost his dad. So what could be so terrible? So dramatic? Who could it be?

Granny stood and beckoned a long, knobbly finger at his sister. "Come on, Lu, you can help me box my tea cozies."

"No, thanks," Lucy said. "I'll help later, Gran, but I wouldn't miss this for an-y-thing."

"Scoot, Luce," shot his mom without breaking his gaze.

Lucy groaned, moaned and did her usual teenage eye roll, but she eventually vacated the room, followed by their grandmother.

"Must be something terrible," mumbled Flynn, collapsing onto a chair. When his mom pulled her stool close and scooped up his hand, his heart went into overdrive. He ripped his hand back, feeling momentarily guilty as hurt flashed across Karina's eyes. But all such emotions were lost when she finally spoke.

"Ellie's coming back."

Flynn opened his mouth but no sound came out. He sat still for a moment, the words echoing in his head.

Then, "Fuck!" He shot out of his chair and stormed onto the veranda.

Ten years! Ten years since she'd left him standing at the altar in a mixture of shock, hurt and embarrassment, questioning why. He thought he'd pulled through, dealt with all those feelings, moved on. But he couldn't have, not the way his eyes were prickling and his heart was pounding.

He spun around, not knowing what to do, before he thumped the veranda post and headed back into the kitchen. Needing to keep his hands busy, he reached for his Coke, but he misjudged and his fingers hit the side of the can, toppling it over.

"Leave it," his mom said. Her lips were pursed and he could tell she was a hairbreadth from tears herself. "It'll be okay."

"No use crying over spilt Coke," he said, trying to make a joke. But his tone wasn't funny and Karina didn't laugh. He knew she was terrified that Ellie's return would send him back to the way he'd been before. She'd already lost her husband. She didn't need to lose her son.

As much as he wanted to retreat to his own space—to forget about the afternoon's game and head to the dam at the far end of their property—he couldn't. He had to maintain the facade for his mom. For the town. He had to pretend he didn't care, pretend the thought of running into Ellie didn't send him into a cold sweat.

It would be easier, he reflected, if he'd found out she'd died. At least that way he'd come to terms with the grief. Surely. Things would be completely different. He wouldn't have to hide photos of her in a box at the back of his wardrobe. People would talk about her fondly, sharing memories, rather than making sure they never uttered her name in his presence. He knew they talked; it's what people in small communities did best. But they never talked about her to him. The town protected him. If people pitied him, he didn't know, but around here, there wasn't any sign that Ellie Hughes had ever existed. It was as if the moment she'd walked out of his life, she'd vacated the planet. In the newsagent, he never saw her face in *TV Week* or on the cover of *Women's Weekly*. But if he went further afield, to Perth or Bunbury, she was constantly in the limelight. Australia adored her. In a way, that hurt Flynn, but it was nothing on the sadness she'd left inside him. The black hole that no attempts at relationships, no casual sex, no nothing, had ever been able to fill.

Working hard to keep his breathing steady, he cleaned up the Coke and recalled some gossip he'd heard at the hairdresser. He might not be able to take his mind off Ellie, but he'd do his damn best to stop his mom thinking about her.

"Some townies are reviving the theatrical society." He ditched the wet tea towel in the sink and leaned back against the table.

"So I heard. Good news travels fast." Karina gestured to the row of tiny nail polish bottles on the table. "Lucy's planning on auditioning. For some reason, she thinks the color of her nails will make all the difference. And of course, she has to test them all first."

Flynn frowned. "You're not going to let her, are you? Year twelve is huge, she should be concentrating on her studies."

Karina raised her eyebrows and smirked. "When did you become so old and stuck in the mud?"

"Don't forget the *wise* bit."

"Whatever," Karina said, waving a hand in front of her face, mimicking her daughter in both language and action. "Lucy won't listen to me. She'll only sulk and pout and ignore her exams altogether if I don't let her get in on this. Besides, it's just a fad. She wanted to start a cheerleading troupe for the Hurricanes last term, remember?"

"Yeah, I suppose."

But his gut felt heavy at the thought of his little sister acting. No matter, the distraction seemed to have worked. His mom was once again stirring her soup with an attentive look upon her face.

Flynn took the chance to slip out the back.

CHAPTER TWO

As the Transwa bus turned into Hope Junction, Ellie tugged the rim of her sports cap down, hoping, with the help of her dark sunnies, that it would cover much of her face. Wearing bland jeans and a man's flannelette shirt, and with her mousy, chocolate-brown hair pulled back in a ponytail, she prayed that no one would recognize Stella Williams—one of Australia's favorite television characters—at least for now. She just wanted the chance to get to Matilda without attention, without anyone confronting her and telling her, in what would no doubt be colorful language, exactly what they thought of her.

But she knew it was only a short-term fix. There were no secrets in the entertainment industry, and even fewer in small towns. Everyone would be on high alert, awaiting her arrival. Next week's glossies would have the news of her sudden departure from the set, with some happy to speculate on the reason while others dug deeper for the truth. Either way, Ellie's return to Hope wouldn't remain a secret for long.

She imagined most people in her situation would be smiling, reminiscing fondly, eager to start adding to their memories. She had fond recollections, too, if she looked back far enough, but they'd all been railroaded by her most painful memory. The memory of making the biggest mistake of her life and, as a result, having to leave the only place she'd ever really called home.

But no one knew the real reason she'd left, not even Matilda. They just thought she was a selfish bimbo, a girl who hadn't fallen far from her parents' tree and couldn't hack commitment any more than she could country life. That hurt, but she'd rather that than the truth.

"Hope Junction," called the driver.

She dared to look up slightly, stealing a quick peek out the window to see if anything had changed. The welcome sign still read Population 1,199, although there'd been at least 1,500 residents when she'd lived here. The Shell servo still had a 1970s feel and the garden center on the corner looked more run-down than ever. The only sign of progress was a new café next to Apex Park—with "About Coffee Time" plastered in big letters across the top of the building.

For a split second, Ellie smiled wistfully, recalling weekends spent in the park, kissing Flynn under the slide, kissing Flynn on the picnic table, kissing Flynn by the bridge, kissing Flynn behind the toilet block. No doubt today's teens would be peeved with the location of the new café and being forced to find alternative premises for canoodling.

"Aren't you getting off here, miss?"

The driver's question broke her reverie. She turned her head slightly. Yep, he was definitely talking to her, but with neither bitterness nor admiration in his voice. He obviously hadn't a clue who she was. Perhaps her tomboy disguise would work after all. Perhaps she'd be able to walk the short kilometer to Matilda's house, dump her things and get to the hospital without causing much of a stir.

If she were honest with herself, it wasn't running into locals that most scared her. It was just the one local, the resident who, despite still being a constant player in her thoughts, she was absolutely petrified to see. How could she ever face him after what had happened? If he ever deigned to speak to her again, to hear her out—and she wouldn't blame him if he didn't—what could she possibly say? *Sorry* wouldn't even begin to cut it.

Not taking any chances, Ellie leaped off the bus, swiped her rucksack and suitcase from the hold and, with eyes trained firmly on the cracked pavement, began jogging toward Matilda's cottage. Although it was longer, she took the back way, past the football oval and the swimming pool, avoiding the main street. Did Flynn still play football? She glanced at her watch, knowing if she hung around a couple more hours—and if the Hurricanes were playing a home game—she'd find out. A shiver shot through her at the thought and she picked up her pace, all the more eager to get to her destination.

In all the years Ellie had been in Sydney, Matilda had visited faithfully every Christmas. And although Ellie was always invited to loads of high-society parties, there was no one she'd rather spend the holidays with than her warm, fun-loving godmother. Matilda had never once questioned Ellie's decision to leave Hope. She never mentioned Flynn, and although Ellie had been desperate on a zillion occasions to ask how he was doing, she'd always been too scared to inquire.

Flynn was always the best-looking guy at school, in the town—hell, the world wouldn't have been an overstatement. Captain of the footy team, tall, strong but still a bit lanky, tanned to perfection. He had a grin that made you feel all warm and liquidy whenever he flashed it your way. It'd be unrealistic—*stupid*—to think that his heart had stayed true to her. Why would it? Lord knows there'd been enough girls waiting on the sidelines. He'd probably moved on quickly and found someone else, married someone else, maybe even had babies with someone else. Happy, settled down, in love. That would be bad, really bad. Ellie couldn't bear to think about it, much less to know, and had avoided finding out for a decade. Flynn Stuart Quartermaine was taboo. Someone Matilda never mentioned and someone Ellie never searched for. But now, now she'd have no choice. Now she'd have to face what he'd become. Whoever that was. Whoever it was with. She tried to console herself. Maybe he'd left town?

For a moment hope sparred with terror in her heart, but then reality knocked. Flynn would never leave Hope. This area was in his blood, part of who he was. Flynn wouldn't be Flynn without his farm and country football.

Ellie came to a stop, realizing that she'd made it to the cottage without running into trouble. She couldn't help but smile at this small success. At the end of an avenue off the main street, it was just as she remembered. Only Matilda could get away with living in a quirky, bright purple house, complete with red roof and yellow awnings. Or rather, *half-repainted* yellow awnings. She closed her eyes for a second, cringing as she imagined the sixty-nine-year-old up there on a ladder doing the painting herself.

"Why must you do such ridiculous things?" Ellie said aloud, looking at the house. If Mat wanted to court danger, she should go bungee jumping or something on one of her holidays. As a respected and once well-known travel writer, money couldn't be an issue for her. And even if it were, Ellie would have paid for the whole damn house to be painted, renovated and decked out in brand-new furniture. Anything to prevent her godmother from taking such a fall. And from that height, she was lucky not to have done *much* worse than a broken ankle.

Ellie shuddered. If Matilda hadn't injured herself, she

wouldn't be here. Life could change direction in an instant; every little decision had the power to affect your existence in unfathomable ways. And other people's. Sometimes Ellie thought it a miracle people had the courage to get out of bed in the mornings.

Enough philosophizing, she told herself. She had keys to find, cars to start, crazy old women to collect and mollycoddle. Because, by golly, Matilda would be mollycoddled. Her godmother never sat still long enough for Ellie to do anything much special for her, to repay her for all she'd done, but now she wouldn't have a choice. Ellie would do everything she could to make Matilda feel loved. She planned on being so focused and dedicated to her role as carer that she wouldn't have time to think or stress about what the locals were saying behind her back.

Although the plastic frog had jumped to the other side of the old wooden veranda, the key was still there, tucked inside, just as Ellie suspected. She stood on the hot-pink welcome mat where she'd first landed as a confused and heartbroken fifteen-year-old, then let herself in, smiling at the bombardment of familiar smells. Matilda had been in hospital for two days now, but this place was so infused with aromatherapy essences that Ellie reckoned it would smell like a flower shop even if she'd been gone a year.

Dumping her bags in the living room, Ellie quickly tidied the kitchen table, wanting the house to be in order for Matilda's return. Her thoughts turned to dinner and what from her limited repertoire she might prepare, but when she opened the fridge, and then the pantry, dismay set in. Both empty, bar half a packet of sugar, two tins of baked beans, some old crackers and Moroccan mint tea bags. What on earth did Mat live on? Whatever the answer, one thing was clear: Ellie would have to go shopping. Deep down she'd known she couldn't hole up in the cottage for the duration of her stay, but it had been a lovely fantasy. Still, it was just after midday. Mat would have eaten lunch already and Ellie couldn't wait to see her.

She found the car keys in the leaf-shaped bowl in the hall and was about to leave when she decided on one final touch. Racking her brain, trying to recall what she'd learned about essences and oils while living in this house, Ellie remembered something about lemon and ylang-ylang being good for convalescing. Once a few drops were in two of Mat's many burners and the candles lit, she smiled and left the cottage.

She started the vintage Holden Premier and turned toward the hospital. Once out on the road, however, the calm instilled in her at the cottage quickly dispersed. Whatever way she looked at it, she'd have to deal with someone at the hospital—nurses, doctors, orderlies, who knows? More nervous than she ever was in front of the camera, she chomped down hard on her lower lip, hoping the pain would distract from the worry. She knew that once she saw Matilda and had been enveloped in one of her magical hugs she could face anything. No one would dare to say a word to her in her godmother's presence. All she had to do was get there. Because, despite what the town thought of Ellie, Mat was a well-respected resident. She was almost a local dignitary due to all the books she'd published, not to mention the fact she did so much charity work. She was held in such esteem that most overlooked her slightly wacky way of living and dressing, while others wholeheartedly embraced her quirkiness.

Sucking air into her lungs, Ellie found a parking

space right outside the entrance and gave herself a final pep talk.

"Think of it as a test. If you survive this, the town will be a piece of cake."

Inside the small, one-ward hospital, she found the front desk unmanned. A sign informed her that the receptionist was on lunch and all inquiries were to be directed to the nurses' desk. One hurdle down.

Ellie headed along the familiar corridor. She'd been here many a time in her teens when Flynn had broken limbs or dislocated things on the football field. Nothing had changed. She kind of hoped there'd be another sign on the nurses' desk directing her back to reception—then she'd simply hunt Mat down on her own.

She had no such luck. Behind the desk stood a glamorous nurse in a short medical ensemble that looked more appropriate for a fancy dress party than the requirements of the job.

The nurse looked up as Ellie padded toward her. She flicked a long, blond ponytail over one shoulder and her perfect green irises glistened as if she were a pirate laying eyes on a monumental treasure.

"Well. Well. Well." She looked slowly up and down as if assessing Ellie's less-than-fashionable attire. "If it isn't Elenora. The runaway bride returns."

Pain speared Ellie's chest. At the nurse's reference to one of the most regrettable moments of her life, she summoned all she'd learned in front of the camera and tried for an air of polite indifference.

"Lauren." Ellie smiled tightly, quaking inside. At the same time, she clocked the nurse's ring finger, her heart relaxing at the absence of any marital bling. Lauren Simpson had always had her sights on Flynn. "I'm here to collect Matilda. Can you tell me her room number, please?"

Lauren scoffed. "This isn't the big smoke, princess. We don't have hundreds of rooms to choose from. She's the second door on the left. I'll get her discharge papers ready."

"Thank you." As Ellie turned, she screwed up her face in disbelief. Some things never changed. On the other hand, never would she have imagined Lauren becoming a nurse. But all thoughts of her archenemy left as she came to Matilda's door, which was slightly ajar. The room was quiet and dimly lit, the antithesis of its occupant. She peered in, noting two foot-shaped lumps at the end of the bed.

"Mat?" she called, knocking at the same time.

There was slight movement under the covers and then a loud shriek. "Is that you, girl? Jeez, Els, you don't have to knock. Get yourself in here quick smart."

Grinning, Ellie pushed the door but almost stumbled as she caught sight of her godmother. She tried to hide the shock on her face. Mat looked ghastly. Usually a towering, well-built woman, she now seemed frail and tiny in this hospital bed. Her face was sallow, and gray bags drooped under her big brown eyes despite the enforced rest.

"What are you gawping at, sweet?" came Matilda's disapproving voice. "Never seen a sick old woman before? Get over here and give us a cuddle."

Relaxing, Ellie rushed to the bed and climbed up alongside her old friend. "The only thing sick about you is your sense of humor." She laughed into Mat's hair as they wrapped their arms around each other and clung tightly. "Golly, it's good to see you again."

They stayed like that for an aeon before Matilda, her

voice slightly choked, pulled back, tugged off Ellie's cap and tucked the stray strands of hair behind her ears. "Don't go getting all sentimental on me. Hysterics won't get me out of this prison. Which better be why you're here."

"Why else?" Ellie shrugged and recognition flashed between them.

Matilda opened her mouth as if about to speak but Lauren swanned into the room.

"Afternoon, Ms. T," she said with a warmth Ellie had never witnessed in her before. Ever. "Looks like today's your lucky day." She turned to Ellie. "Sheila, the other nurse on duty, will be in to help Ms. Thompson get ready. If you can come with me, I'll run you through her pain relief medication and hire you out a wheelchair."

No, was what Ellie wanted to say. *I'll just stay right here, while you fetch the chair and tablets.* But perhaps she was overreacting, her imagination getting away with her. Although Lauren's red fingernails were inappropriately long for a nurse, how much damage could she really do?

"Okay," Ellie said. She leaned over and kissed Matilda on the cheek. "I'll be right back."

They were barely out of Mat's earshot before Lauren started. "You've got some nerve coming back here."

"Still predictable, I see," Ellie replied, before she thought better of it. Probably not a good idea to bait the wildcat.

Lauren froze. Her eyes narrowed and her hands moved to her hips. "What's that's supposed to mean?"

For a split second Ellie felt as if she were back in high school. "I thought you might have come up with something more original, but no, you said what I'm expecting everyone will say."

Ellie saw her opponent's fists bunch. "Whatever. You think you're so fabulous, don't you? Well, not in Hope you're not. Apart from Matilda, no one wants you here. Especially not Flynn."

Ellie's rib cage tightened. She didn't want to talk about Flynn, especially not with Lauren. With false calm, she tried to steer the conversation elsewhere. "I'm only here for Mat." Damn, even she could hear the crack in her voice. "So if you don't mind telling me what I need to know about her painkillers and recovery, I'd like to take her home, please."

"Always about you," muttered Lauren. She turned and headed back toward the nurses' station.

Fifteen minutes later and not nearly quickly enough, Ellie and Sheila had Matilda settled as best they could in the front seat of the golden Premier.

"Are you sure you're comfortable?" Ellie asked as she reversed the beast out of the parking spot.

Matilda shuffled slightly in her seat. "Don't worry about me. Did she leave claw marks?"

Ellie summoned a chuckle. Typical Matilda, worrying about everyone else when she needed all her energies for herself.

"You mean Lauren? She didn't bother me. I just can't believe she's a nurse."

"Stranger things have happened at sea," Mat surmised, quoting one of her favorite phrases. "Besides, everyone knows she only did it for the cute, wealthy doctors."

Ellie couldn't help but laugh out loud. "Has she had any luck?"

"None whatsoever!" Matilda roared. "Oh, we've had plenty of eligible doctors pass through. All are more than happy to pamper her desires while in town. But much to her dismay, none of them ask her to go with them when they move on." Matilda paused, then added with a wicked tone, "Perhaps she should have become an actress instead."

Ellie's laugh was drier this time. "Trust me, there's no surefire success there, either."

On-screen and off, the best love she'd ever had was during her time in Hope Junction. Misfortune had played a hand in the demise of that relationship, and she'd been unlucky in love ever since.

"Here we are," she announced.

A fact about small-town life: it didn't take any time at all to get from one place to another, which wasn't always a good thing. Travel time had its perks—opportunities to ponder, talk, read or just rest. But Matilda's whole face lit up as she stared delightedly at her cottage.

"Now we just have to work out how to unfold the wheelchair and get you inside."

An "ugh" escaped Matilda's lips and the joy on her face softened. She gestured to her plastered limb. "If this is God's idea of a joke, I'm crossing to the dark side."

Ellie smiled. She wasn't sure she believed in God— some days she did, some she didn't, and some it didn't seem possible that there wasn't a divine creator of some kind. More often than not she had her doubts. Matilda's beliefs weren't conventional, either.

"Perhaps God is just trying to tell you to slow down, rest a little."

Matilda aimed her middle finger skyward. "Bollocks to that."

CHAPTER THREE

AT THE HAMMERING on his front door, Flynn shook his head and stumbled from the couch. He'd been there for the past couple of hours, staring at a mark on the wall. His stomach groaned, alerting him to the fact it was probably way past lunch.

"Flynn, what *are* you doing in there?" Lucy's high-pitched shout shot through his head. "You'd better be ready."

"What are you talking about?" He opened the door and felt his body tighten at the sight of his little sister. Dressed in black tights, ridiculously high-heeled boots, a long-sleeved T-shirt that looked three sizes too small and a skirt he practically needed a magnifying glass to see, Lucy was doing a fabulous impersonation of a street-side hooker. He couldn't imagine why his mom was letting her loose like that. Maybe she'd used up all her parenting energies dealing with him in his wayward years.

"Flynn!" She seethed angry air between her teeth and held up her chunky Hope Hurricanes purple-and-orange scarf, proceeding to wave it in his face. "You're supposed to be driving me into town for the game." She looked him up and down, her eyes widening as she took in his holey track pants and scruffy sweater. "And you're supposed to be playing."

"Damn." The game had completely slipped his mind. He rubbed his forehead, which had been pulsing with nonstop pain since he'd heard about Ellie. Running up and down the oval, tackling sweaty blokes and kicking out his tension could be just what he needed, but the rest of it… Having to make small talk, knowing that everywhere he looked people would be talking about him, pitying him. He needed that about as much as a rhino in his top paddock.

"You've forgotten, haven't you?"

"No," he snapped, giving a quick nod to her outfit. "I was just thinking that I should get you an overcoat. You'll freeze in that, not to mention give the boys a heart attack."

"You're not my father, Flynn. Even if you act as if you're about ninety-five." She lifted her chin, daring him to disagree.

"Thank the Lord," he replied, beginning to soften. But Lucy's words made him think. Did he really give off that impression? Was he turning into an old grump? Or was it just all the talk of Ellie that had put him off balance?

"Besides," she continued, oblivious to the churnings of his mind. "This is what all the girls are wearing. You don't want me to be an outcast, do you?"

Flynn had to hide a grin. She was such a drama queen, but her antics were distracting him from thoughts of his ex and lifting his mood. That had to be a good thing.

"Luce, you could never be an outcast. You're gorgeous, intelligent and, most important, you're my sister. That's pretty much got you covered."

"Hardy-ha," she replied, but her full-blown smile told him she'd forgiven his grumpiness.

"I'll be right back," he said, turning toward his bedroom to throw on his gear. He'd play the game, let off some tension and make a quick retreat before anyone could corner him. Footy would help clear his head.

Five minutes later, Flynn turned the ute onto the main road into town. Lucy switched on the radio, grinning as Paul Kelly came blaring out. Paul was the one sound they both liked. The twelve years between them meant there weren't many such bands.

Trying to relax, Flynn tapped his fingers on the steering wheel along to the music. Out of the corner of his eye, he saw Lucy shift in her seat to face him.

"You and Ellie could've been like this song."

He cringed. As if the end of their relationship hadn't been tragic enough. He'd never spoken about Ellie with Lucy, or about what happened after she'd left, and he didn't plan on starting now. Lucy was now the age he and Ellie were when they started going out, but she wouldn't understand. She had one hyped-up crush after another but never stayed with a boy long enough to fall in love.

When he didn't reply, she elaborated. "I reckon Ellie did you a favor running off. I mean, I don't really remember her and she may have been really nice, but Ms. Dawes, our sex-ed teacher, says teen marriages are twenty times more likely to end in divorce than other marriages."

"Is that right?" Frankly, he would have liked the chance to have been in on the decision whatever the outcome of their would-be marriage.

"Uh-huh. Not that that old troll would know," she giggled. "I don't reckon anyone's ever asked *her* to marry them."

Flynn let out his breath, thinking Lucy had moved on to other thoughts. Just to make sure, he raised a new topic. "So, how's school going? Mom said you're doing well."

"S'pose so. Doesn't really matter. For the things I wanna do, I don't need uni."

"You're seventeen, Luce, you have no idea what you want to do."

"Shut up, Flynn, there you are acting all ancient again. You're so boring. No wonder Ellie left you." She gasped and clapped her hand over her mouth.

Flynn's whole body clenched. He'd never entertained the possibility that Ellie had thought him boring—he still didn't—but the words hurt more than he cared to admit. She had chosen a showbiz career and life in the city over a partnership on the farm. Her dreams were bigger than rural Western Australia. And him.

"I'm sorry, Flynn. That was out of line."

"Yeah, it was."

"And it's crap, too. No one thinks you're boring. Jeez, my friends all idolize you and the women in town all drool over you. You could have anyone you want."

He chuckled at the irony. "Perhaps the three women in my life are enough?"

"Three!" Lucy shrieked. "Who's the… Ooh, me, Mom and Gran." She looked disappointed. "I thought I was going to be the first to know something exciting."

"Yep. You, Mom and Gran." He reached out and rubbed her head affectionately.

"Hey, don't mess the hair." She lifted a hand for protection but smiled nevertheless.

For the rest of the journey, Lucy nattered on about the girls at school, the boy they all craved and their plans for Schoolies Week, which, thankfully, was still six months away. It may have been over a decade since Flynn had partied on Rottnest Island during Schoolies, but he knew things wouldn't have changed too much. Seventeen-year-old boys had one thing on their mind and one thing only.

"Crap, we're late," Lucy said as Flynn pulled into the oval and searched for a place to park. Already the field was bordered with cars, people sitting on hoods, eating pies and drinking soft drinks, waving banners as they waited for the game to start. Stupidly, he scanned the crowds for Ellie—she'd been a faithful supporter of the Hurricanes and never missed a game when she lived here, but of course, things were different now. Even if she were in town, it was unlikely she'd make a game of country football a high priority.

Lucy practically jumped out the car before he'd put the hand brake on, and definitely before he'd taken the keys out of the ignition.

"Come straight back here after the game," he yelled, pretty certain she didn't hear him, or at least didn't want to.

DURING THE MATCH, Flynn didn't look at the crowd and tried not to make eye contact with his fellow players. He scored more goals than he had in a while but not enough to give the Hurricanes the victory they'd been missing lately. When it was over, he went to wait for Lucy. He knew his quick departure would provide more fodder for the gossips, but that didn't make him any more inclined to stay around.

Lucy took her sweet time, though, eventually arriving with a giggling teenage friend on each side. Opening the passenger door, she leaned into the car. "I'm going to Kara's," she announced.

Flynn opened his mouth to object—no way was he hanging in town while she had fun with the girls—but she got in first.

"I've already called Mom and she's fine with it. She said I can stay over and she'll pick me up after church tomorrow." She stepped back next to her friends.

"Fine." Flynn's hand was already poised on the gear-stick when pale, delicate fingers—complete with red nails—reached out to hold open the passenger door.

"Hiya, Flynn."

Flynn fought the urge to shuffle closer to the driver's door as Lauren Simpson slipped into the passenger seat. It was hard not to ogle her ample cleavage, which was only further accentuated by her tight silver top. Not many got away with such outlandish fashion in Hope Junction, and most simply wore Hurricanes sweaters to the game, but Lauren was stunning and on her it worked. Still, he'd never found her kind of beauty attractive.

She rested one of her perfect hands on his thigh. He tensed, cursing himself for not changing out of his footy shorts.

"You're not going home, are you, Flynn?" Her sing-song voice grated on his nerves.

"Actually..." That's exactly where he planned on heading. The last thing he wanted to do was socialize right now.

"I understand," she began, in an annoyingly sympathetic tone, "that today would have been difficult for you. But it's times like these you need to be around friends. People who care about you, people who understand you." Her nails drifted a little higher up his thigh. "What do you say? Come to the pub with us?"

He looked past Lauren to see Lucy a few meters away. She was beaming like a loony and holding both thumbs up. *Go on,* she mouthed at him theatrically.

"Who's us?" asked Flynn. He didn't want Lauren getting any ideas.

"Oh, you know, the usual crowd. Rats will be there."

Rats, nicknamed so because he'd had a rat's tail haircut since he was in kindergarten. That is, until a few weeks ago when he proposed to Whitney, who refused to accept unless he cut it off. Rats, who just happened to be the best mate Flynn had.

He still didn't want to go. Pubs hadn't been real appealing since his father's accident, when he'd been forced to get his life back on track. But this wasn't just about the pub. Maybe he should make an appearance and hold his head up high. Show everyone he didn't need their sympathy, that ten years was a long time. Definitely long enough for him and Ellie to be in the same shire without him losing the plot. Again.

"Do you need a lift, then?" He forced a smile to his lips.

"Sure." Lauren's face lit up. She poked her head back out the car for a moment. "Meet you there, girls."

"Shove over. We can fit," said a voice from outside.

Flynn leaned forward to wave at Emma and another local chick, Linda.

"I don't think so." Lauren pulled the door shut before they could negotiate. "Drive on, Flynn. They'll be fine."

Ignoring Lauren, he pushed a button to wind down the passenger window. "If you ladies want, you can hop on the back."

Giggles and shrieks ensued as Flynn hitched the girls up onto the tray. He took the opportunity to pull his jeans out of his bag and tug them on before getting back in. He barely had three hundred meters to drive, so there wasn't much danger. Not on the road, anyway.

When Flynn opened the door at the top pub for Lauren and her friends, however, the hackles rose on the back of his neck. It wasn't that he never came to the pub, but it was rare. Years ago this joint had been his first port of call whenever he'd wanted to drown his sorrows. The place they came whenever they lost a game of football—which hadn't been nearly as often back then—and always where they came to celebrate a win. After Ellie had left he'd come even more. It had become his second home.

Back then, he'd step inside and smile. The aroma of cigarette smoke mixed with beer, sweat and cheap perfume always comforted. The run-down decor? Strangely alluring. The music? Exactly what he would have chosen. The people? Folks he'd grown up with, folks he'd die for. Folks he knew would do the same for him.

But times had changed. Although he still loved his football, he wasn't the carefree larrikin of a decade ago. Not frequently anyway. He was a long way from the Flynn who'd streaked across the oval. In the years since, the law had sent the smokers outside, and although he wasn't one of them, there was something wrong about a pub without that smell. New owners had renovated and The Commercial Hotel had lost its rural character. Its beige walls with a chocolate feature and the leather-upholstered bar stools could have been transplanted from any city establishment. The people he'd loved had moved on or changed. At least the music still had the right vibe.

He barely had the chance to nod at Rats and Whitney or take in the others hanging around before Lauren had an arm round him and was practically licking his ear.

"My shout, Flynn. What are you having?"

"Just a Coke, thanks." He extracted his limbs from hers and moved along the bar to Rats.

"Hey, mate." Rats slapped Flynn on the back and grinned. "Good to see ya. S'pose you've heard?"

"Grapevine wouldn't be working if I hadn't." Flynn looked straight ahead.

"Doubt she'll be here for long," continued Rats. "She's only back to help Ms. T. Surely a broken ankle won't take long to mend. Right?"

Flynn wanted to ask if anyone had seen her yet, but

he didn't want to look like he gave a damn. He *didn't* give a damn. So instead he said, "Free country. She can go where she likes."

"True, true." Rats took a sip of beer and pulled Whitney into his side. "So, mate, we've been talking and you don't have to say yes straightaway but…"

"There's no one we'd rather want as our best man," gushed Whitney, reaching past Rats to take Flynn's hands. "Please, please say yes."

Hell. Flynn supposed he should have seen this coming. His friends hadn't planned a long engagement and Rats had been decked out in the best-man suit the day Ellie had left him standing at the altar of St. Pete's. But today? Just the thought of setting foot inside a church made his skin crawl.

"Sure," he managed. "It'd be an honor."

"Yippee!" As Whitney shrieked, she leaned forward and kissed Flynn on the lips. It was only quick, and entirely platonic, but whoops went up around the pub.

"Did he say yes?" Lauren returned with a bottle of champers, four delicate glass flutes and no sign of a Coke. "This calls for a toast." Behind her were Emma and Linda with another bottle and more glasses.

As glasses were filled, Rats edged close to Flynn. "I'll get you that Coke, mate. You don't have to drink to take part in the toast." Rats was one of the few people who knew just how dependent he'd become on booze before his dad died.

"Don't be stupid," snapped Flynn, suddenly feeling like a tiny shot of bubbles would work wonders for his tension-infused body. "I *can* handle a glass on a special occasion."

"Fair enough." Rats held up his palms in surrender,

but Flynn couldn't miss the worry in his friend's eyes. "Just looking out for you."

Flynn didn't reply. He was tired of people looking out for him, like he was some sort of pathetic child. He took a glass and raised it along with everybody else's.

"To Flynn," Lauren said, staring at him as if he were the only person in the room, "for completing our fabulous bridal party."

"To Flynn," chorused his friends.

He took a gulp and only as the bubbles caressed his throat did he register Lauren's words. Dinner was ordered soon after, and once the pub grub had been devoured the group broke up—some playing pool, others chatting near the dartboard. This was Flynn's chance to escape, but just as he was about to make a sly departure, Lauren pulled up a stool next to him. She barely sat on it, however, and Flynn got the impression she was angling for a spot on his lap, instead.

"You know," she drawled in an unmistakably seductive tone, "the best man gets first pick of the bridesmaids."

"Is that so?" Flynn took another sip to stop himself from saying the first thing that came into his head.

"It's tradition. And it just so happens I'm maid of honor." Was she actually singing her words? "Care for a top-up?" she asked, swaying the half-full bottle in his face and pointing to his glass.

Rats and Whitney were now wrapped in each other's arms, ignoring the rest of the pub. Emma was chatting up the new barman and Linda appeared to be kicking her brother's butt at darts. Flynn looked again at the bottle and then back to Lauren.

"Just one more."

WHEN THE BOTTLE was gone, Flynn ordered Lauren a glass of wine and a beer for himself. For a second he thought twice about the choice. Common sense almost won, but then he glanced around him at the scene of country people having good, clean fun—the music loud, the laughs many, the atmosphere charged and happy—and he wanted that. It'd been years since alcohol had owned him. He'd only have one more.

One became two, two became four and before he knew it, he'd dragged Lauren onto the makeshift dance floor and was partying like it was 1999. As the barman called for last drinks, Lauren sank her arms around Flynn's neck and pressed her curves against the steely length of his body. Of course, he reacted. He wouldn't be male if he didn't.

"I've had a great night, Flynn."

"Me, too." His words slurred slightly.

"You can't drive home like this. The cops will pick you up for sure."

He leaned his cheek against her hair and breathed in her pungent berry scent. "I'll sleep in the back of the ute."

"Now, Flynn…" Lauren's hands crawled down to cup his buttocks and pull him tightly against her. Her words slithered into his ear on hot, wanton breath. "I've got a much better idea."

And then her lips were accosting his. Her tongue took liberties as it swept his mouth, probing for access. His hands floundered as he tried to grab out for balance, to latch on to reality before he did something he might regret, but he got hold of a breast instead, the soft, round orb sending short, sharp messages to his brain. His body took on a life of its own. He couldn't remember the last time he was kissed—the farm had been his sole focus for quite some time—and suddenly it didn't seem like such a bad idea. He was twenty-nine, for crying out loud. He should have a little fun while he could. Besides, since he'd been in Lauren's company, he hadn't thought about Ellie once.

So he kissed Lauren back. Snaked his hands up her spine and then her neck, sliding his fingers into her long, blond locks. He felt his blood pump south and pulled back slightly to look into her eager eyes. "Let's get outta here."

Rats gripped Flynn's shoulder as they headed for the door. "You sure you want to do this, mate?" His eyes were trained on Lauren giggling at Flynn's side. "You've had a fair bit to drink."

Now Flynn knew how Lucy felt when *he* started with the preachy talk. It got old and boring fast.

"Thanks, but I can look after myself."

Outside, Lauren pushed him against the ute, fishing her fingers into his pocket for his car keys. "I'm driving. I only had one drink."

"Of course." Grinning, he leaned back against the vehicle, his hands clasped behind his head as she took longer to dig than was strictly necessary.

"You like that, Flynn?" She plucked the keys from his jeans but, not at all coy, she continued her exploration of his crutch, rubbing her palm up and over the denim at his groin. His hips angled forward of their own accord and he grabbed Lauren's wrist.

"Let's go."

"My feelings exactly."

Lauren opened the passenger door and Flynn slumped inside, his boots kicking a collection of empty Coke cans at his feet. She slid into the driver's side and took in the mess. "I thought you'd take better care of your vehicle, Flynn Quartermaine."

He glanced at her. "Um…" Even his mom didn't nag him about such things.

"Relax," Lauren laughed. She started the ute and, after quickly backing out, laid her hand against Flynn's taut thigh. "It's not your housekeeping I'm interested in."

Chuckling, he sucked in a breath as Lauren's hand again ventured upward. She toyed with his belt buckle, skillfully undoing it without the car veering even slightly off the straight and narrow.

"You nurses are multiskilled," he said, wondering if he should put his hand against her leg or cop a feel of one of her breasts. Both options had seemed appealing back in the parking lot, but now, in the confined space of the car, where his breathing felt constricted by the heady scent of her perfume, he wasn't so sure.

"You haven't seen anything yet," she purred. His eyes almost left their sockets as she opened his zipper and slipped her hand inside his jeans—inside his jocks, in fact.

"You think we should pull over?" He only just managed the words. Her soft, skillful fingers curled around his erection and began to tickle his balls. His breathing intensified. His pulse thudded through his veins. Heat surged beneath her touch. But it was a surreal experience, as if he was hovering outside his body, looking in. He barely heard Lauren's reply.

"It's okay, Flynn, we're almost at my place." Within seconds she'd pulled into a rough gravel driveway. The car came to a stop and a giggling Lauren opened the passenger door.

"You just gonna sit there all night, staring at the real estate?" She wiggled her hips in rhythm to her words.

He winced at the sound of her voice, a sharp jolt rushing through his head. The view of her skinny legs, held together by a denim skirt too short for the season, blurred in front of him. He blinked to clear his vision.

"Had a bit too much to drink, Flynn-y boy?" She reached in and took his hand, trying to pull him out of the car. "Never mind. Nurse Lauren has the perfect medicine. Come on."

Stumbling a little, he trekked up the porch steps, fighting the urge to sit down while Lauren unlocked the door. She switched on lights, which almost blinded him, and offered him a drink.

"No, thanks," he managed, although a voice inside told him a long glass of icy water might be a good idea.

"Hope you don't mind if I do." Grabbing his shoulders, she ushered him into the living room and pushed him down on the couch. "You just wait there. I'll be right back."

He flopped his head against the back of the leather sofa and took a few moments just to sit. Fancy antique vases and massive, gold-framed paintings of famous Aussie landscapes swam around the room—this was her parents' house, but they were overseas at the moment, on one of the travel tours they ran. His gut churned. He was contemplating a dash to the bathroom when Lauren skipped into the room.

"Hey, mister, you're looking a little worse for wear." She straddled his hips, her skirt riding up as she maneuvered on top of him. He realized his fly was still undone. Her warmth seeped onto his groin and he swayed a little, feeling woozy.

"Have you lost your knickers?" he asked, his voice hoarse.

"You noticed." She wiggled her hips more and pressed

down. There was only the cotton of his jocks between them now. She placed a champagne flute on the side table and palmed her hands against his cheeks. "You want me, don't you, Flynn?"

CHAPTER FOUR

ELLIE'S SIDES WERE aching from laughing so hard. Matilda had always been like a drug she couldn't get enough of. But as much as she would love to have stayed up later, listening to stories of what Mat had been up to since they were last together in Sydney, she'd be blind not to notice that her godmother was wilting. She'd counted at least ten yawns in the past three minutes, and the bags under Matilda's eyes were hanging even heavier than before. Her weight loss couldn't be intentional—Matilda didn't believe in fads like dieting. Ellie would never say so, but Mat seemed a lot older than the six months it had been since they'd seen each other. And it worried her.

She feigned a yawn herself. "I'm sorry, Mat, but I'm going to have to call it a night."

"You're not jet-lagged?" Matilda snorted. "First sign of old age, they tell me."

"Like you'd know," teased Ellie, stretching up out of the beanbag she was sitting in at Matilda's feet. "You could do with some rest, too. I don't want Lauren on my back for not looking after you."

"You know I hate this." Matilda sighed, gripping Ellie's shoulder as she got out of the old floral armchair. Matilda had always been so independent—bloody-minded, many would have called it. She'd never married—Ellie guessed she didn't want to be anyone's unpaid housekeeper—and frequently traveled to exotic places not populated by your average tourist.

"I know," Ellie replied. They started slowly toward the bathroom, Ellie trying not to smother her friend but terrified of her taking another fall. "And if you do as you're told, you'll be back to your wicked ways in no time. But I'm here until you are."

Ellie heard Matilda sniff, but she covered it quickly. "You are a true friend. Thank you."

"What? For cooking baked beans on stale crackers and almost killing you with rotten eggs?"

To call dinner a disaster would have been kind. Forgetting that country shops weren't open on Saturday afternoons, Ellie had made do with what she could find: baked beans and eleven eggs from the chicken coop. Matilda assured her that some would have been fresh that morning. But Ellie had been a city girl too long and had forgotten how to test which were fresh and which weren't.

Matilda pressed a hand against her chest and laughed. "I've had a lot worse in my time."

After promising to make it up with a feeding frenzy tomorrow, Ellie stood by while Matilda washed her face and brushed her teeth. She helped her hobble over to the toilet and left the room to give her some privacy. Then she came back to help her up and usher her into her room.

"There. Are you sure you're comfortable?" she asked, sitting down gently on the edge of Mat's bed.

"As comfy as I can be sharing a bed with this." Matilda gestured again to the chunky plaster that went from her toes halfway up her calf.

Ellie knew Matilda's jokes were her way of coping, of lightening the mood. She desperately wanted to snuggle up to Mat like they'd done when Ellie first arrived all those years ago. When she was a lonely, lost, washed-up teen, feeling totally abandoned by the one person who was supposed to love her. But tonight she thought Matilda might take her cuddles the wrong way, as sympathy for her injuries. And if there was one thing Mat hated, it was sympathy. So instead, Ellie patted her hand, kissed her on the cheek and stood.

"Shall I take my old room?"

Matilda cursed and a look of horror flashed across her face. "Oh, I'm a silly old fool." She tried to hoist herself up.

"Sit," Ellie ordered.

"I've been jabbering on all afternoon and you haven't even had a chance to unpack or freshen up. About your room…" Matilda's voice trailed off.

Ellie rushed forward and wrapped her arms around Matilda. She couldn't resist another proper hug. "You *are* a silly old fool. I'm here to look after you and don't you forget it."

In the end, she lay on the bed until Matilda had fallen asleep, which wasn't long at all. The house then seemed quiet without Mat's endless chatter, and Ellie's thoughts returned quickly to the one thing she'd been trying *not* to think about. While Lauren had launched right into the subject of Flynn Quartermaine, Matilda hadn't mentioned him at all. Ellie thought the taboo might have been lifted now she was back in Hope Junction, but it seemed her godmother was leaving that conversation for her to start. And she would. Soon.

Thoughts of just how soon were interrupted as she pushed open the door of her old bedroom. Expecting Mat to have turned the room to other uses, she gasped aloud at the sight in front of her. The room was exactly how she'd left it. *Exactly*. Goose bumps erupted across her flesh.

Matilda had cleaned and dusted, but aside from that, everything was just as Ellie had left it on that fateful morning. Teenage posters, her collection of troll dolls with rainbow hair, scented candles, lots of photos, a pair of bright purple Dr. Martens and...

Forcing breath through her lungs and one foot in front of the other, Ellie stepped into the room and toward the single bed. Her eyes had already been drawn, like magnets, to the simple white wedding dress that lay draped across the mattress. She stared for a second, mesmerized, before scooping it up and sighing at the feel of soft silk between her fingers. She clutched the A-line gown to her chest as if it were a long-lost teddy bear. Her thoughts immediately traveled back a decade, to a day in Perth when she'd felt like the poster child for happiness.

Marrying Flynn was any girl's fantasy, and she'd wanted to be *his* fantasy when he watched her walk down the aisle. Silly, really, but she'd spent hours daydreaming about the expression on his face when he'd see her. She'd loved him so much. So much it made her chest ache if she thought about losing him. Her insides whirled like a roller coaster whenever she even thought about kissing him. And so, when she'd walked past that boutique and seen the most elegant wedding dress with a 50 percent off tag, she'd thought it was fate.

And she'd been euphoric.

The shop had been about to close but she'd dragged in Tegan, her then best friend, and Matilda, and sweet-talked the assistant into letting her try on the dress. When she did, she never wanted to take it off again. It was simply perfect. No need for alterations at all. With Ellie protesting that she'd pay for it, Matilda had handed over her American Express card and someone managed to convince Ellie to take the dress off so the assistant could box it.

A tear dribbled down Ellie's cheek at the memory. At the thought that she'd once been so sky-high happy.

Thinking she was probably crazy but unable to help herself, Ellie laid her fantasy gown back on the bed and stripped to her mismatched underwear. She wondered if the dress would still fit but, if anything, it was a little on the large side. With great effort she wrangled the tiny pearl buttons at her back and managed to do up every last one of them. She twisted to look in the mirror.

What a sight. Her face was stained red with tears and her hair flat from the cap that had trapped it all day long. She didn't look like a bride any groom would get choked up over. She looked scary. But despite her appearance, Ellie didn't look away or remove the dress. She shuddered at the idea of becoming Miss Havisham, but even that miserable vision didn't spur her to remove it. After a while of standing like this, her eyes caught on something reflected in the mirror. Photo frames littered the old wooden tallboy behind her—most of them sickly sweet heart shapes containing pictures of her and Flynn.

She turned and snatched up a photo. A chill raced up her spine. She sank onto the bed, clutching Flynn's image tightly in her hands. He was gorgeous. A heart-throb, sex on legs, a devil in denim and dangerously, deliciously beautiful. His all-Australian country-boy grin lit up his whole face, and the gleam in his sea-green eyes spoke volumes about the kind of fun-loving, hardworking bloke he always was.

She'd tried to forget. In the name of self-preservation, she'd not taken even one tiny wallet photo when she left. She'd not allowed herself to think about the life they would have started together—the perfect house they were planning to build on Black Stump, the babies they'd dreamed of having… But now she realized how monumentally she'd failed. She may have repressed the memories but she hadn't erased them. Looking at him now, tracing his eyes, his nose, his lips with her quaking fingers brought it all rushing back. The intensity of first love, first passion. How he had loved her so completely and stood up for her at every turn. Romeo and Juliet had nothing on Flynn and Ellie. Hope Junction had been up in arms when their golden boy—son of third-generation landowners—had started going out with her. Not only did she not come from farming stock, but her mother had dumped her and her father hadn't even stuck around long enough to see her born. Thankfully, the teenage Flynn had already developed both backbone and morals. He didn't give a damn what the town thought. He saw past her situation to the real Ellie, and before long his dedication won over his parents and the rest of the town, too. Pretty soon Ellie was loved and accepted as if she were a fourth-generation local as well, and that was no easy feat. When Flynn had asked her to marry him, everyone was genuinely ecstatic. The only comments about them being too young came from girls Ellie's age and she wrote off their gibes as simple jealousy.

"Oh, Flynn." Sniffing, she looked down at the photo and tried to push away the millions of what-ifs that floated into her mind. What if things had been different? What if her mother had never asked to meet her in Perth? What if, for once, she'd put her own needs first and said no? What if Flynn had come with her to Perth as he'd said he would? What if she'd stayed and married him anyway? Would they be happy now? Would they have kids? Some would say her life in Sydney as an actress and celebrity was a charmed one, but her whole body ached with the thought of just how magical it could have been if she'd been living it with Flynn.

SUNDAY MORNING, FLYNN WOKE. His head throbbed and a heavy naked weight lay sprawled across his equally naked chest. This realization roused him like no bucket of cold water ever could.

Glancing round the lamp-lit room at his surroundings and then taking a closer look at the woman in his arms, he froze. Scenes of the previous night flashed one after the other. Cringeworthy and stupid didn't even begin to describe what he saw and how he felt. He wanted more than anything to extricate himself from beneath Lauren.

Lauren? Had the drink stolen every ounce of his common sense? Again? He wanted to collect his clothes from wherever they'd landed, flee home, crawl under the bedcovers and stay there all day. He wanted to forget this nightmare had ever happened. But he saw one immediate problem with that tempting scenario. Lauren.

He'd have to be blind, deaf and dumb not to have noticed the mammoth crush she'd harbored for him since primary school. But he'd been fastidious in avoiding her advances—at least until now. Because although she was fun and pretty—if you liked her kind of style—she was also a local. Flings had been few and far between in recent years, but any that Flynn did have, he kept far outside the boundaries of Hope Junction. Local girls were a no-go zone. It was safer and easier that way.

Lauren, on the other hand, was very local. And she was like most single women approaching their thirtieth year. Stars in her eyes when it came to weddings, babies and happily-ever-afters. But after all Flynn had been through with Ellie, he didn't have a marrying bone left in his body.

He cursed himself and his lack of restraint, not so much for not resisting Lauren, but for getting so absolutely hammered that he thought hooking up with her was a good idea in the first place. He'd been dry for eight years now, and although his addiction was always in the back of his mind, he'd forgotten how much of a tool he became, and the kind of stupid choices he made, when he got drunk. It wasn't pretty, nor something he was proud of.

Lauren shifted on his chest. She made a tiny noise like a mewling cat and opened her eyes. Their faces were so close he could do nothing but look straight into her eyes. She smiled like a Cheshire; he gulped like a minnow facing a great white.

"Feeling better this morning, Flynn?"

He couldn't exactly give her the truth—that her face was the last thing he wanted to see first thing in the morning.

"Last night was something else," she went on, crawling her nails up his chest and bringing the pads of her fingers to rest on his lips. He tried not to flinch. "But next time, let's make sure we finish it off, hey?"

His heart skipped a hopeful beat at her words. Could it be possible they hadn't actually had sex? He had to know.

"I'm…really sorry, Lauren, but my memory's pretty hazy about last night. Did we…?"

"I should probably be offended that you can't remember it." She giggled and began toying with the flesh at his ear. He summoned all his self-control not to tap her hand away, raise his voice and demand she tell him the truth. Instead, he smiled the smile he'd been told, on many occasions, was a danger to womankind.

"Well?"

"You passed out before we got that far." She laughed, then added something else. But Flynn didn't take in these last words. He was too busy thanking the Lord for small mercies, promising he'd never touch another drop as long as he lived. But the reprieve didn't last long. Lauren dipped her head and touched her hot, wet lips to his parched ones. A quick worker, she slid her tongue inside his mouth barely before he'd registered her kiss. Where, in other circumstances, his first thoughts might be of his morning breath, in this instance his only concern was how to escape her clutches. Hell, he'd be happy if he had bad breath and it scared her off.

He placed his hands on her bare shoulders and pushed her upward, looking away when her perky breasts thrust themselves into his line of vision.

"Sorry, Lauren, with the ram sale not far away, I really can't afford to have a Sunday off. Work to be done, sheep to check on."

"Damn sheep." Her lower lip practically touched her chest, but she rolled over and scrounged around on the floor for her discarded clothes. If there was one thing a country girl understood, it was that nothing, no one, came before the farm.

Seizing the opportunity, Flynn scrabbled off the couch, located his shirt and boots and yanked them both on in record time. He knew he should stop and apologize to Lauren. He should explain he hadn't meant to lead her on, that he hadn't been thinking straight. But whatever way he put it, she'd be offended and upset. And the honest truth was that he just didn't have the mental energy to deal with this right now. Not on top of everything else.

So without so much as a kiss on the cheek, he thanked Lauren for letting him stay and fled.

AFTER CRYING HERSELF to sleep, Ellie slept more soundly than she had in a long time. Maybe it was the emotion of the day before, maybe it was the jet lag, maybe it was the quiet of the country, but in the morning, it was only the sound of the kettle whistling that roused her. It was a noise she hadn't heard in as long as she could remember. In her other life no one bothered with the time it took to boil a kettle. It was either Starbucks or the staff room machine, which percolated good, strong coffee twenty-four hours a day. It took a second for her to recognize the sound, and then she realized it meant Mat was already up and trying to fend for herself.

Ellie sprang into action. Her hand was on the door handle when she caught a glimpse of herself in the mirror. That was no fancy nightie she saw, it was a wedding dress. *Her* wedding dress. A shiver ran over her skin and a despondent feeling returned to her chest. With what felt like a brick weighing her down, it was an effort to walk even the few steps back to the bed. She sat and stretched behind her to the row of minuscule buttons. If she kept on like this, she was in danger of returning to that dark place she'd gone to when she first left Flynn and gave up everything that mattered to her. A place so gloomy it had taken all her willpower to drag herself out. She never wanted to go there again. Besides, she was in Hope for Matilda, not to revisit past demons.

"Come on," she said, urging her wobbly fingers to steady and coordinate. She'd done them up with only relative difficulty; surely the undoing would be easy in comparison. More twisting, more tugging, but it seemed the only thing likely to come undone was her arm socket.

"Argh!" What was meant to be a silent plea between gritted teeth came out loud and angry. She took a deep breath, concentrated, but as the first pearl slipped from its silken prison, there came a hesitant knock on the bedroom door. Ellie froze.

"Yes?" She managed only just to get the word past the lump in her throat.

"Can I help you?" came the response. Ellie frowned at Matilda's turn of phrase, hoping her godmother hadn't looked in on her while she'd slept and seen her outfit. The thought chilled her.

"No," she said, a lot harsher than she intended. "I'm here to help *you*. What the hell do you think you're doing wandering around without me? Don't do anything else. I'll be out in just a moment."

She focused her attention back on the dress, but the damn buttons refused to budge. Generally calm in the face of a problem, Ellie's pulse raced and the muscles in her neck twitched. Stupid tears prickled at the corners of her eyes. As she saw it, she had two choices. Open the door and, despite the shame and embarrassment she'd feel, ask for help, or...

She took another deep breath, positioned her hands at the back of her neck, one on either side of the dress, and yanked. Hard. Tiny pops rippled as the tiny pearls shot around the room. Ellie shimmied out of the dress, scrunched it into a ball and shoved it on top of a stack of old *Cosmo* magazines at the bottom of the wardrobe. It felt wrong to treat something that had once been so special to her with such disregard, and for a second she hesitated, thought about pulling it out and trying to fix the creases she'd just inflicted. But Matilda's voice sounded through the door again, more anxious than before.

"Ellie? What was that? Are you sure you're okay in there?"

She bit down on her lip, turned and lifted the lid on

her suitcase. There wasn't time to get sentimental. "I'm fine," she said, scrambling around for jeans and a top.

When she finally opened the door and saw the look of worry in the other woman's eyes, she knew that she hadn't been able to hide the truth from Matilda.

"You want to talk about it?"

"Nope." Ellie reached out to take Matilda's arm. "I want to get some caffeine into my veins, get you settled on the veranda swing and get stuck into those awnings you left half-done."

Matilda shuffled alongside Ellie into the kitchen. "Don't think you can change the subject on me, missy. I've let it lie for ten years but it's time. I can see coming back here, to me, to this town, to your room…" Matilda paused and looked deep into Ellie's eyes. Ellie knew she was thinking about the dress. "It's messing with your mind. Therapy is expensive, but talking to an old friend is priceless."

Ellie went to the bench, opened a cupboard and grabbed two large ceramic mugs. Perhaps Mat was right. Perhaps she should talk about why she'd done the unforgivable, why she'd left Flynn standing at the front of a church with the whole town as witness. But Matilda was the only person who'd been there who still believed in her, who could still look her in the eye and not make her feel like the scum of the earth. Hell, she could barely look in the mirror and achieve that feat herself.

No, she wasn't ready to talk, not yet. She turned to the fridge to focus her energies on breakfast and then remembered. No milk. Dammit, she just didn't do black coffee, especially not at the crack of dawn. But another thought followed quickly on the heels of that one. As much as the idea of leaving the house terrified her, it was still early for a Sunday. She was less likely to run into anyone at this time of day, and going for milk and bread—the basic supplies that would get them through the weekend—would postpone the inevitable talk.

"I'm just going to pop up to the Shell and get us some milk. Want any munchies?"

Matilda frowned and sighed. "I'm not one to pass up a chocolate bar, but don't think this gets you off the hook. We will talk. It's well past time."

"I know." Ellie tried to sound nonchalant, as if the idea of raking up the past wasn't uncomfortable or painful. "But I barely function, never mind do deep and meaningful without my morning coffee." She leaned over and kissed Mat on the cheek, then grabbed the car keys and was out of there before her godmother had the chance for further protests.

She smiled with relief as she pulled into the service station. A couple of trucks were parked and their drivers stood between them chomping on greasy breakfast. The thought of eating that kind of food this early turned Ellie's stomach, but she guessed it helped combat the chill of winter mornings. She shivered. She'd been in such a hurry to leave the house she hadn't thought about a sweater or a jacket, never mind actually put one on.

Rubbing her arms, she strode toward the shop, dodging a crusty old ute at the gas tanks and ignoring the chill that ran through her as she noticed it was a Hope Junction license plate. She'd forgotten this about small towns in WA, that you could tell where a car was from by the first letters on the license plate. She was far from the anonymity of Sydney, and this car belonged to a local.

Get a grip, she told herself firmly.

But that was easier said than done. Her encounter with Lauren had reinforced her fears. The reception she would get from townsfolk was likely to be frosty at best, downright nasty at worst. She pushed open the door of the shop, trying to recall what it was she'd come for and crashed head-on into a man carrying a paper and a Coffee Chill. His purchases clattered to the floor and without glancing at each other, they both dived to collect them. Their heads knocked, their hands brushed, and laughter at the silliness of the situation tumbled from their mouths. Ellie felt instantly at ease.

Until they both stood up and the man's warm chuckle died on his lips as he registered who she was.

CHAPTER FIVE

ELLIE REACHED OUT to grab the door for support.

Flynn.

She wasn't sure if she said his name aloud or not. Nothing in her wildest imagination could have prepared her for this. It was as if a million different things were going on in her body. Adrenaline had set off a chain of reactions inside her—her hands got sweaty, her heart was beating so fast and loud it felt as if it would break out of her chest at any moment, and her knees felt incapable of holding her up much longer. Their overexertion probably accounted for the beads of perspiration bursting out across her forehead. But her mind and eyes were feasting on the sight before her, of which her memory had done no justice at all.

The grown-up Flynn was a hundred times more gorgeous than the teenage one—and that was saying something. Not that she'd expected otherwise, but he'd filled out in all the right places, grown into his long, lanky body and become a strapping, commanding presence. Light stubble dusted his jawline and his golden hair was longer than she recalled. And mussed up slightly. It suited him. Yet despite his overbearing good looks, one thing stood out as very different. His lips drew a flat line across his face where once a huge, mischievous grin held prime position. She'd fallen in love with that smile before anything else, and now it was nowhere to be seen.

"Cat got your tongue?"

Ellie snapped out of her trance and realized not only was she practically drooling, openmouthed like a codfish, but also that she hadn't registered Flynn speaking. To her. She tried to reply but something obstructed her words. Like one of those awful dreams where there's a serial killer chasing you and your legs won't function. She had so much she wanted—*needed*—to say to Flynn, and yet her mouth refused to cooperate.

"Ah, never mind," Flynn said bitterly. His eyes narrowed and he shook his head as he walked past, clutching his paper and drink hard against his chest while stepping as near to the door frame as possible. She could only guess he wanted to avoid the possibility of brushing against her. Her heart crumbled at this thought, but still she couldn't find the wherewithal to speak. If only she could turn back time and at least find out what he'd said. But then, if she had such powers, she'd turn back time a lot further and erase other stupid mistakes.

Almost in slow motion, she turned around, but Flynn was already pounding the pavement away from her. He didn't look back. Shivers scuttled down her spine like a thousand nasty, eight-legged beasts. And she started to shake. Uncontrollably. The room spun.

She took hold of herself and tried to moderate her breathing. She was no doctor, but even she knew breathing at such a rate was dangerous. Was this what a panic attack felt like? One of the actresses on *Lake Street* suffered from them, apparently, but Ellie had never bought into the hype.

"Excuse me, miss? Are you okay?"

She registered that someone somewhere was speaking to her, but a sudden, stabbing pain in her chest throttled any reply. She pressed her hand against her breast hoping the pressure would somehow ease the pain, that if the discomfort eased, then so would the dizziness, the shakes and the feeling the room was closing in around her. But it was no good. No longer able to keep a firm grip on the door, her knees gave way and she tumbled onto the hard concrete.

"That's it, I'm calling an ambulance," said the voice.

"Damn straight, looks like she's having a heart attack," said another voice. "Don't want no celebrities dying in my shop. Maybe we should get her a blanket or something?"

No! She didn't want a blanket. She brought her knees up to her chest and rocked back and forth against the door. *I just want to go,* she would have yelled, but her tongue had grown thick and immobile. *I just want to go back to Sydney, where I'm not some kind of freak show, and live my life the best I can.*

Her legs had lost all their strength. She tried to move so she wasn't hunched like a sobbing cripple in the doorway, but the gods were laughing at her. Somewhere a flash went off, but before she had time to comprehend what that meant, sirens pierced the air, egging on her horrendous headache.

"In here," she heard someone say. Then two women in green uniforms were looking over her. One of them crouched down and lifted Ellie's hand, rubbing her wrist, presumably to take her pulse. The other ambulance officer began firing questions at the owner and his employee. Still stunned that this was actually happening, Ellie took a moment to react, but when she heard the word *hospital,* something inside her snapped back into place.

She pasted what was no doubt a less-than-believable smile on her face and looked apologetically into the face of the woman checking her over. "I'm really sorry," she said, extracting her hand and straightening her ponytail. "I'm fine. I don't know what happened, but I'm really fine now. I don't need to go to hospital."

The other, less feminine ambulance officer leaned down and butted in. "It's policy. We have to take you in and have a doctor check you over."

"No." No way in hell was she going back to that pokey small-town hospital and risking another run-in with Lauren. She could only imagine what would happen if she were admitted into that woman's care. "I said I'm fine and I am. You can't force me to go."

"She does seem fine," stated the first officer.

While the two of them discussed protocol and common sense, and the service station owner added his opinion, Ellie flexed her feet and pushed herself up into a stand. Although still shaky, she had every confidence her legs were back in the game. Monitoring her breathing, she trekked slowly around the shop, grabbing chocolates, a big bottle of Fanta, packets of chips, two types of milk and a loaf of white bread. The pickings were slim at the Shell and the prices exorbitant, but she needed to get out of there quickly, with enough provisions to avoid coming back too soon. Tomorrow she'd worry about a bigger shop, although how she'd make it round the Co-op without having an actual heart attack, she had no idea.

"You sure you shouldn't get properly checked out?" asked the shop assistant as she scanned Ellie's purchases through the till. The young woman looked genuinely concerned. Ellie didn't recognize her and judging by her attitude, she deduced that the girl couldn't have been a resident of Hope very long.

"Thanks for your concern, but I just had a shock."

The girl looked at her quizzically, but she wasn't about to start discussing her sordid past with a stranger. No doubt the town gossips would fight to fill her in. Instead, Ellie handed over a fifty-dollar note.

The act of selecting and purchasing items seemed to convince the ambulance folk she was, in fact, physically fine. So, wanting to get this whole sorry episode over quickly, Ellie filled in her details and signed the release.

When Ellie returned to the house, Matilda—sitting in an armchair in the living room—threw her arms up theatrically. "You've been gone an age. I was about to organize a search party."

"Sorry." She walked through to the kitchen and began unloading the sparse supplies. Inwardly she laughed at the idea that anyone in this godforsaken town would give up their Sunday to search for her.

"I almost called the police," Matilda continued, her shrill voice carrying down the short hallway.

"Thank God you didn't," Ellie called back. "I've had my fill of emergency services today."

"You've what?" There was a short silence and then a shuffle. Ellie could hear Matilda reaching for her crutches and knew she was trying to stand up.

"Stay there!" she roared. "I'll get us a drink and make-shift breakfast, and then I'll fill you in." *On everything,* she added silently. It was time.

She took her time making the coffee and toast. She even cut each slice into little triangles, laid them decoratively on the plate and loaded it all onto an elaborate tray Mat had brought back from Mexico a few years ago. When she finally entered the living room, Matilda was leaning forward in the chair, her body tense, the expression on her face desperately curious.

"What happened?"

"I ran into Flynn." Ellie's tone suggested this was an everyday occurrence. She handed Mat her mug, then placed the toast on the little coffee table, positioning it within both their reach.

"Oh." For once Matilda seemed short of words. Then, eventually, "Dare I ask?"

Ellie flopped into the armchair opposite. "It was a complete debacle. He looked like he wanted to vomit at the sight of me and I almost fainted." She laughed a little hysterically. "Someone called an ambulance."

"You've been to the hospital?"

She shook her head. "I refused to go."

Matilda waved an arm in front of her face. "Who cares about the hospital, I want to know about Flynn."

Ellie tried in vain to keep her hands and voice steady as she sipped her drink and filled Mat in on the events of the morning. Yet with every mention of Flynn the effort became all the more impossible.

"My poor girl," Matilda said, gesturing to the tissue box on the table. "You've held it in far too long. It's time to let it out."

"I'm fine." Ellie shoved the box and it plopped onto the floor. That got a skeptical smile and a brow lift from Matilda. "I am," she insisted. "If I hadn't seen the dress, I wouldn't have been in such a soppy and sentimental mood when I ran into him. It's not like I didn't know it was going to happen sooner or later." She paused to collect herself. "Why did you keep it?"

"It wasn't mine to throw away."

"No, I know, but…but…" But what? She'd always assumed Matilda would have given it to the Salvation Army or something.

"At first I left it there because I thought you'd be back. You were so in love with him, no one was more surprised than me when you ran off like that. I knew you better than everyone, aside from Flynn, and he never suspected a problem. He was a wreck. So I was sure you'd be back."

A familiar guilt gnawed at Ellie's heart and she rested her hand against her stomach. Nausea was the standard reaction whenever she thought of what she'd done to Flynn. She did her best to live her life in denial but occasionally—usually on lonely weekends, when all she had was the company of bad black-and-white movies on the telly—her thoughts turned to him. More than once she'd been physically sick.

"Then," continued Matilda, "by the time it became clear you'd made a life for yourself without him, the dress had been there so long. It probably sounds silly, but it made me feel closer to you. You were never as happy as the day you tried on that dress. Sometimes I'd come into the room, look at the dress and wonder if there was anything I could have done."

"No," Ellie rushed, "none of this was your fault." The last thing she needed was for Matilda, who had always been there for her no matter what, to feel guilty, as well. So many times she'd almost spilled her heart out to Mat, but she'd never quite been able to find the words. Mat loved and trusted her more than anyone, so Ellie had been scared. Scared that Mat would think of her differently if she knew. "I don't want you to ever—"

Matilda held up her hand to silence Ellie. "I need to say this. The years passed and you made no mention of coming back. I meant to clean out your room, I really did, but you know what I'm like with my own clutter, I couldn't bear to sort and make decisions about yours. I'm sorry, I should have gotten rid of that dress, but something I can't really explain stopped me."

"It's okay." Ellie's reply was a mere whisper. All choked up, she thought about the crumpled dress in the bottom of the wardrobe. What the hell should she do with it? "I understand," she continued, "but I want you to know that none of what happened is your fault. If anyone besides me is to blame—for leaving, for staying away all these years—it's my despicable excuse for a mother."

"Your mother?" Matilda looked baffled. "I didn't know you two were in touch. I thought the last time you saw Rhiannon was in Perth, just before your..."

Ellie knew she was about to say *wedding*. She shook her head and set her friend straight. "She never turned up."

Matilda's mouth dropped open like a sideshow clown and her eyes grew cold. "But I don't understand. You told me you spent the weekend in the city together, that she apologized profusely about not being able to make it to your wedding. I wanted to hunt her down, give her what for about missing the most important day of your life."

"All lies," Ellie admitted. "I guess I felt like an idiot for thinking she'd care enough to meet up with me, and I wanted you all to think that she did. When she didn't show, I waited in the bar for five hours, treating myself to cocktails to cheer up. I got quite drunk." That was a massive understatement.

In the next hour or so, Ellie spilled the truth about what had happened that awful weekend in Perth. She left nothing out. She cried a lot. And so did Matilda, who cursed herself for not being there for Ellie when she'd needed her support. But not once did Matilda make her feel any less of a person for her mistakes. She didn't pass judgment or even make many comments until the end, when Ellie said, "So you see how I couldn't tell Flynn? He'd have hated me."

Matilda frowned slightly. "I don't see anything of the sort. If there's one thing I've learned in my life, it's to never presume what another person thinks, or how they'll react in a certain situation."

"I suppose." But the truth was, Ellie couldn't have coped with seeing the hurt and disappointment in Flynn's eyes if she had stayed to face her problems.

"Personally," Mat said, "and this is just my opinion, because as I said, I don't know the inside of Flynn's head, but I think he would rather have had you—and whatever came with that—than lose you. He made some bad choices himself after you left."

Ellie's head shot up from where it had been staring down into her lap and a fist full of tissues. "What kind of bad choices?"

ELLIE WOKE ON Monday morning feeling utterly drained. The past couple of days had been exhausting—physically, mentally and emotionally. And she'd be a fool to think the worst was over.

Her guilt had trebled when she heard that for two years after she left, Flynn had gone on a wild bender, becoming best friends with bottles of Jim Beam. And then his dad, Cyril, had been killed in a freak accident on the farm. She could only imagine the pain the Quartermaines would have felt at that deep loss. Flynn and Cyril had disagreed about some aspects of running the farm, and Cyril had been reluctant to take on a few of Flynn's ideas, but mostly, father and son had been great mates. In a somewhat bittersweet turnaround, though, it was his father's death that pulled Flynn out of his self-destructive spiral. Where many turn to alcohol in times of mourning, Cyril's passing shook Flynn enough that he went completely dry. Ellie felt so relieved when Matilda told her that Flynn had reformed, but she couldn't ignore the painful truth. If she hadn't run away, he'd never have gone there in the first place.

Matilda believed the only way for Ellie to truly move on was for her to sit down with Flynn and tell him everything. She shuddered at the thought. Quite aside from the fact that pinning Flynn down would prove a mammoth task, she was scared that in telling him the truth, she risked bringing back hurtful memories for him. Sure, it might get some of the heaviness off *her* chest, but she couldn't jeopardize his well-being simply to clear her conscience.

Bottom line was, she'd never stopped loving him. Seeing him yesterday had made that clear. And what was that old saying? If you loved something you let it go? She reckoned that included not rehashing the painful past.

Her decision made, she climbed out of bed, washed and dressed quickly, and then set to some housework. Matilda rose too and grumbled about being constrained by her cast, so Ellie gave her the important job of drafting the shopping list.

"Leave nothing you desire off that list," Ellie instructed. "I do not want to be traipsing down to the Co-op every day for something we've forgotten."

Just when Ellie thought the house was sparkling so much she couldn't put off the shopping expedition any longer, the doorbell—a yodeling one that Matilda bought on a trip to Austria—sang out.

"That'll be my friend Joyce," Matilda announced, a beaming smile filling her face. "She's going to be your chaperone."

"Chaperone?" Ellie raised a brow while racking her brain for memories of Joyce.

"You haven't met," said Matilda, reading her mind. "She and her hubby, Howard, moved here three years ago when they bought the caravan park. Howard died last year but Joyce is a hoot, you'll love her."

Joyce let herself in. "Everyone adores me."

Ellie looked at the fire-engine redhead. Her first thought was that she'd never seen a female built in quite such a...strong way. She couldn't have asked for a more perfect bodyguard. She smiled. "Well, shopping with me will soon change that. *Nobody* adores me."

Joyce hooted with laughter. "I love her already."

After ensuring Mat had everything within arm's reach, Joyce and Ellie set off in the Premier.

"Mat phoned me last night," Joyce announced as she clicked in her seat belt. "She didn't tell me why you left the Quartermaine boy at the altar, but she said you have your reasons. I want you to know Mat's word is good enough for me."

Ellie's mood plummeted at the idea that Matilda might have told Joyce more, and nausea set in at the thought of Joyce flapping her mouth about town, of Flynn hearing it all on the grapevine. But she quickly relaxed, knowing her godmother would never break her confidence.

"Thanks."

"Don't mention it. Mat's had a lot on her plate recently. She's so happy you're here but doesn't want you being crucified just because she needs you. She wanted someone else in your corner." Joyce's voice was serious in a way Ellie hadn't thought possible, judging by her brassy manner back at the cottage. "And I want you to know, I'm in your corner."

An alien lump formed in Ellie's throat. She couldn't quite get another thanks past it.

"We all make mistakes," continued Joyce, "and I don't believe in beating oneself up about them. But that's your business. If you want to talk, I won't tell a soul your secret, but neither will I press you about it. I just want you to know."

"Okay. I appreciate that." Ellie stared ahead at the road. She didn't really want to make small talk but she didn't want silence right now, either. Besides, she wouldn't mind deflecting the attention from herself. "So, what do you think of Hope? Do you like running the caravan park?"

"Love it. I'm a social butterfly so I adore meeting all the people that come through. And I find the dynamics of small-town life fascinating."

"That's one word for it," Ellie snorted. *Suffocating* and *narrow-minded* were others.

"You obviously don't miss it."

"Actually, I didn't mind it," Ellie said, surprising herself. She'd forgotten. She'd let the horror of her drastic departure overshadow the fact that her years here were the best ones of her life. Busy years, with never a moment's peace. There was always something going on in the town—whether it be a football game, a quiz night, someone's party, a fund-raiser for the Hospital Auxiliary. It was impossible to be idle, and there was something about the way country people pulled together in an emergency that couldn't help but warm your heart. She'd loved being part of that, even if now, looking back, she wondered if she'd merely imagined the act of fitting in.

"I could never go back," Joyce mused. "Not to all those bright lights, crazy streets and people too busy to smile at a stranger."

Ellie could tell from the affection in Joyce's voice that Hope and its people had worked their magic on her. Joyce had fallen in love and the only way she'd ever leave was if they carried her out in a box.

As they found a parking space outside the Co-op, Ellie

fought the desire to bite her nails. People were already turning in her direction. Heads were shaking. Lips were twisting downward.

"You know, Joyce," Ellie said, "perhaps it'd be better if you distanced yourself from me inside. I don't want my unpopularity to affect your business."

"Don't be silly, girl. Most of my business comes from out-of-towners. Besides, if people are that narrow-minded, I don't want their friendship or their money. Give this town a bit of credit. Granted, we have a few silly biddies, but once they've had their moment, you'll be old news. Come on, let's get that moment over with."

Ellie couldn't deny that she felt better with Joyce by her side. As she locked the car—a somewhat unnecessary precaution in the country—Joyce came around to the driver's side and took her arm.

"Just hold your head high and smile," she instructed, and they ventured into the building.

Ellie was used to being the point of focus whenever she went out and about. In Sydney, even though most people didn't go stupid over celebrities, she was always recognized. She didn't mind the attention—she liked talking to fans, and was more than happy to give her autograph when requested. Not that she'd be getting any such requests around here.

The moment they stepped through the automatic doors, Ellie felt the chill of the frozen foods section against her cheeks, reminding her of the reception she was expecting. Her gaze moved to the checkout where she'd once worked after school and on Saturday mornings. There was a queue—two trolleys equaled a mad rush in Hope. The customers met Ellie's eyes and then quickly looked away. She recognized the operator as a girl she'd gone to school with. They'd been quite friendly in the past, but now she wasn't even giving Ellie the chance to toss that smile Joyce had recommended. The woman made sure her eyes didn't come near Ellie's.

Straightening her shoulders and jutting her chin forward, Ellie grabbed a trolley and glanced at Joyce. "Let's do this." The quicker the better, she thought.

In response, Joyce smiled encouragingly and held up their shopping list. As they traversed the aisles, customers stared and were more than generous with reproachful glares. One woman even tsked. Halfway round, Ellie decided she could either let them upset her or she could…

"Hi." She offered a woman in aisle three a huge grin. "Emma, isn't it? We went to school together."

Emma, who had divine, jet-black hair in a catwalk bob, blinked and looked as if she'd swallowed a lemon whole. Ellie's heart stopped midbeat as she waited for a response.

"I'm surprised you remember," Emma said eventually. "Welcome back." Her welcome couldn't be described as warm, and there weren't any polite comments about catching up, but she hadn't spit in her face, either. Ellie put that down as a win.

As Emma walked briskly away, Ellie gave Joyce two thumbs up. They raided items from the shelves and soon filled their trolley. Ellie smiled at a couple of customers she didn't recognize and even stopped to talk to one of her old teachers while Joyce read the labels on different baked bean tins. The teacher—Mrs. Ellery, who taught English and drama—had aged about twenty years in the past ten but she could still talk for Olympic gold. She chewed Ellie's ear off for what seemed an hour, pride shining through as she acknowledged one of her prodigies had made it big. It was funny, drama had never been Ellie's favorite or best subject—not that Mrs. Ellery remembered it that way. Her break was, if anything, accidental.

When she'd arrived in Sydney, Ellie had started waitressing at a trendy, inner-city bar. Located next to a mainstream television production company, it had been the hangout of some top-notch producers. Out of the blue one night, one of them asked if she'd like to be an extra in a location episode he was shooting. Hungry for extra cash and happy she'd only be a shadow in the background, she agreed.

Pretty soon Ellie became a regular extra on *Lake Street* and, as the saying goes, one thing led to another. She was introduced as the long-lost daughter of a much-loved older character, and as the audience adored her, before too long she was a permanent resident on Australia's favorite street.

But if you'd asked her at seventeen what she'd wanted to be, actress would never have crossed her mind.

"We're reviving the theatrical society," Mrs. Ellery said. She caught the first breath Ellie had heard her take in about five minutes and then added, "You should come along. We could do with your wisdom."

"Oh, no, I couldn't." It was all Ellie could do to stop breaking into nervous hysterics at the thought. Venturing out to buy groceries was one thing, but she could just imagine her reception if she tried to wheedle her way into the group. "I'm not here for long, and there are a couple of things I want to do in that time." Painting Mat's gutters and awnings was a much safer bet than what Mrs. Ellery had in mind.

"Think about it, dear." Then, with a pat on Ellie's forearm, Mrs. Ellery doddered off down the aisle pulling her tapestry trolley behind her.

Ellie did think about it, her thoughts distracting her

as she and Joyce finished the shopping. She barely noticed the cold looks and people turning the other way when they saw her coming down the aisle. The town's last production—*Mary Poppins*—had been the year before she'd skipped town. In the middle of winter, it had been the highlight of the cold season. She hadn't been involved, but Matilda had directed and Ellie had often hung around watching rehearsals. The atmosphere whenever the cast and crew got together had been exhilarating.

"Think that's us done now," said Joyce, interrupting Ellie's memory. "Unless there's anything else you can think of."

"No." Ellie stared ahead at the checkout, trying to remember the name of the girl behind the counter. She knew if she acted friendly and not like the snob they all took her for, she'd stand a better chance of not being stoned. That started with addressing people by their names.

As she stopped the trolley at the front of the store, however, her gaze drifted to the newspapers on a stand next to the checkouts. Across the front page of the *West Australian* was her face, large and flushed against the pale cement of the service station floor. The headline: Stella's Soap Opera Past in Rural WA. Flynn's scowling—but still terribly sexy—face was inset at the bottom of the page.

Her heart plummeted at the publicity she neither needed nor wanted. Ten years ago, one particular hound of a journalist had almost uncovered the whole story when she was first starting to make a name for herself. Luckily a well-known cricket personality had indulged in an affair with a newsreader about the same time, and the story of Ellie and Flynn and their nonwedding had died a quick death.

Her mobile began to shrill from her handbag, the un-
mistakable tone of Lady Gaga interrupting her thoughts.
She ripped the zip open and snatched the phone. Not at
all surprised to see the caller was her agent, Dwayne
Wright, she pressed Reject and shoved it back inside.
There wasn't time to deal with Dwayne's fury right
now—she had about five hundred newspapers to buy.

"I'll take the lot," she told the woman behind the
checkout, gesturing to the newspapers. "And if you've
got any out the back, I'll take them, too." Dammit, her
name was Simone, she remembered a moment too late.

"Don't be ridiculous," Simone scoffed, making a de-
rogatory sound between her teeth. "I can't sell you *all*
the newspapers."

"Why not?" Ellie's heart tripped over itself. "My
money's as good as anyone's."

Not deeming her comment worthy of a reply, Simone
leaned forward and spoke into the PA. "Gavin, can you
please come to the checkout? Gavin."

"Who's Gavin?" Ellie hissed to Joyce.

"The manager," Joyce whispered back.

Ah good, thought Ellie, *surely he won't turn down
legitimate sales.* But of course she was wrong. The
manager, whom she recognized as a distant relative of
Flynn's mother, wasn't even sure he wanted to let her
buy one newspaper.

"I don't want you causing havoc in my shop," he announced, his pudgy arms folded over an impressive beer
gut. "Perhaps you should just leave."

To hell with being polite, Ellie had just about had it
up to here with some of the people in this silly, back-of-
beyond town. She thrust her finger at the sign that hung
across the entrance. "Last time I checked, this was a
co-operative." She dragged the last word out, showing

exactly what she thought of him. "And as I recall, co-operative means owned by the community, whereas you are *just* its manager. So I'm buying the damn food in this trolley and I'll buy as many newspapers as I want."

Upset and sweating, Ellie leaned forward and wrapped her arms around the thick pile of papers. She yanked them up and dropped them on the checkout, narrowly missing Simone's fingers. Her sunglasses tumbled off the top of her head and the newspapers fell off either side of the ancient conveyer belt making a mess on the floor.

"I'll pick them up," said Joyce, her voice taking on a warning tone. "You go wait in the car."

At Joyce's words Ellie cringed. She looked at the faces now glaring at her from all over the store. She'd totally lost it, confirming what most of the town probably thought—that she was some up-herself celebrity who thought money could buy everything. Truth was, all she wanted was the chance to prove them wrong. That she wasn't the evil Jezebel they'd pegged her as. What happened to being human? What happened to everyone making mistakes?

Her eyes brimmed with tears she didn't want to shed in public. Years on the small screen had made her very good at being able to turn the waterworks on when she didn't really feel like it, and an expert at switching them off when in the public eye. But right now, she was losing the battle.

Opting to accept Joyce's out, she stooped to pick up her sunglasses, almost poking herself in the eye in an effort to put them back on. She left the store, walking briskly and failing dismally to hold her head high.

CHAPTER SIX

As FLYNN MADE his way out of the sheep yards, where he'd been getting his sheep ready for the big ram sale, he saw Lucy running toward him from the homestead. She was shouting something, her arms waving crazily over her head as she did so. He started in her direction.

"What's up, little sis?"

Despite almost losing it on the weekend and running into Ellie, he'd woken up in a good mood, optimistic about inhabiting the same town as her. The initial meeting was over and, he had to say, it had been less traumatic than he'd anticipated. He'd handled it a lot better than she had, that's for sure. Probably because, when push came to shove, she was the one with something to feel guilty about. If she hadn't loved him enough to settle down with him, she should have been woman enough to say so to his face.

As the gap closed between the siblings, Flynn noticed his mobile in Lucy's hand. Instinctively, he patted his pocket where the phone usually lived. "Careful with that," he said, reaching for it when Lucy approached.

"I wasn't the one who left it on the kitchen table where it's been ringing incessantly and almost vibrating off the edge." She puffed a little to catch her breath. "The house phone's been going crazy since the crack of dawn, too."

Flynn frowned and glanced at the screen. Twenty-two missed calls. That had to be a record.

"*Women's Weekly* has rung, *TV Week,* the *Australian* and even *Sunrise*." Excitement bounced off every word. "Kochie and Mel want to interview you. And Cara says you're on the front page of the *West*. You're famous." Two words he didn't want to hear. Especially not for the reasons he guessed. Why else would the journos come sniffing around?

"Shouldn't you be at school?"

"School holidays," Lucy said with a grin.

He sighed as the phone buzzed again. "No point prolonging the inevitable." He answered. "Good morning, Flynn Quartermaine."

"And a very good morning to you, too, Flynn," sang a woman's voice. "How does it feel to have your first love back in town?"

He gritted his teeth. The audacity of the woman not even bothering to introduce herself, hoping he'd spill some juicy news before realizing she wasn't an old friend. Yeah, right.

"If you're referring to Ellie Hughes, that has absolutely nothing to do with me. Please don't call again."

"But, Flynn…"

He snapped his phone shut. He didn't have time for this in the middle of shearing. But he knew someone who did. "Lucy, what's on your agenda for today?"

She pouted. "We're supposed to be studying for mock exams, but I need to practice my audition for the play. Casting is tomorrow afternoon. Only I've rehearsed so many times, I have no idea whether I'm getting worse or better." Her eyes lit up a moment. "Wanna watch?"

"Yes," he said, and smiled, feeling as if a weight had been lifted off his shoulders. "If you screen my calls today, I'll help you practice this evening. Deal?"

"Hell, yeah." She held out her bawdy manicured

hand—this time with glittery gold nails—for his phone.
"I can handle the media. I can even write you up a press
statement if you like. We learned about them last week
in English."

"Hold fire on the press release," he said. "Tell the
media I have nothing to say and take the name and number of anyone important."

"Got it, captain." Lucy saluted him.

He chuckled, trying to forget Ellie, forget the press
and focus on the work that needed to be done. With not
long until farmers from all around came to inspect his
stock, he had plenty to organize.

"You're a champ," he told Lucy. "And I reckon you'll
knock everyone's socks off at auditions."

"I hope so," she answered, before turning and walking back to the main house.

Alone again, Flynn thought of what the journalist had
said and wondered if they were hassling Ellie, as well.
Yeah, of course they were. The difference was, she probably relished the attention. But in spite of this, he couldn't
stop thinking about her. Damn, she'd looked great yesterday. Not as polished as the photos he'd glimpsed over
the years, her rich brown hair pulled back almost messily,
her complexion paler, her body a little thinner than he
liked but still…sexy as all hell. Sexy even in simple jeans
and a rugby top. Sexier than any other woman he'd ever
met. Just the thought of her had the blood pumping in a
southerly direction. His hormones were only raring up
now because yesterday they'd been suppressed by shock.
He'd known sometime or other he'd bump into Ellie—
Hope was a small town—but he hadn't prepared himself
well. He hadn't thought about what he would say when
the moment arose. Small talk should have been the go,
to show her he'd moved on, that he didn't feel anything

in her presence and that he definitely didn't want to rekindle their friendship. Discussion of the weather or the lack of rain would have been real insulting. Instead, he'd stared like some crazed pervert and pleaded, "Why?"

For a split second, he'd regretted the question. Maybe he didn't want to know if there was an answer beyond the conclusions he'd already come to. Sometimes the truth was best left buried in the past. But he needn't have worried. She'd looked through him as if he was a ghost—a blurry memory from long ago. Simply stared without the slightest inclination to acknowledge him. He'd felt small—real small—and the best thing had been to get out of there before he let loose on exactly what he thought of her.

But as he reflected on it now, and failed to get Ellie out of his head, the question still lay unanswered. Better left alone or not, he couldn't rid himself of the urge to know if there'd been more to her departure than met the eye.

"So, who's in charge of this revival?" Ellie asked as she helped Matilda into the wheelchair. It was Tuesday, just after lunch, and the first official meeting of the theatrical society had been scheduled in the hope of attracting some of the high schoolers to the production. They'd decided walking was easier than Matilda hauling her crutches in and out the car and having to hobble about once there. Ellie had practiced her deep breathing in front of the mirror only moments ago, telling herself it was silly to get all worked up over walking down the street.

"Precious Joyce and your old drama teacher, Eileen Ellery." Matilda sighed. "I was supposed to be the third musketeer, but I'm useless as tits on a bull now. Still, I want to be there for moral support."

Ellie scoffed. "Just because you can't walk doesn't mean you're not worth your weight in gold. I remember all those productions that went off without a hitch due to your fabulous stage management."

"Ah, you're too kind, Els. Still, *you'd* be more use these days." She paused and Ellie could guess what was coming next. "Why don't you come in with me and help us judge the auditions?"

"No, thanks." Ellie was firm as she opened the front door, pushed Matilda through and locked it behind them. A sucker for punishment she was not. "I'll go home and start on the awnings." Before Matilda could press any further, Ellie moved the conversation along. "What play are you putting on? Something traditional or something mod?"

As they strolled down the faded footpath, Ellie kept her head low and Matilda jabbered on happily about the play Joyce had written specifically for Hope Junction. "It's a love story, in essence, but it captures rural life and the community spirit perfectly. It's a story of drought and depression and the effect these have on relationships. Of course, there's a happy ending. One big smooch and the curtains will come down in front of a most contented audience, I reckon."

"Sounds good," said Ellie, biting her lip as the Memorial Hall came into view—she wasn't quite ready for another public humiliation. "Pity I won't be here to see it."

"Well…" Matilda started, but the sentence was lost as they both took in the sight ahead. Cameras flashed and two people Ellie instantly recognized as journalists huddled around a white ute. The same ute that had been at the service station that day she'd fainted. *Flynn's ute.*

Were they harassing him already? Ellie's heart raced so fast she could virtually hear it and she nearly stumbled on a crack in the concrete. She wished the crack were big enough to swallow her. If she knew the media, they would have found Flynn's number and started practically stalking him. Thank God, any contact she had with the press always went through Dwayne.

Ellie and Matilda watched as Flynn stepped out of the car, faded jeans clinging to his buttocks and a scowl on his still incredibly gorgeous face. Not making eye contact with anyone, he strode around and opened the passenger door.

The racing of Ellie's heart stopped as a beautiful young girl slipped out of the car, a smile as wide as a country street on her tanned face. She looked too young for Flynn, but Ellie still felt a jolt of jealousy shoot through her. Jealousy she had no right to—Flynn could date whoever he wanted, even if she did look juvenile enough to be his daughter.

"Have you talked to Ellie yet?" shouted a short, dumpy journo, overstepping the boundary of personal space as she leaned toward Flynn.

"Do you still love her?" called the other, angling his camera for a better shot.

"How did you know I'd be here?" Flynn's voice roared over the top of everyone's.

"Your sister mentioned it when I called yesterday," said the first one. "Very chatty she was."

The gorgeous girl at Flynn's side hung her head and had the good sense to look sheepish. *Lucy?*

Ellie must have uttered the name aloud for Matilda nodded and said, "Yes, she's grown up into a lovely girl. But a bit scatty apparently, can't make up her mind what she wants to do with her life."

"She can only be seventeen," replied Ellie, recalling the seven-year-old with curly, golden pigtails who'd been like the little sister she'd always longed for. Leaving Flynn had been bad enough, but losing his sister and parents, too—it had been like losing a whole family. "She's got plenty of time for serious decisions."

"That's if she lives to see tomorrow," snorted Matilda.

Flynn had angled the journalists out of earshot and was speaking sternly to Lucy. Ellie couldn't bear Flynn suffering this invasive attention and Lucy getting into trouble when she was probably tricked into revealing their whereabouts. Neither of them had asked for this. They weren't the ones with a home on prime-time television. They weren't the ones who'd run away.

Checking the brakes were secure on the wheelchair, Ellie sucked in a deep breath and marched forward. "I'll give an interview," she said, holding up her hands to the two members of the media. They spun around, eyes lighting when they saw her. Immediately the camera flashed. Dwayne would kill her for talking to the press before consulting him, but… "Only if you promise to leave Flynn and his sister out of it."

As she spoke, Flynn turned to face the group and their eyes met. For a tormenting second she saw something there apart from anger. Was it regret? He quickly tugged the brim of his Akubra down to cover his eyes and whispered something to Lucy. Ellie could see the teenager was close to tears, but she nodded and ran into the hall.

"Don't contact me again," called Flynn as he headed back to his ute. Ellie wasn't sure whether he was speaking to the journalists or her. Probably both. The ute started and its engine revved. Flynn did a three-point turn and sped off in the direction of his farm, leaving nothing but a blur of red dust.

Ellie addressed the eager journalists. "I'm going to take my godmother into the hall and then I'll be back."

"We'll be waiting," replied the woman.

I'll bet.

"You want me to stay with you?" asked Matilda as Ellie took hold of the wheelchair once again.

"Nope, you go inside and get everyone focused on the auditions instead of on Flynn and me. This is embarrassing."

"It's not your fault," said Matilda firmly.

Ellie shrugged. "They're just doing their job. If I speak to them, hopefully they'll go away, or at least leave Flynn alone." For a moment she wondered if Dwayne had been right. Maybe she should have stayed in Sydney and simply ensured Matilda had competent hired help.

"Vultures," Matilda spit as Ellie wheeled her past the journalists. They jumped back as if they'd been slapped.

As they entered the hall, Ellie was all too aware that the conversation dimmed. Some people stared while others looked pointedly away. She didn't know which was worse. She pushed Matilda in the direction of Mrs. Ellery, who was holding a clipboard and waving one arm as she chatted to a couple of people near the stage.

Mrs. Ellery's eyes lit up when they caught sight of Ellie. "Elenora!" She thrust the clipboard on the woman next to her and held out her arms. "My star pupil. Have you come to join the group?"

Ellie allowed a quick hug, although she couldn't relax in the other woman's embrace. Nothing about being in this town felt right anymore. She couldn't forget that Eileen's opinion of her was the minority one. "No," she answered, extracting herself. "I've got some…um…things I need to attend to. Can I leave Matilda in your hands?"

"Of course, my dear," Mrs. Ellery gushed. "We're so

glad you brought Mat along. The group wouldn't be the same without her."

As Mrs. Ellery stooped to consult Matilda about the program for the day, Ellie slipped back outside. It was too much to hope the journalists had grown bored and left. Sure enough, they were waiting to pounce the second she exited the building. Ellie made a silent vow to keep control and make sure *she* led the interview. She addressed the two as one. "Let's go down to the park and talk. I haven't got long."

As they trotted down the road, the short and stumpy woman tried to make friends with Ellie, chatting about her character on *Lake Street* and how devastated she'd been to hear Stella was taking a break.

"You will be back, though, won't you?" asked the journo-fan. "After your godmother has recovered, that is?"

"The interview will start at the park," answered Ellie.

That shut her up. She knew she sounded frosty, but right now Ellie couldn't care less. Her mind was like a DVD frozen on the one scene, unable to move on. All she saw was Flynn's face for that brief moment he'd acknowledged her. Stupidly, for that minute moment in time, she'd forgotten their lives had moved on, forgotten she no longer had the right to run up to Flynn and fall into his arms. Her chest throbbed at the thought.

The three walked in silence, attracting the odd stare as a car slowed down to see if it really was Ellie Hughes returned. Country folk loved their gossip, and there was a particular validation from seeing certain things with your own eyes.

When they reached Apex Park, Ellie knew she couldn't put the journalists off any longer. She felt uncomfortable with the subject matter, guilty for not running this past Dwayne first. Bar that one journalist aeons ago, no one had ever asked her about Flynn. She had no rote answers for this.

Ellie sat down on one side of a picnic table and waited for the two to sit. "Okay, this is how it's going to work. I agree to answer three questions. You choose them carefully and promise that if I talk to you, you'll stop bothering Flynn Quartermaine."

"So, you do still care?" The *Lake Street* fan grinned as if she'd just won a Walkley Award.

Ellie looked at the woman. "Is that your first question?"

"Yes."

"Of course I care." Ellie swallowed but it didn't clear the dry feeling in her throat. "Flynn Quartermaine was a huge part of my life. I came to Hope Junction a broken teenager. I was a mess, but Flynn and Matilda, my godmother, saw past the damage to what was inside. They helped me heal. Although Flynn and I didn't work out, he'll always hold a special place in my heart."

"If he meant so much, why did you leave him standing at the altar?" asked the second reporter.

"Ever heard of cold feet?" she said, trying to keep her voice calm. "I was nineteen. I was in love but I was scared. I believe *I do* is forever and, to be honest—" she hesitated, thinking through the ramifications of her words "—I wasn't sure I could spend my life in a small town indefinitely. I wanted to explore. I wanted to see the world."

It was a blatant lie, but it was what everyone already believed and, therefore, convenient. The truth was far more distressing, something she couldn't let herself think about in front of these gossip-hungry strangers.

"How did Flynn cope after you left?"

Both reporters were scribbling her words in their note-books. They were just as Matilda had accused—vultures. They'd love to hear the truth about Flynn and cast her as the villain. She knew how the media worked. Australia had loved her for far too long, and any journalist would be stoked to write the story that brought the star down. Not to mention that rural Australia was all the rage at the moment. *Farmer Wants a Wife* had glamorized the Aussie men and women who worked the land in circum-stances of drought, flood and other unkind conditions. The country would be extremely sympathetic to Flynn's story. A zillion women would write to him offering to mend his broken heart.

"He coped fine, as far as I know," replied Ellie, lifting her chin and trying not to give away any kind of emo-tion. Another lie.

There was a silence—they expected more. Ellie kept her mouth shut, looking from one reporter to the other. She couldn't help feeling a tad victorious.

"I'm afraid you've wasted your time coming here. This story was over long ago. Flynn won't talk to you, and neither will the residents of Hope. I've returned sim-ply to look after my godmother, who fell a week ago, spraining one ankle and breaking the other. She'll be well again soon and I'll be back on the set of *Lake Street*. And I think that's our questions done."

The journos shook their heads at Ellie's saccharine smile, shoving their notebooks into their bags. "Thanks for your time," offered the one who loved *Lake Street*. "Give your godmother our best wishes."

Ellie politely shook their hands. They walked back to the hall and she watched to make sure the reporters took the road out of town and not the one to Flynn's place. Then she made her way to Matilda's to collect the Premier. The interview had gone much better than she'd expected, but talking to the journos had made her realize something. It was time she faced her fears.

If she were to stay in Hope Junction any longer, she needed to face her guilt and speak to Flynn.

CHAPTER SEVEN

A BITTER FLYNN stripped down to his undies and plunged
into the dam. Today was uncharacteristically warm for
August—and especially compared to the weekend—
but it wouldn't have made a difference if it were freezing. He needed to let off steam, to exert energy—and
fast. The altercation with the journalists and seeing Ellie
again had put him in a bad mood. Bad moods he didn't
like. He generally saw the positives in a situation when
everyone else was full of woe—at least nowadays—but
right now the positives could take a hike.

"Argh!" He let out a piercing roar as he came up for
air. *Why? How?* How could he let Ellie take hold of him
again like this? He'd promised Lucy he'd be there to
see her audition, and instead he'd stormed off in a rage.

He swam a couple of laps, trying to sort his churning
thoughts into some kind of order. But it didn't work. The
morning's fiasco played over and over and over again
in his throbbing head. Whether he left his eyes open or
shut them tight all he saw was Ellie. Gorgeous and confident as she'd walked toward the journalists and taken
control of the situation.

Even now, as he turned to swim another lap, there she
was, standing on the edge of the dam, looking utterly
delectable in tight jeans and that mysteriously irresistible rugby sweater. Ignoring the mirage, he dived back
under and charged the other way, and then back again.

Through the water, he thought he saw a golden Premier sitting on the dirt just behind the image of Ellie. He emerged and blinked, hoping she and the car would disappear. That his imagination would stop playing nasty tricks. Instead, Ellie was clearer than ever as she lifted a hand and waved tentatively at him.

She's real!

Her top lifted slightly as she waved and he copped a glimpse of a toned, tanned, terrific stomach. The desire packed a punch and he almost went under.

"Are you okay?" she called out.

Flynn struggled back above the water and saw Ellie running toward him, her deep chocolate hair blowing behind her in the wind. He couldn't believe she still knew where to find him. Dismissing that thought, Flynn swam to the side and scrambled out, yanking on his jeans over wet skin and tense muscle.

"What the hell are you doing here?" he asked. She was kind enough to avert her gaze while he dressed, but Ellie finding him seminaked wasn't the problem. It was her being here full stop. Smoothing his T-shirt over his wet chest, he stared at her and shivered. "Well?"

"I thought it was time we talked." Her voice wavered, and Flynn swore he saw tears welling in her eyes. Eyes almost the same brown as her hair. Her hands were behind her back, making him wonder if she'd crossed her fingers. He remembered holding those hands…could still recall how soft they were.

Stop!

Determined not to let the memories get to him, he let out a derisive snort. "You're ten years too late. Besides, I'm busy."

"Five minutes, Flynn. Please?" The way she looked at him stalled his anger for a brief second. She took her chance. "I know I don't deserve any time at all, that the way I left was unforgivable, but I need you to know it wasn't because of you."

"The old it's-not-you-it's-me, hey?" Flynn's voice seeped disbelief as he bent to pull on his boots. She was once the best friend he'd ever had, and now he didn't know her at all. "Is this supposed to make me feel better or just absolve you?"

"Both," she replied honestly. "I'm sorry for hurting you, Flynn. There's nothing I regret more in the world. I was totally messed up back then, and I truly didn't want to bring you down with me. I thought by leaving I was doing you a favor."

Flynn didn't know which part of that to respond to. He took a moment. "What do you mean messed up? I thought you were happy. I thought *we* were happy."

It was true, Flynn had never been happier than in those years he'd spent with Ellie. It was a high he'd never managed to reach since. She'd ruined him for anyone else.

"We *were* happy." She bit her lip and her eyes brimmed with more tears. "But…you remember how I went to Perth to see my mother?"

He frowned, thinking back. "Yes. I was meant to go with you."

She sniffed. "I wish you had."

"Why?" Without thinking he gestured to a shady spot underneath a nearby tree. Despite everything, he could feel himself mellowing toward her. Although she was older and more refined, there was something about her that he still recognized. Something about her he still liked. Against his better judgment, he wanted to spend a little time with her.

"Thanks." She walked with him to the tree and sat

down cross-legged. He leaned back against the trunk for support. And waited.

"I was so excited about Mom asking me to go meet her, and her promise to come to the wedding." She smiled halfheartedly at the recollection.

He nodded. "I remember."

"Of course you do, Flynn. You were always thoughtful."

He bristled at her comment—it felt like a cheap compliment. It wasn't only the words that irritated him but also the way she said them. As if she'd had elocution lessons and now spoke the Queen's English instead of regular outback Aussie.

"I just wanted to see Mom again," she continued, oblivious to his assessment. "To bring her back to meet everyone who'd come to be a part of my life in Hope. Maybe I wanted to see if she'd changed. I mean, I didn't want her coming here and ruining the life I'd made. I didn't want her doing stupid things and making people think badly of me because of her."

"They wouldn't have." Unsaid was the fact that Ellie had changed everyone's opinion of her without any help from her mother.

"I see that, in hindsight," Ellie said. Her eyes dropped to the dirt and she yanked out a solitary strand of grass to twist around her fingers. She always fidgeted when she was nervous, he remembered. "Anyway, Rhiannon didn't turn up. I waited in the bar at Burswood Casino for hours. I…I endured a number of…come-ons—by men old enough to be my father—but I sat firm, waiting for her. And she never showed."

"Oh, Ellie. I should have been with you." Flynn leaned forward to take her into his arms and then quickly pulled back, terrified by the gesture that had once been second nature. She wasn't his to comfort, not anymore. He cleared his throat. "What did you do?"

ELLIE LOOKED INTO Flynn's understanding eyes and her guilt multiplied. Driving the twenty kilometers from town, facing him, telling him what happened all those years ago—this was meant to help allay the guilt. Meant to help them both move on. But being here, in such close proximity, was stifling. He'd almost hugged her. Almost pulled her into his warm, strong embrace, and she couldn't deny the immense disappointment when he hadn't.

But sitting here under the gigantic old eucalypt, Ellie realized that telling Flynn the whole truth would only hurt him more than she already had. She hadn't told him ten years ago because she couldn't bear to see the disappointment in his eyes. Disappointment in her. She still couldn't bear it. And what good would telling him about something that happened years ago actually do? Could it rewrite history? Would it make him feel any better? Would it make her?

"I got really, really drunk," she answered eventually, after thinking carefully about how much to tell him. "I cried a lot and then I started to ask questions about myself. My mom had been married three times by that point. She had no inkling of responsibility or real love. What if I was like her? What if what I felt for you didn't last?"

Flynn frowned, but even with his forehead lined with creases, he still pleased the eye. "But you went to Perth a month before…before our…"

"I know." Ellie jumped in, not wanting him to have to say wedding, and her not wanting to hear the word, either. "And I thought the doubts would pass, but they didn't. I loved you more than anything, but the future felt uncertain and I just couldn't go through with it. I can't explain it any better than that."

She wasn't exactly lying—her mother's history *had* worried her. But despite more than a few people predicting she'd turn out like Rhiannon, she'd been determined not to. She'd wanted a lasting relationship that meant something. All these feelings she spoke about were real—she'd just left some important parts out.

For a long moment only the squawk of cockatoos high above broke the silence between them. Flynn didn't say anything, but Ellie could feel the disappointment radiating off him like a raging fever. Thank God, she hadn't told him everything.

"I know you can never forgive me," she said eventually, "but I want you to know I did love you." *Still do,* she added silently, knowing it for the truth it was. Knowing he deserved so much more. "I know it'll never be enough, but I wanted to say sorry."

The lameness of the word hung between them and Ellie wished she could erase it. Hadn't she already told herself that sorry wouldn't cut it? She knew if the shoe had been on the other foot, if she'd been jilted, left stranded at the altar, she wouldn't be sitting here now letting him chat. She'd have hacked his heart out with a blunt machete and fed it to the dingoes years ago.

"I do forgive you, Els."

"What?" Her ears had to be deceiving her. Or he was playing a cruel joke? "What did you say?"

He took her hand and held it firm as he looked into her eyes. Ellie's heart pounded so hard she was sure he could see it thumping against her top. His hand was warm, comforting, everything she craved and never found in anybody else.

"I've moved on," Flynn said.

Her heart squeezed. Perhaps he was relieved she'd ended it. They'd been so young that, maybe in hindsight, he'd realized what he'd felt hadn't been love at all.

"Good," she said, trying to swallow the lump in her throat. But it wouldn't go down. In a pathetic attempt to stop the tears she'd hate herself for crying in front of him, she said the first thing that came into her head. "Friends, then?"

Flynn dropped her hand as if it were poison ivy. "No." Shaking his head, he scrambled to his feet. Ellie followed, unsteady. "I can't. I said I forgive you, and I appreciate you sharing why you thought you had to break off our engagement. But I'll never forget it. Do you have any idea what it was like?"

She shook her head as his voice got louder, more agitated.

"*Hell,* Ellie. It was hell. Not only did I have to come to terms with the fact you didn't love me—like I thought you did, like I loved you—but I had to deal with the shame and the pity. With people saying I was better off single. That I should sow my wild seeds before I thought about settling down. That it was a mistake from the start."

She listened as Flynn poured his heart out. Hearing his anguish felt like someone was setting a match to her soul, but she deserved the agony after what she'd put him through.

"I went off the rails, Els. I hate the weak man you made me." The fury in his stare told her he meant it. "It wasn't only me I hurt, either. I broke my mother's heart, Gran's heart. I scared Lucy and I didn't make the most of the last years of Dad's life. That's why we will never be friends. I can't risk becoming that person again."

"Okay." Ellie nodded, unable to say anything more. She knew whatever sympathy she offered would seem insincere. So instead, she said, "I understand. Thank you for listening."

Flynn gave a regret-filled smile. "You're welcome. And thanks for having the guts to come to me. I respect that. Please give Mat my best wishes. I hope her recovery is quick."

Those were Flynn's parting words, before he strode off across the paddock, leaving Ellie alone with only the swish of the trees and the distant sounds of sheep. She stood there for who knew how long, aching at this polite, impersonal end to their heartrending conversation.

CHAPTER EIGHT

AFTER HER CONFRONTATION with Flynn, Ellie didn't know how she would stay in Hope Junction a moment longer, but Matilda had a stream of visitors over the following days, and Ellie practically had a full-time job just waiting on them. Somehow tea and biscuits became a seemingly endless task, then Joyce joined the fray, creating mountains of washing up with her culinary delights.

At first Ellie was anxious about Mat's friends, worried they'd snub her, but either they didn't buy into that nonsense or they loved Mat too much to upset her, leaving Ellie alone in the process. And sure enough, within the week, Ellie had grown to love the old dears, many of whom had ten years or so on Matilda. Their stories of times gone by fascinated her, and she adored it when one of them persuaded Mat to tell stories from her travels.

In her heyday Matilda had been a famous travel writer, favoring off-the-beaten-track destinations over popular tourist spots. Her articles had been published all over the globe, in prestigious publications such as the *New York Times* and the *Guardian,* not to mention every major newspaper in Australia. Some of her articles had been collected in two big coffee-table volumes, complemented by award-winning photography.

Mat had continued to travel widely in the time Ellie had known her, but she no longer wrote for publication. Her brother was as worldly as she was, and she made a point of visiting him wherever he was posted. Her last official expedition had been the month before she'd become Ellie's guardian. Rhiannon's and Matilda's families had been friends when the two women were growing up, and although they were quite different, they'd stayed in contact over the years. Mat was probably the only person Rhiannon could call a friend—for a time, anyway. So when Ellie was born Matilda was the obvious choice for godmother. Later, when Rhiannon's third husband scored a contract overseas and didn't want Ellie tagging along, Rhiannon asked Mat if Ellie could stay with her. Matilda didn't think twice about putting her life and dreams on hold to look after the teenage girl. She welcomed Ellie with open arms and made her life in Hope Junction a good one. But Rhiannon's abandonment had put the nail in the coffin of their friendship. As far as Ellie knew, they hadn't spoken since.

And so for Matilda, Ellie would do anything. Including trying her hand at cooking.

Joyce was a frequent visitor at Mat's house, seeming to spend more time there than she did at the caravan park. Ellie wondered if Joyce's guests simply fended for themselves. But hell, she was grateful for the company of the eccentric woman, who also happened to be a supremely good cook. Her cuisine was better than Ellie had tasted at some of Sydney's top restaurants, and the best thing was Joyce was a great teacher. She took Ellie under her wing, giving her something to think about other than Flynn or life back in Sydney.

She'd be lying if she said she wasn't somewhat homesick. While Mat's place was the only true home she'd ever known, and while she loved spending time with her friend, Ellie missed the routine and familiarity of her life back east. She simply couldn't relax in Hope Junction and she missed the show, her friends and the cast—her home away from home. Emails and the internet were her lifelines. Her iPad was her first point of call in the morning and the last thing she did at night before she went to sleep.

"WHAT'S THAT WOEFUL look on your face?" asked Ellie as she returned to the living room. It was Wednesday afternoon and she'd just waved off Eileen and Joyce, the last visitors for the day.

"Just thinking." Mat smiled, looking anything but relaxed. Ellie flopped into the armchair opposite. "I'm worried you're overexerting yourself looking after me and doing all this cooking."

Ellie rolled her shoulders and pretended to do arm exercises. "I'm using muscles I never thought I had, that's for sure. Can you imagine…me cooking?"

"It's certainly a sight I hadn't expected," Mat said, and chuckled, before adopting a serious look again. "But you're missing Sydney, aren't you?"

A cold washed over Ellie but she shrugged off the suggestion. "It's not easy being here, but I'm glad I came." She forced a smile, hoping she hadn't made her discomfort too obvious. She'd been back almost a fortnight now, and Matilda was right, but she never wanted her godmother to feel like a burden.

Mat made a tsking noise between her teeth. "There you go playing things down again. You've barely left the house in over a week, except to take me to rehearsals."

Ellie offered Mat a reprimanding look. "Hmm, sweetie, I hate to remind you, but that's why I'm here."

Mat tossed Ellie's look right back at her. "You know what I mean. Holing up with an old bird like me isn't healthy for a pretty young thing."

"Stop being silly," said Ellie, starting to feel uncomfortable. She wouldn't put it past Mat to arrange for a group of twentysomething locals to take her out to the pub. She couldn't think of anything worse. "I came here for you and I'm staying until you're free of wheelchairs and crutches and casts. I'd never forgive myself if I left too early and you hurt yourself again. You mean the world to me, you know that."

She saw Mat's determined concern soften as a smile formed on her lips. But then she pressed her hand against her heart, and Ellie wondered, for a second, if she was having difficulty breathing.

"Are you okay?" Ellie leaped to her feet and crossed to Matilda. "Did you choke on something? Can I get you a drink?"

Mat placed her hand on Ellie's forearm and shook her head. She breathed deeply, in and out for a few moments, and then said, "I'm fine, honestly. Just swallowed some air the wrong way."

"Well, good," said Ellie, wrapping her arms around Mat and hugging tightly. "Because I need you around a lot longer yet."

Matilda just smiled.

Despite not having a social life or a day job, Ellie kept herself busy looking after Mat, ensuring she ate a balanced diet and got enough rest, and doing what they did best whenever they were together—talk. She therefore hadn't finished the awnings as quickly as she'd imagined.

"There," she said to Matilda, who was sitting in the wheelchair on the front lawn, catching some afternoon sun. Ellie climbed down from the ladder and admired her handiwork. "Finally done."

"And not a broken ankle to show for it." Mat laughed, knocking on her plaster cast. "What will you do with your time now?"

"Well," said Ellie, dumping the paintbrush in the bucket of metho on the veranda, "I was thinking I might come and watch the rehearsals tonight."

Matilda gasped. "What? You serious?"

Ellie shrugged. "Sure. How bad could it be?" A smile lit Matilda's face as Ellie pondered her own question. She didn't want to count her chickens, but she hadn't had an unkind word from anyone in town for over a week. Granted, she hadn't left the house any more than she absolutely had to, but maybe it was time to change that. Maybe it was time to be brave. She was in a better mood than she'd been in for quite a while. With the benefit of time, she realized her conversation with Flynn had been cathartic. If he could forgive her, what right did anyone else have to harbor a grudge? And with her cheerful frame of mind, she might just tell that to anyone who dared get in her way.

There was the added fact she was itching to be involved with some acting. She missed the comradeship of her colleagues back in Sydney. Hopefully, watching the theatrical group would help alleviate some of the homesickness she felt for *Lake Street*.

"It'll be brilliant." Matilda clapped her hands like an exuberant child. "Let's go get ready."

Ellie glanced at her watch and laughed. "We've got hours before we have to be there."

In those said hours she folded washing, ironed clothes and conjured up two-minute noodles for dinner while Matilda chattered on, telling Ellie the who's who of Hope Junction's reformed theatrical society.

"Lucy Quartermaine pretty much plays herself as the teenage daughter of a farmer."

Ellie's ears pricked up at the mention of Flynn's sister, but she focused on emptying the seasoning sachet and hoped Mat didn't notice her interest. What kind of person had she grown into? Was she good at playing her part? Was she as popular at school as Flynn had been? But she kept her lips firmly shut as she waited for the description of the next person.

Ellie had told Mat the basics of her conversation with Flynn—and managed not to cry at the finality of it—but they'd pretty much gone back to him being a no-go subject since then. It was best that way. Ellie needed to move on, to destroy the stupid hope in her heart that the future may have had a happy ending for her and Flynn. It wouldn't. Yet every mention of him was like a sugar cube dangled before a hungry horse.

By the time Ellie and Mat arrived at the Memorial Hall that evening, Ellie thought she could write a book on the members of the group. They sounded like a quirky bunch of characters and she couldn't wait to watch them from the sidelines. Trying to look inconspicuous, she wheeled Matilda into the hall and led her down to the stage. She sat on a chair next to Matilda and tried not to feel awkward as only a smattering of the people who greeted her godmother bothered to acknowledge her.

Ellie was thankful when Mrs. Ellery took center stage and clanged an old tambourine to get everyone's attention. The chairs around her filled quickly. She cast her eyes about surreptitiously and her gaze caught on the cold stare of Lucy Quartermaine. Her heart lunged toward her throat. If looks could kill, she'd have been sprawled across the wooden floorboards, dead.

She turned back to face the front but could almost feel

Lucy's ice-blue eyes boring into her. *It's sweet,* she told herself. Lucy was just being protective of her big brother. But somehow Lucy's snub hurt more than all the others put together. Lucy had once meant the world to Ellie.

"Okay. Before we start…" Eileen's voice carried right to the back of the hall, much farther than anyone was sitting. Ellie turned her attentions to her former teacher, attempting to forget about Lucy. "I just want to welcome our old friend Elenora Hughes to the group. All the way from Sydney, she brings a wealth of knowledge about the dramatic arts, and I hope you'll all make her feel welcome and pick her brains for advice."

Eileen spoke as if Ellie were here to become part of the group. She thought she should put her straight, raising her hand to speak, but then realized how this might sound. As if she thought herself above everyone else. She withdrew her hand, nodded thanks to Mrs. Ellery and looked around the room. Surprisingly, she met a few warm smiles. She memorized these faces, planning to approach them later. But there was little time to ponder who might be friend and who was definitely foe. Eileen tapped her tambourine again and most of the chairs were pushed back into a semicircle. Ellie felt the excitement pumping through her veins as the rehearsal began. Shifting Matilda back slightly, she stayed seated beside her, following the script in her godmother's lap. Matilda had the role of prompting.

At this stage of rehearsals, it was to be expected that they wouldn't know their lines perfectly. Ellie anticipated some rustiness, but she was taken aback by just how bad the majority of the actors were. No one knew their lines. Some shouted loudly and others could barely be heard. None of them seemed to have been told not to position their back to the audience.

"How long till the production?" whispered Ellie to Matilda.

Mat looked at Ellie and cringed. "They're terrible, aren't they?"

"Well…" Ellie wouldn't say *terrible,* but *diabolical* came to mind. If there wasn't a rapid improvement, the audience would be throwing tomatoes and demanding their money back.

Matilda raised her eyebrows as if daring Ellie to sugar the truth.

"Okay." Ellie nodded. "They're terrible."

As the amateurs continued in front of them, Matilda asked, "Is there any hope?"

"Sure. Some have real potential." She nodded her head at a middle-aged man acting out a scene with Lucy Quartermaine. "Those two are almost good. And I wouldn't say any of them are complete write-offs. They just need a little tuition."

At that very moment Eileen Ellery happened to lean in and heard the tail end of Ellie's assessment. Unfortunately, she jumped to the wrong conclusion.

"Oh, would you mind? I seem to have lost my touch, but I'm sure if they had a professional like you instructing them, they'd catch on in no time."

"Um…" When she arrived two weeks ago, there would have been nothing on this planet—not even Matilda's desperate plea—that would have induced her to join a community theater. Nothing. But a fortnight was a long time. Facing up to Flynn had made her feel stronger. She couldn't change the past but she'd made peace with him, and that, she felt, would make it easier to walk the streets of Hope with her head held high. And a fortnight was a long time to go without doing something you loved.

Although she'd never planned on acting as a career,

it had become everything to her. Her life was her job, and she missed being Stella Williams. The past few days she'd found herself surfing the *Lake Street* website, reading up on the latest news. She welcomed Dwayne's emails every few days, his checking to see how she was, his persistent asking when she'd be ready to return to the show. She couldn't go back yet, but she couldn't just sit around, either. Now the awnings were finished, she needed another pastime. And taking on this task would mean another arena where she got to spend time with Mat. That had to be a bonus. But then Ellie thought about Lucy's cold stare. She didn't want to thrust herself on people who didn't want her.

"I'd be happy to," she said finally to Mrs. Ellery, "but I'd like you to talk to the group about it first. Let them decide if they want me on board. As you know, I'm not very popular around here anymore. I wouldn't want to cause unrest in your group."

Mrs. Ellery sighed and shook her head. "People need to stop holding grudges, but I do understand what you're saying. You're a wise young lady, Ellie. How about you take Mat home and I'll have a quick meeting with the members? I'll pop round for morning tea tomorrow and let you know the outcome."

"Sounds good."

Ellie picked up her bag and checked Matilda was comfortable in the wheelchair before walking them home in the fresh evening air.

She thought she'd sleep well after the manual labor of the past few days, but her mind was abuzz, second-guessing what the members would decide. She tossed and turned, wishing Mrs. Ellery had agreed to call her that night. The more she thought about this opportunity, the more she wanted it. She wanted the chance to show the town the real Ellie. She needed them to see that she could be a team player, that she could be an asset to the town.

CHAPTER NINE

LIFE WENT ON post-Ellie, as Flynn had come to call the conversation they'd had by the water hole. He thanked the Lord it had been busy on the farm in the lead-up to Black Stump's annual ram sale. Getting organized for it had given him little time to think about anything but work over the past week. Aside from driving Lucy into town for rehearsals—so his mom didn't have to drive late at night—Flynn had spent most of his days preparing the ram shed: clipping dags, making up the pens, checking for lameness, cross-checking data. Anything and everything to ensure it was all perfect on the day.

This was also useful in his efforts to ignore the advances of Lauren Simpson. Since he'd fled two Sundays ago, she'd been like a persistent fly at a barbecue, hovering about him as if he were a piece of prize steak. Apart from phoning every day, she'd been waiting in town each time he dropped Lucy off, suggesting they get a drink while he waited. Aside from the fact he needed to stay off the grog, he came up with a number of creative excuses to politely decline.

Yet part of him wished he could accept her offers. Once upon a time he'd craved a woman to love, to come home to, to have a family with. He loved kids. Flynn used to spend ram sales and country shows hanging with any little taggers-on, offering piggyback rides and dizzy-whizzies. But he'd completely retreated from such activities after Ellie left. And then when his dad was killed, he'd been forced back into the business side of farming, unable to mess about. But the desire to have a child of his own hadn't left him like Ellie, or died like his dad. The problem was finding a woman to have children with. And while he dealt with many eligible women—an agronomist, his auctioneer, a number of female farmers, as well as the gorgeous girls he met at football games and social events—he just didn't feel enough for any of them to take things further than a quick roll in the hay. He didn't feel anything like the attraction he'd experienced the three brief times he'd been with Ellie since her return. An attraction that pissed him off and burned like a spotting bushfire. But even if he were willing to forget what Ellie had done, she now led a glamorous life in Sydney and he would never leave Hope.

What the? Shaking his head at the crazy thought, he snicked his chin on his razor and cursed. The last thing he needed on sale day—today—was to have little red spots all over his jawline. And the last thing he needed at all was to start thinking he and Ellie had any sort of chance together. There were some things that just couldn't happen. He ran the tap and washed the cut.

A knock sounded at his front door, and whoever it was let themselves in before he could call out. He knew it would be his mom come to talk about the catering. Every second year Black Stump had the CWA provide the sale food as a fund-raiser. The other years, Mom and Gran, and Lucy if she was in the mood for helping, did it themselves.

Satisfied he had a smooth face and didn't look like Edward Scissorhands, Flynn laid his razor on the vanity. He ran some water through his hair with his fingers and stepped into the hallway, whistling as if he hadn't just spent the past half an hour pondering women and their future in his life.

"Have you eaten breakfast?" his mom asked as Flynn entered the kitchen. She had the kettle on and the fridge open.

"I had a bowl of cereal." He strode to his boots at the back door and stooped to tug them on. "And I'll sample some of your scrumptious cuisine later."

"Flynn," his mom said, and sighed, "Froot Loops aren't food, and you know you won't have time to stop and eat something later. You know we're going to draw a crowd today. You've done such a brilliant job with the SAMMs."

Flynn couldn't help but smile at the compliment.

"Your dad would have been proud. He was man enough to admit when he made an error of judgment. We're both proud of what you've done to ensure the continued success of Black Stump." She walked over and embraced him.

Flynn's eyes watered. "Thanks, Mom, but I wish I could have convinced him before he died. I felt such a prick going against his wishes when he was no longer here to argue for them. Thanks for trusting me."

She pulled back and looked in his eyes. "Of course I trust you, darling. I know that whatever you put your mind to, you'll succeed." She paused a second, then, "Flynn, I—"

He cut her off. The ponderous look in her eyes told him she was about to launch into her favorite topic of late. Happiness, and how she wanted him to find it. Another thing he didn't need was a lecture on how to live his life. "Sorry, Mom, it's getting on. I better get things rolling."

Out of the house, he relished the hard labor that

needed to be done. The sale was due to start at one. He had to put straw in the pens and then he and Rodger, his kelpie, and a couple of workers had the arduous task of collecting the rams from the yards. Potential buyers and company reps usually began to arrive a few hours before the auction kicked off. He needed to be on hand to schmooze—as Lucy liked to put it—and discuss the catalogue with anyone who wanted to chat.

Luckily the auctioneer—the young and extremely efficient Haylee Edwards—had done his last few sales. She was familiar with Black Stump and its genetics, and wouldn't need to take up much of his time beforehand. Not everyone approved of a girl with the hammer, but Haylee ran a clean, quick auction, ensuring plenty of time at the end for a good Aussie piss-up, where the buyers tried to get some of their money back in the form of beer. For this reason, most of the farmers had learned to accommodate her. Flynn was confident that with Haylee's auctioneering, his preparation and his mom's catering, the day would be a success.

LATER, FEELING GOOD about the way the sale had gone, Flynn glanced toward the catering tent. The crowd was dwindling around the sheep pens now and following the aromas of the delights whipped up by his girls. His stomach growled at the thought. He just needed a quick word with Haylee and then he'd be there, too, making sure everyone was happy, well fed and offered a beer if they desired one.

But his plan was interrupted when a group parted and a woman emerged, a pristine white apron tied around her tiny waist and a platter of food balanced on one hand. *Lauren*. What the hell was she doing here? Not to buy sheep, that much was true. Flynn was about to march up to her when he felt a tap on his shoulder.

"Great result, son," came his mom's voice.

He cleared his throat and turned to her. She wore a wide smile and an apron identical to Lauren's. She spoke before he could.

"She's a gem, isn't she?" Her eyes trained to where Lauren was wooing the sale-goers with friendly banter and good food.

"Um…" He couldn't exactly tell his mom that Lauren was more of a pest.

"We ran into each other in the Co-op the other day. I was in a bit of a tizz about how much I needed to organize."

Flynn raised an eyebrow. He couldn't recall a day in his life when his mother had been in a tizz. Even at his father's funeral, she'd been cool, calm and collected. Unnervingly so.

Ignoring his skeptical expression, Karina continued, "I told her about the ram sale and she offered to give up her day off to help Granny and I. I didn't want Lucy taking more time out from study this close to exams. I mean, the play's distraction enough."

"No, course not." He couldn't argue with that. But Lauren?

"You should go over and thank her," Karina finished with a gentle but firm, guiding touch on his arm. He knew matchmaking when he saw it and he wished to hell she wouldn't bother. Lauren needed little encouragement.

Even though it was the last thing he fancied doing, Flynn decided it best to get the conversation over and done with. He waited until the last piece of food had been taken from Lauren's platter and caught her on her way back to the trestle tables.

"Hi, Lauren." It was the first time *he'd* approached *her* since that close-call night.

She glanced up, her pale green eyes widening as if she were surprised to see him. "Flynn?"

He bristled at her velvet tone. "Mom says you offered to help. Thanks."

"Not a problem. I love being out on farms and the atmosphere on these days is amazing." She gestured around at the jovial farmers, Akubras on their heads, bellies bouncing up and down as they guzzled grog and laughed and chatted. "I'd rather be here than just vacuuming at my place."

"Fair enough, but I…"

She broke in, "Look, Flynn, you don't have to worry about me wanting anything out of this, or you giving me the wrong idea. I'm doing it because I want to help and I enjoy it. And I thought it might be the only way to get you to talk to me."

He opened his mouth to lay it straight, to tell her he was sorry, that he just wasn't interested, but she held up her hand.

"You're gorgeous, Flynn Quartermaine—inside and definitely out." She winked and looked him up and down suggestively. "I'm sorry for egging you on with alcohol the other night, but I really, really like you. I know you think coming back to my place was a mistake, and since you do, I'm glad we didn't actually do the deed. But I hate that you won't talk to me, or even look me in the eye. We've got Rats and Whitney's wedding in a couple of weeks—how will it look if the best man and maid of honor can't even look at each other?"

He saw the pain in her eyes and realized how hard it was for her to have this conversation. Hell, he knew all there was to know about unrequited affection—he could write the *For Dummies* book on it.

"You're right. And I'm sorry," he said. "Avoiding you was childish and I really have no excuse."

She shrugged. "I caught you on a bad night. I know that. You weren't yourself and I took advantage of that. Will you forgive me?"

He suddenly saw a whole new side to Lauren. "Forgive you for what?"

"Thank you." Her grin lit up her whole face. Faint freckles danced on her full cheeks. "I promise not to stalk you anymore."

"In that case—" he gestured to the platter in her hand "—let me refill that and you go get yourself a drink. Don't want the word getting around that we're tyrants here at Black Stump."

She smiled and let him take the tray. As she sidled off to the beverage table he hoped some young farmer from the surrounding shires would notice her and strike up a conversation. She'd no doubt make a devoted partner for someone one day.

After finding Haylee and going through the sales of the day, Flynn cracked open a celebratory can of Coke and started doing the rounds. Days like these were good for catching up on the region's gossip—not stuff his mom would be interested in, like who was marrying who and having whose babies, but important things, like which farms were changing hands.

The night was a long but good one. The next time Flynn clapped eyes on Lauren she had her arms up to their elbows in the sink, scrubbing away.

"Is she still here?" he whispered to his mom as she approached.

"Yep." Karina's smile told him how happy she was

with Lauren. "She's surprised me, that girl. A real hard worker, don't know how we'd have gotten through the day without her."

Flynn frowned and watched Lauren from a distance. Could it be he'd misjudged her?

CHAPTER TEN

THE BEST THING about staying sober at a ram sale, Flynn reflected as he cleaned up his breakfast dishes, was not waking up with a hangover the next morning. This way he'd have a clear head for writing up his notes *and* be on top form for football this afternoon.

He whistled as he washed, contemplating Black Stump's best ram sale in recorded history. He couldn't deny that growing the farm gave him a certain buzz. His dad had been a great farmer—one of the best around, locals liked to say—and he wanted to make him proud. He wanted to make his mark as a farmer, and he hoped that one day this was what people would think of when they heard the name Flynn Quartermaine—not the last baby born at Hope Junction Hospital, or his Grand Final streak, or that other thing he'd rather forget. His farming ideas were a bit modern for some, but they weren't crazy or harebrained. They were real good money earners, and yesterday's outcome proved this.

Maybe that was enough, Flynn thought. Maybe living and working on the land was all he needed to feel good about himself and enjoy life.

He stacked the crockery to dry on the side of the sink, grabbed his wallet and keys and left the cottage. He stopped his ute to check in on the women in his life, seeing if they needed anything from town. Surprisingly, Lucy was already awake—actually up and dressed. When he entered the homestead, he found her lounging in front of the telly, her feet on the coffee table, black nail polish drying on her toes. One arm was outstretched as she flicked channels distractedly.

Flynn waved at her —receiving no response—then addressed his mom, who was sorting washing on the big kitchen table.

"I can't understand where they all go." She threw a single bright pink sock in his general direction.

He smiled. "I'm popping into town. Can I get you anything?"

Karina shook her head as she held up a tablecloth and started folding. He was surprised she didn't iron it; she was usually meticulous with that sort of stuff. Dad always called her his domestic goddess. "Nope, but please take her off my hands." She angled her head toward the living room. "I'm going to throttle her in a minute."

"What's up her bum?" Flynn smiled, knowing his mom wouldn't take kindly to his phrasing.

"Who knows? She's been a grouch ever since she came back from theater practice on Thursday. If you can get her to tell you why, you're more woman than me."

"That I sincerely doubt."

"Would you two stop talking about me like I'm not here?" Lucy grumbled loudly and turned the television off with a theatrical swish. Flynn didn't love the idea of Lucy spending time acting—since Ellie had made a life without him on the screen, he'd soured toward the profession—but he had to admit the pastime fit her to a T.

"So, you coming or not?" he asked.

"If you *insist*." Lucy trudged to the door and slipped her feet into her fancy thongs. She stormed out to the ute, arms crossed over her chest and her face contorted in the perfect scowl.

"Didn't Mom ever read you that story about the boy who made faces? You know, the one where the wind changed?" Flynn turned the key in the ignition; Lucy didn't reply. Fair enough. As he swung the car onto the long gravel drive, he turned AC/DC up loud. He knew Lucy couldn't stand this band. And sure enough, before they'd even reached their property boundary, she'd huffed, puffed, uncrossed her arms, crossed them again and then leaned over to turn the music off. He watched all this out of the corner of his eye and did his damn best not to smirk. She glared at him.

"Ellie's joined the play," she finally announced.

Flynn's heart spasmed at her words, but outwardly he tried to not let a flicker of emotion show, maintaining his grip on the wheel as they flew over a pothole. Why the hell should it matter to him what Ellie did?

"Right," he managed. Yeah, that sounded really nonchalant. *Not*. Now it was *he* who felt like the surly teenager. All this talk of Ellie—the fact that she seemed to come up in every conversation—was making him regress. It had to stop. He hoped his voice sounded level and interested as he said, "And what's the problem? Is she vying for your role or something?"

"Hell, no! She's too old to play my part." A hiss slipped between her lips before she continued. "That batty Mrs. Ellery has signed her on as cast adviser or something stupid. But don't worry, I gave her the evil eye. I can't believe we're supposed to take advice from *her*. Can you?"

"Sure. From what I *hear*—" he wasn't going to admit to ever watching *Lake Street* "—she knows her stuff. Maybe you could learn something."

Lucy pressed her finger down hard on the button that

opened the window. She almost gasped in the fresh air. "But, Flynn, that's not the point."

"What is the point?" he asked, wishing they were already in town and this conversation was over. It didn't matter that he'd moved on, every time he talked about Ellie his mouth went dry and he found breathing difficult.

"She wronged you," spit Lucy, with venom and fury in her voice. If he didn't know his sister, hadn't been there every second of her life, he would have been horrified by this raw malice. Instead, he saw her anger for what it was: misguided loyalty.

"That was years ago," he answered simply, although some days it still felt like yesterday. "Ellie and I have spoken about what happened. I've moved on, and so should this town. That includes you."

"You spoke to her? When?"

This was not something he'd planned on discussing with Lucy. After the past week, he hoped he'd never have to speak about that conversation again. With anyone. Ever. But he knew the town was talking, and he didn't want his little sis wasting precious time and energy on this when she should be studying. Besides, he wouldn't wish her rage on his worst enemy. And strangely, he realized, that wasn't Ellie.

He took a deep breath. "A week ago. The day those reporters turned up. She followed me out to the dam and apologized."

Lucy's sharp intake of breath told him that the concept surprised her. "*She* said *sorry?* For leaving you at the altar?"

He tried to make a joke. "Why does everyone keep bringing that up?"

Lucy laughed. "Sorry. But seriously, she came to you?"

"Yeah." His mind flashed briefly to that day by the dam. It wasn't the first time he'd recalled that moment, with Ellie appearing like a heavenly vision, and he banished the image as fast as he could. "And she's not Cruella de Vil. She feels bad about what she did. I think she even regrets it."

"Then why? How could she do it?"

If Lucy only knew how many times he'd asked himself that question over the past ten years. But the same answer always appeared: she didn't love him.

He shrugged. "Not sure I'll ever know. There was a lot going on in her life. She just couldn't go through with it." It wasn't his place to tell anyone else about Ellie's mother. Lucy was back in the present anyway.

"So, like, are you two getting back together?" Her voice was tinged with excitement, in the way that only a teenage girl's could be.

Flynn didn't hesitate in his reply. "No." He spoke a language he knew Lucy would understand. "Not in a million years."

"O-kay." Lucy digested the info.

"But that doesn't mean you should ostracize her. We all make mistakes, that doesn't mean we have nothing to offer. If you're serious about the play, you should soak up as much of her expertise as you can."

Lucy played with her hair, twisting it around her fingers. She always did this when contemplating something deep. "If you're sure," she said eventually. "I mean, I'm loving the play and I think acting is something I could really dig. I want to apply to WAAPA for next year."

What? Flynn clenched his teeth to stop himself shouting. He didn't know what he would've said, presumably something along the lines of, *Get that idea out of your pretty little head right now.* But Lucy had already accused him of sounding like her father.

Flynn had always assumed Luce would go to uni in Perth, that she would study something like teaching or agricultural science, eventually making her way back to Hope Junction. He never entertained the idea that she might pursue a career that would, in all likelihood, move her across the country and out of his life. As well.

"It's really, really hard to get into, though." Lucy sounded more subdued than usual. "Any help I could get would be gold. But I don't want to hurt your feelings by taking advice from Ellie."

Flynn smiled inwardly at Lucy's heartfelt words. The fact she would put his feelings ahead of her dreams told him he would never lose her. He needed to put his fears aside and be as supportive as he could.

"Lucy," he said seriously, "you can do anything you put your mind to. If you want to act, let Ellie help. Understand?"

"Sure thing," she said, taking in the impact of his words. Then a puzzled look came over her. "But who's Cruella de Vil?"

THE RECEPTION ELLIE got on her first night of theater practice warmed her heart. Mostly hellos, how-are-yas and smiles all round, save for the few members who still offered only a cool expression in return for her greeting. But it was the drastic change in Lucy—from frosty to positively friendly—that both confused and pleased her. The Quartermaine girl flounced into the room and made a beeline for Ellie.

"Thanks so much for offering to coach us." Her pink, lip-glossed smile was wide and affectionate, her voice genuinely enthusiastic. "I'm a huge fan of *Lake Street*. I watch it in my bedroom. You know, when I'm 'studying.'" She made the inverted commas with her fingers, her mammoth grin requesting that the information stay confidential. It made sense—neither of them needed to point out that watching *Lake Street* in the lounge room at Black Stump would be a gross faux pas.

Ellie barely knew how to respond to Lucy's sudden kinship. She wanted to grab the younger woman in a warm embrace and shriek with joy, but that might be pushing things.

"Thanks," she managed to squeeze past the lump of surprise and emotion in her throat. "That means a lot." Lucy would never know how much, but for Ellie to feel that she hadn't been completely banished, completely forgotten by those who'd once been friends—that was comforting.

"I can't wait to get started," finished Lucy. She flashed another bright smile and took the seat closest to Ellie. Thirteen other eager amateurs sat in a semicircle facing her, waiting for the rehearsal to start.

Ellie felt glued to the patch of scratched wooden flooring under her feet. Had Flynn spoken to Lucy? She was a seventeen-year-old girl, but this change of attitude was too drastic to be explained away by adolescent hormones, surely. Ellie's heart lifted at the possibility, but she shook her head. She'd made a concerted effort to shift her thoughts whenever they'd drifted to Flynn this past week. It wasn't healthy to be fixated on someone who would never be fixated on you. That much she knew was true. She'd spent her childhood doing everything she could to please her mother, and nothing had made the woman love her. In the end, her desire to please had ruined her. She didn't want to waste the rest of her life feeling the same way about Flynn.

"Good evening, everyone." She addressed the group with a buoyancy she didn't feel. "Thanks for inviting me to help you prepare for the big production. Before we dive into rehearsing, I want us to practice a few key techniques that will enhance our performances." She took some A4 printouts from a clipboard on the seat behind her. "I want you to get into groups of two or three and rehearse one of these short skits. You've got ten minutes, and then we'll come back and perform them. I want you guys to assess each other and brainstorm what you think can be improved. Then I'll offer some tips and feedback. Simple, right?"

CHAPTER ELEVEN

ELLIE THIS, ELLIE THAT! If Flynn heard one more word about the fabulous Ellie, he would not be responsible for his actions. It seemed the town, or at least the theatrical society—and definitely his sister—was warming to Ellie Hughes. Rumor had it she was working wonders for the production, and he was happy about that, he really was. He didn't want people holding a grudge on his behalf. But Lucy's near hero worship of his ex-girlfriend was beginning to get to him.

Ellie was so nice, she said. So cool. So smart. So funny. In Lucy's eyes, Ellie seemed to have it all in the *so* department.

He pulled the protective glasses down over his eyes and drove the circular saw into the wood. He was making a wishing well for Rats's wedding, a task he hoped would also drown out Lucy's chatter. She was sitting on a stool nearby, swinging her legs to and fro, oblivious to the fact he wasn't interested in what she had to say. He'd already asked her if she had any homework to be getting on with. But she'd given him that look again— that he was treading too close to father territory—so he'd shut the hell up.

They talked about the wedding and about the suit fitting Flynn would have in Perth that week. Lucy surreptitiously pried about the bucks' night, and when that topic was exhausted, she moved on to moaning about one of her teachers. Flynn zoned out, wishing the school holidays would hurry up or that Mom would give Lucy some chores to do.

"I told everyone you'd be ace for it," she finished as he cut off the saw. His nerves prickled. What exactly had he missed? "So what do you say?"

He put the saw down, lifted the glasses and looked at his little sister. "Huh?"

"Flynn," she whined, "have you been listening at all?"

"Not really." He gestured to his work in progress. Only a pile of wood a few hours ago, it was taking shape quite well. "I'm kinda busy."

"I know, you're so good at that." She smiled serenely. "That's why I told them you are absolutely the best person for the job."

"You've lost me." Flynn tugged the safety glasses off his head and walked to the bar fridge. He grabbed a can of Coke and chucked a bottle of water to his sister. She was going through one of her health fads and wouldn't drink anything that wasn't see-through. "Start from the beginning. I'm listening now."

"The play's coming along really well. Matilda's got the costumes under control—she's delegated them to a couple of old birds from the Women's Club—and the high school band are gonna cover the music. But we're really struggling with the set. We need someone who's good with their hands." She paused and fluttered her eyelashes. "Someone like you."

He ignored her attempt at buttering him up. "You want me to build the set? I do have a farm to keep me busy, don't forget."

"I know that." Lucy spoke as if he was an imbecile. "You wouldn't have to do *all* the work. There are some boys from school who want to help but they need direc-

tion. Someone to oversee the project. You'd be perfect.
Please?"

I don't think so. That was what he meant to say, what
he should have said, but somehow he heard the word *yes*
slip from his lips. *Yes,* he'd help build the set and *yes,*
he'd come along that evening to chat with the boys he
was to oversee.

If Flynn were into psychoanalysis, which he most definitely was not, he'd read his actions as having something
to do with Ellie. He hadn't seen her since that day by the
dam, and although he'd driven Lucy into town four times
since then, he hadn't caught even the smallest glimpse
of his ex. Either she was already in the hall when he'd
dropped Lucy off, or she was yet to arrive, or whatever,
but he never saw her when he picked his sister up, either.
He guessed she was laying low, not wanting to run into
him again. That was good of her, responsible. Problem
was, there was a small, self-destructive part of him that
wanted to see her. And this was his chance.

Lucy thanked him with a massive hug and a kiss on
each cheek. "You're the best big bro ever."

"And don't you forget it," he called, as she skipped
off in the direction of the homestead.

LATER, FLYNN LET Lucy choose the music as they headed
down the highway into town. She bopped along, practically dancing in her seat as Flynn drove, now seriously
doubting his decision to come tonight. Lucy was rapt—
her word—by his commitment to share his time and
knowledge, but Flynn didn't feel confident about working alongside Ellie. Barely able to focus on anything that
afternoon, he'd rushed through everything on his to-do
list. He'd had livestock to check and repairs to do on one
of the tractors, and only realized he'd been cutting cor-

ners when he arrived home with more than enough time to shower and freshen up for the evening.

He'd been like a teenage girl, preening himself in front of the mirror, agonizing over which pair of jeans to wear and which shirt to top it off with. Which was ridiculous. There wasn't anyone he wanted to impress. In the end, he'd staged a miniprotest and chosen tatty jeans, an old AC/DC shirt and some beat-up Blundstones.

He rocked to Lucy's music, willing time to zoom by. Surely seeing Ellie—or at least the thought of seeing Ellie—should be getting easier. But somehow nerves and tension were taking the reins. Maybe working together would be a good thing. When she was out of sight he seemed to have no control over his mind putting her up on a pedestal. But if he saw her every couple of days, he reasoned, he'd be reminded just how human she was, and just how different they now were. He'd be reminded of what her life had become without him.

"We're here." Lucy clapped her hands excitedly as the Memorial Hall loomed into view.

Flynn parked the ute beside the building, readying himself for the night ahead. As he stepped out onto the gravel, however, a golden Premier pulled up behind them. It felt like a boa constrictor was slowly wrapping itself around him. Would this sick feeling ever disperse?

Then, just as the boa reached his neck, *she* stepped out of the Premier, glanced up and smiled. The constrictor released its hold. There was something about the way certain people smiled that made you feel it all over your body. Just a simple lift of their lips and your bones melted. Ellie had always been that kind of person for Flynn, but he didn't want to feel that way about her anymore.

He nodded, careful not to smile back but unable to resist running his eyes over her body and taking in every perfect detail. From her sleek dark hair, tied back in a high ponytail and showing off her smooth neck, to the black T-shirt and slim-fitting jeans that left little to the imagination. He knew how that skin, how those toned muscles, felt beneath his fingertips. It didn't take much to jolt his memory back to the fun they used to have together. Or that first time he'd caught sight of her without any clothes on.

He closed his eyes and turned away, only to be hit by the strong aroma of a truck full of sheep careening down the hill. The smell brought him back to his senses, reminding him that he wasn't here to perve or reminisce, but to help. To support Lucy in her latest bit of excitement.

"Shit!" yelled Matilda, waving her hand in front of her nose. Ellie helped her out of the car and pulled two crutches from the back. "Literally."

Lucy and Ellie laughed at Matilda's crudeness and Flynn couldn't help a chuckle, as well. Old Ms. T always had a way with words—even more so, a way of putting everyone at ease. Without thinking, he rushed forward to hold the passenger door out of the way as Ellie helped Matilda adjust the crutches under her arms.

"Blasted things," muttered Matilda. Flynn smiled down at her. He hadn't seen Ellie's godmother in quite some time. She'd aged in the past few months, now looking like an old woman, although he knew she couldn't be much over sixty-five. Her fall must have knocked her bad. "Can't wait to use them to shoo the magpies."

"Mat," warned Ellie, as she grabbed their bags from the car. "Don't rush your recovery." She glanced up at Lucy and Flynn and shook her head. "This woman is a terrible patient."

"I can well imagine," said Flynn, feeling slightly odd to be chatting about something so normal with his ex.

With Ellie on one side and Lucy on the other, the four of them slowly made their way into the hall. Ellie tried to make conversation, but Flynn was all too aware of how focused she was on Matilda. Should the older woman stumble, Ellie would catch her in a second.

"So, Lucy twisted your arm, did she?" Ellie asked.

"It didn't take much twisting," Flynn replied honestly. "Where Lucy's concerned I have a problem saying no. Besides, getting involved guarantees me a preview of the show. I'm desperate to see my little sis in action."

"She's got some serious talent," Ellie said. He could practically feel the glow radiating off Lucy at Ellie's compliment.

"She doesn't get it from me. Just the thought of getting up in front of a crowd has always scared me shitless."

"What about football?" Lucy asked.

"That's different," he replied.

"We won't try to lure you into an acting role, then," said Ellie. She was trying for relaxed and friendly, but you could almost see the tension in the air. Like each word they spoke had to be carefully thought out and run past a committee.

Flynn was more than happy when the rehearsal kicked off and Ellie took the cast to the stage. Matilda and Joyce gathered the crew at the other end of the hall and went over where they were at. Flynn nodded at the others as he was introduced as the newest team member. He met the teenage boys who were interested in helping and listened to Joyce's vision for the scenery, making an immense effort not to let his gaze drift to the stage. For a play that wasn't a comedy there certainly was a lot of laughter wafting from that direction. He tried his best to block it out.

"So, Sam," he addressed the taller of the teenage boys. He recognized him as the son of a farmer he knew—his carrot-red hair, lanky physique and goofy grin were dead giveaways. "And Troy, is it?" he said to the other. They both nodded, and Troy—quite stocky and tanned, as if he spent every day in the sun—held out his hand to Flynn. He had a firm handshake, more fitting to a grown man than a high schooler.

"Nice to meet ya." Troy glanced over at the actors and smiled an even goofier grin than Sam. "Lucy said you really know your stuff. T&E's my favorite subject, can't wait to get started."

Flynn liked his no-nonsense attitude, and remembered that T&E—Tech and Enterprise—was his favorite subject at school as well, but the way Troy looked at Lucy irked him.

"You and Luce good friends, are ya?"

Sam snorted. Troy dug him in the side with his elbow and looked seriously at Flynn. "She's a top bird."

Flynn wasn't comfortable with this conversation topic, so he suggested they work out their approach. On two tables they spread out butcher's paper and started to draw up plans. He enjoyed working with Sam and Troy—especially when he didn't think about Troy's feelings for Lucy—and by the time they wound up for the evening he was happy that he'd barely glanced in Ellie's direction. Well, almost barely. A few more nights like this and he might even be able to look her in the eye without breaking into a cold sweat.

"THE NIGHT IS YOUNG," called Matilda, balanced very nicely on her crutches. "Who's coming for a drink at the pub? I think we deserve to celebrate the progress we've made, don't you?"

"Yes," chorused the cast and crew. There was even a whoop and a whistle from someone down the back. Everyone gathered their belongings, and Ellie sidled over to Mat.

"Do you think this is a good idea? Dr. Bates said you still need to rest."

Matilda threw her eyebrows skyward and shrugged. "Bollocks to the doctor. This old woman needs a drink."

"You're not old," Ellie said, and sighed. She was happy to see Mat recovering but was terrified by the idea of facing a rowdy pub crowd. The theater group was one thing—they'd come to accept her and value her ideas—but she worried that stepping out in public would be like putting a tadpole in an aquarium full of crocodiles.

And there was that other little detail: Flynn might come, too.

Every second of tonight's rehearsal, Ellie had been aware of Flynn at the other end of the hall. She'd stolen more than a reasonable number of glimpses, and had sighed longingly at his sculpted arms flexed over the table as he sketched. When she'd come back to town, she'd expected to see Flynn, sure, but socializing with him was another kettle of fish altogether.

"Stop thinking." Matilda glared at Ellie. "We'll all be there to look out for you."

"Um…" And then it hit her—Lucy was underage. It was unlikely that Flynn, only a recent member of the group himself, would come to the pub and leave his sister in the ute outside. Ellie relaxed a little, warming to the idea of chilling out and having a few bevvies. Not many, of course, since she still had to drive Mat home.

"Okay," she relented. "Let's go."

The grin Matilda gave her was reward enough. When they got to the pub, however, Ellie saw Lucy and Flynn walking up the path in front of them. It was only then that she remembered where she was. The rules were different in the country. Lucy was allowed in the pub, as were those boys who followed her around like love-sick puppies, so long as they stayed in the back bar, with adults, and away from the TAB section. And, of course, they weren't allowed to drink.

Her heart rate sped up as she stepped past Flynn, who was holding the door open for them and a number of others trailing behind. He appeared to feel the same appre-hension, for he quickly grabbed himself a drink and sat at a table with Lucy and her mates. Ellie didn't know if he was looking her way at all—she forced herself not to twist her head in their direction. Instead she focused on relearning The Commercial Hotel, which had changed a lot in the years she'd been away, and on the conversa-tion at her table. She told herself Flynn's chuckle was simply extra loud and it wasn't that she was oversensi-tive to his presence.

And after a while she actually relaxed and stopped thinking about him. Her newfound friends—a few young moms, all new to town—didn't care about her past and had welcomed her into the fold. She only saw them on rehearsal nights, but they were a lot of fun. Even though they all kept busy with their kids, she could imagine herself getting friendly with them if she were staying in Hope. Which, of course, she was not.

Sarah, a mother of three boys under three—Ellie could hardly imagine—sculled her last few mouthfuls of wine. "That's me done," she said, glancing around the table with a wicked twinkle in her eye. "Who's buying next?"

"I think it must be me." Ellie rummaged in her bag for her purse and stood up. "Same again, everyone?"

After a unanimous yes, Ellie headed for the bar. She recognized the woman behind it—some days it seemed like everybody in Hope Junction had been in her graduating class—and addressed her with a confidence she didn't feel.

"Hi, Whitney." Ellie tried to smile. Whitney and Lauren had been like Siamese twins at school, and now they were near identical in their Barbie-like perfection. The only time Ellie looked that polished was when she'd spent a couple of hours in hair and makeup. She fiddled self-consciously with her ponytail as she waited for Whitney to reply. When she didn't, Ellie tried again.

"Two lemonades and two house whites, please." Ellie waited for Whitney to acknowledge her order. Whitney turned and walked to the end of the bar. She picked up a couple of tumblers, which Ellie assumed were for the soft drinks, but then started polishing them. Ellie stared, dumbfounded for a good minute before she called out.

"Um, excuse me, did you get my order?"

Whitney stopped, sighed loudly and gave Ellie almost the exact look that Lucy had given her before she'd undergone her drastic attitude change.

"I'm still reeling at your audacity, actually. Thinking you can come in here and ask for drinks like you belong." Her voice rose as she spit poison across the bar. "We don't serve scum."

Ellie blinked, painful goose bumps prickling her skin. She hated to let someone like Whitney get the better of her, but after the pleasant evening she'd been having, this nastiness came as a shock. Tears bubbled at the corners of her eyes. She could just imagine the joy and gossip between Whitney and Lauren if she collapsed in sobs in the middle of the pub. It wasn't a pleasant vision. She had to get out, fast.

Miraculously, she held her head high as she hightailed it out of the bar, the door slamming behind her. It was only when she almost fell down the steps that she re-called Mat—and her crutches—still inside. She halted, grasping the railing for support. Inhale, exhale—she monitored her breathing, fearful of another panic attack.

"Come on, Ellie," she spoke firmly to herself. "You can handle it. Back inside. Now." Wiping her eyes, she was about to turn around when she heard a deep voice behind her.

"Are you okay, Els?"

CHAPTER TWELVE

FLYNN THOUGHT HE'D been doing a pretty good job of feigning interest in the conversation between his sister and her admirers. It appeared Sam had as much of a soft spot for Lucy as Troy did. They weren't bad kids, he had to give them that. In fact, Troy reminded him of himself at that age—besotted with a girl and willing to do anything to impress her.

Yet he'd be kidding himself if he said he wasn't constantly aware of Ellie, of where she was in the room, whom she was talking to and what she was doing. She'd had two lemonades and was smiling a lot as she listened to the others at her table. He didn't know the three women she was chatting with well. Two of them were teachers in town and had ended up marrying local farmers—rarely did a Perth uni grad leave Hope without a ring on their finger and a farmer on their arm. The other one was newer, married to a South African—together they'd bought one of the farms everyone had pegged as unsalable due to the drought. He was glad they'd taken a fancy to Ellie. She'd never really made close female friends at school, so there was no one around—apart from Mat—for her to fall back in with. The company of women her own age would do her good.

He took a long slug of his OJ, settled back and tried to catch on to what Lucy was talking about. The cool liquid was halfway down his throat when he heard Whitney holler across the bar.

"We don't serve scum."

He choked, spilling his glass across the table. Since going out with Rats, Whitney had become like another sister to Flynn, and he knew she felt strongly about protecting him. But dammit, did she need to humiliate Ellie in the process?

The pub door clunked shut, making a loud clatter in the fresh silence. All conversations had stopped, and all eyes were either on Whitney or the newly slammed door. Mouths gaped.

Matilda, wide-eyed with fury, barked at Joyce. "Pass me those sticks!" Joyce moved to the crutches leaning against the table, but Flynn jumped up instead.

"I'll go."

Matilda slumped back against the chair, already breathless with the stress. *Thanks,* she mouthed at Flynn.

He strode toward the exit and down the front steps and, in the dimly lit night, nearly missed Ellie leaning over the railing. His heart squeezed at the sight of her, quietly sobbing. Broken. For a moment, he almost turned back. She wasn't his problem, wasn't his worry anymore—not that he'd ever looked upon her like that—and he'd never been good with tears.... But when he heard her talking to herself, urging herself to trudge back inside like a trouper, he knew he had to say something.

"Are you okay, Els?" *Ellie,* he should have said. Ellie. Els was a pet name, the special nickname he'd used from the moment he'd started flirting with her over the Bunsen burners in chemistry.

She took a moment, but eventually she turned around. By the look on her face, she was anything but okay.

"Come here." Arms open, he pulled her into his chest

before either of them could think twice about it. Physical contact probably wasn't the best idea, but damn, it felt good. As she shed quiet tears against his shirt— already splashed with juice—and her head rested on his shoulder, his body couldn't help but relish the feel of her against him. Again. She'd always been the perfect fit.

They stayed like that for a couple of minutes—Ellie crying, Flynn comforting—as he fought the too-good memories that flooded his mind. Eventually she pulled back slightly, looked up into his eyes and spoke.

"Sorry. I'm messing up your shirt."

He raised an eyebrow at her. "This old thing?" To which she cracked a smile.

"I'd better go back inside," she said, stepping out of his embrace.

He reached forward and lifted her chin, forcing her to meet his gaze. He tried to ignore the satin feel of her skin. "Are you ready for that yet?"

She sniffed and shook her head. "I'm such a mess. This is so embarrassing."

He glanced behind them and saw the many inquisitive eyes peering out the windows of the pub. "Walk with me," he said, putting his arm around her shoulder. He ushered her down the stairs and along the path.

She hesitated a moment, but then her long legs stepped in time to his. He led her into a side street where he knew there was a wooden bench. It was dark, secluded, lit only by a single streetlight on the other side of the road. In a place like this a woman might assume he had ulterior motives, but he knew Ellie wasn't stupid. Out of range of the pub, he dropped his arm to his side. Where once they would have sat as close as physically possible, he waited until she sat before taking a spot at the opposite end.

"Has it been hell coming back?" he asked eventually.

In the shadows, he could only just make out the way she bit her lip, contemplating an answer. Once upon a time she didn't censor her words with him.

"A bit." She wiped her eyes with the heel of her hand. "But I know I deserve it."

"Deserve what?"

She snorted. "This town adores you, Flynn. I'm the scarlet woman. Evil incarnate. People cross the road when they see me or head down a different aisle in the Co-op."

"I'm sorry about that."

"Ha! You shouldn't be apologizing. None of this is your fault." She looked up at the night sky and sighed. "I forget there are so many stars out here. In Sydney, I'm lucky if I can see one or two."

She was changing the subject; he'd be an idiot not to notice. "What's it like?"

"What's what like?"

"Sydney. Your life there."

"You ever been?"

He shook his head. Melbourne, Darwin, Brisbane, Adelaide, Hobart—he'd been to all the capital cities in the past few years, learning as much as he could about how sheep were farmed in different regions, what breeds worked best and how farmers dealt with different conditions. But he'd stayed well away from Sydney. Just in case.

"It's cool. Felt like I'd landed in New York all those years ago, but now I'm used to the hustle and bustle. The nightlife, the shopping, the restaurants, the culture. I love it."

"Do you live with anyone?" He wanted to kick himself in the shins the minute he asked—he hadn't been able to help himself. But was that a slight lift of her lips he noticed?

She shook her head. "I haven't even got a cat." Stupidly, he felt happy about this. "When we're filming, the hours are long and not really conducive to…um… relationships. I've got a couple of great girlfriends, though. One's a makeup artist for the show and the other is my neighbor. I miss them a lot."

"Sure. Well, Matilda's getting better now—you won't have to stay long, will you?"

"No." He saw her shiver but resisted the urge to rub her arms. She continued, "But I'm not leaving until she's off the crutches. I don't trust her not to do something silly. Besides, I love spending time with her. I only get homesick if I think too much about it. Or when people get aggro at me."

"Because of me."

"Don't." Her voice was sharp, annoyed. "It's not your fault."

"But it's not fair, either." A thought jumped into his head and before he had a chance to consider it properly, he put it out there. "Hang with me."

"What?"

"Come to the football on Saturday. It's a home game and we need all the supporters we can get." He paused, realizing he'd just crossed the line he'd drawn two weeks ago. He was about to offer friendship to the woman who had broken his heart. Best he qualify it. "You can bring Matilda if ya want."

"I dunno." Ellie rubbed her lips together. "Why are you asking me?"

He groaned and ran a hand through his hair. Leaning forward slightly, he spoke. "I like you, Ellie, simple as that. Not in the way I used to, but enough that I don't like to see you treated like an outcast in your own town. If people see that I've moved on, then maybe they can build a bridge, as well. You're doing a good thing looking after Matilda, you don't deserve to suffer for it." He paused. "Friends?"

Ellie looked at Flynn. "Okay." She clasped his outstretched hand and shook it firmly but quickly. "Friends."

CHAPTER THIRTEEN

ELLIE WAS WAITING at Matilda's gate when Flynn showed up just before midday. She'd dug out her old Hurricanes scarf and had it wrapped around her neck, the perfect protection from the late-August wind.

He jumped out of the ute and rushed around to open the passenger door. It looked a lot like a date but they both knew it wasn't. There was no kiss hello and he was careful not to brush against her. She smiled her thanks and tried to avert her gaze from his outfit. It wasn't like she hadn't seen Flynn in tight footy shorts and a club jersey before—hell, she'd seen him in a *lot* less—but her mouth went dry at the sight anyway. Men in sports uniforms always did it for her. In Sydney she'd ended up a massive fan of the Swans—and their players—not that she would ever tell Flynn that. Their experiment in friendship was in its very early stages and he was a die-hard Dockers fan.

"Is it just you?" Flynn asked, glancing at the cottage.

"Yep."

Ellie had begged, pleaded, even tried to bribe Mat to come with her, but the old biddy had been firm in her refusal, harboring crazy ideas about her and Flynn getting back together. She hadn't said as much, but Ellie knew the way Mat's brain worked. Although she didn't buy into romance for herself, she thought Ellie needed one to make her happy. And she'd been like a two-year-old on a sugar rush since Ellie and Flynn had walked back inside the pub two nights ago. They hadn't even been walking close to each other, but Mat had jumped to the conclusion that, since Flynn was the one to follow Ellie out of the bar, he must still care about her. In her heart of hearts, Ellie thought this was true. But she knew as well as anyone that caring wasn't enough. Hell, even if he still loved her, he'd made it clear they'd never be more than friends. That they could even try for that was a blessing, and she was grateful for the opportunity.

"Matilda's resting," she qualified. "And footy isn't really her thing anyway."

A flicker of concern flashed across Flynn's face. "Will you be okay while I'm playing? Lucy often comes to the game but Mom's making her study today."

"I'll be fine." Ellie forced a smile and sat down in the passenger seat. She wanted to do this. She wanted to get out for herself, not just on an errand for Matilda. She'd loved this town once and while she was back she wanted to experience it at its best. Footy was one of the things that most reminded her of the country. "I'm actually excited," she said as Flynn slid in beside her and started the ute.

"Great."

The drive to the oval was less than a minute. Not a lot of time for small talk but plenty for reacquainting herself with the feeling of being with Flynn. The confined space of the cabin was the most intimate they'd been in a long time. Memories ambushed her—good memories, sad memories, overwhelming memories. She wondered if the steely expression on Flynn's face meant he was lost in recollection, too.

As the car slowed to a stop at the oval she snapped out of her reverie. She glanced up at the other vehicles bordering the playing field and placed a hand against her stomach. The butterflies there were now more like a swarm of blackbirds. But it wasn't as if she was turning up uninvited; she shouldn't feel so much as if she were overstepping the mark.

"You okay?" asked Flynn.

"Peachy." She flashed him a cheesy grin and grabbed her bag from her feet, as she pondered slinking down and hiding behind the dashboard.

"Liar," he teased.

She raised her eyebrows at him and glared. "How do you know I'm lying?"

"You may be a hotshot actress," he said, rubbing the back of his neck and winking in a way that sent the blackbirds spiraling. "But some things never change. You blink too much when you're lying, Ellie Hughes."

She automatically blinked in response and rushed to press her fingers against her eyes. Did she really? "All right, smarty-pants, you win. Let's get this over with."

Flynn grinned the smile she'd never been able to resist and opened the door. Despite everything, Ellie felt safe getting out of the ute alongside him. He dropped his keys in a sports bag and then threw the bag over his shoulder. In the old days, this would've been where he'd put his arm around Ellie and she'd have slipped her hand in the back pocket of his pants.

"Come with me while I dump my bag," he said. "We might find someone you can sit with." Ellie doubted that. She guessed she'd be sitting on the bonnet of the ute all on her lonesome.

He nodded and waved at a few people as they headed for the change rooms. Ellie couldn't help but notice a few heads do a double take as they saw him with her, but most of them recovered quickly and greeted her with a smile or hello. They were almost at their destination when she heard someone call, "Ellie!"

She turned toward the giggly voice and smiled to see Sarah from the theater group waving crazily at her. Jolie, another one of the trio, was at her side and both had chubby, chocolaty toddlers perched upon their hips. Behind them deck chairs were set up in front of dust-covered four-wheel drives.

"You go say hello," said Flynn, "I'll pop back before the game starts."

"Okay." Ellie was glad to find the genuinely friendly faces and walked briskly over to them. Jolie and Sarah hugged her enthusiastically, and the sticky hands of Jolie's daughter caught in Ellie's hair as they pulled apart.

"I'm so sorry," Jolie gushed, putting the toddler down and digging around in a big black bag. "I've got some nappy wipes here somewhere to clean you up."

Ellie waved off her apology. "Don't be silly, I don't mind." She pulled out her hair elastic, ran her hands through her locks and redid her ponytail. "Are you gals here to watch your hubbies?"

"Yep. Anything to get out of the house, away from washing and ironing," said Sarah. "Here, take a seat."

They sat down on the deck chairs, of which there were a couple spare—presumably for absent husbands—and the children started playing noisily with cars at their feet.

"What's with you and Flynn Quartermaine?" asked Jolie conspiratorially.

"Nothing," Ellie answered far too quickly. She felt her cheeks flaring with heat.

Jolie and Sarah raised their eyebrows and smiled in a way that said, *Sure, we believe you.*

"He doesn't take just anyone to the footy," Sarah said, opening a bottle of water for one of the children.

"I heard they used to be an item," mentioned Jolie, as if Ellie weren't there.

"Okay, okay," snapped Ellie, smirking at their obvious ploy for gossip. "It's true, I left him at the altar. I'm an evil bitch and he, well, he's just an all-round nice guy who doesn't want me to suffer for it."

The other women laughed and glanced up, catching sight of Flynn as he headed back to them.

"You must have had a damn good reason, girlfriend," Sarah said in a hushed voice, "because that is one hot bod right there."

Don't I know it, thought Ellie, succumbing to a good old perve herself. He really was particularly easy on the eye.

Flynn, oblivious, approached them smiling. He held out a brown paper bag and a can of Fanta for Ellie. "Thought you might need some sustenance." She peeked inside the bag to see a perfect meat pie steaming back at her, but it was the can of soft drink that made her fingers tingle as they closed around it. Her favorite drink.

"I hope you still like it," he said with a touch of anxiousness. Of course she did, but she couldn't recall the last time someone remembered this about her. The fact he did touched her heart in a dangerous manner. How was she supposed to keep an emotional distance if he kept doing sensitive things like this?

"I love it," she replied. "But you'll be sad to know it still makes me hyper."

"Not at all." Flynn grinned and gestured with his thumb to the field behind him. "We need all the cheering we can get, especially against Tambellup. Fanta is all part of the plan."

"Well, thanks."

"You okay with these guys?" Flynn asked in a lowered voice.

She nodded. "Don't worry about me, just go play. And win."

"Yes, boss." Flynn saluted her, waved goodbye to Jolie and Sarah and jogged off to join his team.

Sighing and not knowing what to think or feel, Ellie caressed the icy Fanta can. She tugged on the ring pull before taking a long, thirst-quenching drink. Then she leaned back in the deck chair and waited for the game to start.

As FLYNN JOGGED toward his teammates he prepared himself for the barrage of questions. Blokes didn't usually indulge in gossip or deep and meaningful conversations, but there were certain things that warranted attention. He knew his friends—some of whom he'd been close to since high school—would want to know why he'd brought Ellie along.

Problem was, he was still asking himself the same question. When they'd spoken on the day of the media frenzy, he'd made a conscious decision to stay away from her. But even then, he could feel himself mellowing toward Ellie. Perhaps it was true that time healed. Perhaps, after ten years, he'd rather have her as a friend than not at all. He may have once blamed Ellie for his journey down that destructive path, relying on alcohol to get through each day, but no matter what she'd done, he now accepted that his actions were his own responsibility. He'd chosen to be weak on his own accord, something he wasn't proud of. Now he was choosing to be friends.

"Mate," called Rats as he approached. The players had already started warming up, so Flynn launched into a hamstring stretch alongside his friend.

"G'day guys." His greeting was met with an array of raised eyebrows.

Rats leaned in close. "What's Ellie doing here?"

"Watching the game, like everyone else."

"Don't give me that crap, you know what I mean." Rats finished a stretch and started jogging on the spot.

Flynn straightened up. "Whitney tell you what happened at the pub?"

"Yeah." Rats nodded.

"Well, that's why. I don't appreciate people treating her like dirt with some perverse notion that they're protecting me. I want to move on, not dwell in the past."

Rats's eyes widened. "You're getting back together?"

"No." Flynn scoffed. "I don't want *any* relationship, much less one with her. We're trying friends, that's it."

Rats shrugged and linked his hands behind his back in an arm and chest stretch. "Admirable. Don't know if it's something I could do."

"Just as well you don't have to worry about it, then, hey, mate?" Flynn's comment sounded harsh, but when he winked and nodded to the sidelines—where Whitney was sitting with her girlfriends—Rats caught his meaning. "She's besotted."

"Do you blame her?" The groom-to-be puffed up his chest theatrically and flexed his arms.

"You're a dag," said Flynn, but he was glad the conversation had shifted away from himself.

They did a few more warm-up exercises before the siren signaled the start of the match. Flynn launched himself into the game he loved, with no time to worry about Ellie or what people were thinking. It was rowdy, it was rough, it was sweaty, it was invigorating. The Hurricanes hadn't been playing well this season, but today they were pumped. The home crowd shrieked as Flynn scored another goal.

When the game was over and the Hurricanes were miles ahead on the scoreboard, he could have roared with satisfaction. Despite the sweat pouring down his back and off his forehead, he felt more alive than he had in a long time. His team had almost forgotten the sweet taste of victory, and he hoped this was the start of a change of luck. But whatever the future, one thing was certain: the festivities would be long and loud in the club rooms that night.

"Great game, boys." Whitney met them as they came off the field and wrapped her arms around Rats. "Are we celebrating?"

"Of course," Rats replied, one arm around Whitney's waist. "I'll just get changed and be there in a sec."

Lauren, at Whitney's side, tossed Flynn a smile. "You coming, Flynn?" He couldn't help but notice the optimism in her voice.

"Sure. I'll just go tell Ellie." He turned tail before anyone had a chance to say anything or ask any questions. He hoped they'd take their cue from him and be nicer to Ellie, but he wasn't holding his breath.

After a quick shower, Flynn changed into jeans and a clean shirt and found Ellie already inside the club, with Sarah and Jolie. He watched her from the door, wondering whether she was as relaxed as she looked sipping Bundy and Coke from a can. Acting was her bread and butter, but she really did look comfortable in the room full of noisy Hope locals. His plan seemed to be working.

A friendly slap between the shoulder blades jolted Flynn from his thoughts. "Mate, you played bonza out there." The voice belonged to Jimmy, a retired player who still celebrated every Hurricane goal as if he'd kicked it himself. "What's your secret? You wearing lucky jocks or something?"

"Something," chuckled Flynn, his eyes drifting back to Ellie.

"Can I get you a drink?" asked Jimmy, sculling his can, then crushing it in his hands.

"Yes. I mean no." Jimmy was, without a doubt, offering him an alcoholic beverage. And Flynn wasn't going there again, not with Ellie *and* Lauren in the room. He chatted a few more moments with Jimmy, listening as the older man reminisced about winning goals and past glory. When he went to the bar, Flynn ventured farther into the room. Ellie had moved on from Sarah and Jolie and was now surrounded by a bunch of the younger players. He decided to go over and see what she was saying that had them so mesmerized.

"Hi, Flynn." Ellie threw him a smile when he nudged into the group. "Can I get you a drink?" She held up her can.

"I'm right for now," he said.

"Els was just telling us about her job on the telly," informed Grant, a fullback who thought himself a lot better than he was. Flynn bristled at the way he shortened Ellie's name.

"I reckon I'd like to be one of those blokes that surf all day," said Tim, a hardworking farmer Flynn generally got along with. "Does anyone have a real job on *Lake Street?*" Everyone laughed, then someone asked a more serious question about life in front of the camera. Ellie spoke openly and honestly, generous with information about the life she'd made in Sydney—both on and off screen. Flynn couldn't help but notice the happiness and pride in her voice as she spoke about her friends there and her apartment in Bondi Beach. In many ways she was the girl he'd loved all those years ago, but in others she was a total stranger. This last thought helped ground him.

Ellie seemed perfectly capable of holding her own, so Flynn excused himself from the conversation—barely anyone noticed—and went to buy himself a can of Coke.

ELLIE LOOKED WISTFULLY after Flynn as he headed for the bar, not because she was harboring any ridiculous fantasies (à la Matilda), but because she was finding all the attention a little overwhelming. Everyone was being very friendly, which was great, and Flynn's pledge to befriend her seemed to be contagious.

After fielding another round of questions, Ellie slipped off to the ladies' room. She washed her hands and put on some pink lip gloss—that was about as far as she went in the makeup department when she wasn't on-screen—and was about to go back into the main bar when Lauren and Whitney walked through the door. They stopped and blinked, as if shocked to see her there. Ellie felt like saying, *Yes, I pee like everyone else,* but simply smiled politely.

"Elenora." Whitney smiled back, looking awkward. "Nice to see you tonight." Which Ellie knew really meant, *What the fuck do you think you're doing here?*

Ellie tucked her lip gloss back into her bag, held her chin high and replied, "Yeah, great to see you, too." Which translated as, *I was hoping to never to see your stuck-up face again.*

Lauren entered the conversation. "I see you came with Flynn." She didn't bother with a fake smile.

"Uh-huh."

There was an awkward pause before Whitney spoke again. "Look, I'm sorry about the other night." Her voice softened surprisingly. "I love Flynn like a brother and I just don't want him to get hurt."

Startled at her blunt and open confession, Ellie replied with equal honesty. "I don't want that, either."

"So, you'll be heading back to Sydney soon, then?" Lauren grinned eagerly as she said this, telling Ellie she still maintained her high school crush on Flynn.

Whitney elbowed her friend and spoke again. "If you'll be around for a while, maybe we could catch up, for old times' sake?"

Ellie wasn't sure what old times she was talking about. In high school these two had only bothered speaking to her if it was to tell her to get out of their way. She couldn't believe that Rats, the lovable rogue, had ended up with a princess like Whitney. But then, who was she to question true love?

"Yeah, that'd be great," she lied, thinking she'd rather spend two weeks camping in the outback, without a toilet *or* showering facilities, but that if it made things good for Flynn she would. She needed to show that she was making an effort with the locals. "Well, I'll see ya round."

After exchanging polite goodbyes, Whitney and Lauren each slipped into a cubicle and Ellie went off to find Flynn. She saw him chatting with a girl by the jukebox and her heart constricted. She didn't have the right to be jealous but, dammit, she was. Painfully so. The woman flicked her long, copper hair over her shoulder and laughed daintily at something Flynn said. Ellie turned in the opposite direction and headed to the bar.

After what seemed an age Flynn arrived by her side. She'd talked to a number of people in between but wouldn't have been able to recall who or what they'd chatted about.

"Enjoying yourself?" he asked, leaning against the bar, his gorgeous arm propping up his jaw.

"Yes." She bit her tongue on her snarky response. This was harder than she'd imagined—being with Flynn but not being with him. "But I think I'm gonna call it a night. I really should get back to check on Mat."

There was silence for a moment as he mulled this over. She wondered if—*hoped*—he would offer to drive her home.

"Are you sure?" he asked. "As Matilda would say, the night's still young."

She nodded, pushing aside the thought of what might happen, of who he might end up going home with if she didn't stick around. "Yeah."

"Okay, then, guess I'll see you around."

"Bye." Ellie turned and made her way through the crowd. She offered a quick goodbye to Sarah and Jolie but was careful not to make eye contact with anyone else. This felt too odd, too surreal—being in her old stomping ground but being a total stranger to it all. It would take time, she realized, to become part of Hope's close-knit community again.

Unfortunately, time was something she didn't have. As if on cue her phone buzzed in her bag, alerting her to a text message. She dug it out and smiled. It was from Saskia, her makeup artist best bud, and read: Miss you, gorgeous, we're hitting Zona tonight and it's not the same without you, xox

Zona was a hip, upmarket nightclub in inner-city Sydney. Ellie always felt a fraud there, even after Saskia instructed her on what to wear and did her hair and makeup. But tonight Zona would be easy. Being there wouldn't be full of memories that were once sweet but now held only sadness. Being there wouldn't make her feel things for Flynn she'd spent ten years trying to repress.

CHAPTER FOURTEEN

ON TUESDAY, ELLIE dropped Matilda off at her CWA meeting and then headed to the Co-op. Her reception there was drastically different from her first visit just over two weeks ago. Simone, on checkout again, flashed her a smile when she walked in the door and asked if she was after anything in particular.

"Just a few groceries," replied Ellie, trying not to let her surprise show.

"Oh well." Simone shrugged good-naturedly. "If you need any help, just let me know."

Ellie enjoyed pottering round the shop, picking things off the shelves and reading their labels before deciding whether to buy them. Play practice was tonight and it was Ellie's turn to provide supper. She wanted to make something that would show her appreciation to the group that had accepted her so openly. Thankfully, Joyce had promised to help her. She threw two tins of condensed milk into the trolley and wandered to the next aisle, almost crashing into Flynn, who was carrying a red shopping basket under his arm.

"Well, good morning," Flynn said. He sounded genuinely pleased to see her and Ellie couldn't help the lift of her heart. "What are you up to?"

"Oh, this and that," she replied, gripping the handle of the trolley. "Mat's at CWA and I'm really just putting in time. What about you?"

"I had to drop Rodger at the vet. He's got a growth on his side—they need to cut it out and see if it's benign. I'm killing time till it's over, too."

"Puppy Rodger?"

He chuckled. "It's more Old Man Rodger now. But yeah, he's the pup I got the year we left school."

"Wow. I hope he's okay." And then, before she had the chance to check herself, Ellie said, "Would you like to get a coffee?"

"Yeah, sure," he replied. Peering into her trolley, he added, "And you can tell me what you're making with all those yummy ingredients."

"'Tis a secret." Flynn would be working on the set tonight, and she didn't want him expecting something special when she wasn't sure if she could deliver.

"Fair enough." He shrugged and gave a broad, warm smile. Her traitorous heart flipped. "I'll just pay for these and meet you at the café, shall I?"

"Sure." But then, as she watched him stride down the pasta, sauces and tinned veggie aisle, as if he didn't have a care in the world, Ellie remembered that she hadn't been to About Coffee Time yet. Who owned it? Who would be working there? How would they treat her? It was ridiculous to get caught up in these concerns, especially when she would be there with Flynn, but she just couldn't rid the feeling of being on edge in this town. Everywhere she went, she was waiting for someone to get nasty.

Flynn was sitting on the funky, plastic outdoor setting when Ellie arrived at the new café. New to her meant it had sprouted up sometime in the past ten years, which meant it might not be that new at all. He sat with one foot up on his opposite knee and was reading the newspaper. As she approached, he stood and took off his cap. She smiled and tried to ignore the glow inside as he held the door for her. She couldn't start thinking about his being a gentleman, and the fact that such people were few and far between—it wasn't kind to her mental health. So instead she focused on her surroundings. The modern decor, the music, the divine smells wafting from the kitchen. She was more than impressed.

"This place is fabulous," she announced, still looking around and grinning like a loony.

"Glad you approve." The female voice behind her was neither warm nor icy.

Ellie swung round and set eyes on possibly the tallest woman she'd ever encountered. She wore a white apron and had a kind face. She was terribly thin, too, and Ellie couldn't help but think of one of Mat's favorite sayings—something about never trusting a skinny cook. Still, if the smell was anything to go by, she had to be doing something right.

Flynn spoke first. "Sherry, this is Ellie. Ellie, this is Sherry—her family moved away from Hope when she was a toddler. She was very popular when she came back and opened About Coffee Time."

"I'll bet," said Ellie warmly. "Hope Junction really needed a good café."

Sherry smiled her appreciation. "And you don't need any introduction, *Stella*. I absolutely love *Lake Street,* watch it every night."

Ellie relaxed at the other woman's confession but she noted Flynn stiffen at her side.

"Can we order?" he asked, tucking his newspaper under his arm.

"Sure." Sherry grabbed a pen from behind her ear and a notepad from her apron pocket. "Where do you want to sit?"

Ellie and Sherry followed Flynn over to a table in the corner. Ellie quickly sat in the seat where she'd have her back to the window. She didn't want to be staring out at the park, which would no doubt ignite numerous Flynn-and-Ellie memories. They came fast and furious these days, and right now she wanted to focus on the real Flynn in front of her.

Flynn ordered a meat pie and a flat white; Ellie went for the same, but with a latte. They chatted while they waited for Sherry to fill their order. Flynn mentioned he was going to be best man at Rats and Whitney's wedding. Very soon, too—it wasn't shotgun in the normal sense, but when they'd decided to get married, they hadn't seen the point in waiting years, or even months, for the pleasure. Flynn talked about his plans for Rats's bucks' night next week and his other best-man duties. He clearly didn't have the paranoia about weddings that she had.

"What?" Flynn asked.

Ellie blinked, wondering if she'd said something. "I'm sorry?"

"You look like you've seen a ghost."

"Oh…no…um…" No way was she going to tell him. He'd laugh his socks off if she confessed that she'd barely been able to step inside a church since *that* day, never mind attend a wedding. She'd tried once—a colleague from the show had tied the knot at St. Mary's Cathedral in Sydney, but Ellie hadn't even been able to make it up the steps and past the elaborate front doors.

"It'll be my first wedding since ours," he admitted, as if reading her mind. She couldn't believe he'd brought it up. But she admired his guts for doing so.

"Are you scared?" she asked, then added, quickly, "I'd be petrified."

He nodded, glancing down at the table as if ashamed. He looked like a cute puppy, and she wanted nothing more than to lean forward and cuddle him.

"I'm sorry," she said.

"You don't have to keep saying it," he replied, looking up at her again. "If we're to be friends, it has to be a level playing field. We start afresh."

Start afresh? Did that mean there was the chance that one thing could lead to another, like it had when they'd first met?

"Okay," she said, firmly pushing that hope out of her mind. Quite aside from their history, there were a zillion *now* reasons it would never work. "If we've just met, I'd love to know why you're scared of attending your best friend's wedding."

He threw his head back and laughed. "If you must know, I was jilted at the altar by the love of my life."

Her belly somersaulted at his turn of phrase. *Love of his life!*

"Good God," she said faux theatrically. She wished she had her coffee already so she could wrap her fingers around it and take comfort from the warmth. This was an odd and awkward conversation.

As if sensing her wish, Sherry landed with their lunch and drinks before either of them could say another word. They thanked her politely and each took a forkful of the homemade pastry. Near identical moans of goodness escaped their mouths.

"Tell me," Ellie said, resting her fork against the plate and picking up her glass.

"What about?"

"About what happened after I, after *she* left." She swallowed. Flynn had been very guarded about his past when they'd talked at the dam. He'd skated over the facts, telling her the bare minimum, and Matilda had told her a version but, call it perverse or self-defeating, Ellie wanted to know more. She wanted to know Flynn's version. Even if she hadn't told him all the facts about her. When Flynn didn't say anything, she pushed a little more. "I noticed you don't drink alcohol anymore. Is that because…?"

"Ellie." He sighed and took a sip of coffee. "I'm an alcoholic."

She gasped, not expecting such a blatant confession. When Matilda had said he'd turned to drinking, she'd imagined some wild nights and bad-boy behavior, but not addiction. Flynn had always been so together, so controlled. It was one of the things she admired about him—he and his family were in stark opposition to the mayhem of hers. She'd had a brush with the bottle herself in the months after she left, but he was the last person she'd expect to lose it. Tragedy did strange things to a person.

Ellie swallowed, not quite knowing what to say next.

"Shocking, isn't it? I'm surprised the town still respects me after all I did."

Did she really want to know? Didn't she carry enough guilt as it was? She couldn't help herself. "What *did* you do?"

"Became a resident of the pub. Spent all my money on booze and drugs."

"Drugs?" Her eyes widened at the impossibility. The Flynn she knew was vehemently against drugs, whether it was recreational use or steroid abuse in athletes.

"A bit of marijuana to start with, but that soon lost its edge and I sought stronger stuff. The only time I could stop the memories was when I was drunk and off my face. I hit a bloke in the pub once because he knocked over my beer. The cops let me off with a warning, but only 'cause the man was an old friend of Dad's, he didn't want to lay charges.

"Mom and Dad didn't know what to do with me. I could see I was hurting them but I couldn't stop. So I went bush. I followed the road north and ended up on a cattle station. No one knew me there—no one knew what had happened. I started getting my life back together. I got a job on the station, was working, getting clean." He paused for a second, and then sighed deeply. The mood between them was no longer fun and jokey. "Then Mom called one day and told me Dad had had an accident. He'd been cutting a tree with a chainsaw. It'd fallen on a fence during a storm. Somehow he lost control and a branch came down on him. He didn't stand a chance."

Ellie's hand rushed to her mouth. She knew Cyril had died tragically, unexpectedly, but it sounded so much more awful coming from Flynn. She wished she'd been around to comfort him.

"I should have been here," said Flynn, anger coming into his voice. "I should've... I came home and haven't drunk since. Except for once."

Although he'd piqued her curiosity—big-time—she didn't ask about that once. He was already guilty enough. She knew the signs. How much more guilt would he feel if he knew what really happened to her in Perth? The answer made her certain she'd never tell him.

"Don't play the *should've* game, Flynn. You can't re-write history."

"Would you?" he asked suddenly.

"Would I what?" She licked her lips, which felt like the Sahara.

"Rewrite history." He looked at her earnestly. "Having had time to live with it, would you still leave me, if you could make the decision again?"

Oh fuck. How to answer? She must have hesitated too long, because his cheeks blushed and he waved his hand in front of his face as if to dismiss the conversation. But it wasn't that straightforward. She opened her mouth to say as much but couldn't push a sound past her tonsils.

In the same circumstances, she couldn't be sure she wouldn't make the same decision again. And if it were as simple as rewriting history, she would give herself a different beginning in life. Parents who cared, a stable childhood. But that would mean she'd never have met Mat, much less Flynn. She shuddered at the thought. As much as she'd like to believe in fate and all the storybook stuff about destiny, she had to be realistic. If Flynn really was The One, then her mistake wouldn't keep them apart. But so far it had. She didn't know how to put any of this into words.

"Flynn, I…" Instinctively she reached for his hand. It felt warm and hard and brought her comfort when that was supposed to be what she was offering him.

Flynn's phone buzzed in his pocket. As if grateful for the opportunity to extract his hand, he retrieved the vibrating mobile and pressed a button. "Flynn Quartermaine….Really? That's great….Okay, thanks….Yep, I'll be there in five."

"The vet?" guessed Ellie as he ended the call.

"Uh-huh." He nodded with a relieved smile.

"Rodger's okay?"

"A bit woozy, apparently, but they've cut the lump out and it doesn't look dangerous. Of course, they have to send it off for tests…." He grabbed his wallet, pulled out a twenty and laid it on the table. "Don't suppose you want to come see him?"

FLYNN COULD'VE KICKED himself. It was a stupid thing to ask her, considering she'd just all but said she was happy with her decision to have left him. Her honesty hurt like barbed wire around his heart, and yet he kept going back for more. Spending time with Ellie was not a good idea. Sure, he was over her—it had taken years but he'd moved on—yet being in her company unbalanced him. He was man enough to admit that. He decided to avoid being alone with her after this.

"Okay, let's go," he said, standing up.

"I'll pay," she argued, opening her purse.

"It's fine," he said, a little more forcefully than necessary. "I may not be a famous television star, but I can afford to shout a friend lunch."

"Thanks," she replied, although she looked a little taken aback.

She followed him to the clinic, where they parked in the gravel parking lot out front. "Shall I come in, or do you want me to wait out here?" she asked, juggling her keys in her hands. She was suddenly acting nervous around him.

He nodded at the front door of the converted cottage. "You may as well come in." As they crunched across the gravel, silence reigned between them. He longed for the easy conversation they'd had in the Co-op, even their chat in the café before he'd gone and asked that tragic question. He couldn't help the image that came into his head as he held the door open for her. Of how life should have been. Of them working alongside each other on the farm, living the country life and doing important things together—like getting their sheepdog from the vet.

"Afternoon, Flynn." The vet, Craig, reached out to shake Flynn's hand. He hadn't been in town more than a year and wasn't the type to gossip, so Flynn didn't expect him to give them a hard time. Instead, he did a double take when he saw Ellie. "You're that sheila from *Lake Street*."

Ellie giggled awkwardly and nodded. "Don't hold it against me."

"You kidding? My missus loves it. Wait till I tell her you were in my clinic today."

Flynn could tell Ellie was uncomfortable, and he didn't love the conversation much himself. "Can we see Rodger, Craig?"

The vet straightened up, looking slightly embarrassed. "Sure, sorry, mate. I'll go get him." Craig traveled down a corridor and returned a few minutes later with a very forlorn looking kelpie. Flynn dropped to his knees and held out his arms. He hated to see Rodg looking like this—so vulnerable, so *old*.

"Come here, mate."

But Rodger looked right past Flynn, visibly perking up as he noticed Ellie. Looking pleased with herself, she stooped a little and held out her hand. "Well, hello there, old friend."

Craig let go of the leash and Rodger shuffled forward to greet Ellie, wagging his tail as much as he could while still groggy from the anesthetic.

"I think he remembers me," Ellie said, delight in her voice. She knelt and wrapped her arms around the dog, not even flinching as he licked her all over her face. "Amazing."

Not really, thought Flynn, she was pretty unforgettable.

Still, he felt somewhat put out that Rodger didn't seem the slightest bit happy to see him, yet was embarrassingly all over Ellie. If the dog were human, this reunion would have been quite inappropriate.

He cleared his throat, loudly. "Rodger, lay off the poor girl."

"It's fine." Ellie giggled and almost lost her balance as Rodger upped his antics.

Flynn couldn't help but smile at the interaction in front of him. This was the old Ellie—a girl who loved animals and country life and couldn't give two hoots about getting dirty.

This was the girl he'd loved.

CHAPTER FIFTEEN

"WHAT'S YOUR SECRET?" Matilda asked the second Ellie got her settled in the front seat of the Premier.

"What are you on about?" Ellie smiled down at her friend.

Her smile was met with Mat's raised brow. "You're glowing. I can practically feel the happiness radiating off you. Do you have good news or what?"

"Nope," Ellie shook her head. She closed the door and trekked round to the driver's side. She almost whistled but caught her lips between her teeth as she realized how it would look. Inside her was a big ball of happiness. She felt light-headed, lighthearted…and it had everything to do with Flynn. She should push the feeling aside, repress it but, dammit, she just wanted to enjoy it. Ellie couldn't remember feeling so wonderful about just spending time with someone. Not for a while, anyway.

"Well?" Matilda glared at Ellie expectantly as she started the car.

"Well, what?"

"Your news? Have you heard from Dwayne or something?"

"Huh?" Oh, that's right, she was an actress on a prime-time television series. She hadn't thought much about the show or Sydney for a few days now. She'd been too preoccupied with Mat, the play and, if she were honest with herself, Flynn.

"It's him, isn't it?" Matilda had a knack for reading minds.

Ellie thought through her options. She could deny it or she could save a lot of time and cut to the chase. "We had lunch together at the café."

"Ooh." Matilda's utterance was packed with meaning.

Ellie's cheeks burned. She felt like a schoolgirl sharing her first crush. A sigh slipped from her lips at the complexity of what she was feeling. Of what she *shouldn't* be feeling. "*Ooh* is one word for it."

"So, what did you discuss? Are you, you know, seeing him again?"

"It's not like that," Ellie rushed. "We're not dating." The truth in her words hurt her more than they should. "We're just friends. It's nice."

"Is it?"

Although Ellie focused on the road, she felt Mat's eyes boring into the side of her head. She gulped and tightened her grip on the steering wheel. She couldn't talk about this, not now, not with Matilda. Not when her belly was fluttering at the mere mention of *him*. She pointedly changed the subject. "What are your plans for the arvo?"

Mat took the hint. "Are you still cooking with Joyce?"

"She's going to teach me how to make a caramel slice and then, if I conquer that, we might try a batch of scones."

"Sounds delicious. I might keep out of your way, then. Have a quick rest and start sorting my stuff."

"Your stuff?" Ellie thought of the cottage, swollen to the brim with knickknacks and souvenirs from Mat's expeditions around the globe. "What do you mean?"

Mat sighed. "I'm not getting any younger. These feet have shown me that, and I just thought—"

"Anyone can break bones, Mat," Ellie interrupted.

She refused to think about Matilda getting old. "It's not a reflection of your age, more your stubborn mindedness—believing you can do everything without help."

"Still, it's got me thinking. You're all I've got in this world. And you're busy with your own life. I'd hate to think of my leaving you with all that junk to get rid of."

"As if!" Ellie shrieked in outcry. "You have treasures, not junk. I'd never get rid of it."

"Get serious, girl, you couldn't keep it all in that tiny apartment of yours. I was thinking there might be certain things you'd like to keep as a reminder of me. And while you're here, well, this is a good time to do a clearout. That way you can let me know what you'd like when I'm—"

"Don't say it. You can spring-clean if you like, but all this morbid chatter is creeping me out."

When they got home, Ellie settled Mat on the couch to rest her legs for a while. She made them both sandwiches and scoffed hers down in record time, wanting to get the kitchen prepared for Joyce.

"Ready to cook up a storm?" Joyce was punctual as usual, arriving at two on the dot, her arms laden with recipe books. Not the type that Ellie had been given by friends who liked to pretend they could cook; there wasn't a Jamie Oliver or Nigella Lawson in sight. No, Joyce's books were old and splattered with food stains and smelled like homemade delights.

"Definitely." Ellie opened the screen door and took some of the heavy load. She knew if anyone could teach her to make something actually worth eating, it was Joyce.

"How's Mat?" Joyce asked, pushing her large sunglasses up over her head and peering into the living room. Ellie looked in behind her to see Matilda propped up by half-a-dozen mismatched cushions, her mouth gaping. She was already fast asleep.

"Tired," Ellie answered, frowning. "She's sick of the crutches and not being able to do anything—she hates to be so dependent on me. Hopefully, the doc has good news when we see her next week."

"Hmm." Joyce pursed her lips as if thinking deeply about something. "Will you go back to Sydney soon, do you think?"

Sydney. Ellie's heart froze in her chest. Of course that was what she'd do. She couldn't go on like this forever—pottering from day to day, effectively jobless. When she arrived in Hope Junction, she'd wanted nothing more than for time to speed by so she could leave. But this holiday from city life had been surprisingly fabulous. Now the thought of packing up again, of saying goodbye to Matilda, to the town and to Flynn put her in a panic. The thought of leaving before the play was awful, too—she felt part of that now, completely.

"Um, I haven't really given it much thought. I mean, I'm enjoying myself, and I'd really like to get my mentees a little closer to their debut."

Joyce grinned. "So good old Hope isn't that bad after all?"

"No." Ellie tried to keep a straight face. "It has its merits."

"Right, then, let's get to work."

JOYCE AND ELLIE spent the better part of the afternoon baking, and Ellie found it a strangely relaxing pastime. Joyce was easy to get along with—Ellie was glad Mat had such a good friend close by. It made thinking about her return to Sydney that tiny bit easier. Joyce was also a fabulous teacher, and pretty soon Ellie was surveying

the kitchen table with a large smile. The spread was—
if she said so herself—splendid. Alongside the caramel
slice and the oversize scones was a rich chocolate mud
cake. Joyce praised Ellie's enthusiasm. What she didn't
know was that mud cake was a longtime favorite of
Flynn's, and that Ellie had lovingly toiled all afternoon
with him in mind.

Sometime between the scones and the mud cake,
Matilda woke up and shuffled into the kitchen to watch.
She seemed exhausted despite having slept about four
hours, and Ellie couldn't help but notice Joyce fuss over
her. Ellie wondered if there was something else going
on. She was probably making mountains out of mole-
hills but, nevertheless, she made a mental note to talk
to Joyce about it soon.

The opportunity didn't come that afternoon, though.
Joyce stuck around until teatime, and the three of them
pored over Mat's old photo albums and travel journals
until it was time to go to rehearsal.

ELLIE GRINNED AS the first full rehearsal came to a close.
She applauded as loud as she could, as did Matilda,
Joyce, Mrs. Ellery, Flynn, Troy and Sam. The thirteen
actors still had a fair bit of work to do before opening
night—a mere five weeks away—but they'd come such
a long way since they started. Ellie couldn't help being
proud of the part she'd played in their improvement. Everyone deserved the celebratory supper they were enjoying that evening, and as Ellie helped Joyce lay out the
food on a couple of old trestle tables, she was glad she'd
been able to contribute.

But glad didn't begin to describe the emotion she
felt when Flynn sidled up to her, his hand full of a slice
of mud cake. She rubbed her lips together, waiting for

him to take a bite. When he did, she watched his reaction closely.

"Phwoar," he said as he swallowed the first mouthful, his eyeballs almost glazing over. "This is heaven. Joyce is amazing."

"That she is." Ellie smiled, resisting the urge to wipe a crumb from Flynn's lip. The last thing she needed was to feel her skin against his. "But, as it happens, that's one of my creations."

"Really? I didn't know you could cook."

"I'd like to tell you I'm a whiz like Joyce but, fact is, I'm only learning." She shrugged. "I like it, though, and seeing a reaction like yours makes even the washing up seem worthwhile."

"In that case, I'll have to get you to make another."

"That'd be the test. This one could have been a fluke."

"So, you didn't cook much in Sydney, then?"

Ellie shook her head. "Not unless you count scrambled eggs. I'm usually so exhausted after filming that I can't be stuffed cooking a meal for one. Guess I never really gave myself the chance to find out if I was any good."

"How did you get the gig on *Lake Street?*" he asked, swiping another slice of cake from the table and leaning back against the wall. He looked as if he was willing to listen for the long haul. Ellie loved the idea of having Flynn's undivided attention, but she was wary of the vibes he'd been giving off about her acting. This was the first time he'd spoken of it without the muscles in his neck constricting. "You never mentioned you wanted to act to me," he added, and she'd be an imbecile not to notice the pitch of accusation in his voice.

"That's because the idea never really crossed my mind," she answered honestly. It wasn't very feminist of her to admit it—so she rarely did—but back then she hadn't thought much about a career of her own. She'd just assumed she'd work with Flynn on the farm, his partner in every way. "It just kinda fell into place."

He raised a skeptical brow. "Lucy reckons she wants to become an actor. She's under the impression it's a hard profession to get into."

"She's wise beyond her years, that little sister of yours. And she's right, but there's an exception to every rule, and you're looking at her."

"So what happened?"

Ellie told him the story of arriving in New South Wales without knowing a soul, barely a penny to her name. How she'd taken a bed at the first hostel she'd come across and found a job the next day at the pub down the road.

THE THOUGHT THAT things had fallen into place for Ellie from the day she left was a heavy one. Flynn ignored the twinge in his heart and focused on her words. She spoke about being an extra before getting a permanent place on *Lake Street*. Her history was interesting as long as he forced himself to forget that her career had been at the expense of a life with him. He listened as if she were someone he'd just met. He could do this—he could talk about her job, her life, and not feel completely bitter about it. Still, when a pause came in the conversation, he welcomed the opportunity to escape.

"It's getting late. I better be getting Lucy home."

"Sorry for rabbiting on," Ellie said, tucking her hair behind her ear.

"No, I enjoyed it," he lied. Even if it were bad for him, he liked being around her—that he couldn't deny—it was

talking about her other life that irked him. "But Luce
has exams soon and needs her rest."

"Fair enough." Ellie nodded and they both glanced
around the room. There was no sign of Lucy. Flynn
frowned but relaxed a little when he saw Troy polishing
off the scones at the other end of the table. "Maybe she's
popped to the toilet," Ellie said, as if reading his mind.
"Do you want me to go check?"

"Yes, please." He tapped his boots against the dusty
floor for what seemed like forever, waiting for Ellie to
return. When she did, Lucy was not by her side.

"Well?" he asked.

"Not there." She pursed her lips, her eyes twinkling
as if she were trying to smother a smile.

"What's so funny?" he asked.

"I think you'd better come with me."

"Don't play games, Ellie. Did you find her?"

"Yes, well, not in the bathroom, so I checked outside.
She's fine." Ellie touched his arm slightly and nodded
in the direction of the main doors, urging him to follow.
Feeling like a cranky old man, he did so. Pressing one
index finger to her lips, Ellie used the other to point into
the shadows. Flynn narrowed his eyes, trying to make
out the details in the dingy alley.

"Is that who I think it is? Is that *what* I think it is?"
His stomach churning, he tried to charge forward, but
Ellie had a surprisingly firm grip on his arm.

"Shh," she hissed, but neither his voice nor hers appeared to be a problem. Lucy and Sam were altogether
too consumed in each other to notice anyone else. *Sam?*
And he'd thought Troy was the one to watch.

"I can't just stand here and watch him grope her,"
Flynn whispered, yanking his arm free.

"He's not groping her."

"As good as," Flynn scoffed. His eyes boggled as Sam's hand disappeared from view. "That's it."

"We did much worse, Flynn." This stilled him for a moment as red-hot memories came rushing back. Oh boy, had they done much worse. And enjoyed every fucking moment of it. But this was Lucy, this was…

"She's my little sister, Ellie. I have to do *something*."

"Flynn." Ellie's voice was low but firm. "Will Lucy appreciate it if you go barging over there? She's seventeen. If you don't want to alienate her, you'll give her some privacy. Let's go back inside and call her mobile."

Her words made some degree of sense, but they did nothing to release the tension in his body. He clenched his fists and looked at Ellie. "What if she gets pregnant?"

"Last time I checked, you couldn't get pregnant from kissing, Flynn."

"You know what I mean." Still, her humor worked to relax him a little.

"Look, if you'd like, I could have a talk with her," Ellie suggested. "Friend to friend, rather than big bro to little sis. She might be more receptive if *I* check she knows all about…being careful."

Flynn let out a frustrated growl and ran his fingers through his hair. He didn't want to think about his little sister and contraception in the same sentence. "Okay, but sooner rather than later—Troy and Sam are coming over on Thursday to paint the set. Why don't you come and help, engineer some way of talking to Lucy?"

"Sounds good."

"Great." Yet Flynn felt only marginally better as he trekked back inside to call Lucy and break up the lovebirds.

CHAPTER SIXTEEN

ON THURSDAY, ELLIE collected Lucy, Troy and Sam from school so they'd get to Black Stump quicker than on the bus. As she cruised along the quiet gravel roads, Troy sat in the front, munching on a packet of Smith's chips and chatting to Ellie. He reminded her a lot of a young Flynn. His interests were definitely the same—food, football and his family's farm—and their conversation helped keep her mind off what lay ahead. This would be her first proper visit to Black Stump—where she was once almost part of the furniture—since she'd left for Sydney. She'd ventured onto the periphery when she'd visited Flynn at his dam, but the location of his secret place meant she hadn't had to drive by the homestead to get there. The swarm of blackbirds was back in her stomach.

Meanwhile, Lucy and Sam sat in the back, their arms around each other. They acted in a manner quite understandable for their age but one that would, nevertheless, make Flynn's blood boil. She pondered how she was going to get Lucy away from Sam, on her own long enough to have that talk. She tried to ignore the fact that she was likely about to see Flynn's mother and grandmother for the first time in ten years. By some small miracle, she hadn't yet run into either of them in town.

Before she knew it, the impressive dry stone wall bordering the entrance to Black Stump loomed into view.

Ellie slowed the car up the potholed drive despite the urge to turn tail and speed back into town. The bumping of the car echoed the thumping in her heart. She tried to ignore both while reacquainting herself with the sights of Flynn's world: the large wheat silos you could see from the road; the massive tin sheds not far from the homestead used to store feed; the wooden shearing shed, which had seen over a century of sheep seasons; and the old windmill that still turned with heavy gusts but which hadn't been used for years. She wound down the window and breathed in the scents of the farm—animals mixed with fresh, clean air—which she found more alluring than the most expensive perfumes. Aromas that had once been so comforting but now only highlighted the fact she was really here and couldn't turn back.

Her chest relaxed when she saw Flynn waiting a good distance from the main house, waving to them cheerfully. She was nervous about this visit, but not so much that she didn't notice how totally scrumptious he looked. Wearing denim jeans, a long-sleeved black tee and his faithful Akubra, he looked every bit the iconic Aussie farmer, leaning back on the picket fence that surrounded the homestead. Her heart fluttered like a real-life romance heroine. It was no mystery why *Farmer Wants a Wife* was a huge hit with women her age. Flynn's kind of rustic attractiveness trumped gym-buffed men in suits any day.

"Watch out!" Troy's shout through a mouthful of chips startled Ellie—she slammed on the brakes. Rodger was lolloping toward them, in the direct line of the car. *Crazy oaf of a dog,* she thought, but silently thanked the Lord she hadn't hurt him. The last thing she needed was to cause Flynn any further grief. She glanced behind her and saw that the jolt had had the unintended effect of breaking the lovers apart. Lucy was tucking her hair behind her ears and straightening her school uniform, but neither Flynn nor Karina were born yesterday—the rosy flush on Lucy's cheeks would give the game away immediately.

Ellie unclicked her seat belt and the others followed suit. Flynn grabbed Rodger by collar and Ellie heard him scolding the dog as they got out of the car.

"Sorry," she said, "I didn't see him till the last second."

Flynn shook his head. "Not your fault, the fool went psycho the moment he heard the car coming down the drive. Must've recognized the sound." He let go of the collar and Rodger jumped up against Ellie. She tried to steady herself, but there was nothing to grab on to, so she ended up falling gracelessly on her butt in the dirty, red mud. Rodger immediately took advantage, positioning one paw on each shoulder and pushing her back as he licked her face relentlessly. She couldn't help but laugh, which made it hard to keep her mouth clamped shut and avoid being French-kissed by a kelpie.

She heard Flynn's stern voice, "Rodger, get back. Now." He strode to her, hauling the dog off. Rodger growled his annoyance, but Flynn was stronger. He offered his free hand to help Ellie up, which she took, making a concerted effort to ignore the warmth that shot through her at his touch. She straightened to a stand before brushing herself off, but the mud stuck hard and fast. Troy and Sam sniggered at the sight. Lucy shot them a warning glance.

"Sorry," mumbled Flynn again.

"S'okay." She shrugged one shoulder, thankful she'd decided on an old sweater for painting. Aside from the dirt, however, she was now soaked from the back of her neck to the crease behind her knees.

"Lucy, have you got some clothes you could lend Ellie?" Flynn turned to his sister, his grip still firm on the scruff of Rodger's neck.

She nodded and smiled. "Sure. Ellie, come into the house and we'll find you something while the boys get to work."

"Slave driver," Sam muttered teasingly.

In reply, Lucy stuck out her tongue at her boyfriend before scooping up Ellie's hand to lead her to the house. Ellie had a brief moment to worry about the fact she was about to set foot inside Karina Quartermaine's house for the first time since she'd hurt the woman's son.

"Maybe I should wait here, on the veranda," Ellie suggested as she and Lucy climbed the front steps.

"Don't be ridiculous. This is a farmhouse. We're not scared of a bit of dirt. Just take your shoes off."

Swallowing, Ellie toed off her sneakers. She held her breath as Lucy opened the front door. The coast was clear. Ellie sighed her relief as she stepped into the impressive old house. The decor had been redone since she'd last been here but the stamp was still Karina all over; classy but modern, homey but minimal. She followed Lucy through the lounge room and into the kitchen, relearning the family photos that still held pride of place on all the walls. She resisted the urge to linger on them, thinking it best to get cleaned up and dressed and back outside as quickly as possible. Simply being here gave her the heebie-jeebies.

"Ellie?"

She froze, openmouthed, staring at a photo of a teenage Flynn and little-girl Lucy. *Karina*. Fear surged through her before she managed to turn around and greet the woman who was once almost her mother-in-law. Just her luck that the first time they met again Ellie was a mud-covered mess.

"Hello, Karina." Her voice sounded shaky. Perhaps she should have called her Mrs. Quartermaine.

Karina had always been lovely to Ellie, but she was the kind of person who said things how they were and didn't pretty up the facts. She wouldn't blame Karina if she told her to get the hell off her property and never return. Ellie's shoulders tensed, and she braced herself for the onslaught. But it didn't come.

Lucy spoke first. "Ellie's come to help us paint the set. Rodger got a bit excited with her outside, so I'm just going to grab her some clothes." She spoke as if this were a perfectly normal occurrence and then flitted off down the hallway, leaving Ellie at a loss as to whether she should follow or stay where she was.

"You'll need a freshen up, too," said Karina, moving closer to Ellie. She called after her daughter, "Bring the clothes to the guest bathroom."

Ellie felt her stomach turn as Karina stopped in front of her. She stood like a toy soldier as the other woman wrapped her arms around her and hugged tightly. To say she was shocked would be an understatement. Gobsmacked was closer, but either way, and as much as she wanted to return the embrace, she was incapable of even lifting her arms.

Karina didn't seem to notice. She pulled back slightly and, still clutching Ellie's upper arms, took a good look at her. "You look good, sweet. I've missed you."

With words like that how could she do anything but choke up? She looked at Karina, wondering where to start.

Karina took Ellie by the arm. "Come and let me run you a bath."

They walked in silence to the bathroom and Ellie watched, feeling she was in some sort of trance, as Karina leaned over the vintage claw tub and turned on the taps. It wasn't long before she got down to business. "Flynn told me he'd invited you and I must admit, although part of me couldn't wait to see you, the other part was wary for my boy. You hurt him so much, Ellie."

"I know." She fought the urge to hang her head and stare at the floor tiles.

"I'm not trying to chastise you," continued Karina. "I know you wouldn't have left him lightly. Flynn assures me that you've talked about it and he understands your reasons. If he's okay with them, then so am I."

Ellie sucked on her lower lip, guilt growing as if she'd been hit over the head with a great big bag of the stuff. Would Flynn and Karina be so forgiving if they knew the whole truth? She really didn't know how to talk about any of this.

"Thanks," she said, trying to pump some warmth into her voice. She didn't want to seem standoffish, but this was just plain awkward. The other woman straightened and gazed at the water creeping up the side of the tub. Ellie sensed she was about to say something serious.

"But, Ellie, nothing can happen between you two again. You know that, don't you?"

She nodded, seeing her head bob up and down in the mirror. Of course she knew that, she'd always known that, hadn't she? Just because she worked in television didn't mean she had her head stuck in the clouds. But that didn't make her feel any less like a naughty child.

"Flynn's a good man," Karina said, a mother's pride shining through her reserved smile. Ellie couldn't argue with that. "I'm so proud of him for wanting to help you after…after everything, but I don't want you holding him back."

Oh, Lord, Karina was warning her off. She was scared Ellie's being around would stop Flynn hooking up with someone else. "My life's in Sydney now," she offered. "I'm here to look after Matilda. You have nothing to worry about."

"That's good," Karina said. The bath only half-full, she leaned down to turn off the taps. She pulled open a cupboard and took out a fluffy apricot towel. "I'll get Lucy to leave your clothes at the door."

As Ellie pulled her sweater over her head and unbuttoned the fly on her jeans, she realized she was shaking, positively trembling. It wasn't the shock from being bowled over by Rodger—she couldn't care less about a bit of mud on her clothes. It wasn't even Karina's warning, carefully couched in her kind words. No, it was the realization that had come with those words. Ellie didn't want Flynn finding anyone else. Not now. Not ever. She still wanted him for herself.

She gripped the edge of the vanity so as not to faint into the bath and, after a few deep breaths, slowly lowered herself into the lovely warm water. She welcomed the opportunity to just think for a few moments. Still, all the time in the world wouldn't be enough to figure out what to do now that she understood, without a doubt, she was still head over heels, crazy in love with the very eligible Flynn Quartermaine. When there were oh so many reasons not to be.

But right now, she needed to get on with the afternoon as if nothing had changed. She scrubbed the few smudges of dirt that had somehow gotten onto her face, and clambered out of the bath. As she toweled herself dry, Lucy's knock sounded at the door.

"I'll just leave the clothes out here and wait in the lounge room for you," she called. "I brought you a selection to choose from."

"Thanks." Not that Ellie cared what she put on. There were far more serious things to worry about.

Ten minutes later, Ellie and Lucy entered the shearing shed where the guys had set everything up for the afternoon. Ellie breathed in the stale sheep smells, glad to have something hands-on to do for the next hour or so. As Flynn turned and smiled at her, she remembered the talk she was supposed to have with Lucy. *Bugger.* How could she tell him Lucy's love life had slipped her mind the moment she'd started thinking about her own?

"How's it going?" she asked, surveying the big wooden backdrops the boys had been constructing the past few weeks. "These look fabulous already." She hoped to distract Flynn so he didn't drill her about Lucy.

"Really good." Flynn handed her a paintbrush. "You okay?"

"Just your mother," she replied, deciding to be honest.

"Oh." He stopped painting for a second. "She wasn't horrible to you, was she?"

Ellie shook her head. "Relax. You don't have to protect me from everyone." Although the prospect pleased her more than it should.

"Fair enough." Flynn returned to the backdrop, dipped his brush in the tin at his feet and raised his arm to resume his work. Ellie thanked God for peripheral vision as she started painting the leaves on a tree. Without having to obviously perve, she could see his arm muscles flexing— and it was as sweet a sight as she'd seen for a long time. She wiped the back of her hand against her brow. Sweat lingered, but not from exertion. Now that she'd admitted she still had feelings for him, it seemed her sexual reflexes were letting loose. He was a meter away from her, reaching up to paint the sky, but she could still feel the heat emanating from his body. It sparked crazy responses in her; she was helpless to fight the thought of her heat combining with his. Her pulse ran rampant as images and emotions swirled in her cerebellum. She tried to banish them all, knowing they were blow-ins from a fantasy world. If she thought she and Flynn could really get past everything—everything she'd done to him, the distance that now stretched between their lives, his mother—then she really was living with her head in the clouds. But knowing that they couldn't…

The paintbrush fell from her fingers as she felt the signs of a panic attack coming on. She pressed one hand against her chest, trying to quell the physical reactions before they took hold. She took a deep breath, forcing herself to concentrate solely on breathing in and out and remaining upright.

"You okay?" Great, now Flynn had noticed, and all eyes had turned to her. Flynn and Lucy wore almost identical expressions of concern.

She summoned a carefree smile. "Sure, just a little bit hot. I'm going to grab some fresh air." She all but ran from the shearing shed, her sneakers pounding the rough floorboards. Outside, she stopped, scanning left and right for a place to sit. It seemed all she'd been doing since she arrived back in Hope was running from one thing or another—the Co-op, the pub and now Flynn's shed. And the tears…what was with that? She'd barely cried in years and now every little thing seemed to trigger her tear ducts. Being in love wasn't supposed to feel like this, that much she knew.

She felt something cold and wet against the skin between Lucy's track pants and her sneakers. *Rodger*. Instinctively, she reached down and rubbed her palm over the back of the dog's head. His fur was soft and warm. Comforting. Pets were another thing lacking in her real life. There just wasn't time for them in her filming schedule, or room for them in her Bondi flat. "Walk with me."

The dog followed her to a nearby gum tree. She checked the ground, and when it didn't appear wet, she slid herself down and leaned back against the trunk. Rodger settled beside her, his head happily resting in her lap, and reveled in the attention. She closed her eyes and breathed in the aroma of damp dirt, eucalypts and hundreds of sheep. It was the perfect thinking spot, and she had loads to think about.

IN NEED OF a little oxygen himself, Flynn left the others in the shed. He worried what Lucy and Sam might get up to in his absence, but he hoped with Troy there they'd at least have a little decorum. Right now he was finding it hard to be too irritated by Sam's behavior anyway. His inner teen had reared its hormonal head and he was busy fighting his own urges. No one else seemed to notice, but he couldn't miss the fact that Lucy's clothes were about a size too small on Ellie. Every time she bent to dip her brush in the paint, the fabric of the black trackies stretched across Ellie's pert butt. It took all his strength to keep his libido under control. It wasn't usually hot in the shearing shed at the beginning of September, but he felt like an ice cube in a sauna.

Outside, he relished the cool afternoon air as he made his way down the steps. His gaze immediately located Ellie twenty or so meters away, sitting under an old gum. He hung back a moment, watching the way she gently ran her hand back and forth over Rodger's back. From the dog's stance, he was obviously enjoying the attention. Ellie looked peaceful, too, like this was where she was meant to be. Then she raised a hand to her eyes and swiped at something.

Was she crying? God! His heart clenched at the thought. She'd caused him more pain than anyone—more than his dad dying, or his grandfather before that—and yet he still couldn't stand the thought of her upset. Without hesitation, he approached her, instantly annihilating the distance between them.

As he stopped in front of her, she looked up and blinked three times in quick succession. Obviously trying to cover up the fact she was near to tears.

"What's up, Els?" He knelt and gave Rodg a quick tummy rub.

"It's…" She trailed off.

"Don't say *nothing*. I know you better than that."

"I was going to say *stupid,* not nothing."

"Okay, then." He smirked at her feisty response. "What's stupid?"

She paused, as if contemplating her response. "The way I feel about your mother, I guess. She was nice as pie, but her request that I stay away from you hurt. We used to be such good friends."

This time, *friends* referred to Karina. And it was true, they'd been close once. Anger bubbled in Flynn's veins that his mom had to stick her nose in his business. He knew she was just looking out for him, but dammit, he wasn't a child.

"I'm sorry she confronted you, Ellie. She had no right."

Ellie rubbed gentle circles around Rodger's ears. "At least she gives a damn."

Flynn tensed. He'd be stupid not to pick up on Ellie's bitter comparison to her own mother. "Did you ever see your mother again, I mean, after her no-show in Perth?"

She shook her head. "I didn't want to. I still don't. I just don't care anymore."

Her words were tough, but he saw past her bravado to the raw hurt inside. He didn't blame her. "Fair enough."

"I don't," she insisted.

Even as a teenager, Flynn had known what a selfish woman Ellie's mother was, how different she was from Karina. He knew if his mom were in her position, she'd have acted totally different to Rhiannon. No way would she leave her child with a stranger because the new boyfriend didn't want kids. He and Ellie had talked about this over and over in the past.

"Mat's been more a mom to me than she ever was. If I have kids someday, I hope I take after her. I just pray maternal instinct isn't in one's genes. If it is, they may as well tie my tubes now."

"Don't be ridiculous," he scoffed. "You'll be a wonderful mother. You were always good with Lucy, still are."

"Thanks." She smiled meekly. "But it's a moot point. First I'd have to find a man to have kids with."

As if that would be difficult, he thought. Did she really have such a low opinion of herself? Without thinking, he reached out and brushed his fingertips along her cheek, tucking an errant strand of hair behind her ear. She caught his hand against her cheek, holding it there as they gazed into each other's eyes. His pulse thrummed hard and fast. He felt himself leaning forward, losing his balance and much, much more as he stared at her lips and imagined them playing erotically across his. One hand still pressed to her cheek, he reached the other up to steady himself against the tree and dipped his head.

Right before Lady Gaga's latest hit started blaring from Ellie's pocket.

DAMMIT. ELLIE CURSED her phone as Flynn's head snapped back. Her ringtone had broken the moment. It was set to loud, and wasn't the kind you could easily ignore. She swallowed her disappointment and resisted the urge to lick her lips, which felt as if they'd been robbed of a vital liquid. He had been about to kiss her. *Flynn had been about to kiss her.*

"My phone," she explained, her focus still on his lips.

"I figured." He raised his eyebrows at the vibrating bulge in the pocket of Lucy's track pants. "You going to answer it?"

"It could be Mat. I think I'd better." Her heart sinking, she let his hand drop from her face. She dug about for the offending item and then glanced at the screen. She grimaced apologetically to Flynn. "It's my agent."

"Take it." Flynn gestured to the phone before leaning back to rest on the palms of his hands. He looked totally at ease; a pretty good actor, she thought. An onlooker wouldn't guess that, only seconds ago, they'd been that close to stepping across a line she'd drawn a decade ago.

"Hi, Dwayne," she answered, trying to inject some normality into her voice.

"Babe," he drawled down the phone.

Ellie angled her head so the phone was as far from Flynn as possible. Not that it would do any good—her agent had the kind of voice that carried much farther than the telephone. She could guess what Flynn would make of a guy like Dwayne. Even she could only take him in small doses and she'd had years to acclimatize.

But while he had the most flamboyant personality of anyone she knew, and while he could rarely see past how anything affected himself, he was a good agent. "How you going?" she asked.

"Struggling without my best client."

"Always the sweet-talker." She shook her head and glanced across at Flynn, but he was engrossed in rubbing Rodger's belly.

"I'm serious, babe. How long till you're back? The writers have done a great job writing you out these past weeks, but the boss is getting tetchy about your absence. Not getting any ideas about leaving for good, are you?"

"No." Her reply wasn't as determined as she'd meant it to sound. She wouldn't admit it, but she was already contemplating the idea of extending her stay a little longer. "Why would you think that?"

"Journos, why else? Haven't you seen the articles I'm sending?"

She pursed her lips before replying. "I've been kinda busy. You know, looking after my godmother."

"So, it's not because of that ex of yours?"

She looked across at said ex. Placing her hand over the mouthpiece, she stood up and said, "I'm just gonna finish this over here."

Flynn nodded.

"What exactly have they been saying about us?" she demanded as soon as she was out of Flynn's earshot. It had been remiss of her to not keep track of what was being written, but since she'd started helping out with the play, she'd only given the occasional thought to her job.

"That he's a spunky, hunky monkey, and locals say you're getting mighty close again."

Grr. She gritted her teeth. Somewhere there was a leak. That must be why the media knew about her break from the show so soon. *Lake Street* was filmed months in advance, an absence like hers usually didn't make itself known for some time. But who?

"One, Dwayne," she started, "you shouldn't believe everything you read. Two, Flynn and I are on speaking terms again, but that's it." She refrained from telling him she'd been sitting under a gum tree with the accused only moments before. From saying how wonderful it felt to have him back in her life, and that they'd just almost kissed, and that, right then, she'd wanted it more than anything.

"Ah, well, that's a relief."

"Is there anything else?"

"In a hurry to get away, are we?" Dwayne joked.

"No, it's just…" She glanced over her shoulder and realized Flynn had already gone back into the shed. Disappointment weighed heavily on her.

"Never mind," Dwayne said. "I've got loads of work to do, just wanted to check in. How many more weeks do you think you'll need?"

"Matilda has a doctor's appointment next week, to see how long until she's off the crutches," Ellie replied. "I'll give you a definite time then. Speak soon."

"Bye, babe."

Ellie turned off her phone and shoved it back in her pocket. She looked at the shearing shed. She wanted to go back inside, to talk to Flynn, to hang out with him, but she was scared, as well. Terrified that the more time she spent in his splendid company, the less she'd want to leave.

One near kiss didn't mean Flynn would get over what she'd done. She couldn't go off on such foolish, fantastical tangents. Besides, as she'd told Karina, her life was in Sydney now—her job, her apartment, her friends.

But despite all this, she had to acknowledge that Hope Junction was getting under her skin again. And it was becoming harder to deny it had almost everything to do with Flynn Quartermaine.

FLYNN WANTED TO punch something, but dabbing the backdrop with globs of brown paint would have to do for now. Foolish should have been his middle name. Ignoring the jibber-jabber of Lucy and the boys, he threw himself into the task, but he sensed Ellie's presence the minute she walked back into the shed. He didn't even have to see her to know she was there, and he hated himself for it. She was getting under his skin. Again.

He acknowledged her with a nod as she sashayed up beside him and retrieved her brush. In his head, Flynn could still hear that sleaze's voice asking her if she was staying in Hope. Of course her answer was no, without a moment's hesitation. Flynn was foolish all right, foolish for thinking that Ellie might have been harboring similar feelings for him as he was for her. Yeah, right. He was pathetic. What could he offer her now that she hadn't turned down years ago?

Everything he'd overhead of the phone conversation made him despise her career even more. He hated the thought that Lucy wanted to become a part of that world, too. He tried to tell himself that just because the bloke she'd been chatting to—*babe* this and *babe* that— sounded like a total tool, it didn't mean everyone in the industry was like that. Ellie certainly seemed grounded enough. Simply returning to care for Matilda proved that, but the extra stuff with the play, with the cooking and with painting Matilda's house—all that showed Flynn that her celebrity status hadn't gone to her head.

It wasn't her fault if he was having trouble remembering the boundaries.

Maybe instead of feeling bitter, he pondered, he should be thanking his lucky stars the call had interrupted what could have turned into a very big mess.

CHAPTER SEVENTEEN

"NICE EVENING?" MAT'S voice floated down the hallway before Ellie had even shut the front door.

She tried to school her smile so it wasn't a dead giveaway of what had gone down between her and Flynn. Not that, technically speaking, anything had actually gone down, but something had shifted between them today. A candle of hope had been lit in her heart—a candle she hadn't known was there until the moment when he'd leaned intimately toward her.

"Yes, thank you." She stopped in the doorway of the living room to find Matilda and Joyce surrounded by half-full boxes. "Looks like you two have been busy, as well."

"Never mind these," said Mat, giving the box nearest to her a good shove with one of her crutches, as if to prove her point. "We want to hear about *your* night."

Ellie glanced at Joyce. Nice lady, sure, but still not someone she wanted to spill her secrets to. She shrugged and perched on the arm of the couch. "Well, I got bowled over by a dog and covered in mud. We painted, talked and painted some more, and then we had Karina's minestrone for dinner."

"That soup is definitely a meal," Joyce said, heaving herself up off the floor. "I've begged her for the recipe but she won't budge. And speaking of food, I must be off. The cats will be wondering where I am with their dinner."

Ellie saw Joyce out and locked the front door for the night. "Shall I make us some hot chocolate?" she asked Matilda.

"As if I need to answer that," Mat replied.

Chuckling, Ellie headed for the kitchen. She whipped up two big mugs of cocoa, topped each with three marsh-mallows and then carried them into the living room, where Matilda already seemed to be nodding off. Ellie frowned as she put the drinks on the coffee table; it was a miracle she could find a spot amongst all the clutter. At the thunk of the mugs against the table, Mat startled and opened her eyes.

"Thanks, m'dear."

Ellie sat on the couch next to Matilda, biting her tongue. She stopped herself asking whether her god-mother was overdoing it and pushed aside the niggling worry that there was more going on here than a broken ankle. Mat didn't like being fussed over. And despite Ellie thinking she deserved such fuss, she understood where the other woman was coming from. Matilda was the most independent woman she'd ever met. The per-son she admired most. A true inspiration to the female gender. Sticking around a bit longer would give Ellie the chance to make sure Matilda recovered properly, and if she was still tired once her ankle healed, Ellie could make the doctor find out if there was anything else going on.

"Would you mind if I stayed a little longer?" Ellie picked up her mug. "Say, another month or so?"

Matilda's smile stretched from ear to ear, but she took a moment to speak. When she did, Ellie noted her words were slightly choked. "I would absolutely love that." She scooped up Ellie's hand and squeezed it gently. "What's brought this on? Is it Flynn?"

A delightful warmth flooded Ellie at the mere mention of his name. She swallowed, trying to regulate her feelings. She didn't want to go getting Mat's hopes up, or her own. "He has something to do with it, yes, but it's you and the theatrical society, too. I'm enjoying myself."

"I knew it." Mat punched the air in triumph, ignoring the bit about herself and the play. "Something's happened between you."

"Not exactly," Ellie replied. It was perilous to talk about this but she desperately wanted to share it with someone. And in Hope Junction, Matilda was the only someone she could trust.

"Come on, girl, don't be coy."

"Okay." She lowered her voice, even though the closest possible eavesdropper was old Mrs. Willet next door, who had hearing aids in both ears. "We almost kissed."

"Ooh." Matilda pressed her hand against her heart and positively swooned. Ellie frowned, she'd never known Mat to be so gung ho about romance. Or to say "ooh" so often. "Tell me more."

Ellie took a deep breath. "It's all a bit of a blur, but sometime this afternoon I realized I still love Flynn. I guess I never stopped." Mat nodded as if this were yesterday's news and waited for Ellie to continue. "He's such a lovely, strong man, but he's also incredibly charismatic and good-looking." She couldn't help but blush a bit at this confession. "For the past ten years, I've tried to keep busy—so I wouldn't think about what life would have been if I'd stayed, if I'd told him the truth. But really, I've thought of nothing else. Coming back here, to the town, to Black Stump, confirms what I always suspected. I never gave up that dream of being married to

Flynn, I just repressed it. I thought Hope would make me feel like an outsider, unwanted." Feeling herself choking up again, she took another deep breath. "And it did at first, but now that's passed and I feel as if I've come home. Sydney, my career, it all seems like an alternate universe, like this is where I'm meant to be."

On the one hand, this admission felt like a heaviness had been lifted from her shoulders, but on the other, she now had more weighing her down than ever. Like the prospect of telling Flynn how she felt. And how her life could—*would*—change dramatically, whatever his answer. God, she couldn't even begin to fathom what Karina would say if she knew.

If Flynn wanted to give their relationship a second chance, she would have to decide what to do about her career. Flynn's life was in Black Stump; leaving the farm would crush his whole essence and everything she loved about him. But could she really give up acting so easily? It had been her lifeline for so long—the only stable, certain thing in her world—but suddenly it didn't seem that important. If she got the chance to choose, she knew, with absolute clarity, that Flynn, Matilda, Black Stump, Hope Junction would be the winners. She loved working with the theatrical society, so if she stayed, perhaps teaching was an option. She could do her degree by correspondence and teach at the local school, or even just run private lessons. That way she could keep a hand in her career and be in Hope.

Stop! Her mind was running full steam ahead to fantasyland, but she couldn't jump on board just yet. Maybe never. Despite Flynn still feeling something for her—the chemistry between them had undeniably sizzled—he was fighting it. Every time they started talking deeply, getting close, he withdrew or changed the subject. Or her bloody phone rang.

"You're not listening to a word I'm saying, are you?"

Ellie blinked, realizing she'd been in a trance. "Nope. I had no idea you were even talking."

Mat snorted, but there was a certain understanding in her voice. "Love will do that to you every time."

With those words, Ellie realized she'd never asked Matilda about her own loves. She must have had a few in her time—she wouldn't be surprised if she'd had one in each port—and it seemed strange now that they'd never covered this ground. She wanted to ask, but—

"I've had a few special men in my life, you know," Mat announced.

Ellie knew better than to be surprised by Mat's telepathy. "You've never mentioned them," she said.

Matilda settled back into the cushions. "Most of them were long ago. Just flings in my late teens and early twenties, but there was one…" She took a moment, clearing her throat before continuing. "He ruined me for anyone else. He's not easy to talk about."

It sounded dramatic but Ellie understood. She'd been on odd dates in Sydney—trying to prove to herself that she'd recovered from the nightmare in Perth. But it wasn't that memory that stopped her getting intimate with anyone else; it was her comparing every suitor to Flynn.

"I'd like to hear about him," she said.

Mat nodded and gestured to the now-empty mugs on the table. "And I would like to tell you, but we'll need a refill. This is not a short story."

Ellie stood and picked up the mugs. "I'll be right back."

Five minutes later, they were both settled on the couch

again, one at each end, Matilda's ankle propped up on a burgundy-and-gold ottoman. Ellie had also brought in a box of chocolates, and rested it between them. In her limited opinion, it was always good to have ample chocolate options when discussing loves lost. Mat took one immediately, unwrapped it, smoothed out the paper and then carefully chewed it before speaking.

"His name was Tom. And he was my first love. We were in high school together. Crazy about each other. I can blame him for never becoming the doctor or lawyer my parents hoped I would. Having my tongue down his throat was far more interesting than having my nose in a book."

Ellie sniggered and took a sweet. She popped it in her mouth and sucked off the chocolate while Matilda continued.

"He was younger than me by a year but not to look at. He was so…built, so charismatic." Ellie couldn't help but notice that Mat used the same word she'd used for Flynn. "We stayed together through my last year of high school, and then his, but then he got a scholarship for a university in Melbourne, and I was in my second year of English in Perth. We decided it would be best to try and see other people." She paused. "Okay, he decided. It broke my heart, especially when, as we kept in touch and stayed friends—best friends—he wrote to me about girls he'd take to the theater and to swanky restaurants. Still, through all his liaisons, I was his only constant. And he mine. As I said, best friends. I held on to the hope that one day he'd realize we were meant to be together. Forever."

"But he didn't?" Hearing about Mat's broken heart almost felt as if it were happening to her.

"Oh yeah, he did." Mat nodded, confusing Ellie. "But by that time, I was engaged to Dougal."

"*Dougal?* Hang on, you were married?"

"Don't sound so surprised," Mat tsked.

"Nothing should surprise me about you, but it does. Why hasn't anyone ever mentioned it? Did Rhiannon know?"

"It was long before I landed in Hope. Everyone here assumes I'm a crazy old spinster, and I have quite a lot of fun playing that part." Her smile was a little bit wicked. "And sure, your mother knew. Dougal was a mutual family friend, but Rhiannon wasn't interested in anyone's romances but her own."

"Don't I know it." Ellie didn't bother to hide the bitterness in her voice. "Forget Rhiannon, I want to know more about Tom, and Dougal." She crossed her legs.

"I started seeing Dougal when I realized Tom was a lost cause. Dougal was five years older than me. He was a lovely, kindhearted banker, but not very exciting. He didn't ever make me *feel* the way Tom did. But I wanted to have a family, kids, a house and a picket fence, so I gave Dougal a chance. When he asked me to marry him, I settled. I said yes."

Ellie's mouth gaped. She couldn't imagine Matilda settling for anything. "You didn't love him?"

"No, I certainly loved him." Matilda nodded insistently. "I loved him like a good friend, a family member, but not like you should love the one you spend the rest of your life with. I wasn't on fire for him." She took a sip of hot chocolate. "Don't look so surprised, lots of people marry for the wrong reasons. And most of us aren't gutsy enough to run out on a wedding once the dress is bought and invitations are sent."

Ellie shut her mouth and ignored the reference to herself. She didn't think leaving Flynn had been gutsy—it had been a coward's way out. "So what happened? Where's Dougal now? What happened to Tom?"

Mat held up a hand. "One question at a time, girl." She took another chocolate and Ellie tried to control her impatience while Matilda ate it. "Okay, so three weeks before the wedding, Tom came back to Perth and begged me to break off my engagement to Dougal. He said he loved me with all his heart, always had, and couldn't live without me."

"Aw." Ellie's spine tingled at the romance of it.

"His declaration made me miserable, shattered my heart into a zillion pieces. Dougal was a good man. If I left him, it would break his heart, too. I couldn't bear to do that. So, yes, I married him. I settled. Eventually, we found out that I couldn't have children. And our marriage, built as it was on shaky foundations, crumbled. Our separation was a mutual decision, but by the time it was legal, Tom had married someone else."

"Oh, Mat." Ellie reached out a hand and squeezed her godmother's, blinking to stop the tears. She knew all too well the double heartbreak Mat had been through. "Did you keep in contact with Tom?"

Matilda shook her head. "Too painful. But we have friends in common. I hear about him. He had kids, made a good career as a geneticist and became a widower two years ago."

"His wife died?" Ellie sounded happier than she probably should have.

"Cancer."

Despite the tragedy of it, Ellie couldn't help feeling a little bit excited for Mat. She imagined the lovebirds getting back in touch and making a life together. Better late than never, right? The way Mat spoke about this man, Ellie knew she still had feelings for him.

"Why didn't you contact him?"

"He needed time to get over his loss."

Ellie raised her eyebrows. "Two years? Come on… let's go on Google, try and find his phone number." She unfolded her legs and was leaping up to fetch her iPhone when she felt Matilda's firm grip on her arm.

"No." The word was like a gunshot.

Ellie flopped back against the couch, disappointed. "Are you sure?"

"Yes." Her godmother's voice was shaky but her words were clear. "Some things are better left in the past. He has a family—kids, grandchildren—me suddenly appearing in his life could disrupt what he holds nearest and dearest. It's different for you. I told you about Tom because I wish, more than anything, that I'd followed my heart. I should have left Dougal and gone with Tom. I should have been honest with everybody." She paused and looked seriously into Ellie's eyes. "You have that chance. You've been honest with yourself, but can you be honest with Flynn?"

CHAPTER EIGHTEEN

THAT SATURDAY, AFTER the game—another Hurricanes loss—Flynn, Rats and a group of mates piled into a school minivan driven by one of the footy-playing teachers, Simon, and headed northwest, bound for the big smoke. Normally, Flynn would have been uneasy about two nights of drinking and partying—it was Rats's bucks' weekend—knowing he'd be the only one sober, surrounded by temptation, but today he relished the opportunity to get away from Hope, to put some distance between himself and Ellie.

Since their near kiss by the shearing shed, he'd thought about precious little else. And he couldn't afford to be distracted at the moment. Following the success of the ram sale, he had plenty on the farm to keep him busy. Some of the ewes had started lambing now and checking them was a full-time job in itself. But he still woke with thoughts of Ellie, thoughts and images that stayed with him through the day and long into his restless nights.

"Chuck us another beer," yelled Paul, one of Rats's cousins.

Rats dug into the cooler at his feet and threw a can of Emu Export across the van. Flynn resisted the urge to ask for one, as well. He could put Ellie out of his mind without alcohol, he decided—he'd managed it pretty well for the past eight years.

But they were still an hour from Perth, and already he and Simon were the only two not half-sloshed. Which was a little worrying given their first stop was to get the groomsmen fitted for the big day.

As if reading his mind, Rats leaned in. "Relax, old man, this'll be my last one till tonight. And I'm not going to go mad then, either, can't wait for tomorrow."

For tomorrow, Flynn had organized for them to do some laps in a V8 Supercar at Barbagallo Raceway. Rats had been a racing fan for as long as he could remember. Personally, Flynn could take or leave it—he preferred the hands-on physicality of football and other team sports— but right now, he couldn't wait to get in the hotted-up car, put his foot down and let off some steam. Once he'd rid his body of the tension that had been eating him the past few days, maybe his head would be clear enough to make a logical decision about Ellie Hughes.

AFTER THEIR TALK on Thursday night, Ellie thought about nothing but Mat's advice, about her belief that she should talk to Flynn. She rehearsed over and again exactly what she would say when she next got a minute with him, but such an opportunity wasn't forthcoming. For weeks Flynn had been popping up wherever Ellie went, but now he seemed to have done a disappearing act. She was unsure whether this was simply a coincidence or perhaps on purpose. But then, unlike her, he wasn't on leave from work—he had plenty to fill his days.

A week after they'd nearly kissed under the gum tree, Ellie started feeling anxious. Flynn didn't make an appearance at Tuesday's play practice and now, on Thursday night, the rehearsal was nearing an end, with no sign of his irresistible self. Sure, he'd been away on the weekend, and he didn't need to be here now that all the set work was being done off-site. But Ellie thought it odd when he didn't even venture out of his car to drop Lucy off.

Was she being paranoid, or now that she thought about it, had he looked a little relieved when her phone rang that day? She touched her lips at the memory and then glanced across the room. Lucy and Sam were entwined like trained rosebushes. She hadn't forgotten she still needed to talk to Lucy. Perhaps if she did, she'd have a legitimate reason to talk to Flynn. She marched across the hall, stopping a meter or so in front of the teenage sweethearts, and cleared her throat.

"Lucy, do you have a moment?"

"Sure, how can I help, Els?" Lucy let go of Sam's hand and he, as if sensing this was women's business, crossed to the supper table.

Ellie pursed her lips, hoping Lucy wouldn't take this conversation the wrong way. She stalled a second. "Is Flynn picking you up?"

Lucy shook her head. "Mom is. Flynn's got a rehearsal for the wedding."

"Oh, right. That's this weekend, isn't it?"

"Yep, Saturday. Personally, I'll be glad when it's over. The town can't seem to talk about anything else."

Ellie supposed she should be glad the focus was now on the wedding rather than her. But Lucy, realizing her gaffe, covered her hand with her mouth.

"Oh, I'm so sorry. You probably don't like talking about weddings."

Lucy was right, she didn't, but Ellie liked to think she was capable of doing so. Or maybe she just had other things on her mind right now. She shrugged. "It'll be fine. What about you? Are you going?"

Lucy shook her head. "I'm too young, apparently."

She rolled her eyes. "I'd much prefer to hang with Sam anyway."

"Hmm…" This was Ellie's cue. She could feel the color rising in her cheeks already, but if she wanted an excuse to approach Flynn, she needed to see this through. "About you and Sam…" she started, "things are going well there?"

"Fabulous." Lucy's own cheeks flushed and her eyes twinkled. She glanced across the room, to where Sam was digging into a plate of scones and beamed. It was almost identical to the glow the seventeen-year-old Ellie had had whenever Flynn was near. Ellie didn't want to burst that bubble, but young love burned fast and bright. Aside from Flynn's concerns, she cared about Lucy and didn't want her ending up in a predicament similar to her own.

"If you want to talk about anything to do with Sam, you know, about being…intimate, I'm here." God, this was awkward. Now Ellie knew how parents felt when they had to have *the talk* with their children.

Lucy giggled, clearly not nearly as uncomfortable as Ellie. "Thank you for your concern. Am I right in guessing this is coming from Flynn?"

Ellie didn't say a word.

"Tell him not to worry about me," Lucy continued. "Sam is the best, but I'm not rushing into sex. I'll put out when I'm ready and when I'm ready only, not a moment before. If Sam can't wait, his loss."

Wow, she was so wise and confident. Flynn had never taken Ellie for granted, but she'd been a ball of nerves and self-doubt at Lucy's age. Ellie admired her, wishing all the more that things had turned out differently.

"I'm glad to hear it." Ellie smiled. "But if you ever change your mind, you know where I am."

"Thanks." Lucy leaned forward and put her arms around Ellie. "You're the greatest, you know that? I'm so happy you and Flynn are friends again."

CHAPTER NINETEEN

RATS AND WHITNEY had planned a wedding that reflected who they were. They wanted it to be casual and fun, a celebration of their love, shared with the people they looked upon as their closest friends. The fact that they considered about two hundred locals to fit this definition meant Whitney's family's shearing shed—decked out in silver and pink balloons and a zillion fairy lights—was full to bursting when the bride turned up at dusk.

Flynn proudly stood beside the bloke who'd been his best mate since their first day at school and grinned at the sheen of sweat across his brow. "You okay?" he whispered. Whitney was only five minutes late, but if anyone could understand the groom's anxiety, it was Flynn. If the improbable ever happened and Flynn came to be tying the knot himself—again—he'd learned one thing: weddings should be held early in the day to reduce the opportunity for nervousness.

But Rats didn't hear him. At the roar of the vintage ute on the gravel driveway he lifted his head and relaxed his shoulders. The tense line of his lips transformed into a crazy smile as he glanced out the doorway and caught sight of Whitney riding on the back of her dad's 1960s Holden FB ute. That vehicle was legendary in these parts. It had been Whitney's granddad's last car; the poor bloke had rolled it and died. But Whitney's dad refused to let the ute go with the old man, spending years lovingly bringing it back to life.

Still, Flynn shouldn't be thinking about the transport when everyone else had their eyes glued to the bride. Whitney was a vision atop the ute in her white, ruffled dress, her two bridesmaids giggling on either side. It was a sight you'd only ever see in the sticks, but if Flynn knew Whitney, she'd have made sure that tray was cleaned to within an inch of its life, so that not so much as a single black speck could mark her pristine gown.

The guests held their breath as they watched Whitney and her bridesmaids disembark. Beside Flynn, Rats let out a wolf whistle, making everyone break into laughter. Whitney's smile was the largest of all as her eyes followed the sound and caught on Rats, dressed to the nines in his swish black suit. From that moment, everything about Rats and Whitney's country wedding was relaxing and, Flynn had to admit, romantic. Not the mushy kind of romance his mom, gran and sister went gooey over, but ridgy-didge romance—the kind he'd seen between his parents growing up, the kind he'd always assumed he'd have himself one day.

As the ceremony began, some people stood, while others sat on hay bales in semicircular rows around the couple of the hour. When Rats spoke his personally written vows, there wasn't a dry eye in the shed, including Flynn's.

"I, Jordan Kage O'Donnell, take you, Whitney Rebecca Browne, to be my lawful wedded wife. I promise to love and adore you, to be there whenever you need someone to laugh with or a shoulder to cry on. I want to travel the world with you, to have babies and grandbabies with you, to grow old with you. I dream of us sitting on the veranda at the end of a long day, drinking beer and just being together. You are my best friend, my soul mate, and I would do anything to make you happy—yes, I'll even wash the dirty dishes every night. I thought nothing could top the day you agreed to become my wife. But each day with you is better than the last, and I know we have so much to look forward to. Whitney, I love you with all my heart."

Whitney's response was hard to make out, choked up as she was from Rats's heartfelt vows, but hers were equally genuine. And the look in her eyes when she gazed at her husband told Flynn, and everyone else in the shed, that these two would be very happy for a very long time.

Even the Anglican minister struggled to speak when the rings were called for. Flynn slipped the two simple gold bands out of his pocket and laid them on the Bible before him. When he stepped back he realized his hands were shaky, along with his legs. What the hell was wrong with him? He thought he'd gotten over his queasiness with weddings. This setting was about as far from his near miss in the church as one could get, and he couldn't be happier for his friends. He tried to focus on his balance, watching in awe as Rats and Whitney placed the rings on each other's fingers. Something inside him squeezed, something hurt. And then they kissed.

While everyone else was whistling and hooting cheers around him, while Rats's mouth explored his new wife's for a lot longer than necessary, Flynn had an epiphany. He still wanted this. He'd lived ten years in denial, thinking that happiness could be found in other things—first alcohol, then the farm—but it wasn't true. Not for him anyway. The only real thing in life was love and family, and dammit, he wanted that more than anything.

Just not with Ellie, he thought. As much as he loved

her company, she'd hurt him irrevocably, and she'd moved on. The call from her agent had rammed home that fact: she would never be his again. What would he do once she went back to Sydney? And to think, he'd been that close to kissing her…

Flynn knew he couldn't keep up the pretense of friendship, but now he felt that even avoidance wasn't enough. He needed to move on. Not only did he need distance from Ellie, he had to stop comparing every woman he met to her. He had to make an effort.

"Flynn, what are you waiting for?" Lauren's voice brought him back. He swallowed and looked up at her. In one hand she held a pink bouquet; the other was perched on her hip, her elbow held out to him. He realized they were supposed to link arms. This was his cue to follow Rats and Whitney down the aisle—the middle of the shed—and out into the paddocks where they were scheduled to have photos. Thankfully, everyone was too busy kissing and congratulating the newlyweds to notice that the best man and maid of honor were still dillydallying.

He shook his head, trying to clear his thoughts. "Sorry, Lauren." Her took her arm.

"What were you thinking about?" she asked as they smiled and nodded at the gathered guests.

"Nothing important," he muttered quietly, so as only she could hear.

"What would you give me if I guessed?" Lauren stopped and hugged Whitney's mom. "Great wedding, Tanya."

Flynn followed suit to hug the parents of the bride and groom, then turned back to Lauren. "What would you want?"

"One dance."

He took in Lauren's curvaceous body in her hot-pink

bridesmaid's gown. She was nothing like Ellie but…hell, he'd just made a promise not to think about Ellie. Lauren had grown from the ditsy girl at school into a very attractive woman. Flynn had seen a different side to her at the ram sale, too.

"I thought, as best man, that I had to dance with you?"

"Jeez, don't make it sound like such a hardship." She was trying to make a joke, but her disappointment was tangible.

He grabbed her hand and squeezed. "Lauren, I'd love to dance with you. But—" he saw the hope in her eyes "—first we have to suffer photos." She smiled at him and he felt a warm glow spread through his body. Maybe there was light at the end of the Ellie tunnel.

After agreeing with every guest that Whitney was the most divine bride ever created, and that, yes, Rats had scrubbed up quite well, too, Flynn and Lauren emerged into the early-evening air. On the horizon, orange and purple melded together to create the most amazing sunset Flynn had ever seen.

The photographer caught him looking and said, "I want to get a few snaps of the bride and groom before we lose the backdrop. You two," he directed two fingers at Lauren and Flynn, "stand by for group shots."

Nodding, they sat down on a couple of old logs and watched the newlyweds smile, hug, kiss and generally play up for the camera.

"How's your family?" Lauren eventually asked, breaking the silence.

"Good, thanks. Busy. Mom keeps talking about you, saying we should invite you round for a thank-you dinner. You know, for helping with the sale and all."

"As I said before, it was a blast. Since Dad sold the

farm, I don't get to go to many ram sales. To be honest, I miss them."

"Did you ever think about taking on the farm yourself?"

She shook her head. "Not really. Dad never gave me the option anyway. He always said farming was men's business. Although I couldn't have done a much worse job than him."

Flynn didn't say anything. He'd never had much to do with Lauren's father. The story round the traps was that he'd inherited the family property only to discover that the love of farming hadn't carried down the generations.

"Mom and Dad are much happier now with their travel business."

"But you still stayed in Hope?" Apart from Whitney and Lauren, most of the girls from school had fled the moment they got their driver's licenses.

"Of course I did. I may not have land anymore, but I'd choose the country over the city any day."

Flynn couldn't hide his surprise, but before they could continue, the photographer summoned the entire wedding party and began issuing orders. Flynn obeyed reluctantly. He never enjoyed being in front of the camera—he didn't mind taking photos but always felt awkward when the lens was turned on him. Whitney's little sister, Sharni, brought out a tray of pink champagne in crystal flutes. Rats downed a couple, and although Flynn thought he could do with a little Dutch courage himself, he steered clear and forced a brave face.

Thankfully the fading light was against them and was soon no good for outdoor photos. Anyway, Whitney seemed to have had her fill—she was as eager as a Border collie to get back into the shed and rejoin the celebration. The photographer told Whitney he'd do the formal family shots inside, but Flynn didn't like his chances of pinning Whitney down again. She was a girl with love in her eyes and partying on her mind.

The reception wasn't at all formal, and loud music was already pumping from large speakers at both ends of the shed. Half of Flynn's class from school were bopping away when they entered. Trestle tables were laid out along one wall and the enticing smell of roast meat and veggies was wafting from the makeshift kitchen. Once again, the CWA ladies were outdoing themselves.

"Why are you standing there like a roo in lights?" asked Whitney, grabbing his hand. "Come dance."

"I thought the bride and groom had to dance together first?"

"Pooh-pooh to tradition!" Whitney shrieked, waving her ring finger in front of his face. "I'm a married woman and I'll dance with whoever I damn well please."

Rats threw back his head and laughed as Whitney dragged Flynn to the middle of the floor. Flynn relaxed a bit and got into the groove.

"You're a great dancer," Whitney said.

He'd never admit it, but Flynn didn't mind dancing. When the music was good, and loud, letting go on the dance floor was a fabulous way to forget about life's troubles. And in the absence of alcohol, he needed all the natural endorphins he could get.

"Thanks," he replied, spinning her round under his arm.

She laughed, then caught Lauren's eye. "Sweetheart, do you mind taking over? I think it might actually be time I danced with my husband." She swelled with pride on the last word.

Flynn knew a matchmaker when he saw one, but for

once it didn't bother him. It was hard to be annoyed at the blushing bride. He smiled encouragingly at Lauren.

"I didn't set that up," she gushed as he took her in his arms.

"I know. Relax. It's a party, let's just have fun."

He listened to his own advice and banished Ellie from his mind for the evening. He talked to nearly everyone in the room, danced some more, ate some delicious grub and stayed until the early hours, long after the bride and groom had hit the road. Throughout the night, Lauren had turned out to be far more fun and interesting than he'd imagined. And this time alcohol wasn't blurring his judgment.

"So what about all those emergency-room scenes?" he asked. They were sitting on hay bales, struggling to keep their eyes open but not yet ready to leave. Somehow they'd gotten chatting about medical television dramas and how unrealistic they were.

"Besides all the shagging on stretchers, you mean?"

He laughed. "Yeah, besides that."

She took another sip of champagne. He'd lost track of how many drinks she'd had. He guessed he was the only person in the shed without a drop of alcohol in his body.

"There are elements of reality in them, but I'm amazed by how many facts and procedures they muck up."

"So, if it's not all sex on stretchers and gagging-for-it doctors, why'd you become a nurse?"

The look in Lauren's eyes changed to serious. She shrugged a shoulder. "I like looking after people. It feels good to help. When I'm at work and someone comes in who's in a dire state, I almost become someone else. Someone efficient, logical, respected. And I'm fascinated by the human body and how it works. As you know, Frank is a doctor..."

"Your brother, yeah?"

She nodded. "Every time he came home to the farm and talked about his studies, I was riveted. Uni was a slog for me, but whenever I went into hospitals for training, I knew it was what I was meant to do. Guess it's like you and the farm."

Lauren got him. Few women did. They didn't understand that farming wasn't something you chose to do, it was something you were born to do. Something that got under your skin. Which wasn't to say it wasn't tough. He had plenty of mates who'd left their family farms, who'd felt trapped by the lifestyle, kinda like Lauren's dad. But Flynn thrived on it. Ellie had understood that, or at least he thought she did.

At about two in the morning, Lauren yawned and flopped her head against his shoulder. She quickly snapped up and apologized. He felt like a prick for making her so jumpy and neurotic.

"Think it's time I hit the road. Want a lift home?" It was the least he could do.

"If it's not too much trouble," Lauren replied with another yawn. "My car's here but I probably shouldn't drive."

"Definitely not," Flynn said, catching her as she tried to stand and swayed.

"Sorry. You must just think I'm a blonde bimbo." She took his offered hand as he led her to his ute.

"Not at all." In fact, many of his notions about her had been shattered that night. She spoke passionately about her job as a nurse and seemed to love the land almost as much as he did. He wondered how many other women he hadn't seen properly all these years. All because he'd been hung up on Ellie.

Not that he would have admitted it to himself at the

time. Hell, he didn't even realize he still had these feelings. But now that he owned up to them, it was a release. He felt as if he could breathe again. Flynn had always been a man of logic and action. Now that he knew what he was dealing with, he could work out how to face them and move on. He *wanted* to move on.

He contemplated this all the way to Lauren's house—wondering how soon was too soon—but when they arrived at her driveway, it just seemed right. "So I was wondering—" he felt ridiculously nervous "—if you'd like to come round for lunch tomorrow? I mean, today. Whatever it is. Mom goes the whole hog every Sunday and there's always too much food for the four of us."

In the glow of the streetlight, he saw Lauren's cheeks flush. She waved a hand coyly in front of her face. "Tonight's been sweet, Flynn, but that's not necessary. Your mom's a darling, but you don't have to ask me round when you don't want to."

"I *do* want to," he replied with conviction. It was time to move on, to look at women who weren't Ellie as if he might like to get to know them better. Lauren was in his mom's good books, she was friends with Rats and Whitney, she liked living in the country, she was good company and she'd never made it a secret that she liked him. He'd need to tread carefully, but she seemed as good a place to start as any.

Her eyes widened. "Are you sure?"

"Definitely."

He got out and opened the passenger door, offering a hand to help her up. But he didn't kiss her good-night. This was all too new and he wanted to take things slowly, for everybody's sake.

CHAPTER TWENTY

After washing up the lunch dishes, Ellie made sure Mat was comfy in front of the Sunday movie and then went to her bedroom to dress. Today, no matter how daunting the idea was, she was going to have that talk with Flynn. She had Lucy's love life to break the ice, and her future was riding on the real conversation. She wanted to look her best. For Flynn.

She pulled her hair out of its usual ponytail, heated up her straighteners and gave them a run through the lengths. Fitted indigo jeans were selected from her suitcase and a floaty pink top that, although a little flimsy for winter, made her feel feminine and pretty—the idea being that Flynn would get the same impression. To top it off, she smoothed on fresh foundation, dusted blush over her cheeks and ran a gloss called Cotton Candy across her lips. Despite her pulse racing at the thought of what lay ahead, she looked at her reflection and smiled at what she saw.

First stop was a kiss on the cheek for Matilda. "Wish me luck," Ellie requested as she bent over.

Mat looked into her eyes and smiled. Warmth and excitement shone there. "You won't need luck, my darling. Some things are just meant to be." Ellie's heart swelled three sizes at this. Mat's words gave her the boost of faith she needed to follow this through.

Next was the twenty-minute drive to Black Stump.

Her hands were a little shaky as she poked the key into the Premier's ignition, but she managed to start the car on the second shot. Unfortunately, the dodgy radio decided not to play music, so Ellie was stuck with her thoughts. These were like a whirlpool—spinning round and round but never seeming to settle on any one thing. Twice she almost turned back, recalling Flynn's adamant words that day by the water hole. But things had changed since then. Her life had become clearer in her head, and she had the feeling Flynn had been doing some soul-searching, too. Now it was a case of either confronting him with the truth and risking rejection, or living with what-ifs haunting her forever.

She drove on autopilot, barely noticing the crop paddocks flying past on either side of the red gravel road or the dust that rose up behind her. To quell her nerves, she found herself singing the last five minutes of the journey. There was a reason she'd never been asked to sing on-screen, but in the confines of the car, the act had a calming effect. And it passed the time. Before she knew it, she'd turned into the familiar long driveway.

Flynn had told her he now resided in the cottage that had been his grandparents'. When his grandfather died a few years ago, his granny had moved into the house and Flynn had welcomed the chance to fly the nest, sort of. This meant Ellie could bypass the homestead and Karina altogether—which could only be a good thing.

She spared a glance at the homestead as she drove past slowly, trying not to alert anyone inside to her arrival. A sporty red hatchback was parked under the old jacaranda just outside the picket fence. Ellie didn't recognize the car, and assumed Karina must have visitors. For a split second, she wondered if Flynn might be inside, too, but it was well past lunchtime. Even if he'd been invited to dine with his mom and her friends, Ellie knew Flynn would've made an excuse to get away the first chance he got. Being cooped up inside making polite banter just wasn't his thing. She'd try his cottage, and if he wasn't there, she knew she'd find him somewhere on the property, checking sheep or fixing fences.

With the cottage now in her sights, Ellie took a deep breath. She maneuvered round a couple of large potholes and parked in front of the old residence. Out of the car, she glanced up and smiled at the quaint little place. Flynn hadn't changed it much—the garden out the front still swam with waterwise native plants, and she recognized the twin antique rocking chairs on the veranda. It was strange that Granny Quartermaine hadn't taken her faithful rocker with her, but then again, Ellie couldn't imagine the porch without them.

There were two big, muddy farm boots resting by the door. Ellie sighed in relief—Flynn was home. He was inside and she was here, less than twenty meters away. Only a few short moments from confronting him with the past and what she wanted from the future. The fact that her pulse galloped wildly shouldn't surprise.

Another deep breath and she forced herself to start walking. One foot in front of the other. When she was younger, she used to count paces and stairs from one place to another. There was something comforting about keeping track. But right now she didn't have the capacity to add up, she just had to get there.

She padded up the steps and crossed to the door. Her hand was poised on the dangly bit of the old-fashioned doorbell when she heard laughter. The high-pitched noise of a woman's giggle mixed with Flynn's low, sexy chuckle. The shock caused her hand to jerk, yanking the bell loudly as it did so.

She froze. The noise coming from inside died.

It was probably Lucy, Ellie reassured herself, as heavy footsteps approached. She and Flynn were friends as well as siblings, and she imagined Lucy would want to escape Karina's guests as much as her brother.

But when the screen door flew open and she registered the discomfort on Flynn's face, she knew she was wrong. He was well dressed—his best jeans, a good shirt and short riding boots. They stared at each other for what seemed long enough to boil an egg.

"Who is it, Flynn?" came a singsong voice down the hallway. Not Lucy's voice—her voice held more warmth. Good God, Flynn had female company. Ellie wished the wooden planks of the veranda would split and suck her under the cottage.

As if the voice had woken him from a trance, Flynn stepped quickly outside and shut the door. "Ellie?" He sounded as though he'd been caught stealing food from old people.

Ellie opened her mouth to explain but before she had the chance, the door opened a crack behind Flynn. A head of long, blond, shiny locks poked through and peered over his shoulder. Ellie's hair efforts seemed very amateur in comparison. She pressed her hand against her tummy as it rocked in revolt. *No!*

"Hi, Ellie." Lauren's smile looked like an ad for artificial sweetener. "Flynn and I were just getting ready to go riding." She came out onto the veranda. In her hand she held a chocolate-brown riding cap, which Ellie was certain wouldn't have a detrimental effect on her hair even after hours of it being on her head. "I'm still full from Karina's scrumptious lamb, but Flynn assures me he'll go easy." Flynn looked awkward. "I didn't dress for it, so it's lucky I fit into Lucy's stuff." She gestured to her perfect body adorned with tartan jodhpurs and short leather boots. In just a few sentences, Lauren had succeeded in rubbing Ellie's nose in a whole load of manure.

"Oh. Well." Ellie tried to inject some confidence into her voice. "I won't keep you, then. I only came to talk about Lucy."

"She's a doll, isn't she?" Lauren still grinned ridiculously as she laid one hand possessively on Flynn's shoulder.

"Lauren, could you give us a moment?" Flynn asked, shrugging her off.

As Lauren's lips formed the perfect pout, Ellie's mouth spit, "No." Her emotions were only just balanced on the edge of a very high cliff—there was no way she could have a normal conversation about Lucy. Not now. Yes, she could act, but not when her heart was at stake, that would be asking too much. And what if he tried to explain about Lauren? She shuddered at the thought of such a painful humiliation.

Already retreating, shaky words fled her mouth. "I can see I'm interrupting, and I've got loads of things to get done anyway." Right at the top of that list was exorcising any fantasies about Flynn. A close second was booking a flight to Sydney. There was no way she could stick around now. It had been foolish to even entertain the idea. Matilda's doctor's appointment couldn't come fast enough.

"Never mind, nice seeing you again." Lauren wiggled her fingers in an irritating wave. Ellie stared at those manicured hands and imagined them running freely over Flynn's body. Her nausea stirred again, like a sucker punch to the gut. She didn't want to think about Lauren or her fingers, unless that thought was of snapping each and every one of them off.

Nice? "Yeah, right." Ellie didn't pretend she felt anything of the sort. She let her gaze swing to Flynn. "You don't need to worry about Lucy. See ya." Pointedly, she didn't add a *soon* or *around.*

The look he gave in return told her they both knew this was goodbye. If he could give his Sunday afternoon to plastic Lauren, then the past few weeks must have meant nothing to him. It was better she found this out now than after spilling her heart.

Ellie focused on the Premier, not allowing herself to look elsewhere as she headed back down the driveway. She didn't need any more memories of Black Stump; it was going to take long enough to erase the ones she already had. As she drove into town, she felt like the stupidest woman in the history of the planet, one of those characters known in the movie world as too-stupid-to-live. Not that she'd done anything obviously wrong, like enter a house known to be occupied by a serial killer without even a golf club for protection. No, her mistakes were far more mundane, far more unforgivable. She'd blown Flynn's kind actions out of proportion, conjured up feelings that weren't there.

The worst thing about it—well, the thing that was making her sick at this precise moment—was that she had to go home and tell Mat about it. Mat would feel her pain. Mat would want to hug her tight and feed her consolatory chocolates. Mat would want to make it all better. But it could never be better. Not in this world anyway.

As Ellie's grip tightened on the wheel, the urge to take the road out of town almost overpowered her. But once had been bad enough, doing it twice would be inexcusable. She could just imagination the busybodies gossiping that she was just like her mother—flighty and irresponsible.

She'd come back to look after Matilda, she reminded herself, not to fall in love and have her heart broken all over again. Still, this didn't stop the tears careening down her cheeks and making it hard to focus on the road ahead. Trying to summon sense, she pulled onto the gravel shoulder and killed the ignition. A road train screamed past, honking its horn long and loud, the driver clearly thinking Ellie had pulled up too suddenly. Once upon a time, she'd have raised her middle finger to the bad-mannered truckie. Today, though, she had neither the energy nor the inclination. Everything from the tips of her fingers to the core of her being felt heavy.

She let the tears fall freely. Lately it felt as if she housed a never-ending supply of salt water in her body, but hopefully she was wrong. Maybe she only had a certain number of tears in her, and once she'd shed them that would be it. Maybe, if she were lucky, losing all that liquid from her body would make her feel lighter. It was a futile hope, but the tears were coming fast and furious whether she liked it or not—she may as well wish for the best.

Hours passed as Ellie sat on the side of the road. The sun began to set, painting a vivid blood-orange and royal-blue painting in the sky. The temperature began to fall. When a kangaroo stopped in front of her at the sight of headlights ahead, she realized she'd been there too long. She reached a finger to her eyes. They were dry now, but her heart still felt like a canoe with a cruise ship's anchor.

After Ellie left, Flynn saddled up his black gelding, Elton, and his mother's white mare, Marilyn, and forced a smile at Lauren. She looked a little nervous, almost sheepish, as she stood beside him in the stables, hug-

ging her arms around her chest. He was no longer in
the mood for social riding, but it wasn't Lauren's fault.
Likewise, he shouldn't feel guilty about Ellie finding
him with another woman. He hated that he did. Hated
the hold she had over him. He was so irritated that all
he wanted to do was to jump on old Elton and ride until
his thighs burned. Burned so bad that he could think of
nothing but the physical pain.

But that wasn't going to happen today. Unofficially,
this was a first date—he'd wanted it to be. He swallowed and offered to help Lauren onto her steed. "Are
you ready?"

"You betcha," Lauren said, and took his hand. It was
soft and comforting, but there was none of the spark he'd
hoped to find at her touch, not with the ghost of Ellie
hanging around. He had to give her—*them*—a chance.

"Great. I haven't had a good ride for an age." He
helped Lauren and then heaved himself up onto Elton.
He pulled the straps of his small backpack taut—it held
a few provisions for the afternoon—and racked his brain
for something to talk about. Something other than Ellie's unexpected visit. He hoped Lauren would follow
his lead and not raise the subject.

He knew she'd come to talk about Lucy and that he
shouldn't feel bad, but he could read Ellie like a book.
Still. The encounter had wounded her pride, definitely,
her heart, maybe. Not that she had any right to feel such
things—she'd lost that privilege the day she'd left him.
But fucking hell…he still felt like a prick. Horseback riding had been *their* thing. On their first dates he'd taught
Ellie to ride, and riding had given them an excuse—as
well as the means—to get far away from the farm and
civilization, to be alone. He'd even bought a horse for
her as a wedding present, not that she ever knew about

that. Dammit, would he never be able to spend time with another woman without feeling like this?

"You okay, Flynn?"

He looked up. Usually he did his stewing in solitude. He nodded. "Sure. Fine. Why wouldn't I be?" He sounded like a rambling fool.

"No reason, it's just…" Lauren's mouth stayed open for a second but no words came. Smart, she snapped it shut.

He needed to say something. Anything to take his and Lauren's minds off the bane of his existence. To bring the tone of the day back to fun and relaxed. He'd been enjoying Lauren's company until Ellie turned up. Eventually he said, "Fancy a bet?" When she raised a confused brow, he explained. "Let's wager how long it'll be until Rats puts a bun in Whitney's oven." It was stupid, but it was the first thing that came into his head. Up until now, their friends had been the only thing they'd had in common. "Closest guess wins. Loser buys the winner dinner at the roadhouse."

"The roadhouse? You're all class, aren't you, Flynn Quartermaine?"

"Sure am, Ms. Simpson." He tipped his cap and winked, willing the tension in his body away. He was a strong believer in mind over matter. It was his mind that had pulled him from the abyss eight years ago. He could relax and enjoy the afternoon with a good-looking, eager woman if he put enough energy into it. "So, what do you say?"

She leaned slightly off her horse and held out her hand. "It's a deal. I like a good bet. And for my money, I think we'll hear the pitter-patter of tiny feet within a year. If Whitney has anything to say about it, that is."

"A year?" Flynn scoffed. "Rats isn't stupid. He's heard

enough stories of what happens once a baby arrives. I'm saying two."

Lauren giggled knowingly as the horses began to trot. "I didn't know you were a betting man, Flynn."

"There's probably a lot you don't know."

"Is that a challenge? You should know I like a challenge as much as I like a bet." They rode slowly side by side. "And I want you to know, I usually win."

She was flirting. Or at least trying hard at it. The thought had his heart thumping, but he couldn't tell if it was in a good way or a bad. Regardless, he wasn't in the mood for flirting back.

"Is that right?" He glanced ahead, drafting an idea. A plan in which he wouldn't have to worry about flirting or making conversation. "How about a race, then? First one to Oak Smith Reserve is the winner."

She followed his gaze, a slight frown creasing her perfectly plucked eyebrows. It crossed his mind that she was a lot more polished, more preened than Ellie. Her beauty a lot less natural.

"How far is Oak Smith?" she asked eventually.

He shrugged. "About three K."

"Well, since most of that is on Black Stump land, I'd say you have the distinct advantage. I'd want to be playing for something decidedly worth my while. Not a dinner at the roadhouse."

"Okay, then, if you win, I'll take you to Perth for the weekend. We'll dine at an establishment of your choice."

Her eyes danced with anticipation. "And if *you* win?"

There was no *if* about it, but he'd humor her. "You bake me a couple of cakes to take to practice on Tuesday night. It's my turn to bring supper."

The light left her eyes and her shoulders visibly

slumped. Her pout was more pronounced than that of a pug. "I really didn't think drama was your thing."

He didn't want to talk about the play or his subconscious motives for getting involved. He wanted to ride, fast. "Well, are you up for it? That direction." He pointed north.

Lauren flicked her hair over her shoulder and turned to face north. "On your mark," she said, eyeing Flynn sideways. "Get set…" She readied herself at the reins, pausing longer than necessary. "Go!" She kicked her legs, surprising Marilyn. The horse yanked her head up high and launched into a fast gallop.

This was an ingenious plan, thought Flynn, urging Elton on in pursuit. He could ride away his anger, ride away his confusion. On another day, in another mood, he might have played a bit and given Lauren the chance to win. At least let her think she might for a little while. But not today. He rode fast to catch up, and as man and horse cantered past Lauren and Marilyn, Flynn gave an arrogant wave. He didn't look back as the dust kicked up behind him.

When he got to Oak Smith his heart was pumping so hard he had to huff out breaths to calm it. He felt high, exhilarated, free and in control of his emotions. Exactly what he wanted. He didn't have to wait long before Lauren came charging out of the trees, a smile on her lips and her hair whipping around her face. As she slowed to a stop, he saw that she was flushed—the first time he'd seen natural coloring enhancing her cheekbones.

She let out a "phew" and tipped her hat to him. "You win."

"Not by much." Ensuring Elton was grazing happily, he went over to help Lauren down. "That was impressive riding."

She beamed and placed her hands atop his shoulders to jump off Marilyn. "I'm not just a pretty face, you know."

"So I see." He couldn't help thinking that it was a fairly conceited comment, but he brushed the thought aside. There was no sin in being proud of what nature had given you. He unzipped his backpack and offered Lauren a can of Diet Coke. Somehow he'd known she'd prefer that to the real deal.

After searching carefully for a patch of soft, fluffy grass, she sat down and drank. Flynn plunked down beside her, taking another drink and a packet of choc-mint biscuits—his favorite—from the bag.

Lauren scrunched up her nose and shook her head. "I don't eat chocolate. It doesn't agree with my skin."

"Fair enough. Sorry, I don't have anything else." He shoved the packet back inside his pack.

"That's okay, you go ahead. I had more than enough to eat at lunch. I don't mind."

Now that he thought about it, she'd eaten like a mouse at lunch, but he didn't need to be asked twice on the biscuit front. He wolfed down two in record time.

"So, if you don't eat chocolate," he said, wiping the heel of his hand along his lips to check for crumbs, "what do you eat for pleasure?"

She thought for a moment, fiddling with her pearl earrings. "I keep veggie sticks in the fridge, and if I deserve a treat, I buy a tub of hummus."

He couldn't help it, but his eyebrows rose. If they weren't going to find common ground with food, he'd have to try something else. "Favorite movie?"

"*Clueless*. Yours?"

"*The Fast and the Furious*."

And on they went, doing the typical first-date thing,

playing twenty questions about likes, dislikes, hobbies, etc. It was a pleasant enough afternoon, but this time he really did need to check on the lambing ewes and get a couple of odd jobs done before he lost the light. Lauren understood. Although they didn't race back to the cottage, the air was starting to bite, so they rode fast enough that they were unable to chat.

When they'd unsaddled the horses and settled them back into the stables, Flynn walked Lauren to her car. She turned at the driver's door, twiddling her keys between her fingers as she looked up at Flynn.

"I had a really great day, Flynn. Thank you."

He nodded. With Ellie haunting his thoughts most of the afternoon he was unable to echo the sentiment. It wasn't fair to Lauren, but he couldn't lie, and he couldn't kiss her when she tilted her chin up and leaned into him. Instead he stepped back a tad, and disappointment flashed in her eyes. He found himself telling her he wanted to take things slow. That he didn't want a repeat of that disastrous and embarrassing night at her place. She seemed to accept this, especially when he asked her on another date.

CHAPTER TWENTY-ONE

IF ELLIE HADN'T already made up her mind to go back to Sydney, the sight at the Memorial Hall on Tuesday night would have done it for her. Her pressure on Mat's back tightened unintentionally as they entered the hall, and it was all she could do to not let sickness take hold of her gut again.

As they walked through the door, all eyes swung in her direction, but not for the reasons they had that first night she'd come. She saw pity in their faces this time, pity from these people who had become her friends. Pity because there was another woman in the room. Another woman with Flynn.

If she could talk to Flynn now she would ask him this: *Of all the women in town, why did you have to take up with Lauren? And why did you have to bring her here?*

Lauren, who had never made any effort to hide her opinion of Ellie. Lauren, who had ribbed her about her tomboy appearance and op-shop clothing when she'd first arrived in Hope Junction. Lauren's parents had bought her clothes, music, anything she damn wanted. She'd made fun of the fact that not only could Ellie's mother not afford those things, but that she didn't even want to.

Then again, Ellie had to concede *who* Flynn was with wouldn't have made any difference to her feelings.

She swallowed but it didn't get rid of the lump in her

throat. She settled Matilda down to watch the rehearsal, trying to block her ears when she heard Lauren proclaiming loudly about the fabulous, healthy cakes she'd made for Flynn. Carrot-and-zucchini slice didn't sound delicious, but what would she know? Maybe Flynn's tastes had changed in the past ten years. She certainly couldn't attest to his taste in women having improved.

While Flynn led Lauren to the end of the hall, presumably to show her his handiwork on the set, Ellie threw herself into helping the actors perfect their lines. For the first time since she'd joined the group, she wasn't looking forward to the supper afterward. Thankfully Matilda made an uncharacteristic fuss about being cold and tired and Ellie jumped on this as an excuse for not staying. It probably didn't fool anyone—certainly not Lucy, who stopped her at the door with a comforting hand on her arm.

"He didn't ask her here," she told Ellie. Neither of them had to say who he or her was. "It all stemmed from the wedding. I'm sure Lauren invited herself to lunch, or Mom encouraged her, and then they had some silly bet…" Ellie was lost in Lucy's ramblings, but the sentiment touched her all the same. "He can't be interested in *her*."

"It doesn't matter, Lucy," Ellie lied. "He can be interested in whoever he wants. I'm leaving soon."

Lucy made an angry noise between her teeth and twisted her fingers around a lock of hair. "I'll miss you."

"And I'll miss you, too, but some things just aren't meant to be."

Mat waited until they were in the car before she opened her mouth, her words more accusatory than Ellie had expected. "I thought you were extending your stay."

Ellie winced, trying to focus on turning the car around. "I can't. I'm sorry."

"I won't pretend I'm not disappointed. I was looking forward to having you around a bit longer. I love your company, and I hate to see Flynn pushing you away like this."

"It's not Flynn, it's me. Flynn has a right to get on with his life…whoever that's with. But I can't stick around and watch. It'll kill me."

Out the corner of her eye, Ellie saw Matilda nod. "I still think you should tell him."

"It won't change anything."

They'd been over this already, talking it through when Ellie had finally returned on Sunday night. As stubborn as each other, this was just something about which they'd have to agree to disagree. Still, she tried to explain again.

"Fact is, if Flynn felt for me what I do for him, he wouldn't be dating Lauren, or anyone else for that matter. He's too noble, too committed. So there's no point in raking up the past. It'd be hard enough talking about it, I can't handle Flynn's guilt and pity, as well."

As they turned into Matilda's street, the older woman snorted and said, "Maybe I should take matters into my own hands and tell him myself."

"No!" Ellie shrieked, almost losing control of the car. "You wouldn't."

Mat took a moment before replying. A moment in which Ellie's heart stopped beating. "No. I wouldn't," she said. "But I think you're making the biggest mistake of your life."

Matilda wasn't one to hold a grudge, but Ellie knew her godmother was angry. That night she was even more stubborn than usual, insisting on getting ready for bed on her own and refusing their ritual nighttime hot chocolate. Her rejection hurt almost as much as Flynn's. Well, maybe not quite that much. Matilda would come around.

ELLIE THOUGHT THE tension would disperse overnight, but in the morning, you could still cut the air with a knife. Mat let Ellie drive her to the hospital for her checkup but made it clear she didn't want company when she went in to see the doctor.

Ellie sat on the cold plastic chairs in the waiting room, flicking through ten-year-old copies of *New Idea* and *Woman's Day*. She'd never pay for these rags in real life, but burying her nose between the pages was a good tactic for avoiding Lauren. She'd bet her life savings that if Lauren could engineer a way to talk to her—or rather, to gloat about her time spent with Flynn—she would.

An orderly mumbled a hello to Ellie as he stopped to sweep under the chairs. Ellie smiled quickly and lifted her feet to give him access. Time ticked by and Mat stayed with the doctor for longer than Ellie expected. Maybe it was the cold she was coming down with. Ellie twisted her watch around on her wrist and tapped her feet against the floor. Finally, the door to the examination room opened. She stood, ready to help Mat, but only Lauren came out

As the door clunked shut, Ellie sat back in the chair and lifted another mag up to her face. Her heart beat wildly, thumping so hard she swore she could hear it. She was furious that Lauren made her feel this way. So nervous, so on edge. Was she going to say something? If not, why the hell didn't she just walk past?

"You like reading upside down, do you?"

At Lauren's mocking tone, Ellie took a good look at the page and realized it was about a colleague's drug addict son. And it was upside down. Why couldn't she think of something witty to say in response? Something incisive, something to show Lauren she couldn't get to her. When nothing came to mind, Ellie simply turned the magazine around and kept pretending to read. She prayed to the God she wasn't sure existed, begging him to make Lauren disappear. But nobody up there was listening.

Lauren sniggered. "Don't think you're in there this week. A month off set and you're yesterday's news. Although I'm sure they could write a story about how cold and callous Channel Nine's darling is. Perhaps I'll give them an exclusive interview."

Cold and callous? Had Flynn called her that? Her heart cramped at the thought. She knew she shouldn't bite. Ignoring the bait was the only way to handle people like Lauren. But dammit, she had to know.

"What the hell are you talking about?"

Lauren smirked, wicked dimples forming as she did. "Running away again, what else?"

Ellie hoped the look she gave Lauren screamed scathing and annoyed. "If you mean returning to Sydney to my job, then yes, I leave on Friday."

"Typical."

Don't bite, don't bite. "What's that supposed to mean?"

"You, your habit for leaving the people who need you."

"Flynn doesn't need me anymore, Lauren."

She laughed at that, loudly, and in a most unladylike manner. "Of course I know that. I didn't mean Flynn. I meant Matilda."

Stunned, Ellie shook her head as Lauren strutted off down the corridor. "Wait," she called. "Matilda?"

For a moment, Ellie didn't think Lauren was going to stop. But when she did—turning around agonizingly slowly—her smile was pure evil. She marched back just enough that she didn't have to raise her voice. "Oops." She pressed her fingers against her cherry-red lips. "You mean she hasn't told you? I just assumed because you two were so close..." Her voice trailed off and then she shrugged. "Forget I said anything. It's not my place."

Lauren twisted on her heels and marched away again. Ellie's body went cold with fear. Her heart was thumping again and she wondered if what Lauren said had any truth in it. Perhaps it didn't. Surely even Lauren wouldn't risk her job—patient confidentiality and all that—simply to manipulate her.

But as she thought it over, little things began to add up, and the sum total pounded her skull like an angry fist. Mat looking frail and weary after two nights in hospital. Her fatigue, her constant need for nanna naps. Feeling the cold more than she ever had before. *Oh, Lord!* Sorting her stuff and packing up her house...

Goose bumps swam like a plague on Ellie's skin. Her breath raced. She stood, sat, stood and paced the poky waiting room, trying to calm herself.

Don't overreact. It could be nothing. But her little pep talks did nothing to placate her anxiety. Inside, she knew. Something was wrong. Something was terribly, horribly wrong with Mat.

And she had to know what it was.

The door of the examination room opened again. Ellie stopped pacing and turned. Dr. Bates had a steadying hand on Matilda's back as she helped her through the doorway.

"So, I'll see you again next week," she said. "And please, think about what I said. Please?"

Matilda nodded. When she looked up at Ellie, the fight of the morning was gone. She smiled, but it didn't quite reach her usual heights. Ellie regarded her mother figure—her best friend—and her eyes brimmed with tears. It wasn't fair for either of them to have the conversation here.

"I'll go get the car," she said. Her feet pounded the cold linoleum and raced across the parking lot. It was raining, so she pulled up right in front of the hospital entrance. She helped Matilda into the car and ran round to the driver's side. "How was your appointment?" she asked, trying to focus on driving and not on the crippling fear in her bones.

"Fine. What do you feel like for lunch? I could make us some nice scrambled eggs."

"I'm supposed to be looking after *you*."

"Then you can make the scrambled eggs," said Matilda, an edge to her voice.

Two could play at this game. "When does the doc think you'll be able to put pressure on your ankle?" Ellie asked surreptitiously.

"Soon." Matilda glanced out the window as they arrived at the cottage. "Oh look, Joyce is here."

Ellie wanted to kick something. She should have gotten straight to the point. Now she'd have to wait until Joyce left, and that could be hours. Mat and Joyce talked faster than anyone Ellie had ever known, and when they got together, getting a word in was impossible.

Ellie sighed. Joyce came out to help Mat up the steps, so Ellie went on ahead to put the kettle on. She banged cupboards and the fridge door as she thundered around the kitchen, collecting cups, milk and coffee. Patience wasn't one of her virtues at the best of times, but when worry was thrown into the bargain, she didn't have any at all. The kettle seemed to take aeons to boil and the coffee didn't want to dissolve. In the end, she only made two cups, deciding she'd leave Joyce and Mat to their gossip and take herself off for a bath. But when she turned down the hallway to deliver the drinks, their hushed and hurried voices stilled her. At a sudden halt, coffee slopped over the edges and over her fingers and onto the carpet, but she stood, oblivious to the heat and the mess, her ears stretching to hear the conversation.

She placed the mugs on the side table next to a vase, and crept closer to the door. Someone had gone to the effort of almost closing it, but the tiny gap was enough to make out their words.

"You have to tell her," Joyce muttered. Her voice conveyed a forcefulness Ellie hadn't yet witnessed in the jovial woman.

"I can't," Mat's replied irately. "I don't want to hold her back."

"Bah humbug. Or to put it your way, *bollocks*. How do you think Ellie will feel when she finds out from someone else? Or when it's too late?"

There was silence in the living room as Mat pondered her response. Ellie waited a moment before deciding it was time to announce herself. Forgetting the coffee, she pushed open the door and stepped into the room. It lacked the usual warmth found in Matilda's house. She stood straight and tall, her tight fists on her hips. She glared first at Mat and then at Joyce.

"What is it you need to tell me?"

Joyce rubbed her lips together. She stared at the carpet as if the ancient weave were worthy of museum status. Mat looked up and tried to smile but her face crumpled. She seemed small and weak and it scared the living daylights out of Ellie. Her shaky hand patted the spot on the couch beside her. "You'd better come sit down."

Thoughts flashed through Ellie's mind. First and foremost that nobody ever said "sit down" before good news. What was going on? She sat down and prepared herself for the worst. But the words that left Mat's mouth next were ones you could never be prepared to hear. Nightmare words.

"I have cancer, Ellie. Bone cancer."

Ellie took a few moments to process the diagnosis. There had to be some mistake. Mat had never smoked. She'd always derided Ellie for her terrible eating habits. And she came from sturdy stock. Her mother, who died only last year, had lived to nearly a hundred. There had to be a misunderstanding, a medical mix-up.

"Since when?"

"Since a few months ago. It's all right, everyone has to go one way or another."

"Hold on…rewind a second. We'll talk about the dying later." No way in hell would she let a disease rob her of the only mother she'd ever known. "If you've known a few months, why didn't you tell me?" Hurt and confusion threatened to bring forth tears.

Mat shuffled over and put her arm around Ellie. "What use would it have done? You'd only have worried yourself sick."

"And that's my right, dammit! You've worried about *me* long enough."

Joyce cleared her throat. "I might leave you girls to it. If you need me, just call." She slipped out, almost unnoticed.

Matilda locked eyes with Ellie. "I'm sorry, but I needed some time. I had to make a couple of decisions on my own."

"What decisions?"

"What I should do. Whether I should fight it."

Ellie jolted from Mat's embrace. "What do you mean *if?*"

"The cancer is quite aggressive, Ellie, it already was when I was diagnosed. I could have done chemo and radiotherapy, but they couldn't give me any guarantees—besides the fact it'd be an absolute hell. The symptoms could fill a book—vomiting, hair loss, fatigue. Bunch them together and there's no quality of life. I decided against it."

"You what?" Ellie couldn't keep the fury from her voice. She shot up, needing to move around before her negative energy took over.

Mat reached for her crutches and tried to struggle up.

"Stay there," Ellie growled. Her muscles had never felt so tight. She wanted to start hurling antiques and souvenirs, screaming at the top of her lungs. She stopped and ran a hand through her hair. Her fingers caught in the elastic of her ponytail at the precise moment that nausea whirled in her gut. She covered her mouth and fled the room.

In the bathroom, she slammed the door and fell onto the tiles. She gripped the toilet bowl as sobs and vomit combined in a cocktail of fear, anger and grief. When she thought it was finally over, she reached for the toilet roll and tugged. The whole thing began to unravel. She tore off long lengths and scrunched them up, swiping at her cheeks and eyes. The last time she'd been this sick was in this very bathroom. Only a week or so before her wedding.

Shivering, she tossed that thought aside and looked around. The sobs had slowed, but as she contemplated the bathroom—one that could only be Matilda's—the feelings resurged. The walls were covered in sayings, poems and crazy jokes her godmother had collected over the years. Many a first-time guest had been known to spend hours in here, simply reading. It was like a collaged history of all the places she'd been—a quote or a poem from every city and village, a testament to a woman in love with life and the world around her. How could she not fight this?

"Els?" Mat's voice sounded through the door. "Can I come in?"

"No." Ellie pouted. She couldn't look at Mat without the anger welling up again. She loved her more than anyone, but she just couldn't see her right now.

"Please, Ellie, come out. We need to talk about this."

"No."

"This is childish, Ellie."

"Now that's the pot calling the kettle black." Ellie glowered at the bathroom door. "Not seeking treatment is childish. *And* selfish."

"Now look here, young lady, you can call me a lot of things, but don't you dare call me selfish. I've never been that. Especially not to you."

"Sure seems that way from where I'm sitting." Ellie crossed her legs and arms and leaned back against the door.

"So it was selfish of me to turn down one of the best offers of my career, was it? To take on a child who wasn't mine?" Ellie had never heard Matilda raise her voice in this way, at least not to her. And she'd never mentioned this sacrifice before. "To house her, feed her, clothe her, love her?"

Another sob slipped from Ellie's lips. There were so many damn thoughts, so many damn emotions going through her mind and body she didn't know what to feel. But life without Mat wasn't worth thinking about. When she didn't respond, neither did Matilda. After a while—

Ellie couldn't be sure how long—she heard the slow *click-clack* of Mat's crutches against the floorboards as she walked away. Ellie stayed there until her bum went numb. Despite the pins and needles, she still wasn't ready to see her godmother. Not yet.

Eventually, she washed her face and ventured out into the kitchen. Mat's bedroom door was shut, Ellie guessing she'd retreated there for a rest. She hesitated by it for a moment before pulling the hood of her sweater over her head. She couldn't face Matilda right now, but there was someone else who could give her answers.

CHAPTER TWENTY-TWO

ELLIE STRODE DOWN the main street past the shops, keeping her head down. She turned at Apex Park and walked briskly toward the caravan park. It was on the other side of town to Mat's house, one block back from the main street. Ellie hadn't been past since her return. Joyce had asked her round for a cuppa numerous times, but between looking after Mat, fixing the house, helping the theatrical society and dealing with her emotions, she just hadn't found the time. But right now, she needed Joyce's thoughts and opinions. Joyce and Mat were close, and if Joyce believed Mat needed to try proper medical treatment, then maybe she and Ellie could launch the battle together.

Not that Ellie wanted to fight Matilda—that had and would never be the case—but she needed to lodge a persuasive argument. Make the stubborn old bat see just how important and needed she was.

She stopped at the entrance to the caravan park to gather herself. The paths between the camping and van plots were weed-free and neater than Ellie had ever known them. The ablutions block had been repainted since she'd last been here, and signs scattered the park telling visitors what activities they could partake in around town. An abundance of flowers grew in big tin pots on the veranda of the caretaker's chalet. Joyce's chalet. Ellie took the steps to the front door. Unsurprisingly, it was wide-open, a sign that all and sundry were welcome.

She knocked, her nose catching the aroma of freshly brewed coffee. Just what she needed to bring her tension down a notch.

"Ellie?" She turned at the voice behind her. Joyce, with an arm full of washing, approached. "How are you?"

"Not good." Through her hoodie she rubbed the goose bumps that still littered her arms. It wasn't that chilly a day, but her bones felt icy.

"Come on in." Joyce marched ahead of Ellie and dumped her washing on the table. She had the kind of home one felt comfortable in—a lot like Mat's. There was a profusion of clutter and, despite the small size, lots of nooks to curl up in and read or rest or watch TV. "I'm glad you came," Joyce announced. She gestured to her impressive-looking percolator. "Can I twist your arm?"

"No twisting required." Ellie helped herself to a wicker armchair. "Feel free to put in a shot of something stronger if you like."

Joyce chuckled but didn't reach for any secret stash. She finished making the brews and then laid them on the table with a plate of homemade choc-chunk cookies. "Help yourself."

Ellie picked one up to be polite, but she was unable to stomach even one bite. Now that she was here, she wasn't quite sure how to start this conversation. Joyce was, in essence, a stranger. They'd never talked about anything more meaningful than baking.

Joyce sensed her hesitation. "I take it you and Mat had *the* chat?"

Ellie shook her head. "Not exactly. Conversation kind of blew up after you left." The cookie crumbled in her hand as her fist clenched. She'd forgotten it was there. "Sorry." She attempted to wipe the crumbs onto a plate but Joyce waved a hand in front of her.

"Don't be silly. Leave it. Why did things blow up?"

Ellie crossed her arms. "Because I'm furious. And Mat can't seem to understand why."

"Are you angry because she didn't tell you, or because you don't agree with her decision?" Joyce cradled her mug in her palms.

"Both. I don't understand, either. When did she tell *you?*"

"Four months ago. The day she was diagnosed."

Joyce's admission was like a shot in the back. Ellie had always thought of herself as the closest friend Matilda had.

Joyce knew what Ellie was thinking. "Some things are hard to share with those we care about the most."

Ellie scoffed. "What a crock. And you should have told me the moment I arrived. Does anyone else know?"

"No one, aside from the medics. Mat didn't want them to." At Ellie's scowl, Joyce raised her eyebrows. "How would you feel if Matilda had told me your secret?"

"Betrayed."

"Exactly." Joyce nodded. "And didn't you only tell her yourself recently? Some things are hard to confess. I desperately wanted to tell you. I've been begging Mat to tell you since she told me. She speaks about you constantly, she's so proud of everything you've achieved. I knew you could handle this."

"So why didn't she?" Ellie felt herself succumbing to tears yet again. She reached for the tissue box on the table. "I could have made her see sense."

"And there lies your answer," Joyce replied sagely. "She doesn't want you to change her mind."

The tears trickled silently down Ellie's face. "I don't get it. She's always loved life. Why doesn't she want to live? Why doesn't she want to beat this?"

"As you say, she loves life. She's done amazing things, met amazing people, always been independent. My feeling," Joyce said, "is that she doesn't want that independence taken away. She doesn't want chemo—and all that it entails—to deprive her of it, and she doesn't want to go through treatment alone."

"She wouldn't have to," Ellie rushed. "I came home for an ankle, I'd have moved mountains for this. I would have been by her side through it all. If only she'd given me the chance."

"So you'll stay now?"

Ellie swallowed. "Of course." An image of Flynn jumped into her mind. She pushed it away. There were more important things to think about than her heart. "Do you know how long we've got?"

"Yes. At least, the doctor's estimation anyway. But you need to talk that through with Mat. As much as she doesn't want to need anyone, the road ahead won't be easy."

"Thank you." Ellie lifted her mug and took a long, comforting sip. Now that she'd had time to calm down a little, she realized how awful she'd been to Mat. She'd screamed and yelled and acted like a spoiled child when she should have been understanding and giving. "I was horrible to her," she confessed, looking across at Joyce. "I just don't want to lose her."

"I know." Joyce reached across and held Ellie's hand with hers. "I don't want to lose her, either. But we have to respect her wishes."

"I guess so." But it pained Ellie. "I better go," she said, taking a final sip. "Thanks for the drink, and for listening. And thanks for being there for Mat. I only wish she'd trusted me enough to be there for her before now."

"I know. Tell her."

"I will." Ellie said goodbye and wandered back through town. She passed by the Co-op and bought a pizza from the deli counter, knowing that neither she nor Mat would be in the mood for cooking.

When she arrived home, the cottage was silent. Eerily so. She wandered slowly about the rooms, looking through Mat's many possessions—some worth lots, others only of sentimental value. She fingered the collection of snow globes from around the world. They'd always been special to Ellie. As a teenager, she would choose one an evening and ask Mat to tell her stories about where it was from. She wanted these when Mat was gone.

This thought startled her so much that she almost dropped a beautiful globe from Salzburg. She clutched it tightly to her chest and tried to remember what Mat had said about it. In the silence, she heard a tiny sob come from her godmother's room. Guilt swamped her.

She moved to the door. "Can I come in?" she asked, pushing it open. Her heart cramped at the sight: Matilda huddled up in bed, a box of tissues in her lap, most of its contents used and scattered around her.

Mat looked up, a tiny sparkle in her eyes as she registered Ellie. "Of course." She patted the bed beside her.

Then at the same time they both gushed, "I'm sorry."

Ellie rushed to Mat, forgetting to be gentle as she landed on the bed. The other woman bounced a little but wrapped her arms around Ellie—the girl she thought of as her own—and pulled her close. Ellie hugged back, squeezing like she'd never let go. They stayed like that for some time, neither of them saying anything. Words were unnecessary. Tears were shed and the tissue box was empty before Ellie finally asked the question burning inside her.

"How long do we have?"

Taking a deep breath, Matilda answered, "Three to six months. As long as I don't come down with anything else."

"Three months." Ellie tested the words, thinking that was nowhere near long enough. Then a thought struck her. Terrified, she asked, "But what about your cold?"

"It's nothing." Mat shook her head and began to stroke Ellie's hair. "Only a sniffle, and I've been taking my vitamins and minerals."

Her touch had always soothed Ellie but today it didn't work. A zillion thoughts blurred together in her head. "You shouldn't have gone out the other night. It was freezing."

"I was rugged up."

Ellie shivered. She had to ask. "Is it too late for treatment?"

"Yes." Mat's voice was firm. "Even if you tried to change my mind, it would do no good now. The only thing is to keep on living. Which means—" she paused "—you should go back to work for a bit. I'll let you know when I'm close."

"No." Ellie felt sick. It was as if they were talking about someone else, some*thing* else. Something trivial. "I love you, Mat. I owe you everything."

"Darling, you don't owe me anything."

"I do. But I'm not staying out of duty, I'm staying because there's nowhere else I'd rather be."

"What about Flynn?" asked Matilda.

"What about him?"

"Well, if that's the way you want to play it." Her sense of humor was returning.

"It's the only way we're going to play it," Ellie retorted. "Now, can I get you some supper? I've got a pizza in the fridge and we can crack open a bottle of white to go with it. Then you can tell me some snow globe stories."

"Yes, ma'am." Mat pushed herself out of bed and shuffled down the hallway after Ellie. She sat at the kitchen table while Ellie put the pizza in the oven and poured the wine. "Do you know how blessed I am to have you in my life?" she asked after a while.

Ellie shook her head. "I think it's the other way around." And she did. Ellie's few years under Matilda's guardianship had made her the woman she was today. Mat had taught her independence, self-sufficiency and, most important, confidence and faith. Now it was her turn to give back. And give back she would.

If they only had three months, Ellie would make them the best three months of Matilda's life. She would look after her better than if she were the queen.

CHAPTER TWENTY-THREE

THE BUSH TELEGRAPH wasn't a myth—news, both good and bad, traveled fast in country towns. Flynn usually didn't listen to gossip, but when he was at the bank on Friday morning, he heard Natasha behind the counter mention how sad something was. Then, when the woman she was talking to—the minister's wife—nodded and said, "Bless Matilda's soul," he had to know.

"Excuse me, but what's wrong with Ms. Thompson?"

The minister's wife pressed a hand to her breast and sighed sadly. "Haven't you heard? She has cancer, love. She requested the prayer chain pray for Ellie."

The prayer chain was a group of women from the local church, including his mother, who rang each other whenever there was an emergency or someone was sick. If something bad happened in the district, everyone knew to ring the first link of the chain, the minister's wife. She'll say a prayer, then ring the next link, and so on. Pretty soon half the district would know about the issue and a dozen or so prayers were sent skyward. Whether it worked or not was anyone's guess, but Flynn couldn't see the harm.

"This town won't be the same without her," Natasha said. There were murmurs of agreement amongst the staff and patrons, who all seemed to have heard the news already.

Flynn's first thought was for Ellie. According to Lucy,

she was going back to Sydney today. Would she still leave? She'd not mentioned Mat's illness, but then, why should he have expected her to? What right did he have to know? His eyes closed for a moment as he contemplated her devastation. The bond between Ellie and Mat was one of the strongest he'd ever seen, and he knew what it was like to lose a parent. His instinct told him to go to her.

He shoved his card back inside his wallet without conducting his business and started for the door. Once outside, however, he called himself on his actions. Aside from the day she'd turned up when Lauren was visiting, he hadn't so much as spoken to Ellie in two weeks. Since that day on the farm when they were painting the sets, when they almost…

He couldn't just drop in. Besides, he'd already arranged to meet Lauren for lunch.

He leaned against the wall of the building and cursed. It seemed higher powers were committed to disrupting all his dates with thoughts of Ellie. She didn't even have to be near him to be a distraction. Would this ever change?

"Flynn."

He stood to attention at the sound of Lauren's voice. Guilt weighed heavy on his heart. Lauren was in a tiny white uniform—the kind that sassy nurses on television shows wore—but all he could think about was how Ellie would be feeling.

"Hi." He cleared his throat, wishing it were as easy to clear his head. "You look lovely."

Her cheeks gave away her joy at his compliment. "In this? You are such a sweetie." Before he could anticipate it, she leaned forward and pressed her lips to his. It was just a quick peck, but it took him by surprise all the same. He smiled and resisted the urge to wipe his mouth.

"Eat in, or takeout in the park?" he asked.

"Takeout in the park sounds very romantic."

Not feeling the slightest bit romantic, Flynn let Lauren take his hand and listened to her chatter as they walked down to the café. Unable to think through the options, he ordered a simple toasted sandwich, but they had to wait an age for Lauren's tofu-and-paella salad—whatever the hell that was.

In the park they sat against an old eucalypt. The tree had been the topic of much debate amongst shire councillors over the years. Many thought its height and reach would be a threat if a storm came through, while others believed the ancient tree was part of Hope Junction's iconic history. Flynn agreed with the latter, and thought about this while Lauren chatted away. He wasn't in the mood for conversation—a grumpy and doleful disposition seemed to be his norm lately. And although he didn't like it, he couldn't quite find a way to shake it. For a while, Lauren didn't appear to notice, content to natter on about her emails from Whitney—she and Rats were now on their honeymoon—from her brother, and general local gossip. She didn't mention Matilda. Flynn knew this much as he made sure he paid enough attention to make the right noises at regular intervals.

But eventually Lauren noticed his lack of interaction. "Flynn, what's up with you today? You've barely said a word."

"It's…" He meant to say *nothing*. He probably should have, too, but he wanted information and Lauren, working at the hospital, might have some. "Have you heard about Matilda Thompson?"

She nodded. "Who hasn't?"

"I only just found out in the bank. How long has it been?"

"Quite a while." She took a sip of Diet Coke. "But she didn't want anyone to know. Not even Elenora."

"Ellie," he corrected.

"*Ellie,* whatever. Sorry."

There was silence for a moment. "I don't want you to break your vow of silence or whatever it's called, but how bad is she?"

Lauren sighed. "Bad. She's not doing chemo, so she's got maybe a couple of months."

Flynn gasped, he couldn't help it. "That's awful."

"It is," Lauren said simply. "But Matilda has a full life with friends who care. There are many who have no one."

Flynn heard professional sympathy in her voice. He understood the need to develop a thick skin as a nurse, but Lauren seemed overly detached. This wasn't just anyone who was dying—this was a special member of their community. This was Matilda. Ellie's Mat. He tried to think of a way to help without getting involved. They didn't need money, and he couldn't offer physical comfort, but he hated feeling so damn helpless.

"Perhaps we should organize a local event, a dinner to show how much we all care or something."

"There'll be someone already thought of it," said Lauren absentmindedly. She dug her phone out of her bag and began scrolling. "Matilda's got plenty of friends."

She was right. The eccentric, lovable Ms. T was as much a local identity as the statue that stood in Apex Park. Mat would have visitors aplenty and everything she needed. But what would Ellie have? Who would be there to offer her the support she needed?

CHAPTER TWENTY-FOUR

ELLIE TURNED ON the kitchen light and made a beeline for the kettle. Through the window the first glow of dawn made a violet strip along the horizon. Every day she made sure she rose before Mat and prepared a cup of tea and her painkillers for the moment she awoke. She'd put *Lake Street* on hold—the script team found a way to explain her absence—and the producers had expressed their sympathy, happy to hold her job for as long as she needed.

Mat's strength astounded Ellie. She never got the grumps about her situation and rarely complained about the pain, even though the doctor said it would be increasing. Eventually it would become almost unbearable, she'd told Ellie, and it was likely then, if some other ailment didn't take her first, that Mat would give up her fight.

Hating the thought, Ellie filled the kettle and flicked the switch with more force than necessary. Even now, Mat slept a lot in the daytime and got tired from just doing a crossword.

Life simply sucked sometimes. Today, cleaning, cooking and movies were on the agenda. She had to keep busy or she'd go insane. And although she'd made enough soup and scones to last them till judgment day, it helped her feel she were doing something useful.

While the water heated, she swallowed her own vitamins—a concoction she'd requested from the pharmacist to help her stave off any errant illness. She didn't want any germs in the house, anything that would make Mat's last months harder than they already were.

She took the oats out of the cupboard and set about making porridge. Another sacrifice for good health—she'd much prefer a good old bowl of Froot Loops.

Froot Loops. Flynn's favorite, too. A spasm of jealousy hit as she imagined him sharing breakfast with Lauren. Mat's visitors gave precious little away, but one had let slip they'd seen him lunching in the park with Lauren. She guessed he was too busy with his new girlfriend to offer his sympathies to an old one. She didn't know what she expected from him, but almost every other person in town had made some sort of gesture—a card, an email, a phone call—and his silence angered her.

Argh, the smell of burning oats broke her thoughts. She'd forgotten to stir and the porridge was stuck in big clumps to the bottom of the pan. Swearing, she took the pan off the heat and dumped it in the sink. Toast would have to do.

She took care over the toast and laid it nicely on a tray next to Matilda's tea. When she knocked at the door, she only just made out the sound of Mat telling her to come in.

"Morning," she said, flouncing into the room with feigned enthusiasm. "How are you today?"

"Fine," she said, but Ellie could barely hear the words. It sounded more like the noise a frog would make.

"What's wrong?" Shoving the tray onto the bedside table, Ellie sat on the bed and took Mat's cold, papery hand in hers.

Mat hesitated a moment, contemplating her answer. Ellie gave her a firm look and she relented. "I have a sore throat," she admitted, her voice thick and rusty. "Need more tissues."

Ellie glanced at the empty box and the mountain of scrunched up white on the floor. She tried to keep the horror from her face. "Right. I'll call Dr. Bates and see what she recommends. In the meantime, do you think you can manage some toast and tea?"

Mat peered at the tray. "What happened to porridge?"

"Don't ask." Ellie propped some pillows behind her godmother's back as she struggled to sit upright. She rested the tray on Matilda's legs and smiled. "Dig in, I'll be right back."

Outside the bedroom, Ellie let her face and shoulders fall as she slumped against the wall. She rocked forward, her head coming to rest in her hands. This was not good. The prospect of another sickness—and its implications—terrified Ellie. It was all too soon. There were still so many things she wanted to say to Mat—she wanted to thank her more, hear more stories, ask more questions, cherish her opinions and ideas. She needed as many months as possible with Matilda.

The sound of another nose blow reminded Ellie she needed to get on to the doctor ASAP. Anything to help Mat fight off illness would be a godsend. Picking herself up, she sought the telephone and dialed the hospital. The surgery wasn't open yet, but the nurses said they'd get the message to Dr. Hannah Bates.

Less than half an hour later, the doctor was listening to Mat's breathing, checking her blood pressure and doing a variety of other tests. With a beautiful bedside manner the doctor sat and held Matilda's hand in the same way Ellie had done thirty minutes earlier.

"You've got this ghastly cold that's going round. I'll

give you some antibiotics, just in case there's anything underlying it. But basically, the doctor orders bed rest and TLC." She smiled at Mat and glanced at Ellie. "Is that chicken soup I smell?"

Ellie nodded. "I have tons of the stuff."

"Good. Keep fluids up—water, herbal tea, lemonade, hot chocolate, whatever takes your fancy—and keep warm. Sounds like a contradiction, but a little fresh air would do wonders, too. If it gets warmer this arvo, rug up and get outside for a while. If not, open the window a fraction." The doctor patted Mat's hand and stood, stooping to collect her bag. "I'll pop by again this afternoon to check on you, but if you have any questions or start to feel worse, get Ellie to call me."

Ellie saw Dr. Bates to the door, thanked her immensely and went back to Mat. "Would you like to go into the living room and we can watch a movie?"

"Thanks." Mat's reply was soft.

They deviated to the bathroom so Matilda could relieve herself, wash her face and brush her teeth. Ellie was happy that she'd managed the tea and half the toast while waiting for the doctor.

"I'll just get you settled and then pop down to the pharmacist. Is there anything you need before I go? Anything I can get for you while I'm out?" She'd be quick. She hated the thought of leaving Mat on her own, even for short periods. Would it be overreacting if she called Joyce to come and watch?

"I'll be fine," Matilda said, as if she had a hotline to Ellie's inner thoughts. "I like my own company."

"Have I been smothering you?" Ellie asked.

"Not exactly, my sweet, but you are very…attentive.

Why not have yourself a cup of coffee and a nice piece of cake while you're out. I promise not to move."

Ellie laughed. "Great idea. I'll get you one of each, as well."

FOCUSED ON HER medicine mission, Ellie parked the Premier outside the chemist and rushed inside. She went straight to the counter—it was unusually quiet—and handed over the prescription. Dr. Bates wasn't too concerned about Mat's cold, but Ellie agreed it was best not to take any risks.

"How is Matilda?" asked the pharmacist, a woman who'd come to Hope Junction as a graduate, met the love of her life and never left.

"Good and bad," replied Ellie. "Her spirits are surprisingly high, but she's caught a nasty cold. It's so not fair."

"Life never is, is it?" She offered a sympathetic smile and held up the prescription. "Let me fill this for you. Won't be a moment."

Ellie nodded and stepped back to wait. She picked up a packet of jelly beans as the bell at the door jingled. She glanced up, almost dropping the candy as she registered the figure of Flynn. Their eyes met for the shortest of seconds before they both quickly looked away. Her cheeks flushed and she moved from the counter to let him step up.

Mere meters away, she stared at the creams, nail polish, glossy mags and hair ribbons in front of her, but later she wouldn't be able to recall any of it. Every cell in her body wanted to turn back, to soak up the essence of Flynn, to take a snapshot in her mind to go alongside all the others. She racked her brain for something to say, any excuse to start a conversation.

"Hey."

She jumped at the sound of his voice. Her heart beating wildly, she took a moment before turning around. "Hello," she answered eventually. It seemed forever since she'd been this close to Flynn.

He stood there, hands shoved in his pockets as if he didn't know what to do with them. He was still illegally gorgeous, and she still had dangerous thoughts whenever he was near. She squeezed her nails into her palms. It was almost impossible to suppress the instinct to reach out and touch him.

"How are you doing?" he asked, making him the first person—aside from Joyce—who'd asked how she was. Everyone else thought first and foremost of Matilda— and she wouldn't have it any other way. But the fact he'd thought of her caused a lump to form in her throat.

She tried to talk over it. "I'm okay."

He raised his thick blond eyebrows and shuffled in his shoes. "You sure?"

She glanced around to check that no one else was lurking in the chemist. "Okay. I'm a mess. Happy now?"

"Not at all." He scratched the side of his neck, stepped toward her and then quickly back again, as if she might infect him with a horrid disease. "Is there anything you need?"

Besides you to stop seeing Lauren and pick up where we left that near kiss? Her cheeks burned at the thought. She couldn't think about kissing him. Not now.

"No." Talk about awkward. And painful. She glanced at the counter, but the pharmacist was still busy fixing Mat's prescription. When she looked back, Flynn was looking at her funny, his head tipped to one side like a confused puppy.

"Okay, then. But if there is, you can come to me, you know. Mat was like a second mom to me when we were together. If there's anything I can do for her, or you, I will."

His words worked to balloon the lump in Ellie's throat, but then something came over her. Instead of thanking him, which would have been the right thing to do, she snapped, "And what would your girlfriend say to that?"

He didn't deny he had a girlfriend. "I'm sure Lauren would be quite happy about me helping a friend in need."

A friend? Somehow she managed to suppress her snort. If one thing had become perfectly clear, it was that Flynn had been right that day at the dam. They could never be just friends.

CHAPTER TWENTY-FIVE

"ARE YOU SURE you don't want to give these to the state library? Or the national one? They'll get more publicity there than in the local library." Ellie closed the lid on the box of manuscripts. She'd taken to helping Matilda sort her stuff with as little emotion as possible, treating it as a task that needed to be done without dwelling on the reason why.

Mat, propped up on the couch by her collection of crazy cushions, shook her head and made to speak, but all she managed was a wheeze and a half cough. She barely had the energy to splutter these days. Forgetting the box, Ellie knelt next to her godmother and took note of her symptoms. Her eyes were bloodshot, her nose red and peeling from too much blowing, and her chest hissed like an angry blue-tongued lizard.

"I'm calling Dr. Bates again," Ellie announced, rising to her feet. She should have called earlier, she thought to herself, instead of listening to Matilda's proclamations that she was on the mend. While she was on the phone in the kitchen, Joyce popped her head in the back door.

"Morning," she sang in her usual cheerful manner.

Ellie gestured to the phone. Joyce closed the door quietly behind her and waited. She listened, her smile dimming as she heard Ellie's half of the conversation.

"That's what I love about small towns," Ellie said as she pushed the off button on Mat's cordless, feigning high spirits. "Home visits. No way you'd get that kind of service in the city, not unless you were on death's door." She caught her breath and put her hand over her mouth, any attempt at normality quickly washing away. "Oh, Lord—" she glanced at Joyce in horror " I didn't mean…"

Joyce came to her, easily reaching her arms around Ellie's slender frame. "I know you didn't, darling." She rubbed Ellie's back as the younger woman relaxed into her embrace. "What did the hospital say?"

"Dr. Bates will be here in an hour." Ellie sniffed. "They're getting a bed ready for her just in case." A knowing look passed between them. Matilda had already stated her case for staying out of institutionalized care, and they both wanted to respect her wishes.

"Okay, then," Joyce said, taking charge. "I'll make us all a nice drink, and we'll go sit with Matilda while we wait."

Joyce made hot chocolate with marshmallows. Mat managed to down most of hers, but it was cold comfort to Ellie. Apart from this, she'd barely eaten anything the past couple of days. She said she just wasn't hungry.

"How's the play going?" asked Mat, handing her near-empty cup to Ellie.

"Fabulous." Joyce smiled. "Ellie's worked wonders with the cast. I thought they'd be struggling to be ready for opening night, but looks like I'll be proved wrong." They chatted a little more about the theatrical society and then the doorbell rang. Joyce leaped up to let the doctor in.

"Morning, ladies." The doctor offered a smile all round, making a beeline for her patient as she opened her medical bag. Her brow creased as she took a good look at Mat. "Are you having difficulty breathing?"

"A little," Matilda conceded. Ellie glared at her and she added, "Okay, a lot."

"Hmm." Hannah listened to Mat's chest. She took some time before she announced, "We need to get you to hospital for an X-ray. I'll arrange an ambulance."

Mat tried to argue but Dr. Bates was well practiced in the care of stubborn sick people. She instructed Ellie to help Mat dress warmly, and an hour later, Mat and Ellie were on their way to Katanning, the nearest hospital with a radiology department.

"I hate hospitals," Mat grumbled as they wheeled her out of the ambulance on a stretcher.

"I know you do." Ellie squeezed her hand. "But I'm right here. This won't take long."

Ellie sat on the cold, hard plastic seat and flicked through another batch of antiquated magazines while she waited. They wouldn't get any results until they were back in Hope with Dr. Bates, but she had a sick feeling in her gut. The speed at which Mat had been rushed for an X-ray scared her. She wished she knew someone in the medical field that she could ring to get more insight, but Lauren was the only person who came to mind.

Shoving a twelve-year-old *New Idea* aside, Ellie decided to pass the time checking emails on her phone. It had been a couple of days, but aside from an email from Dwayne, one from Saskia and a handful from organizations she subscribed to, there wasn't much going on. Amazing how quickly life could change. She checked Facebook and updated her status—*I hate the smell of hospitals*—when the doors to the waiting room finally opened. One of the ambulance officers came in to tell her they were loading Mat into the van. Ellie followed hurriedly down the corridor and out through the emergency-and-ambulance entrance where they were all waiting.

Inside the van, the other officer and a nurse from the hospital were propping Mat up on the stretcher to help her breathe easier. She coughed a little and scowled. Ellie could feel her discomfort as she sat down beside her.

"Tell them I want to go home, Ellie." She looked fearful, like a scared animal or a child in need of grown-up protection. Ellie took her hand. She glanced at the nurse.

"What's going on?"

"Ms. Thompson has pneumonia," explained the nurse. "We're not taking any risks—she'll be taken to Hope Junction Hospital. She needs stronger antibiotics than can be administered by mouth. We've informed Dr. Bates."

Ellie wanted to follow Mat's wishes but she couldn't go against medical advice. "How long will she have to be in there?"

The nurse glanced at her watch—fleetingly, but long enough to make her point. "I really can't say. Dr. Bates will explain everything when you get there. Bye, Ms. Thompson." The nurse left the ambulance before Ellie could blink. She turned back to Mat and shrugged apologetically. She felt her backbone had deserted her.

"We'll sort something out, I promise."

FLYNN SLOWED THE ute as he approached the paddock. Resting the phone against his shoulder, Lauren talked, making arrangements for their date later that evening. He hopped out to open the gate, needing to do a quick check for any new lambs.

"Look, Lauren, I'm—"

She spoke over him. "Sorry, Flynn, I have to go. The ambulance just arrived with Matilda Thompson. I'll see you tonight."

"The what? What's wrong with Matilda?" When Lauren didn't answer, Flynn stared at his phone—she'd already hung up. He looked at the mob of sheep before him, cursed and shut the gate. Getting back into his ute, he rammed the gearshift into Reverse, then spun around to head for the homestead.

"Anyone around?" he asked, barging through his mother's kitchen door. The house was suspiciously quiet. He found his mom on her exercise bike in the study. "Have you heard anything about Matilda?"

She stopped cycling, took her earphones out and pointed to his boots. "They're supposed to stay outside."

"Forget the boots, Mom. Matilda's been taken to hospital in an ambulance."

"What?" Karina climbed off the bike and picked up a towel. "Has something happened?"

"I don't know," he said, *that's why I'm asking you.* Women were so frustrating sometimes. "I came to see if you'd heard."

She wiped her neck and forehead. "I've been in here all afternoon. I'll check the answering machine to see if the prayer chain's got anything."

Flynn got to the machine first and, seeing the flashing green light, pressed Play. "Hi, Karina, its Carol. Sorry I missed you, I'll jump the list and ring Bethany, but could you pray for Matilda Thompson when you get this, please? She's been admitted to hospital with pneumonia. Not good on top of the cancer. I'll see you Thursday for CWA." The dial tone sounded.

"I have to go to Ellie," he said.

His mom grabbed his hand as he started to turn. "Do you think that's a good idea?"

"What do you mean?"

Karina cleared her throat. "I know you want to help, Flynn, I love that about you, but you don't want to send mixed messages. You can't go running to Ellie whenever there's a crisis. What will Lauren think? What will *Ellie* think? Don't give her the wrong idea."

You mean, don't look like a lovesick puppy, he thought. He took a breath. He didn't love Ellie anymore, it was just weird getting used to her being in town. Especially now that their relationship was so different.

"She'll need someone," he said. "I can't just sit back while she deals with this alone."

"Okay." Karina nodded. "Would it make you feel better if I went? I could take Lucy—they seem to get on."

The idea didn't sit well with Flynn but maybe she was right. Ellie wasn't his responsibility, nor his problem. She'd chosen not to be, no matter what his instinct told him to do. "All right." He sighed. "I should get back up to the paddocks anyway. Promise me you'll call when you know how Mat is."

"Promise," his mom said, and smiled.

"Can we come in?"

Ellie looked up from the game of Uno she was playing with Matilda, almost jumping when she saw who was at the door. The last person she expected to turn up was Flynn's mom. Not that it should have surprised her—Mat being who she was. Ellie smiled. "Sure, come on in."

Karina and Lucy entered as Ellie gathered up the cards. Lucy was trying her best to look cheerful, but Ellie could see she didn't know how to react to the sight of such a fragile Matilda. She offered the teenager an encouraging look and gestured her over to the bed.

Karina was another story. Refined and well dressed, as usual, she didn't look uncomfortable in the slightest, barely sparing a glance for Ellie as she took the empty chair on the other side of the bed.

"I heard you were in here," she started, "and I knew how much you'd hate it, so I brought you some of the puzzle books you love. Also, a selection of new releases from the library."

"Thanks." Matilda's face glowed as she took a book off the pile and read the blurb.

"You're welcome." Karina beamed. "Is there anything else we can do for you? Flynn's busy with the sheep but he said to send his love."

Ellie's heart froze at the mention of Flynn, wondering if he'd really said that or Karina was just being polite. Mat made to respond but instead began to wheeze again. Ellie leaned her forward to ease her breathing, her eye on the emergency buzzer, but after a few moments the difficulty passed. Mat reached for her lemonade. Ellie moved her hand to help but Mat pushed it away.

"I can do it myself," she barked, and the cup tumbled onto the cold linoleum floor, sending liquid over the bed and making a clatter that echoed in the bare and sterile room. All eyes stared at the puddle of liquid until Karina launched into action.

"Lucy, go and ask the nurse for a cloth. And do be careful not to slip in those ridiculous shoes you're wearing." Lucy all but fled the room as Karina stooped to pick up the cup.

"I'm sorry, Mat." Ellie's throat closed over. The last thing she wanted to do was lose the plot in front of Flynn's mom and sister.

"It's okay, sweet. It's my fault," Mat said shakily. She reached out for Ellie's hand, which Ellie gave freely. "I'm just tired."

Sheila, the nurse, entered the room, followed closely by Lucy and an orderly wheeling a mop and bucket. "I think you've had enough visitors for today," Sheila announced, taking the clipboard with Matilda's records from its holder at the foot of the bed. She smiled at Flynn's mom. "I'm sorry, Karina, but I have to insist that everyone leaves to let Matilda rest."

"That's fine. We just popped in to say hello." Karina moved closer to Matilda and patted her hand. "If there's anything else we can do, please let Ellie know."

"Thank you."

Ellie swallowed, preparing herself to speak. She summoned a smile for the Quartermaine women. "Thanks for coming."

As Flynn's family headed for the door, Ellie lowered herself back into the chair, placing the books on the bedside table. Once the nurse had done her observations she would see if Mat wanted to watch a movie. Uno was perhaps a little more energetic than Matilda could handle.

"Ellie, maybe you should go, too." Sheila spoke softly and gestured to Matilda. Ellie saw that she was already asleep again. Before she knew it, the nurse had lured her out of the room, the hand at Ellie's elbow a firm, albeit kind reminder of who was in charge. In the corridor, Sheila lowered her voice even further. "Lucy said Matilda got angry at you."

Ellie nodded, embarrassment flushing her cheeks.

"Don't take it too badly," Sheila said. "Being here has been difficult for her. And we know things aren't necessarily going to get better. Although she needs your love and support at the moment, she also needs time to digest her fate. At this stage it's not unusual for a sufferer to withdraw from those close to them. I'm not saying that's what's going to happen with Matilda, but she might need some alone time. Do you understand what I'm saying?"

Ellie ran a hand through her hair and caught her fingers in the knots. She couldn't recall the last time she'd given it a proper brush. "Yes, but...I can't just leave her."

"She's sleeping. You should get some rest, too. Have a shower, take five minutes for yourself. It's getting late now—she'll likely sleep all night. Go home and come back fresh in the morning."

Reluctantly, Ellie agreed.

CHAPTER TWENTY-SIX

FLYNN TUGGED A sweater over his head. He ran a hand over his face and decided he had neither the time nor the inclination to shave—he would visit the homestead instead. He glanced at the microwave clock as he headed into the kitchen. Half an hour till he was due at Lauren's. She was making him dinner. It was the first night they would stay in rather than go out, and the thought left him a little uneasy.

He pushed his reservations aside, grabbed his keys off the table and left. After parking his ute outside the main house, he let himself in through the front door rather than the kitchen, where he usually appeared, hoping to locate Lucy before his mom knew he was there. The plan worked.

"What are you doing here?" Lucy accused as he slipped into her room. She'd been snarky with him lately, but he'd just put it down to teenage hormones.

"You studying?" he asked, disregarding her question. She'd been on a social networking site he didn't recognize, but the way she clicked back to something schoolish when he came in gave her away.

"Yes," she answered crabbily.

"Good." He sat down on her bed and ignored the way she was glowering at him. "How was Matilda?"

Lucy's scowl lessened. "I *knew* you cared."

"Of course I care. Matilda Thompson is a great old bird."

"It's Ellie you care about," snapped Lucy insightfully.

He weighed up whether to deny this or admit he was worried about his ex-girlfriend. "Ellie's... Ellie *was* a friend," he said eventually. "Of course I'm anxious about her situation."

"Do you still love her?"

"It's complicated, Luce, but I'm not really here to discuss my love life."

"So it's okay for you to butt your nose into *mine* but not the other way around?"

"Since when have I butted into your love life?" he asked, not sure if he wanted to know the answer.

She raised her eyebrows. "Getting Ellie to talk to me about Sam—that ring any bells?"

Come to think of it, yes, but she'd never told him the outcome of that conversation. "Well, what *is* going on with you and Sam?"

"Not that you would understand," Lucy started, relaxing a little in her swivel chair as a glow flushed her face, "but I'm in love with him. He's all I've ever wanted in a boyfriend. Loving, caring, interested in me and supportive of my dreams."

Flynn didn't know what to think of this, but he hadn't come here to raise his blood pressure any more. "Good for you," he lied. "Now, what happened when you visited Ms. T?"

"It was awful," Lucy confessed. "I mean, it's only been about a week since I last saw her, but she's so much worse. She looks so weak and vulnerable, like she couldn't raise a flyswatter to kill a mosquito."

"How bad is the pneumonia?" he asked.

Lucy shrugged. "Everyone kind of just used small

talk, pretending it was all normal. I heard Sheila say to one of the other nurses that it didn't look good, though, so..." She shrugged again.

"And what about...?" He didn't need to say her name, Lucy knew what he was asking.

"Ellie's devastated, but completely on eggshells. She accidentally made Matilda spill her drink while we were there and Matilda snapped at her. Ellie looked like she was ready to burst into tears."

He nodded, feeling even stronger now the pull to go and visit Ellie. If he didn't have a date with Lauren, he very well might have. "Thanks," he said. "Now get back to studying."

"Yes, boss," she answered, smiling. Her tone was far more jovial than when he'd first entered the room, making him glad he'd spoken to her.

LAUREN MET FLYNN at the door, a glass of something sparkly in one hand and a beer in the other. She kissed him on the cheek—that was as far as things had gone since that night at the pub—and offered him the beer.

He smiled but shook his head. "I don't drink, Lauren." She knew this—he'd told her before, twice, but it didn't seem to have registered.

"Oh, I keep forgetting." She waved a hand in front of her face. "Are you sure you can't just have one?"

"Definitely not." He strode into the lounge room and felt her hands on his shoulders a few seconds later. She rubbed her fingers across his shoulder blades and whispered seductively into his ear, her strong perfume enveloping him.

"It might help loosen you up," she said.

He shrugged her off. "I don't need loosening up."

Then, in an attempt to change the subject, he asked, "What's for dinner?"

"My famous vegetarian lasagna and rye garlic bread." She sounded a lot more excited by the prospect than he felt.

"Sounds delicious," he managed. "I'm starving."

"Let's go eat, then." Lauren tried to be upbeat, but there was a tension between them. Everything she said seemed to annoy Flynn, and although he knew this wasn't fair to her, he just couldn't help it. She fetched him a glass of orange juice and served their dinner on perfectly white porcelain plates. When they sat down, Flynn raised his glass and clinked it with Lauren's. He took a swig before his first mouthful, which, he reflected afterward, probably saved a complete disaster, as the citrus slightly masked the taste of her creation. It was ghastly. Trying not to grimace, he swallowed the next mouthful without chewing at all. He'd never tasted anything so horrible.

"You like it?" she asked on his fifth reluctant spoonful.

"Hmm… It's interesting," he replied, psyching himself up for another round.

Lauren kept trying to ignite the conversation but Flynn just couldn't show enthusiasm, making the night even more of a challenge. He wondered what the hell he was doing there, why he was pushing for something so obviously wrong. If Ellie hadn't come back, would he have even contemplated dating Lauren? The answer shamed him.

"What's up with you, Flynn?"

"Nothing." He hoped his nose wasn't growing.

"It's Ellie, isn't it?" Scorn filled her words.

"Yes. And no." He didn't want to talk about this with

Lauren. No one understood how Ellie made him feel. Complete, yet totally lost—all at the same time. Simply knowing she was near made him unable to focus on anything else. Talk about tragic. Because that's what it was. That's what *he* was.

Lauren poured more bubbly into her glass and downed half of it in a single shot. "I honestly don't see what's so fabulous about her. Is it just a case of wanting what you can't have?" she asked. "Because she doesn't want you, Flynn." It was a cruel thing to say, each word slicing deep into his pride. "The only reason she's still here is because of poor old Matilda Thompson. Ellie's just waiting for her to drop off so she can get back to the high life. Back to Sydney. Without you."

Flynn looked at the woman in front of him, shocked by the bitterness of her tongue. He swallowed, withholding the angry words he wanted to spit back. Whether she was right or not, he knew one thing for sure. He needed to cease this ridiculous attempt at a relationship. It was his fault they'd gotten to this point. He shouldn't have been so delusional as to think he could simply shift his interest to someone else.

Standing up, he said, "Thanks for the lovely meal, Lauren, and I'm sorry I'm not very good company. I don't think anything will ever work between us."

She shrugged as if she couldn't give a damn. He nodded and hovered awkwardly. Kissing her on the cheek wasn't a good idea—she might very well slap him, and he wouldn't blame her—but it seemed rude to walk out without some sort of goodbye. The room was silent for a moment.

"Well, I guess I'll see you round." He walked briskly to her door. She didn't follow and he tried not to think about the state she'd be in after he left. He felt like a right tool, but breathed a deep sigh of relief that the evening was over.

As ELLIE CLOSED the door of Mat's cottage, she doubted rest would come easily. She caught her reflection in the hallway mirror and remembered the knots in her hair. If Saskia could see her now, she'd be appalled at her appearance. Such things were never high on Ellie's list of priorities, and now they seemed practically insignificant. Still, she needed to do something to pass the time and so decided a shower was a good idea.

Despite the strict water restrictions for the region, Ellie couldn't bring herself to hurry. Standing under the hot water relaxed her muscles, and washing her hair made her feel she was doing something useful. Feeling cleaner, and slightly better, she plodded to her bedroom, dressing in her faithful old flannelette pajamas. She recalled one of the scriptwriters from *Lake Street,* a woman who used to write magazine articles before she got a gig in television. She always bragged about writing being the best job in the world because you could stay at home and work in your pajamas. Doing up the buttons, Ellie could see the appeal. The flannelette, combined with her fluffy slippers, was like a much-needed hug. Now all that was missing was comfort food and a movie she knew inside out.

Although she hadn't done much of a shop recently, there was a packet of Deb instant mash in the cupboard. That, and a bit of grated cheese, would make the perfect dinner.

She took her meal into the living room, selected *Mary Poppins* from Mat's collection of DVDs and sat down on the couch, covering her legs with a CWA crocheted blanket. The first spoonful of Deb was halfway to her mouth and the wind was blowing in Cherry Tree Lane when a loud knock sounded at the front door.

Ellie started, and a clump of mash fell onto her top. Sighing, she contemplated ignoring the caller, but curiosity got the better of her. After wiping the potato off, she went to the door and switched on the porch light. She peered through the peephole and almost jumped back. Her hand shot up to cover her mouth, stifling a gasp as she glanced down at her dire attire. She thought about rushing down the hallway to at least throw a sweater over the top, but settled for running her hands through her hair. Whatever reason Flynn had for being on Matilda's doorstep, it surely wasn't to serenade her, so she might as well relax about her appearance.

She opened the door. "What are you doing here?" Her question sounded more accusing than she'd meant it to.

He grinned at the pink and purple owls covering her body. "Nice pajamas."

"I wasn't expecting guests," she said, her voice softening.

"I won't stay for long." His hands were tucked in his pockets again—perhaps he was nervous, more likely he was bloody cold. A sickly floral smell hung about him.

"It's okay, I wasn't doing anything. You coming in?"

"Sure." He nodded and stepped inside, then sniffed. "Did I interrupt dinner?"

She laughed. "If you could call it that."

"It smells delicious."

She led him into the living room and gestured to her bowl of mashed potato. "There's plenty more if you're hungry."

Now he laughed. "Hasn't Joyce taught you main courses yet?"

She tried to scowl but couldn't quite hide her amusement at his comment, or the glee in her heart at his presence. "First my pj's, now my cooking? Did you come here to insult me or do you have some other agenda?"

"Sorry." He hung his head in surrender. "It does smell good, though. Do you really have more?"

"Sit down. It won't take long to make some." Thankful for the chance to gather herself, she went into the kitchen, flicked the kettle on and measured out the potato powder. "Do you want cheese, too?" she called down the hall.

"Yes, please. And tomato sauce if you have it."

She grimaced a little but retrieved the sauce from the cupboard nevertheless. This felt strangely normal—despite the fact she never imagined she'd be sharing a meal with Flynn tonight.

"There. Dinner—" she plunked the bowl down in front of him "—of a sort." She retrieved her own and took the other end of the couch, mindful to leave a secure distance between them.

She took a mouthful, as did he. Comfortable silence reigned, and then he said, "It's delicious. Much better than—" He stopped himself midsentence.

"Better than what?" She scrutinized his expression.

"Never mind." He shook his head and set about devouring more of the mash.

She got a whiff of that shocking aroma again and screwed up her nose. "Have you already been out to dinner?" Not that she had the right to know, she thought, or a right to the spear of jealousy that was piercing her gut.

Flynn looked sheepish. "I was at Lauren's place. We were on a date. She made me dinner."

Ellie sucked in a breath, not sure how to respond,

the reminder of her nemesis killing the camaraderie between them.

"It wasn't good," he said, filling the silence.

"The dinner or the date?" she asked.

"Both."

"I see."

Ellie was happy to leave it at that, but Flynn seemed intent on explaining. "She made some ghastly vegetarian dish—the texture was all…" He made his face into a look of horror. "And it was so bland I couldn't even decipher what veggies she'd used. I mean, I'm sure it's good for you, but I think I'd rather be unhealthy."

Ellie swallowed another mouthful of cheesy Deb, wondering why he was telling her all this, not to mention why he was here. Still, she couldn't help the joy that came at his less-than-kind words about Lauren's cooking. That probably made her a callous bitch, but then, she didn't pretend to be a saint when it came to Lauren.

"Isn't that a nasty way to talk about your girlfriend's cooking?"

"She's not my girlfriend," Flynn answered, perhaps too quickly.

"Oh?" Inside her, every bone and muscle and nerve ending sang in delight, bringing on a rush of endorphins. Ellie only hoped Flynn didn't notice.

"Not anymore, anyway. Though I'm not sure she ever really was."

"I see," she said again, but she didn't really, nor did she know how to treat this conversation. "Rumor is, you two are dating."

"We were." Flynn sounded ashamed. "But sometimes you go out with the wrong person, you know?"

"Hell, yeah." Ellie thought of all the useless men she'd

dated over the years. "So why did you go out with her? Was it to make me jealous?"

He blinked at this. "Did it?"

"A little," she confessed. There didn't seem much pointing in lying.

"Good." He sat upright, looking pleased with himself. "But that's not why. I did it because I want to have a family one day. And if that's gonna happen, I need to try dating people."

"I suppose you do," she said, her heart clenching at the thought. She didn't know where this was all going, and she wasn't sure that she wanted to. She tried to change the subject. "So if you didn't come here to insult me, and you didn't come for dinner…"

Flynn placed his empty bowl on the coffee table and looked serious all of a sudden. "I came to see if you were okay. As okay as you can be. Are you?"

Ellie felt the now ever-present lump in her throat expanding again. Holding in her emotions was almost impossible, but she didn't want to lose it in front of Flynn. Not when he was contemplating happily-ever-afters without her.

"I'll cope." She smiled weakly.

"You don't have to be so stoic, you know."

She swallowed, hating him for being this comforting and sympathetic. She wanted to ask how she was ever supposed to get over him when he kept being such a gorgeous gentleman, but she was scared that if she did, he'd leave. And right now, she didn't want him to. She didn't want to be alone with her woeful thoughts.

"I'm not trying to be stoic," she said eventually. "To be honest, I don't know how to talk about all this. I'm angry at Mat, and I'm guilty for feeling that way. I want to be there for her, but I can't help being upset that she didn't tell me. And I can't understand how she can be so resigned to death."

He shrugged a shoulder. "It's hard to empathize with something like that, but in the end, I guess it's her decision."

"I know, and I need to respect that, but I just want more time." She wiped her eyes quickly to block the tears, trying not to get hysterical. "I came back to spend time with her, and now there's this, and she doesn't have long left, and she's stuck in the hospital for who knows how long."

"Ellie, *Ellie*." He tried to calm her down. "It'll be okay. With a doctor like Hannah, Matilda will be back with you in no time. I'm sure of it."

"Thanks." She appreciated his positivity—he'd always been a glass-half-full kind of guy. "And thanks for coming. But don't you have anything better to do on a Saturday night than sit around with a Moaning Myrtle like me?"

He raised an eyebrow. "I thought we already established that I don't?" As she laughed, he gestured to the television, paused on the opening scene of *Mary Poppins*. "If you're still going to watch that, do you want some company?"

"That'd be nice," she replied. On the one hand, it was surreal to be sitting here with Flynn—hanging out, chatting, offering each other support—but on the other, it felt as if they'd always been like this. The few weeks where he'd avoided her now seemed insignificant. She needed him to be here tonight, and she was too tired to reason otherwise.

So she didn't. They sat alongside each other, not touching but not too far apart. They watched the children's classic for the umpteenth time, and for a little while Ellie was able to forget her concerns and simply relax. Then they watched *Sister Act 2,* which was playing late on channel seven. Somewhere in the middle, Flynn got up to make hot chocolate and microwave popcorn. When it was almost midnight, Ellie yawned, knowing she was now tired enough to fall asleep without tossing and turning in worry.

"I'd better go," Flynn said, slipping on his boots. "Will you be okay?"

"Yes." She nodded and stood up. "I'll get some sleep so I can get back to Mat first thing. Thanks."

"No worries."

There was a meaningful silence as they walked to the door. Like soldiers, they marched in time, accidentally but with their backs straight, arms swinging close but not close enough to touch. Heat emanated from Flynn's body. She'd felt it all night, had been trying to ignore it as it raged like an inferno within her, as well.

They reached the door. As he opened it and stepped outside, she licked her lips. He turned on the mat and stared into her eyes. It felt as if he were drilling into her soul, as if he saw every need and desire playing across her pupils. She couldn't hide anything in her heightened state. She rocked back and forth on the balls of her feet, desperate to feel his lips against hers. This was when the guy usually leaned in and kissed his date good-night, Ellie thought. But she was all too aware that this wasn't a date, no matter how much her tingling body disagreed. Yet still he stood there, staring at her. Usually at ease and confident in his actions, Flynn now hesitated, kindling a hope she'd been terrified to contemplate before. Her pulse raced. If this went on any longer, someone was going to have to acknowledge the situation.

"Ellie." He leaned toward her.

Her stomach flipped, her legs trembled, and an inebriated feeling rushed to her head. This was it. He was really going to kiss her.

But then he sighed, heavily, and ran a hand through his hair. He looked at her, remorse and sadness filling his big green eyes. Tucking his hands back inside his pockets, he said, "If you need anything, just call me."

CHAPTER TWENTY-SEVEN

"SHE'S REFUSING THE ANTIBIOTICS."

"What?" Ellie looked into the eyes of Bonnie—an agency nurse on the morning shift—and wished someone she knew better was around. Someone other than Lauren, of course.

"Dr. Bates was in this morning," Bonnie continued. "The patient's condition has worsened overnight, but she's asked to forgo all forms of treatment."

"I'll talk to her," Ellie announced.

"It's better if you leave that discussion to me, Ellie," said Dr. Bates, appearing behind her. She wore a sympathetic expression, but her tone was unyielding. "I've tried to convince her otherwise but she's quite adamant. I don't want you upsetting her in these last few days."

"Days?" Ellie's knees threatened to fail her. She stepped back and collapsed onto a plastic chair.

"Yes, Ellie. Days."

Those words were her undoing. Her hands and legs began to quiver and she bit her lip to stop the flood of tears. It didn't work. Ugly sobs escaped and salt water streamed down her cheeks just as Lauren turned up. Ellie fled to the bathroom.

The one-toilet visitor bathroom was a tiny cubicle that didn't smell quite as disinfected as the rest of the hospital. Ellie flicked the lid down and sat. Once again, toilet paper became her tissue as she swiped at her eyes.

Anger burned within her, making her feel sick. She couldn't believe it, couldn't believe it was going to happen, couldn't believe Mat was going to let it happen. How could she? How could she just pick and choose when to die without a thought for those left behind? If she took the antibiotics and let the nurses look after her, she could recover from the pneumonia, maybe have another couple of months. They could go on a road trip, sort through her things properly, even write that play they'd always joked about. Wiping her eyes again, Ellie decided she couldn't just leave things as they were. She'd never forgive herself if she didn't try to make her godmother see sense.

She blew her nose and splashed water on her face. She didn't want to use emotional blackmail by going to Mat looking like a wreck—she wanted to present reasoned and sincere arguments. Yet when she entered Mat's room a moment later, all thoughts of these evaporated.

Ellie swallowed at the sight before her. Mat looked even grayer and more listless than yesterday. The scene tore at Ellie's heart. She forced herself to breathe, to try to act as normal as possible as she approached the bed.

"Morning, gorgeous," Matilda managed to say, reaching out for Ellie's hand.

"How are you feeling?"

"On top of the world," she joked, sounding surprisingly chirpy.

"Good." Ellie took the chair next to the bed. She didn't quite know what to say. If she wasn't going to confront Mat, should she just pretend everything was peachy?

"I'm sorry, Els." Mat looked deep into her eyes.

"It's your decision, my darling." She sniffed but amazingly held back the tears.

"You've always been such a sweet thing," Mat said,

stroking Ellie's hair. "I remember when you were five years old. We were at a Christmas party."

Ellie knew this story well but settled back to listen to Matilda reminisce. It was much better than contemplating the inevitable, and she wanted to hoard as many memories as she could.

"You were so in tune with animals, you wanted to help them even if they didn't need helping."

"I vaguely remember," Ellie said. "Mom had just broken up with Dad Number Two, and was looking to get back in contact with everyone."

"That's right. Rhiannon had brought you to see us all. What a cherub you were. It broke my heart to see how roughly she treated you." There was a meaningful pause. "Anyway, the people who were having the party had just gotten a kitten and you were besotted with it. But no sooner had you caught it than you walked straight into the swimming pool. Everyone was screaming—one man even jumped in to save you." Matilda's chuckle was hoarse and weak. "All you were worried about was the poor, bedraggled cat."

"I always wanted a cat," Ellie mused.

"You could have one in your flat, couldn't you?"

"Probably, but it never seemed fair getting one. I'm out all the time. Maybe one day."

"If you moved back here you could have fifty cats."

Ellie laughed. "One, what would I do with fifty cats, and two, what would I do here?" She was glad she hadn't mentioned to anyone the idea of staying to teach acting. When Mat was gone, she wouldn't have any reason to hang around, even if she wished, more than anything, that things were different. Changing the subject, she said, "Tell me about that time you went to Mumbai and auditioned for a Bollywood film."

Ellie thought Matilda would have been a great hit in the world of showbiz—she was sure of it—but as her godmother then recounted, she'd missed out on the part, moving on to other creative pursuits.

OVER THE NEXT few days, more memories and stories were exchanged between the two. Matilda's closest friends came to visit, but nothing like the stream of visitors she'd had when people first found out about her illness. This relieved Ellie, giving them more quality time together. Joyce and Eileen took turns giving Ellie breaks—even though Mat slept much of the time, they didn't want her to be alone, and she seemed content to have them by her side even if she were too tired to converse. Ellie only left the hospital to go home, wash and change her clothes. She lived on cheese sandwiches made by the kitchen staff at the hospital. That and cheap hospital coffee. She hadn't checked her email or Facebook for days, and she asked Dwayne and her Sydney friends to give her some space. She didn't know what was happening in Hope Junction, never mind the world outside it. She didn't care.

Somehow Ellie managed to stay strong while Matilda went rapidly downhill. Without antibiotics, Mat went into heart failure more quickly than she would have with only the cancer. The nurses did their best to keep her comfortable, but she stopped eating, and even with the morphine, she was sometimes overwrought with pain. Every time Mat tried to cover a wince or a cringe, Ellie's own bones ached. This woman had done everything for her and now she could do nothing to ease her suffering.

She knew Mat's torment wouldn't be for long, though. The nurses were careful not to pinpoint an exact date, but everyone accepted its imminence. Their focus now was simply letting her die in peace.

Ellie spent the final day sitting next to Matilda, holding her hand and stroking her hair. Mat managed a few jumbled words here and there, but was basically out of it due to the high dosage of painkillers. Despite this, and despite knowing how little time they had, Ellie was still shocked when that last breath was taken.

Her fingers, linked as they were with Mat's, stilled. Her own breathing stopped momentarily, and a cold crept to the ends of her limbs. She'd not seen a dead person before, much less witnessed someone die. It was strangely peaceful. Surreal. Swallowing, she looked down at Mat, feeling a bone-deep sadness that she'd never experienced before.

She didn't get up and tell the nurse right away. She wanted some time with the best stand-in mother a girl could ever have, before she was finally taken away from her. Ellie kissed Mat's cheek, and both her hands, and then leaned over and hugged her.

"I love you, Matilda Thompson. I'll always love you."

She stayed like that until Lauren found her.

CHAPTER TWENTY-EIGHT

TAPPING OUT AN email at the computer, Flynn started a little when his mobile rang. He glanced down at the caller ID and rolled his eyes.

Lauren.

He thought he'd been quite clear that nothing could happen between them. Why did she insist on prolonging the agony? He toyed with ignoring the call, but then decided it might be easier to just answer.

"Flynn Quartermaine."

"Hi, Flynn." Lauren sounded subdued. "How are you?"

"Not bad, just doing some books. You?" The small talk was inane, and he wondered when she'd get to the point.

"I'm okay, but I'm not calling for me." She paused a moment. "Matilda just passed away."

"Oh. Fuck." He should have been expecting the news, not that it would have lessened the shock.

"I won't pretend Ellie's my favorite person," Lauren continued, "and this might confuse things, but in a professional capacity, I'm worried about her. I don't think she's got anyone else."

Flynn was already out of his seat, tugging on his boots. "How's she coping?" he asked, the phone wedged between his ear and his shoulder.

"Not sure." Lauren lowered her voice, as if she didn't

want other people to hear. "On the surface she seems totally fine—hasn't shed a single tear and is acting very
matter-of-factly, talking about arrangements and so forth.
But I'm not buying it."

"Yeah, she's not a professional actress for nothing,"
Flynn said. "I'll be there in ten." That would be driving
fast, but some things were more important than speed
limits.

When Flynn entered the hospital, a somber mood
hung in the air. The receptionist gave him a regretful
smile and nodded down the corridor. He started along it
just as a stretcher, covered in a white sheet, was wheeled
out of one of the rooms. His breath hitched in his throat
and a chill scuttled down his spine. He closed his eyes
for a moment. When he opened them again, he saw that
Lauren was at one end of the stretcher and an orderly was
at the other. He stepped back to let them ease Matilda
past and then noticed Ellie in the doorway.

She stood there, frozen like a beautiful ice sculp-
ture, her arms hugging her body as she stared after the
stretcher. Although her eyes were trained in his general
direction, they appeared vacant. He understood. Ellie's
whole world had just shifted. He could only imagine the
paralysis he'd have felt if he'd actually seen his dad off.
He didn't know whether or not he should feel anything
for her, but he had to admit he did. When she ached,
dammit, so did he.

Joyce came out of the room and stopped alongside
Ellie. She placed her hand on Ellie's arm and murmured
something to her, but Ellie didn't respond. Noticing
Flynn, Joyce shrugged at him, wiping a tear from the
corner of her eye.

He nodded back. Joyce made herself scarce and he
walked over to Ellie. He put an arm around her shoul-

ders and led her into the visitor room, closing the door behind them. Ellie was in a daze, seemingly confused, glancing around and blinking a few times. Then her eyes landed on Flynn. He saw the first sign of recognition there. And a vulnerability few souls ever glimpsed.

"I can't believe it's true," she whispered.

He wished he could tell her it wasn't. His mom always teased him about his protective side, which Lucy called *stifling,* but in moments like these, he just followed his instinct.

"I know," he said. Then, unable to offer any words that would hold true comfort, he pulled her into a hug. She was warm and soft, all the things he remembered from that night outside the pub and their many times together in the past. As her head fell onto his shoulder, he breathed in the sweet scent of her hair. It wasn't silky or freshly washed, and it didn't smell of floral or citrus shampoo—it simply smelled of Ellie. And he couldn't help but like it.

Then he reminded himself where he was and how inappropriate these thoughts were. Ellie sniffed, and he braced himself for tears, the tears of which she'd no doubt cry rivers.

But she didn't cry. Instead, the pair stayed in the visitor room, simply holding each other, his hand on the back of her head, for what seemed like an hour. So many thoughts ran through Flynn's mind in that time, and not all of them were sensible. Each moment being this close to Ellie felt excruciating, both physically and emotionally.

"Thank you, Flynn." Her almost formal words came out of the blue, startling him. She eased herself from his embrace. Her eyes were still dry.

"Don't thank me." They stood staring at each other.

He was still searching for the words that would make things better. "What happens now?" he asked eventually, not entirely sure what he was referring to.

She swallowed, cleared her throat and spoke. "I'll collect Mat's things, I guess. Then go home, start making calls, let her friends and family know."

"Okay."

He worried that she wasn't crying—she appeared so completely detached—but perhaps that was normal following a loved one's death. By the time he'd arrived home after his father's death, his mother, Lucy and Gran were almost drowning in their tears. It was hard to know what was normal, and he imagined Ellie was similarly confused. He wished Ellie wasn't the one who had to make the calls, but then again, maybe having something to occupy her would be good.

"I'll come with you," he said.

Her eyes widened and she shook her head. "You don't have to."

He took her hands in his and looked down into her tired eyes. "I know I don't have to."

She took a deep breath. "Okay. Let's do this."

Not caring what anyone thought, but wanting Ellie to know he was there for her 100 percent, he took her hand. They walked out into the corridor, where Lauren and the other nurse looked up from the desk. As he met their eyes, they quickly looked away. He wanted to get Ellie out of there fast, away from inquiring eyes. They approached the desk, Flynn ready and willing to speak on Ellie's behalf, but she was a picture of calm and control.

"Is there anything you need me to do, or can I just fetch Mat's things?"

Lauren shook her head and tried to smile. "No. If the doctor needs you to sign anything, she'll come and see you tomorrow. Or the next day." She paused. "I'm really sorry, Ellie."

"Thanks," Ellie replied civilly.

Flynn watched as she cleared the room of Mat's few possessions: a photo of Ellie and Mat, a couple of puzzle books, library books, pajamas, socks. Ellie put them all in a big, green garbage bag as if she were just taking them down for dusting.

"Let's go."

She moved as if in a trance. Flynn wasn't sure how to snap her out of it, or if that was a good idea, but he didn't want her to be alone like this. He took the bag from her as they left the hospital.

"How's the farm?" she asked as they crossed the parking lot.

The farm? "It's fine," he said. "Our sale was a huge success and we've got more lambs on the way than ever." It felt bizarre to be discussing work, and he wondered if he should make Ellie talk about the elephant in the room. He decided to give it time. "I really can't be a complaining cocky this year."

She gave a halfhearted chuckle. "That's great."

They arrived at the cars. "Are you okay to drive?" he asked.

"Sure. Why wouldn't I be?"

He frowned. This wasn't going how he'd imagined it at all. "Okay, then, I'll follow you."

"Thanks." She smiled as if he'd just offered to make her a cup of tea.

Once on the road, Flynn mulled over the fact that he had no idea how you were supposed to act around someone who was grieving, didn't know what to say or do to help them process everything. He contemplated calling his mom, but annihilated the thought immediately. As far as Karina knew, he wasn't talking to—much less comforting—Ellie, and he wasn't in the mood for a lecture. Hell, if his mom found out she might even turn up at Mat's place to keep an eye on things. And if Flynn knew only one thing about grief, it was that Ellie wouldn't want many visitors right now. Especially not his mother. She might not even want him, but something told him not to leave her just yet.

She turned into the drive in front of him and he parked behind her. He took in the sight of the cottage with its purple walls, red roof and yellow awnings. What would happen to it now? Would Ellie sell it? He couldn't imagine anyone but eccentric old Matilda Thompson living in it.

When he stepped into the hallway the place already felt odd, as if he were entering someone's private space without permission. His eyes skittered about the living room. When he'd dropped in on Ellie a few days ago, he'd noticed the half-packed boxes, the knickknacks and souvenirs already cleared away. But it had still been a home then, the walls and floors and everything between had still told a story about the amazing woman that lived there. Now the house felt cold and empty. And if this was what he felt, he could only imagine the desolation Ellie was experiencing.

"I'll put the kettle on," she announced, dumping her keys in the leaf-shaped bowl on the side table. "And you must be hungry. There are a hundred different casseroles in the freezer. What do you fancy? Chicken? Beef? Lamb?"

"Els." He stepped in front of her, blocking the way to the kitchen. "You don't need to feed me. Why don't you go sit down, I'll get us a bite to eat."

"No." She flicked his hand away. "I'm quite capable of heating up a meal."

He wasn't saying otherwise, he thought, but refrained from pressing the point. Her eyes were wild, as if she might fly off the handle at any moment. He held up his hands and backed away. "Suit yourself."

Leaving Ellie to the food, Flynn pottered around the living room, taking in Matilda's remaining paraphernalia. He looked at some things and picked up others, trying to remember if she'd told him the stories behind each of them. *She'd been around, that old duck,* and she had some seriously cool stuff to show for it. He hated to think of Ellie sorting through it all on her own, but who else would know what was gold and what was junk? Hopefully, Joyce or one of Mat's other friends would lump in.

Jeez. He paused, his hand wrapped around a vase in the shape of a naked woman. *She really was gone.* His throat thickened as he tried to imagine Hope Junction without Matilda. She'd come to the town when he was just a child and had been a whirlwind of activity ever since. There wasn't a local charity or group that Mat wasn't a member of. She'd even led the Boy Scouts at one stage, and he recalled sitting round the campfire, Matilda telling more poo jokes than any of the boys. A tear trickled down his cheek. *No,* he thought. He had to stay strong for Ellie. As he wiped the back of his hand against his eyes, a colossal crash came from the kitchen.

Flynn almost dropped the naked woman. Swearing, he laid her down on the coffee table and hurried into the other room.

Ellie stood, frozen, peering down at a mess of shattered china. He could only just recognize the pieces as belonging to Mat's teapot collection. She raised her head, her eyes wide and glistening as she spoke. "I wanted these," she said. "Out of all her treasures, these were the ones she loved most."

He stepped toward her. "There's still plenty more," he offered, but the moment the words came out he knew they were the wrong ones, dammit.

She shook her head, her hand covering her mouth. He couldn't tell whether she was about to be sick or just trying to stop the flood of emotion. "I'm such a clumsy fool," she said, and then it happened. The tears he'd been anxiously waiting for fell like a winter storm. Harsh, messy, unforgiving.

The microwave pinged. They both ignored the tantalizing aromas drifting through the cracks around the door.

"You're not a fool," he consoled. "Anything but. Come here." He met her halfway across the kitchen. She came willingly, accepted his embrace. If anyone were the fool, he thought, it was him, because right now, standing so close you couldn't slide a ruler between them, he wanted her. Bad. And he felt terrible for it.

ELLIE LET FLYNN lead her into the living room, where he gently eased her onto the couch. Her head fell against his hard shoulder, which was anything but uncomfortable. She watched her tears splash down onto his sweater, unable to stop them, unable to care. All she could think about was Matilda. All the things she wanted to say but she'd never have the chance to.

Flynn put his hand on her back, rubbing the heel of his palm in tiny circles. Although it was platonic, she felt sparks of awareness shooting down her spine and lingering in parts of her that hadn't seen a spark in years. She stiffened, so minutely that he didn't seem to notice, not because she didn't like the feel of his touch—the complete opposite, in fact—but because his attentions were taking her mind away from where they'd been. Away from Mat.

What kind of a daughter, what kind of a friend did that make her, if she could be so easily led astray? And when, as far as she knew, Flynn wasn't even aware of the effect of his actions? He was just being Flynn. Kindhearted, always-there-for-a-friend-in-a-crisis Flynn. He said she wasn't a fool but he was wrong. She'd let herself be taken from him by one cowardly decision. And that made her the most foolish person she knew.

She looked up and twisted her head so she was gazing into his sea-green eyes. He looked back as if he, too, were lost in serious contemplation. Without thinking, she raised her hand and palmed the stubble on his jaw. Rough as sandpaper, she could run her fingers over his face all day and never tire of it.

"You're beautiful, Flynn Quartermaine."

"Don't, Ellie," his voice warned, but it wasn't irritation she saw in his eyes. A muscle twitched in his throat; she had muscles twitching all over her body.

"But it's true." Boldly, she crept her fingers up his face and into his mussed-up hair. A moan escaped her lips. He echoed it, his eyes closing and his head rolling back against the couch. She took the opportunity, moving quickly to straddle him. He opened his eyes and before he had the chance to voice any opposition, she pressed her lips against his. And kissed him.

Hard. Deep. Aggressively. Gently. Imaginatively. She couldn't stop, couldn't make up her mind. His lips were divine, too fabulous.

But the best damn thing was that he kissed her back. Wholeheartedly. Roughly. Lovingly. As their tongues entwined, his fingers slipped through her hair, drawing her closer to him. Deepening their kiss even more.

Once upon a time they'd been able to make out like this for hours, but right now she wanted more. Emotionally exhausted, physically wrung out, mentally drained, she wanted something that would help her forget all else. If there really were such a thing as right and wrong, then being with Flynn would definitely be categorized as the latter, but losing Mat had given her a different perspective. Life could be short. If she lost hers tomorrow, she didn't want it to be with any regrets.

Her cheeks flushed, her body sweltered. She broke her connection with Flynn just long enough to peel her sweater over her head. The expression on his face gave her all the encouragement she needed.

She climbed off him, stood up and smiled, offering her hand. For a brief moment, he hesitated. Staring at her hand but not making a move with his. He hauled in a breath, running his fingers through his already tousled hair before placing them in her palm.

Her heart lifted. She grasped his hand and pulled him toward the bedroom where she'd lost her virginity. To him. He stopped at the door and glanced around. She hadn't changed anything since she'd returned, so it still looked much the same as when she'd left, ten years ago—aside from the wedding dress, of course. She shuddered at the thought of him seeing it and sent up a prayer of thanks when she saw that the wardrobe was closed.

Not wanting to think about her bedroom, or the past, or the future for that matter, she turned back to Flynn and stepped close. Fingering the bottom of his sweater, she lifted it up over his head. He didn't help but neither did he struggle. Underneath he wore a simple, tight black tee. She inhaled and held her breath at the sight of his muscled torso.

"Don't just look," he whispered, his eyes glazed and dreamy. She knew then that he wanted this as much as she did. To hell with the consequences.

She slid her hands around his back and under his shirt. He sucked in air at her touch—she guessed her hands must feel like icicles against his burning skin.

"Sorry," she whispered.

"Don't apologize," he said gruffly, leaning down and capturing her mouth. Where she'd been the instigator up until now, he suddenly became the assertive one. And if she'd ever been kissed like this before, she couldn't recall. It was how two lovers would kiss in the middle of a bushfire, breathless and urgent, desperate to hold on to a forever they may not have.

And then Ellie couldn't think anymore.

Flynn walked her backward till her knees hit the single bed and she tumbled onto the ancient mattress, almost drowning in an abundance of cushions. One by one he threw them off, staring down at her with a ravenous look in his eyes. Still fully clothed, she'd never felt so on fire, so desirable. If he didn't start undressing her this moment, she'd rip off her clothes with no thought to ever needing them again. She wanted nothing but skin between them.

He stood at her feet. Her eyes couldn't help but be drawn to the evidence of desire rising in his pants. "You sure this is what you want?" he asked.

"Yes." She wanted him inside her taking everything she had.

"Thank fuck." And with those words he sank onto the bed, reaching out to make quick work of her shirt buttons. Within seconds she was naked from the waist up, her nipples erect and her whole body shaking with need. He ran his hands over her bare skin as if reacquainting himself, cupping her breasts before he stooped down and wrapped his lips around one nipple.

She arched up off the bed and gripped his back with her fingers, the need between her legs growing with each passing second. Flynn gave her other nipple equal consideration as he rid her of her trousers. Warmth flooded through her and her heart spiked as his fingers slipped under the cotton of her knickers. She wanted to touch him, too, but didn't know if she had the energy or the wherewithal in her bamboozled state.

She tried to fight the rise of pleasure at her core, wanting to make him writhe, too, wanting to come together at exactly the same moment. But it was impossible. With a few deft strokes he had her shuddering, panting and whispering his name as she came around his fingers.

"You're still so gorgeous when you come," he said, smiling down at her. His words worked to build up her desire again. That had been nice—much better than nice—but now she wanted to be truly together again.

"Do you have protection?" she asked.

He pulled a little foil packet from his back pocket. "I wasn't a Boy Scout for nothing."

"Thank fuck," she said, giggling as she took the condom and pulled him on top of her.

CHAPTER TWENTY-NINE

ELLIE WOKE WITH a heavy weight pinning her to the bed. She opened her eyes, discovering that the weight was a forearm lightly speckled with hair. A very sexy forearm. Her eyes widened. She shook off the last remnants of sleep as the events of the day before came rushing back to her.

Mat's death. She swallowed but the lump in her throat didn't budge.

Flynn coming to the hospital.

Flynn coming back here.

She jumping his bones like a nymphomaniac.

Embarrassment and regret visited her briefly, but before they could take hold, Flynn whispered, "Good morning," into her ear, tightening his lovely, strong hug. She relaxed in his embrace, resting her head against his manly chest. Refusing to think about how wrong this was.

"How are you feeling?" he asked eventually.

"A little broken," she admitted. "I just…can't believe it."

"That's not surprising." He nuzzled closer, which wasn't hard in the single bed. "I still sometimes forget that Dad is gone. I'll be doing something on the farm and think of something to ask or tell him. Sometimes it takes a good few minutes before I realize I can't. And then the hurt comes back."

"So the thing they say about time? Is that a myth, then?" She didn't know how she could live with this clamp on her heart forever.

"Not exactly." Flynn brushed her hair away from her face and looked into her eyes. "You'll never really forget, but living with it becomes easier. With time."

"I see." Right now, though, she didn't want to live beyond this bed. Didn't want to think about crawling out from beneath the covers, facing the shower, breakfast, the world outside. "I suppose I have to talk to someone about the funeral."

"What about Mat's brother?"

"No." Ellie shook her head. "Mat told me what she wants. Must be in Hope, she said, and no one is to waste money on flowers, and the music can't sound like funeral music."

He laughed. "Well, the Co-op is an agent for the funeral directors in Katanning. Speak to them."

They lay there a few moments in silent contemplation before Ellie remembered that Flynn was a farmer. She glanced at her watch—it was almost ten. The exhaustion of it all must have overwhelmed her. Pulling gently out of his embrace, she said, "Don't you have sheep to check or something?"

"Or something." He laughed again and pulled her back against his chest. "I woke a few hours ago when you were channeling Sleeping Beauty and called Mom. She's going to do a couple of jobs for me this morning."

Ellie chomped down on a grin and raised her eyebrows. Flynn had rearranged his day to be with her. "Bet she was pleased about that."

"Let's not talk about my mother," Flynn said, which told Ellie that Karina had *definitely* voiced her opinion. Oh well. She didn't want to waste time on what Karina thought of her, but it led her to think about something else.

"How'd you find out so quickly about…about Matilda's passing?" she asked, a new chill coming over her at the recollection.

"Lauren called me," Flynn said matter-of-factly.

She blinked and snapped her head back in surprise, almost tumbling them both off the bed. Once he'd pulled her back on and secured the covers around them, she said, "Wow. Maybe she's not as evil as I thought."

He chuckled. "She's not evil, Els, she's just not…" He stared meaningfully into her eyes. She recognized something from long ago there, and a moment of intense silence followed. *Not what?* She wanted him to go on, but at the same time didn't. She couldn't handle that conversation on top of everything else. If they'd made love under different circumstances there'd be all sorts of ramifications. They'd need to talk about why they did it, what it meant for each other and their futures. But under different circumstances, would it have even happened? They'd probably have managed to ignore the lust and think with their heads. As it was, they'd both seemed to accept that sleeping together was inevitable, a need to be fulfilled but not pontificated on.

He kissed the top of her forehead. "Why don't you have a shower and I'll whip up something to eat?"

"You don't have to," she said.

This time it was his turn to raise a brow. "I'm starving, and you know I make a mean pancake." He patted his stomach.

Smiling, she climbed out of bed and pulled her old robe around her naked body. Flynn being here made it easier to face the day and all the horrible decisions that lay ahead. Still, she took her time in the shower, letting

the hot shards of water pour over her as she cried again.
Not that she was afraid or embarrassed of crying in front
of Flynn, but more because she didn't want him to stay
out of pity. Or because he worried she might do something stupid if she were alone. She wanted him to stay
because he wanted to, because he felt the same strong
need to be with her as she did to be with him.

FLYNN USED THE task of cooking breakfast to take his
mind off last night. When he'd woken before Ellie, his
first thought had been whether or not he'd taken advantage of her. He'd stressed about this for hours, worrying
over what it said about him as he waited for her to wake
up. When she did, he'd looked into her eyes and seen
the truth. She was neither angry nor regretful. Not yet.
It was his job to make sure she stayed that way.

He whisked the pancake batter he'd managed to throw
together from Ellie and Mat's measly provisions, and
then paused. *Mat*. That was the strange thing about
death—you set about doing something normal and totally
forget what happened, then all of a sudden—bam!—
something snaps, reminding you that the world isn't the
same as it was the day before. Flynn felt a sharp pain in
his chest and could only imagine the ache Ellie would
be experiencing.

Looking at the batter, he'd never felt so useless or
helpless in his life. Well, aside from that day in front of
the church, waiting for Ellie to turn up. He'd been certain
then that something had gone wrong, that there must be
an explanation. Not knowing where she was or how to
contact her had been hell. What if she needed help, what
could he do? And then, when it turned out she'd gone…

He shook his head. The last thing he wanted to do was
ponder that day. He spooned two dollops of batter into

the frying pan and watched them sizzle and bubble. He took care, focusing on the task, and not on all the other places his mind kept trying to go to.

"Wow." Ellie entered the kitchen, a towel wrapped like a turban around her head, her skin still shiny from the water. "I forgot you know how to cook."

He gulped, feeling like a stereotypical male—unable to be in close proximity to a hot, barely dry woman without getting a hard-on. He turned back to the bench so she wouldn't see his horniness.

"Yes, it's one of my few uses."

"If you're digging for compliments, just say so," she said, coming up close behind him. "Because I can think of plenty." It seemed her mind was scraping the bottom of the gutter, right alongside his.

Just as he was turning around to kiss her again, a knock sounded on the back door. Ellie sprang back as if they'd been caught defacing the *Mona Lisa*. Flynn watched as she tugged off her towel-turban and shook out her long, wet hair. She tucked it behind her ears as she held her head high, opening the door to Joyce.

To Joyce's credit, she barely batted an eyelid at the sight: Flynn, standing in yesterday's clothes, cooking at the kitchen bench, with a just-showered Ellie nearby.

"Morning, Ellie, morning, Flynn."

"How'd you sleep?" Ellie asked, embracing the older woman.

Joyce shrugged. "Like there was a boulder under my mattress. I was worried about you, and spent all night wondering if I should come see if you were okay."

As Ellie's cheeks turned a lovely pink, Flynn returned to flipping pancakes.

"I'm okay," Ellie answered demurely. "To be honest, I don't think it's really sunk in yet."

Joyce nodded and pulled a chair out from the kitchen table. She sat down. "It won't till after the funeral, when life goes back to normal. That's when you really need your friends. Or, will you be going back to Sydney straightaway?"

Flynn's ears pricked up. He stiffened.

"Hmm." There was the scrape of a chair on the old floorboards as Ellie sat down, as well. "I haven't really thought that far yet."

What did that mean? His grip tightened on the spatula as he told himself to cool his thoughts—along with his hormones. Now wasn't the time to be questioning these things. He tuned back in to Joyce and Ellie's conversation.

"I'll call the Co-op in a moment," Joyce said, "and make the appointment for you. Would you like me to come with you?"

"That would be lovely, thanks."

"Don't mention it." Joyce turned to Flynn. "Now, are you making cuppas, too, or should I?"

"I'll do it," Ellie said, jumping up—Flynn could tell she wanted to keep busy. While she set about making the drinks, he laid the table and placed a plate of pancakes in the middle. Then they all sat down and shared breakfast. He was glad to see Ellie eating a good fill. When they'd finished and washed up, and the women were readying to go to the Co-op, he made his excuses.

"I'll be back this arvo," he told Ellie, wondering if she'd object or push him away. But instead she smiled her thanks and showed her appreciation with a kiss goodbye.

He sat in the ute out front, turning the keys over in his hands as he glanced back at the house. How the hell was he supposed to concentrate on work for the next few hours when his mind was on a permanent replay of last night? Groaning, he put his head on the steering wheel. Heavy labor was the only answer.

Ellie entered the Co-op with Joyce at her side, the older woman's fingers closing encouragingly around hers. Solemn faces met her, and she accepted each sympathetic apology, every word of condolence, even the occasional hug. But part of her still felt detached from it all. When she'd arrived back in Hope Junction a mere two months ago, she'd never imagined it would come to this.

Trying not to dwell on what she'd lost, she sat and faced Gavin, the man who'd gone ape at her over the newspapers all those weeks ago. Neither of them mentioned that embarrassing incident now—it felt like a lifetime ago. Whether it was Flynn's friendship, Mat's death, or a bit or both, Ellie seemed to have been accepted once again into Hope society, and a small country town looks after its own.

"I'm so sorry," Gavin said, clasping his hands together on the desk in front of him. "I can't begin to express how much Matilda Thompson meant to this town. To lose her so suddenly, so cruelly, is just inconceivable. I want you to know the staff and directors of the Co-op offer you and Matilda's family our sincerest condolences. If there's anything we can do, please just ask."

"Thank you." Ellie thought she'd already shed her daily quota of tears in the shower, but her throat tightened at his sentimental words.

For the next half hour, Ellie, Joyce and Gavin planned the funeral, going over every detail. They chose a low-key, relatively cheap coffin, as Matilda hadn't believed in paying good money for something the worms would chew through. She'd have preferred a cremation to any coffin at all, but that would mean holding the service outside Hope, in a bigger town, and Matilda had made her wishes quite clear about that. She hadn't wanted any fuss, so a burial it would be. A burial in Hope, with music from around the world and the reading of a poem written by the Dalai Lama.

By the time they left Gavin's office, everything from the celebrant—no one religious for Mat—to the notices in the newspaper were organized. Joyce had been in touch with a number of local women who'd put their hands up to cater for the wake, which would be held at the bowling club, where Mat had been an active member.

But rather than relieving Ellie, she left the Co-op with a feeling of emptiness. She didn't want to think about this new hole in her life, and she really didn't know what she was going to do to keep her mind off it the next few days.

This, however, turned out to be an unwarranted worry. It soon became apparent that no one planned on leaving her alone long enough to even blow her nose in private. She didn't know whether there was an actual roster for Ellie-sitting, but she had a constant stream of visitors. Flynn came every night, and during the daytime she received Matilda's friends, her own friends from the play, as well as Lucy, Sam and Joyce.

She couldn't help but wonder what it would be like if she'd lost someone close to her in Sydney. City people were different to country folk—showing emotion or getting too close to people scared them. She'd become like that, she realized, making only a few close friends there. If one of her neighbors died in the city, it could be days before anyone raised the alarm, but here...

"A never-ending packet of Tim Tams for them?" Flynn's voice snapped Ellie out of her thoughts.

"I'm sorry?"

"You know, for your thoughts," he said, making a

reference she hadn't heard in a while. He stood beside her at the kitchen sink, his outstretched arm proffering a chocolate biscuit. She was still holding the tea towel she'd been using to dry the lunch dishes, but she now discovered that he'd not only finished washing them, but also dried and put them away. He laughed at the bemused look on her face. "You looked like you were in some sort of trance." He winked suggestively. "Thinking steamy thoughts, were you?"

Shaking her head, she flicked him with the tea towel and took the biscuit. "I was actually thinking about how different city and country life is. How in the city there's not such a strong sense of community. I don't know, maybe there is, maybe I just never found it."

Flynn chomped down on a Tim Tam, swallowing and then grinning. "Sounds like you don't think we're all that bad out here in the sticks."

"Of course I don't. In fact, I'm thinking there might be more pros than cons to country life."

Flynn almost choked at this. She laughed at his surprise, but once he'd recovered, the look he gave her was serious. "I like the sound of that." He took a step toward her. The tingles her body reserved only for him erupted all over her in anticipation, but he stopped before he reached her. "Ellie…"

Her heart hitched a beat as she waited for him to continue. Before he could, however, the room echoed with another knock on the back door. *More visitors.*

"Hello," said Lucy, followed by another knock.

Ellie welcomed Lucy and Sam into the kitchen.

"It's freezing out," Lucy said, leaning into Sam as he rubbed his hands up and down her arms. They made such a sweet couple. Every time Ellie saw them she remembered how she and Flynn used to be, before life had tainted things. She couldn't help but ask herself whether they'd be in the small percentage of high school romances that lasted a lifetime.

"Flynn's got the fire roaring in the living room," Ellie said. "Head on in. You guys want a hot drink?"

Sam looked to Flynn in apparent confusion, but Flynn jumped in, albeit clumsily. "I've got a couple of jobs to do back at the farm, actually, and I need to bring some more of the set into town. And Sam offered to help. We thought Lucy could stay here with you and watch a movie. Or something."

Lucy held up five DVDs, fanned out in her hands. At a glance, Ellie saw they were all chick flicks that she'd seen before and loved.

Ellie opened her mouth to say she didn't need a babysitter, but the looks of concern on the others' faces warmed her heart. With Mat gone, she hadn't thought it would be possible to feel so loved again, but Flynn and the people of Hope were teaching her it was.

Love. That was the second time she'd thought about Flynn and love in the same sentence these past couple of days. She couldn't help but wonder what he would have said had they not been interrupted just now.

Forcing such contemplation aside for now, she smiled at Lucy and the guys. Pointing at *27 Dresses,* she said, "We'll need an extralarge box of tissues if we watch that one."

That settled, Flynn and Sam disappeared, and Ellie followed Lucy into the living room with the rest of the Tim Tams.

"I think the last movie I watched with you was *The Little Mermaid,*" she said to Lucy once they'd settled into armchairs and the opening credits were rolling.

"Oh, my gosh," Lucy squealed, "I used to adore that movie. I wanted to be Ariel when I grew up."

"Was it the tail or the handsome prince?" Ellie asked.

Lucy pressed her hand against her heart and pretended to swoon. "The handsome prince, of course."

"Think you may have found him, then, my dear. Sam is quite a spunk."

Lucy glowed. "Isn't he just?" She paused for a moment, and Ellie could almost see the cogs of her brain ticking over. "Do you think my brother is a spunk?" she asked delicately.

Ellie gulped. Flynn still topped the charts in terms of spunkiness, but she wasn't sure that was the right answer for Lucy.

"I'll rephrase that," Lucy said, sitting upright. "Are you still in love with Flynn?"

Ellie blinked and chewed on her lower lip. Lucy had asked her the question she'd been avoiding for a week now. Did she? She'd certainly loved him ten years ago, and that first peek at him when she'd returned had made her think she still might. But what she felt now was stronger than that, if such a thing were possible. In the past, she'd been in love and lust with a boy; the man Flynn had grown into made her heart flutter in a deeper way. For this type of love, she'd sacrifice everything—everything she'd worked for and built up these past few years. And she wouldn't look back.

"Yes," she answered honestly. "I think I am."

"That's so cool," Lucy said. "What will you do about work, then? Are you going to quit the show and move back here? That would be great. We could—"

"Whoa." Ellie held up her hand to stop Lucy's runaway imagination—next she'd be picking out crockery patterns for their registry. "Flynn and I haven't spoken about any of this, we've just been…" She stopped short of confessing things Flynn may not want his little sister knowing.

"Having sex, I know." Lucy giggled and rolled her eyes. "Flynn still thinks I'm a baby, but I know what goes on between consenting adults." She shrugged. "It's none of my business, sure, and with Matilda gone things have been intense these past few days, but you guys can't go on like this forever. Flynn never speaks about how he feels about you, but I'm certain he wants you to stay. I guess I'm just hoping it's a possibility. He's my big brother—I love him and I want him to be happy."

"I can understand that." Not having any brothers or sisters herself, Ellie always envied the special sibling bond, like that between Flynn and Lucy. "I haven't really had time to think about this, and I haven't asked Flynn what he wants. But I want you to know, Lucy, I never wanted to hurt your brother the first time round, and I'll do my utmost to make sure it doesn't happen again."

And she would. Still, her insides twisted at the thought. Her intentions were true, but Ellie wasn't sure she'd be able to protect Flynn from hurt again, or herself for that matter. That big, black secret still hung like a dark shadow between them. Mat had urged her to speak to Flynn about it, but the idea still terrified her. She'd given him one version, which he seemed to accept, which she'd hoped would be enough. But she knew that if there was any chance for them to be together again, she'd need to start their relationship with a fresh slate. And that meant telling him everything. Finally.

CHAPTER THIRTY

"FLY-YNN!" KARINA'S VOICE floated from the direction of the homestead. He and Sam had just loaded a life-size wooden cow into the ute, and turned to see her heading toward them. Flynn let out a frustrated breath, thanking the Lord Sam was here to stop Karina giving him an Ellie lecture. As if sensing Flynn's mom's wrath, however, Sam promptly announced he had to pop to the loo.

Dammit. Flynn would have to chat to him later about blokes sticking together.

"Nice of you to grace us with your presence," Karina said, huffing slightly as she arrived in front of him. He'd barely been home since Mat died, and the times he had, he'd been too busy drafting sheep to socialize.

"Hello, Mom." He ignored her dig.

"Were you planning on coming over and saying hello or are you too preoccupied to spend time with your old mom?" She folded her arms over her chest. This wasn't typical Karina behavior. Normally the first to help a friend in need, he'd never heard her say a jealous or resentful word in his life. And if it were anyone else Flynn had been supporting, he was sure she'd understand.

"Well, as you've guessed, I'm headed back into town." He leaned against the ute, daring her to voice a complaint. "Ellie needs me at the moment, Mom. You raised me to look out for others. I thought you'd be glad to see me doing this."

Karina shook her fists as if she could uncharacteristically punch something. "Argh! Don't make out like you're with her because of your upbringing. You're with her because she makes you feel things no one else does."

He blinked at his mom's insight. Then nodded.

"I've been there, Flynn," Karina continued. "That's how I felt about your dad. I understand your craving. But she left you once, and it terrifies me that she'll do it again. It almost killed you last time." She wiped a tear from her eye, then gestured to the land around them. "What are Lucy, Gran and I supposed to do here without you?"

"It won't get to that," he said firmly. "I'm older now, and we're not engaged. I'm sorry, Mom, but I can't not be with Ellie just because you're scared. All I can promise is that whatever happens, I'll be stronger this time. I won't touch the grog."

And he meant it. He didn't know what was going to happen, but things *were* different now. Three nights ago he'd made the snap decision to sleep with Ellie, and now he was taking whatever he could get, enjoying the ride. Having fun with Ellie during the day, helping her come to terms with her loss, then churning up her bedsheets at night. Just being near her had his body reacting in ways it never did around other women. The sex he'd had in the past ten years wasn't always worth writing home about, but sex with Ellie was too hot for words. And he wasn't man enough to turn it down. In the past few days, they'd consummated their lust time and again with the urgency imposed by an end date. Waiting for Mat's funeral was like living in a kind of limbo where they could ignore reality for a short while. And they had.

He tried not to think about what would happen after that end date, though—tomorrow, when they officially laid Matilda Thompson to rest. He didn't want to contemplate saying goodbye to Ellie just yet. Until this morning he hadn't entertained the possibility of anything long-term between them, but the things she'd said today—and, when he thought about it, over the past few days—made him hope that maybe they would have longer.

"I think things might be different this time," he said eventually, then shut his mouth. He didn't want to get his mom's hopes up, or look like a dill if he were wrong. "But I'll be okay, even if they're not."

"I hope so, Flynn. I really hope so."

Wanting to offer more assurance, he leaned forward and wrapped his tiny, strong-willed mother in a tight hug.

BY THE TIME Ellie heard Flynn's ute in the drive, her chest felt so tight she could barely breathe and her palms were so slick that wiping them on her thighs marked her jeans. Lucy hadn't appeared to notice, moving on from the conversation about Flynn and Ellie the moment Ellie asked about her acting ambitions. She'd been trying to pay attention and hoped she'd done a good job of sounding interested. She *was* interested, it was just that the thoughts about Flynn whirling through her mind were distracting. Almost as distracting as the man himself.

Half an hour ago, she'd determined to talk to him about it, but not until after the funeral. They'd enjoyed each other's company for three fabulous nights, and without him, Ellie didn't know how she'd have gotten through the days. All that time they'd managed to not analyze or speculate on what they were doing, one more night wouldn't make a difference.

"Guess they won't be interested in watching this," Lucy said, as she aimed the remote and flicked the television off. "Besides, my eyes are getting sore. We must have been watching for four hours."

"Something like that." Ellie didn't have much of a concept of time these days. She stood to stretch her legs and greet the guys as they barged through the front door. Her heart flipped at the sight of Flynn, slightly ruffled from working on the farm. She shouldn't really be surprised by it anymore, but each time she saw him, a jolt startled her, and often she had to grip something to keep from toppling over.

"Did you do what you needed?" she asked, pleased she'd kept the quaver from her voice. Her nerves were ricocheting around and bouncing off each other as if she were on a first date. Ridiculous.

"Yes." He topped off his answer with his usual country grin and her insides melted a little more. He held up a plastic bag of takeout. "And I brought dinner, so we don't have to cook and wash up tonight."

"Fabulous plan." That kind of thinking she could get used to. She turned to Sam and Lucy. "Are you guys staying for tea?"

"Ah…" Lucy looked to Sam, but Flynn made the decision for them.

"Nope. Mom wants them both at home tonight, make sure they actually do some study. Besides, I only got enough for two." He looked at her as he said this last line, his eyes speaking suggestively. Then he turned and headed for the kitchen.

With a look like that there had to be hope, but would it still be there after she'd told him? Her knees threatened to stop working and she flopped back against the couch.

"Looks like we're going, then," Lucy said with a touch of snarkiness. She leaned forward and hugged Ellie.

"We'll see you tomorrow. If there's anything you need in the morning, just call."

Huh? Ellie looked up at Lucy as if she were speaking in tongues. Then it hit her—Mat's funeral. Guilt jabbed her in the chest, she needed to get her head straight. Flynn, and the conversation they had to have, would still be here tomorrow night. For the time being, she needed to focus on farewelling her closest friend.

"Thanks." She summoned a smile for Lucy and Sam. "I appreciate your support."

"No worries." Arms around each other's waists they headed out the door, shouting bye to Flynn as they left.

Moments later, Flynn wandered in with Matilda's Mexican tray laden with roadhouse cuisine. Ellie surveyed the feast of hamburgers and chips. Two cans of Fanta at the side. The sight brought a smile to her lips, but she didn't feel her stomach could handle a single bite. Again, ridiculous. This was Flynn sitting next to her. The first person she'd ever kissed, the man with whom she'd lost her virginity. Aside from Matilda, he knew more about her than anyone, and she hadn't felt one bout of nerves the past few days. But that was before she'd started thinking beyond tomorrow.

He settled into the couch beside her and leaned forward to pick up his hamburger. He wrapped his long, sexy fingers around the bun as if he hadn't a care in the world. He obviously couldn't read minds. Determining to act normal despite the hyperactivity of her brain, she plucked a chip, dipped it in sauce and then chomped down on it. She chewed slowly, then managed another. She couldn't yet tackle the hamburger, but one chip at a time seemed to be working. Until, that is, Flynn scooped up the television remote. He switched the TV on and starting changing channels like a typical male. Like they were in a typical relationship in a typical house on a typical night.

Almost choking on a chip, she swallowed quickly and turned to face him. "Don't you find this weird?"

"What?" He frowned at the television. Someone on *Neighbours* was snogging their husband's brother. "It's downright immoral, but I don't know about weird."

She let out an exasperated sigh. "Not them. Us." She thrust her finger back and forth between them, stopping short of jabbing him in the ribs. "You, here with me. We're acting like this is normal. Like we're an item, a couple, when we both know that's not how it is."

He put down his hamburger and turned off the soap opera. "Do you want me to leave?"

"No." The word came out fast and firm. Her hands went immediately clammy and her heart began to hammer at the prospect. "I didn't say that."

Neither of them spoke then for what seemed like a long moment, but the air sizzled. Again. He only had to look at her for her libido to kick into overdrive, but right now she needed to ignore such urges and get serious. She stared at him, waiting for him to respond, kicking herself for starting this conversation *now,* racking her brain for how to negotiate it here on in.

They stayed that way, suspended, until time seemed to start up again, and Flynn leaned slowly toward her. Her hammering pulse stopped completely. If she weren't so anxious about what lay ahead, she'd be concerned her heart was going to collapse. Yet when he reached his hand up to her neck and trailed his fingers past her ear, into her hair, she realized her heart hadn't stopped at all, jolting as it was with every touch. Following his hand, he leaned in closer with his mouth. So close she could feel his breath against the skin at her collar. Her tongue darted out instinctively to moisten her lips. Her head lolled back as her body anticipated the pleasure, but as his lips landed on the sensitive hollow between her neck and shoulder, instead of succumbing to her burning desires, she pulled back, pushing her hands against his chest.

"Don't you like that?" Flynn's voice was husky, his eyes slightly bemused.

"On the contrary," she groaned. "I like it very much."

"Then I can't see the problem." His hands sneaked toward her again.

She stood quickly, dodging his grasp. "The problem is that if I get any more of you, I won't want it to stop. I don't know where we stand, Flynn. I don't know what's going to happen after Mat's funeral, and although I shouldn't care, I do."

It was as close to confessing her love as she'd come, so she bit down on her tongue to shut herself up. For all she knew, he was simply having a bit of fun while looking out for her. Maybe he hadn't given a second's thought to what happened after tomorrow.

The humor in Flynn's face fled and a slow, tentative smile replaced it. "To me, that there is music to my ears." He paused before continuing. "I wasn't going to say anything until tomorrow, until after the funeral—I didn't want to confuse things, or upset you—but I can't stop thinking about what my life could be like if you were in it permanently."

She gulped. Her knees wobbled again, but she wasn't sure that sitting next to him was a good idea. "What are you saying, Flynn?"

"Is being in my life again something you'd consider?"

Her stomach did a flip. He was offering what she'd dreamed of for the past ten years. But could she accept?

Could she leave her job, her friends, her life in Sydney to return here? The answer came like a blinding light from the sky. *Yes*. Yes, she could leave it all in a second. Sure, she liked acting and had her friends, but Sydney wasn't home. It never had been. Because Sydney had never had Matilda or Flynn.

She opened her mouth to reply, but that lump had lodged in her throat again, and her eyes watered once more, despite having cried more tears in the past week than she had in years. So she simply nodded, hoping he read her happy smile as a yes.

"You're going to have to say it," he said, his voice shaky. "I don't want to get my hopes up for nothing."

The way he sat before her, like a nervous schoolboy inside a man's handsome, strapping body, sent warmth flooding through her. It pained her to think of all she'd put him through in the past. Looking back, she didn't know whether she'd done the right thing… Every time she played the what-if game she came up with a different answer.

"I'm still waiting," he said.

She realized her silence might appear like hesitation. Anything but. She knew—with every cell in her body— that she wanted him now and forever, but she'd promised herself she'd tell him the truth. If she didn't, there'd always be something between them. She'd know she hadn't been honest, even if he didn't.

"Yes," she managed, "I want to be in your life again. I want nothing more than to move back to Hope Junction and be yours, all yours."

"But?" He looked up at her warily. "I'm sure I hear a *but*."

She swallowed and finally sat down beside him. "It's not a but, more of an explanation."

He held up his hand and shook his head. "You've said yes, I don't need an explanation."

"Yes, you do. When I told you why I left before, I wasn't 100 percent truthful."

"You lied?"

"No," she shook her head adamantly. "I didn't lie. I just didn't tell you everything."

CHAPTER THIRTY-ONE

FLYNN LOOKED INTO Ellie's eyes, searching for answers. He didn't want to believe she'd had the chance to be honest and had fed him some cock-and-bull story. The confidence he'd been feeling only seconds ago was now seeping away.

"I'm listening," he said.

"Thank you." She gathered herself. "I told you about Perth and my mother, that when she didn't show up, I was a mess." He nodded. "I always knew she only cared about herself, but when she didn't even bother… Anyway, I told you I drank and drank, trying to drown my sorrows. I didn't tell you I got chatting with this guy."

He flinched at the mention of another man. Never, in all these years, had he contemplated a third party was involved in the demise of their relationship. He needed to know. "Did you sleep with him?"

"No." She looked genuinely appalled at the thought, but her next words knocked him even harder. "Well… not exactly."

His whole body tensed. Bristling, he said, "You can't half fuck someone, Ellie."

"Please, Flynn," her voice shook. "Listen."

"Okay." And he would. He reminded himself that this had all taken place over ten years ago. That it was the here and now he was interested in. The future.

She picked up her can of Fanta and downed it as if

it were something much stronger. Then she sucked in a breath and let it out slowly. "This guy found me at the bar—looking all forlorn, I guess—and bought me a drink. He asked a few questions and listened as I poured my heart out about Rhiannon. When I'd spent all my words, he nodded knowingly and told me his own awful story—physical and emotional abuse, he only escaped it by running away from home, hitting the streets at fourteen. Or so he said. I could barely believe it—he seemed so together.

"Anyway, more drinks were bought. When the bar closed, he suggested we go back to his room to keep chatting. I never once thought there was anything sinister in it. Shows how naive I was."

"What do you mean?"

"He raped me."

Time slowed and her words hung in the air for what felt an eternity. All sound stopped, save for the thumping of Flynn's pulse in his ears, before everything whirled back into place, hitting him like a freight train.

Ellie continued, "He said I'd been gagging for it, and what did I think? That all the drinks he'd bought me were free?"

Something inside Flynn snapped. He grabbed the tray off the table—leftover chips, burger, rubbish and all—and flung it across the room. But it did nothing to defuse his anger. He clenched his fists and looked at her, hating himself for not protecting her. Hating that someone had violated her and he hadn't been there to stop them.

"Son of a bitch. I'll kill him."

Ellie sniffed and smiled grimly. "Thanks, Flynn, but I don't even know his name. It happened years ago."

Her words just drove the point home further. He should have been there.

"Why didn't you tell me? I could have supported you. We could have gone to the police."

"I knew what you were like, that you'd blame yourself. I didn't want you to feel guilty."

With his fingers digging into his palms, he rocked on the couch, taking his mind back to that weekend. He'd had a game. She'd asked him to go with her to meet her mom, and he'd turned her down for football.

He looked up at her. "But on some level you do blame me, or else you wouldn't have thought about my guilt." And she'd be right to blame him. What kind of boyfriend, what kind of fiancé, chose sport over the woman he loved? Regret washed over him as he thought of what life could have been had he made one better choice.

"That's not true. I blamed nobody but myself." She reached out her hand and clutched his.

Flynn didn't know what was worse—thinking she'd left him for bigger, better things, or knowing that one awful night had ruined everything. Had changed and damaged her so much she didn't think that their relationship had stood a chance. He felt angry and despondent. He stared at her hand, going dizzy as a zillion thoughts shot about in his head. He grabbed at one.

"Okay, if that's true, and you don't blame me, why did you run away? I don't get it."

She pressed her lips together as if fighting back tears. He appreciated that. If she started now, he was sure he'd fall in a heap himself.

"I found out I was pregnant."

Whoa! He took a moment to digest this new piece of information, then voiced the first real thought that came into his head. "It could have been mine," he croaked. He couldn't help but picture a little kid with her hair, her smile, his passion for the land. And with that came a new rush of emotion and anger. "What happened to it? Did you adopt it out? Did you get…rid of it?"

She spoke matter-of-factly. "I lost it. And yes, it could have been yours. It most likely was—but without tests, I wouldn't have known. And without telling you, there couldn't be tests."

He ran his hands through his hair, falling short of tugging out chunks. "I don't know what to say, Ellie."

"It was torture, Flynn, and it was torture leaving you, but I didn't know what was going to happen. I didn't want you to have to make a decision if the baby wasn't yours, and well, it's shameful to admit, but if I'd known I was going to lose it, I probably would have stayed, tried to keep all this secret. But I didn't know, Flynn, I just didn't know."

"What kind of decision?" He was baffled. She'd been raped—the woman he loved had been raped. He hated the thought of some scum touching her, but he'd never have deserted her. Never.

As if reading his mind, she said, "See, you don't believe there *was* a decision. I know you, Flynn. You're the most honorable man I've ever met. Whether you wanted to raise another man's child or not, you would have stayed with me, looked after me, simply because that's the kind of man you are. But I know what it's like to not be loved by your parents, and I didn't want that for my child."

He shook his head. She was right—he would have stuck by her—but she was also so wrong. She'd made a decision on his behalf, based on what she thought he'd do. But he wouldn't have stayed out of duty he'd have stayed because, back then, he couldn't imagine spending his life with anyone else. He still couldn't. And if a baby had been a part of that, he'd like to think he'd have learned to love it as his own. He'd never have held the sins of the father against the child. But she'd doubted him. She'd doubted his love, commitment and devotion.

And that was a kick to the gut.

The fact she hadn't thought his love strong enough, the fact she'd doubted his ability to love her, for better or for worse, hurt a hundred times more than being jilted at the altar.

Half an hour ago, he'd asked her to come back to Hope and live with him. But no matter the passion, the love, the intensity in everything he felt for Ellie, after this conversation, he could never be sure she trusted him. Never be sure she believed. And never be sure he trusted her. Was that what he wanted for the rest of his life? Always wondering if his partner was questioning his motives, questioning his love? And him forever striving to prove how much she meant to him? Hell, that sounded exhausting.

"Are you going to say something?" she asked shakily. "Please, say something."

Ellie quivered with the combined relief and fear of what she'd just told Flynn. It felt right to have it finally out in the open, for him to know the truth, that she hadn't left him because she didn't love him. The opposite, in fact. But the look on his face left her cold.

He sighed deeply. "I can't believe you thought that little of me."

"Flynn, I never... You were my world."

He held up his hand. "You say that, but your actions tell me something else. You didn't trust me—first, to confide in me about what had happened, and second, to believe I would love you *and* the baby. You made a decision on your own, a decision that should have been ours to make together. You jumped to conclusions, assuming the worst of me."

His look of anger turned to one of revulsion as he edged away from her. "All these years I thought you left because you weren't happy. That hurt like hell—I ached that I wasn't enough for you. It took me years to recover from that. But now I find out it was worse than that—that you left because you didn't have faith. You didn't think our relationship was strong enough to survive. What's changed, Ellie?"

She swallowed. "What do you mean?"

"If you didn't trust me then, why do you trust me now? Relationships are rocky roads. Who's to say you won't run at the first sign of difficulty?"

"I'm not the same person I was then. I've grown. And you're not the same person, either. I've fallen in love with you all over again since coming home—I've fallen in love with the man, not the boy." And she meant it, felt it with all the certainty of her heart. "I don't know if I truly knew what love was back then, I was such a mess when I came to live with Mat."

His eyes widened and he scoffed at her words. "And it gets worse still. You don't *know* if you loved me? What was I to you? Just a little bit of fun while you worked out what you wanted?"

"You're twisting my words, Flynn, that's not what I mean." Frustration clawed at her.

"That's the difference between you and me, Ellie. I *know* I loved you. Everyone else might have thought we were too young, but I had faith, I believed." He paused before delivering the fatal blow. "It's only now I'm not so sure. Everything I thought I loved about you was built on a lie. I don't know what to think anymore." He pushed up off the couch. "I've always known my heart where you were concerned, but now I'm not so sure I should follow it."

No! She trembled as she clutched Flynn's hands. She looked into his eyes and begged. "Please, Flynn, we've already wasted ten years. Don't let this ruin us again."

"And whose fault would that be?"

He shook her off, or tried to, but she held on tight, desperate not to let him go. She'd been so close and she'd blown it. Again.

"Let go, Ellie. I love you, but right now I don't want to be with you. I can't."

He tugged his arm free with a force she couldn't fight. She knew that if he left tonight, he wouldn't be coming back. And she knew the heartbreak that awaited her if that happened. She may have been the one to break off their relationship last time, but that didn't mean she hadn't ached. In the weeks and months following her departure, there'd been days she hadn't thought life worth living. He wasn't the only one who'd turned to alcohol. After losing her baby, and with nothing left to live for, she'd hit the bottle pretty hard. Being offered a permanent gig on *Lake Street* was the only thing that pulled her out of the abyss. This time, she wasn't sure work would save her.

"Please, Flynn," she cried again as he thrust his feet into his boots and strode toward the door. "Don't do this. We can make it work."

He looked back briefly, sadness in his eyes as he shook his head. Despite the past few days, despite his admission that he still loved her, she knew what would happen if he walked through that door.

FLYNN DIDN'T MEAN to slam it, but he left in such a hurry and with such anger that the boom of the door echoed in the night air. He stormed to his ute, contemplating his roller coaster of a life as he started the engine. The past few days back in Ellie's life, back in her bed, had felt so right. That was why he'd avoided talking about what they were doing. He hadn't wanted anything to break their magic bubble.

He'd known that real life would intrude sooner or later, but he'd thought it might have waited until after the funeral. He'd imagined they'd address their feelings for each other with an emphasis on the future, not the past. Call him gullible, but he'd believed Ellie's story about her mother and being confused. He hadn't for a moment considered there was anything like rape and miscarriage in her past.

He'd never felt so conflicted. Part of him wanted to turn around and go back to her, to be there for her now as he wasn't ten years ago, to tell her the past didn't mean a thing. But you couldn't rewrite history. He'd grown up watching his parents' relationship, admiring the comradeship, passion and trust between them. All of which made up what he believed was love. Real love—the kind that was there for you in life's highest moments, and the lowest. He'd always imagined that one day he'd share that with someone. But that kind of love needed to be mutual, and he didn't know if Ellie was capable of it. With him, anyway. How could she be, if she'd kept such a huge secret from him? If she'd let it ruin their relationship?

He stopped the car. Without paying attention, he'd ended up outside The Commercial.

Fuck. He wanted to punch something. He also, obviously, wanted a drink. Apart from that night with Lauren, he hadn't touched any grog—hard or soft—in just over eight years, but he'd never forgotten the taste or the effect. Not only did the liquid numb your thoughts and pain, but in a pub, you could always find solace in another drunk. Someone who'd listen to your woes and tell you that one more bourbon might just make it all go away. Someone who wouldn't judge you, someone who didn't make out that life wasn't as bad as you said it was.

But that wouldn't happen in this pub. Nor in the town's other drinking hole. Not where every fucking person and their fucking dog knew his life story.

Still, they had to serve him. He'd earned every cent he had through hard manual labor and deserved to bloody well spend it however he pleased. He didn't feel like talking to anyone anyway. Maybe he'd just go through the drive-through. One of the out-of-town attendants wouldn't bat an eyelid if he bought a bottle of Beam and a two-liter Coke. That's all it would take. Just one night to get himself straight.

CHAPTER THIRTY-TWO

ELLIE MANAGED TO drag herself up from the couch where she'd spent the night trying not to drown in tears. Her heart ached as if it had been put through the wringer and then trampled in the dirt. Her eyes stung, and when she made it to the bathroom she saw they had an appearance to match—it looked like both had been bitten by mosquitoes, so swollen and red were the lids.

She groaned loudly. She had about an hour until Joyce arrived and the funeral car came to pick them up. She wondered what she'd say about Flynn's absence. All she wanted right now was to curl up under her duvet and disappear. But that was impossible today. She had to pull herself together—get washed, get dressed, focus.

Her determination lasted all of two seconds before her mind returned to Flynn. Maybe he'd arrive before Joyce, just so she wouldn't have to explain why he wasn't there. He was nice like that.

Yet, as she turned the taps and forced herself into the shower, she knew he wouldn't be coming. She'd get a glimpse of him at the cemetery, looking all handsome and dapper in his dark suit, but that would be it. She'd pushed this Mr. Nice Guy to his limit. Tears threatened again at the realization of just how much she'd stuffed up. Her life, his... If only there was an option to start over.

She dressed in the skirt and dressy shirt she'd asked Saskia to courier from Sydney. She did her hair and

slapped on more makeup than usual. Toast was pushed
down her throat bite by bite, which in her current state
was quite an achievement. She was just about ready when
she heard a car pull into the driveway. Joyce was early,
she thought, but as she peered through the kitchen blinds
she almost choked on her last mouthful.

Karina. What was she doing here?

Ellie watched from the window, wide-eyed and frozen, as Flynn's mom got out of the car, followed by
his little sister. They both looked somber yet stunning, dressed in near-identical black dresses. As the
two women walked up the garden path, Ellie dusted the
crumbs from her mouth and made her way to the door.
She opened it as Karina stepped onto Matilda's bright
pink welcome mat. She didn't know what she'd expected,
but the warmth and sympathy she saw in the older woman's eyes was not it.

"Morning, Ellie." Karina smiled softly.

"Hi," Lucy said.

"Hello," Ellie replied, somewhat bemused. She felt
like a fool standing in the doorway, but she wasn't sure
what else to do. She waited for Karina to launch into
an angry tirade, but she didn't. Instead she pulled Ellie
into an awkward hug. Well, it was awkward to Ellie. Her
head rested on Karina's shoulder, where it felt as if she
were wearing shoulder pads. Karina pulled back. Ellie
didn't know anyone who still wore shoulder pads, but
on Karina it looked stylish, and not at all out-of-date.

"Flynn told me he wants to be with you," she said,
tucking Ellie's hair behind her ears so she could look
into her eyes.

Relief flooded Ellie. If Flynn had told his mother they
were getting back together, then he hadn't gone for good.

"I can't deny how worried this makes me," Karina

continued, "but I have to trust that you two know what you're doing. He never got over you, Ellie, and part of me is rejoicing that you are back in his life."

"Thanks," Ellie managed, heartened by Karina's words. Flynn had said he still loved her last night. Maybe she'd been bawling her eyes out for nothing. Maybe he just needed some time.

"This makes you family, Ellie. And family is there for each other at times like these. Is there anything we can do to help you today?"

"Um…" Ellie didn't quite know what to say. Perhaps she should ask if Karina knew when Flynn would be back. And she wouldn't mind one of them making her a cup of tea. She'd been too shaky to make one herself.

But Karina spoke first, stepping into the hallway. "So, is Flynn in the shower?"

"What?" Closing the door behind Lucy, Ellie turned back to Karina.

"Flynn. Where is he?"

"He left last night." As the words left Ellie's mouth, dread sank in. "When did you talk to him?"

Karina's brow creased and her eyes narrowed. "Yesterday afternoon, at the farm."

Ellie swayed and palmed the wall for support. The hallway suddenly felt claustrophobic. Once again, she wished she'd kept her secret buried. Karina was being so lovely—thinking Ellie was back in Flynn's life—but now, now that she had to tell her the truth, she didn't want to think about the kind of wrath the woman was capable of.

"Oh," Ellie managed.

"Oh?" Karina's voice wasn't sweet and supportive now.

Ellie cringed, anticipating the outcome of what she

was about to say. She breathed deeply. "Last night I told Flynn why I left."

"Yes?"

"It upset him. A lot." She sniffed, determined not to cry. "We broke up again, not that we were officially together, and he left. In a hurry."

Karina sighed angrily. "What is it with you, Ellie Hughes? Why did you have to lead him on again?"

"I didn't." Ellie fought back on instinct, tired of being the villain. She hadn't led him on, she'd merely apologized. He was the kindhearted soul that suggested they hang together, the one who stopped the town from ostracizing her, the one who came to her when she most needed someone. Who could blame her for falling in love with such a noble heart? "And I don't really want to discuss this with you, or anyone, right now. Maybe you should talk to Flynn instead."

"I would, if I knew where he was. We thought he was here, with you." Karina's words stung. She took her mobile out of her clutch. Lucy didn't say anything, she just looked at Ellie with a baffled expression.

Ellie shivered and her knees locked, her thoughts paralyzing her. What if Flynn had gone on a bender again, because of her?

Karina seemed to have the same fears. She was already on the phone to Rats, who must have only just returned from his honeymoon. "Jordan, it's Karina….Yes, I'll be there….I'm just wondering, have you seen Flynn this morning?" There was a long pause, then Karina grabbed Lucy's arm and nodded toward the door. "No, he's not with her."

Shrugging apologetically to Ellie, Lucy opened the door for her mother and followed her out. Ellie stared after them, hearing snippets of Karina telling Rats that

Flynn had been dumped again. For the first time in her life, Ellie felt like punching something. It was only the thought of not wanting to break any more of Mat's things that stopped her.

She took a deep breath. This was the day she was laying Matilda to rest. She'd be damned if she let Karina Quartermaine or any other member of Hope Junction ruin it.

Shutting the door, she caught her reflection in the hallway mirror. Ugh. She looked like a bad clone of Morticia Addams. She glanced around at the bright colors of Matilda's home and imagined her godmother scowling at her grim outfit. She'd hated funerals—she would've avoided having one altogether if it were legal—and she'd be appalled to think the whole town was dressed in a dour fashion because of her.

Ellie wandered through the house, taking in Mat's wonderful array of treasures. She lingered in each room, knowing that when she returned tonight, Mat would really be gone, and she'd be more alone than ever.

Flynn wasn't at the cemetery. The whole town had turned out, or so it seemed, but Flynn was noticeably absent. As was Mat's younger brother, but that was more understandable—he was unable to leave his overseas posting at such short notice. Mat hadn't believed there was any point in him coming to see a dead body anyway, and had told him so in no uncertain terms. She'd visited him plenty in the past few years—although she was officially retired from writing, the travel bug was not so easily repressed. She'd followed him around the world, visiting him at every place, and he would miss her dearly.

Ellie also thought briefly of Mat's lost love, Tom, and wondered if she should have told him. Then again, she'd stuffed up enough in her own life lately, it was probably best she let Tom be. Joyce had informed Dougal, who'd sent his condolences.

Mud-covered cars lined the streets leading up to the burial site. The coffin would be carried by four young farmers for whom Matilda had been Scout leader. Ellie went ahead with Joyce to stand at the front of the procession.

The two were quite the sight. Ellie couldn't change the fact that locals would follow tradition and wear customary funeral clothes, as they had, but in the end she'd decided not to join them. Today was about celebrating Mat's life, not having a contest over who could be the most downcast and depressed. So instead she'd changed into a bright fuchsia maxidress—perhaps a little cool for the September weather, but her black woolen shrug would deal with the chill. She knew Matilda would have loved the massive flowers splattering the skirt.

She'd also picked one of Matilda's pink spider orchids to go in her hair. Its luscious scent instantly recalled Mat tending her garden.

"They were one of her favorites," Joyce said. In terms of outfit, she'd come to the same decision as Ellie. Her bright purple-and-orange dress looked like something out of a Bollywood film. When Joyce had come to collect her, Ellie couldn't help laughing, a bubble of tension popping inside her.

"Do you think we stand out awfully?" she asked now, her speech folded in her hands.

"Well, not *awfully*." Joyce laughed. She carried a wicker basket, which was available for anyone who wanted to donate to Mat's chosen cancer charity. She'd insisted on no flowers, but people liked to feel they were doing something.

Locals were gathering and Ellie smiled at people as she passed them, wondering who knew about her fight with Flynn. She didn't think Karina or Lucy would be broadcasting the news, but Rats knew, so Whitney and Lauren were probably already popping the champagne corks. And even if they kept their big, lipstick-primed lips shut, his absence spoke volumes. She certainly felt it. Like a brick at the bottom of her stomach.

Pulling her shrug around her shoulders, Ellie tried to push thoughts of Flynn from her mind. She breathed a sigh of relief when the music started wafting from the stereo. Joyce put her arm around Ellie's waist and Ellie leaned into her for comfort as the celebrant took her position before the crowd.

"Thank you, everyone, for coming here today to celebrate the full and vibrant life of Matilda Jean Thompson." The celebrant glanced around as the sun moved behind a cloud. It didn't stay hidden long, shining brightly for a spring morning, in complete contrast to the darkness filling Ellie's heart. It were as if the weather was reminding her to think about the happy memories, to celebrate a good life and not dwell on loss. Ellie zoned out and lifted her head to the sky, wondering if, somewhere up there, Mat was looking down and giggling at the gathering.

See Norma Rickart? she imagined Matilda saying. *She bought that dress in 1975. Only ever brings it out for funerals and her wedding anniversary.*

Ellie suppressed a grin as her heart began to thaw. Then she heard the celebrant call her name. It was time for her to read the eulogy. She'd written most of it on her own, praise of Mat flowing freely from her fingers onto the page. Flynn had listened to her read it a couple of times and suggested a few additions. She'd gone over it on her own as well, so much so, it turned out, that when she stood before the crowd of mourners, not far from the coffin, she barely needed to look at the piece of paper in front of her.

Ellie's words were heartfelt and raw. Her speech had a visible impact on the gathering—not because of her acting training, but because it was borne of the deepest, most honest emotions. By the end of it, there was not a dry eye to be found.

"Mat was one of a kind," she said in closing. "Every town has someone who's a little eccentric but all heart, willing to do anything for her friends and family, even for strangers. When Matilda Thompson took me into her home and heart, she taught me what love, family and community meant. She taught me to live life to the best of my ability and not to harbor regrets. I didn't always manage to live up to her mantras, but they were always here." Ellie touched the spot just above her heart. "And I will never forget them. Just as I will never forget her."

She recalled the flower in her hair, pulled it out and laid it on Mat's casket.

"I love you, Mat," she whispered. Tears splashed freely from her cheeks onto the wood of the coffin. *I'm sorry I didn't always listen to your advice,* she added silently.

Mat had believed in her and Flynn. She'd urged Ellie to tell Flynn the truth the moment she returned to Hope, but Ellie'd been too scared to listen, too scared to act. Would things have been different if she'd told him straightaway? She couldn't think like this. *No regrets,* she reminded herself.

Taking a deep breath, Ellie stood and walked back to Joyce. After the eulogy, the celebrant did something a little unconventional—something Mat would have loved— and asked people to share their memories of Matilda.

Ellie loved listening to everyone's anecdotes. It seemed that Mat had touched the hearts of almost everyone in Hope Junction.

So it wasn't surprising when the bowling club filled quickly for the wake. Ellie made an effort to do the rounds, talking to as many people as she could and thanking them for coming. She especially thanked those who'd shared their memories of Matilda. But every person she spoke to made Flynn's absence even more conspicuous. No one asked her about him, but she got some strange looks. At one point she overheard Karina brushing someone off when they asked where he was.

Despite being in a room full of loving, supportive people—even Lauren offered her condolences—Ellie felt utterly alone. She couldn't wait until the crowds dispersed and she could escape back to the safety of Mat's cottage. She needed to make some heavy decisions, and as much as she wanted to put them off, she knew she couldn't.

As the last of the stragglers closed the door behind themselves and the CWA volunteers cleaned and tidied in the kitchen, Ellie saw Joyce coming toward her.

"Was a good funeral, as far as funerals go." Joyce offered a supportive smile.

Ellie nodded. "Mat would have liked it. Not at all pompous or morbid."

"Shall I walk you home?"

"No, thanks." As much as Ellie appreciated the offer, she wanted to be alone, to not have to keep putting on a brave face. When Joyce didn't say anything, Ellie felt the need to explain. "I'm really tired, I just want to crawl into bed and catch up on some sleep. But thanks anyway. And thanks for everything you've done for me and Mat in the past couple of months. I don't know how we would have coped without your support."

"Oh, nonsense." Joyce held her index finger like a schoolmarm. "I just did what any friend would do, and you've been equally supportive of me in my grief."

There was a solemn moment between them before Ellie said, "I'm glad."

Ellie went to thank the CWA crowd and Joyce went to turn off the lights in the bathrooms. When Ellie stepped outside a few minutes later, however, Joyce was waiting for her. She opened her mouth to speak, but Joyce held up a hand to silence her.

"Where's Flynn?" she asked.

Ellie's stomach muscles tightened. She tried to keep the quaver from her voice. And failed. "I don't know," she confessed.

"Do you need to talk about it?" Ellie couldn't help but notice how Joyce said *need* rather than *want*.

"You can walk me home," she said by way of reply.

Joyce simply nodded as they walked, waiting for Ellie to talk in her own good time. Ellie told Joyce what had happened, complete with the truth of why she'd fled to Sydney all those years ago. This was the third time she'd opened up to someone about this, and she wasn't sure if the conversation was getting easier or harder. Either way, Joyce's response was much more relaxed than Flynn's—which was understandable. There was less at stake, and she was so like Mat in her nonjudgmental, down-to-earth outlook.

"I'm scared," she told Joyce.

"Of what the town will say?"

Ellie shook her head. "I couldn't care what anyone but Flynn thinks. If he turns back to the drink because of me, I'll *never* forgive myself. I don't know what to do. If only I'd approached the conversation a different way. I just blurted it all out, really. I need him to give me another chance."

"Is that what you want?"

"Yes," Ellie replied emphatically. "I want *him*. I've always wanted him. I don't seem to be very good for him, but I'd give anything to change that."

"And if he gives you the chance?" Joyce asked. "Will you quit your job and stay here?"

"It wouldn't even be a sacrifice. If he let me in, I'll have won the world."

"Then you need to be patient." Joyce put her hand in Ellie's and squeezed as they approached Mat's house. "As the saying goes, If you love something, set it free. I know that isn't easy, but you need to trust your heart. And his."

"Thanks." Ellie gave Joyce a hug and then hurried up the driveway. She closed the door behind her and leaned against it.

Patience.

Easy for Joyce to say, she wasn't in Ellie's position. How was she meant to be patient? Just hang about and not even try to contact Flynn? He could have fallen into a pit of self-destruction, and it was all because of her.

She switched the radio on to drown out the painful silence. Taking her phone out, she clicked to her recent calls list. Flynn's number sat right at the top—he'd called her from the Co-op yesterday morning to see if they needed milk. Yesterday morning, when they'd been living in an alternate reality.

She clicked the call button, holding her breath as she waited for the dial tone. But it never came.

The phone you are calling is switched off or unavailable. Please leave a message after the tone.

Dammit. The resounding beep rang in her ear.

"Flynn. It's me. Ellie. Please call me. I know you need

time, but I'm worried about you. I'm sorry, so sorry. I just need to know you're okay." She hung up. Her message sounded clichéd, but she really didn't know what else to say. As she thought about this, her mobile began to ring and vibrate in her hand. She answered without a glance at the caller ID. "Flynn?" She was past caring about sounding desperate.

"No, *Dwayne,*" said the voice, with a slight chuckle.

"Oh, hi, Dwayne." Ellie's heart sank.

"Sorry to disappoint. I was just calling to see how you were after the funeral."

"You're not a disappointment," Ellie assured him, "it's just…" Dwayne didn't take his percentage for listening to her woes. She stood straight and tall and adopted her most professional voice. "Thank you for the call. I'm doing okay, just tired." She thought she sounded like a broken record with the tired line, but it was true. Emotionally, she was exhausted.

Dwayne cut to the chase. "I don't want to hassle you, but now your godmother has gone, I've got the producers on my back. How long do you think you'll need to wrap things up?"

She glanced around at the things Matilda hadn't managed to pack or give away. The idea of wrapping things up seemed so cold and disconnected. And then there was Flynn. Joyce's words about being patient rang in her ears.

"I'm not sure. I'm going to need some more time. A couple of weeks, at least."

"Aw, Els," Dwayne groaned down the phone line. "It's been two months already. I don't know how much longer I can keep them hanging."

She swallowed, all too aware of the tightrope she was walking. A couple of false steps and she could lose Flynn *and* her career. But she had to show him how much he meant to her. That she was prepared to fight for him.

"I understand that, Dwayne, but my hands are tied."

CHAPTER THIRTY-THREE

STACEY GREENWAY LOOKED up from behind the bar of The Imperial, a pub in the far north of Western Australia. "Flynn Quartermaine!" she squealed, rushing to capture him in a warm, friendly hug. "Oh, my gosh, what are you doing here? Wait until Sean finds out." She pulled back to look at him. Flynn saw that she'd barely changed in the eight years he'd been away. Sure, she carried a few extra kilos, but she'd delivered four little boys in that time, so who could blame her?

"You look great," he told her. "I needed a break from the farm and I haven't seen you guys for a while, so I thought I'd drop in."

"I'm so glad," she said. "I'll fix a room for you."

"No." He waved his hand at her. "I'm staying at the motel. I don't want to put you out and…" His voice trailed off but Stacey understood. He couldn't put himself through the temptation of staying in a pub.

"Let me get you some lunch, then. Did you fly?"

He shook his head. "Drove. Took us three days."

"Us?"

In answer to her question, Rodger ambled in, yawning and stretching his legs. "Us," Flynn echoed.

Stacey scoffed. "I can't imagine being stuck in a car that long. How long are you staying?"

Flynn shrugged. "Not sure. I have a few things I need to think through."

She looked worried. "Anything you need to talk about?"

"No, but thanks. I can't get my head straight at the moment, so talking about anything else will help."

"All right." Stacey smiled and pretended to zip her lips. "I won't ask again, and I'll tell Sean to butt out, too."

Flynn chuckled. He hadn't realized how much he missed his distant friends until he was here again, back in the place he'd stopped eight years ago and finally started to recover. "How's your dad?" he asked. "The station? Your boys?"

"Hold up, one question at a time." Stacey fixed him a pint of Coke and pushed it across the bar. "Dad's good. My brother Kyle's pretty much taken over the station now. He thrives on it. And the boys, well, you'll get to meet them when you come round for dinner tonight. You will come, won't you? I've got a couple of backpackers who'll be happy to man the bar, give Sean the night off."

"I'm there." Flynn took a slurp of his drink and glanced around the pub. He'd only had a few drinks here before taking up residence on Stacey's dad's station. Stacey and Sean were newly married back then and had just bought the place. Aside from making babies, they'd done a lot of work to the old girl in the past decade. For a back-of-beyond establishment, it oozed character. You couldn't help but feel welcome the moment you walked in.

Stacey and Sean had been good mates to Flynn at a time when he was pretty hard to be friends with. Having grown up in the pub industry, Sean recognized Flynn's problem pretty much immediately, and had offered an ear rather than a lecture. By that stage, Flynn was ready to clean up his act and the Greenways made the perfect cheer squad. He owed them a lot.

Stacey served a group of Main Roads workers who had come in for lunch, and Flynn took his time finishing his drink. He wasn't quite sure what he was doing here, he just knew he had to get away from Hope Junction—and away from Ellie—for a while. Thinking of her, he took his phone out of his pocket and turned it on. Within seconds the beeps bombarded him, signaling a message, and another, and another, and another. He already knew they'd be from Ellie and his mother. Both women had persistence down to a fine art. But Rats was the only person Flynn had spoken to since he left. Once he was out on the road he'd made a quick call to his best mate to ask him to keep an eye on Black Stump for a bit. Rats was happy to supervise the workers and make sure things kept ticking along smoothly. Flynn didn't know how long he'd be; Rats had told him to take all the time he needed.

He listened to his mom's messages. Hearing the anxiousness and sadness in her voice, he resolved to call her and let her know he was okay. He'd been a prick not to call until now, but he just couldn't deal with the prying questions and told-you-so opinions. As much as he adored her, he needed space.

His heartbeat slowed as he listened to the next message. Another one from Ellie. It sounded like she was still in Hope Junction, waiting for him. This revelation gave him a kick he wasn't sure he wanted to feel.

Hi, Flynn. It's me. Again. I miss you. Please come back.

Back to what? More heartache? She'd been unrelenting in her efforts to contact him, calling ten times a day, sending emails that he'd picked up on his phone. He wanted more than anything to believe that she loved him and would stay, but her confession, her lack of faith in their relationship, had more than shaken him—it had near on broken him again. He'd been practically at the counter of The Commercial's drive-through when he'd thought better of it. Instead of giving in, he'd gunned it, stopping only to pick up Rodger before hitting the road. And then he'd just kept on driving. Three days avoiding the pull of each liquor store and pub, of denying himself the drink he desperately craved.

He deleted the messages and dialed his mom before he had time to contemplate Ellie's words.

"Hi, Mom."

"Flynn!" Karina all but shrieked down the line. A couple of the Main Roads blokes looked his way and he shrugged apologetically. "Where on earth are you? Are you okay?"

"Relax, Mom. I'm up north. And before you ask, I haven't had a drink."

"Thank God for that. If only you'd called before now. I've been worried sick."

"Have you talked to Ellie?" he asked.

Karina's voice went cold. "She's the fool, Flynn, if she doesn't want you."

"Stop. I don't need sympathy. Or a lecture. I don't even want to talk about her, I just want you to know that I'm okay. Has Rats been popping round?"

Karina sighed. "Yes, Jordan has been a godsend. He's a good friend, you know, but you can't rely on him to keep things going forever."

"I know, Mom. But I'll repay him sometime. Please don't stress about the farm, or me."

A scornful hiss came down the phone line. "You can't tell a mother not to stress, Flynn Stuart Quartermaine. You just up and leave and don't call me for three days, what do you expect?"

"Rats knew where I was. I told him to let you know." When his mother didn't reply, he added, "Is it too much to ask for a little understanding?"

Another sigh. More regretful this time. "Of course not, darling. I'm trying. But this is *your* home, and she'll be gone soon. You can't let her keep you from being near the people who care about you, who love you."

Gone? His gut clenched. Of course she wouldn't hang around forever. "When's she going?"

"I'm not sure. She's keeping very much to herself. Lucy might've seen her at theater practice, but your sister's not saying anything to me at the moment."

Karina wanted a definitive answer about when Flynn would return, but he couldn't give her one. Every time he tried to think about his future, Ellie's face popped up. He needed time to work out what this meant. He promised to check in every couple of days.

He devoured a pie and chips for lunch, and said goodbye to Stacey. He had a much-needed nap at the motel and then headed out to Shamrock Station, where he received almost as warm a welcome as he had from Stacey. Grant, Stacey's father, took Flynn in his arms as if he were a long-lost son and asked, half jokingly, half hopefully, "Are you here to work again? Never since you left have we been able to find such a good worker."

"It's true," nodded Kyle, his scruffy curls barely confined beneath his Emu Bitter cap.

"Sorry, guys." Flynn shook his head. "Mom'll kill me if I don't go back. But if you need an extra hand the next few days, I'm more than happy to lend one. I've never been that good at being idle, even on holidays."

"You got a deal," said Kyle excitedly. "But first, you're just in time for Mom's prizewinning scones."

Flynn stood by his word, eagerly helping out around

the station. He was a sheep farmer through and through, but he relished the experience of working with cattle for a short while. Over the next few days, he worked hard from dawn to dusk, the manual labor exhausting his body and his mind, which he was thankful for. He was finally able to get a few good nights' sleep, free of dreams of Ellie.

Guilt weighed on him for deserting his own farm, but he checked in with Rats daily. Rats loved the freedom of managing Black Stump anyway; his father was still head honcho on his property and reluctant to give up the reins. This made staying away easier for Flynn, but it didn't stop the barrage of calls from his mom. And Ellie.

Three days on the road with no one but his dog for company and nothing but Ellie to think about, then four more about as far from her as he could get, and he was still none the wiser about what he should do.

CHAPTER THIRTY-FOUR

THERE WAS ONLY so much comfort Fanta and chocolate a girl could scoff, Ellie discovered, and only so much cleaning she could do to keep her mind off things. She also found that you could live on the remnants of an understocked cupboard for five days—the same amount of time it took to completely clean a house the size of Mat's.

On the morning of the sixth day, she lay in bed longer than usual and contemplated her next move. She'd never been good at twiddling her thumbs, and her favorite movies—rom-coms—were out of the question in her current state.

She rolled over and picked her mobile up off the bedside table. Call her desperate, but she was still phoning Flynn two or three times a day. He'd been gone almost a week now. She felt utterly lost and bereft and helpless, but she figured she had nothing to lose and everything to gain. If she harassed him enough, maybe some of the walls he'd built around himself would start to crumble.

"Good morning, Flynn," she said to his voice mail. "Joyce said she heard you're up north somewhere. Hope it's a bit warmer there. I've been sorting through Mat's things and found some old Hurricanes memorabilia you might like. The things that woman collected you wouldn't believe. She didn't even like football." Ellie forced a laugh. "Anyway, I hope whatever you're doing, you're keeping safe and happy. Miss you."

She hung up and clutched the phone against her chest, letting out a deep, mournful sigh. Although they went unreturned, leaving messages still made her feel closer to him. She tried to keep her calls relatively normal, the aim being simply to remind him she was still here, waiting. She'd heard through Joyce, who must have spoken to Karina, that he wasn't on the booze, but she was still none the wiser as to his location, or his state of mind. Flynn staying away from the farm this long seemed unthinkable, and she worried about him more and more. If she knew where he was, she would simply get in the Premier and drive there. Immediately. Even if he wouldn't accept her apology, her declaration of love, she just wanted to see him again, needed to know that he was okay.

A knock dragged Ellie from her thoughts and out of bed. She pulled an old dressing gown of Mat's around her—she'd been wearing it because it smelled like her godmother—and went to answer the door.

At the sight of Lucy and Sam, her knees threatened to give. "Is it Flynn?" she asked, in lieu of a greeting.

Lucy shook her head. "No, Flynn's okay," she rushed, "well, physically anyway. We're not sure when he's coming back." She sounded apologetic.

Ellie looked at the couple, again making the comparison to herself and Flynn. But where the youngsters' love was new and innocent, Ellie's was jaded and losing hope. On the one hand, she felt relief at hearing Flynn was okay, but on the other, it reaffirmed that he'd kept contact with others—and not her.

"That's good to hear," she managed to say. She even offered a smile, which she considered quite an accomplishment.

"We were wondering if you'd like to come watch our

final dress rehearsal this afternoon." Lucy smiled, her eager eyes full of warmth. Ellie wanted to hug her.

She nodded. "Sure. I'd love that."

THE REHEARSAL GAVE Ellie the incentive to pull herself together—to get dressed and make more of an effort with her appearance than she had in the past few days. She went to the Co-op—which, despite building it up so much in her mind, was largely uneventful—and bought enough supplies to last another week. She hoped that, in that time, something would let her know just what she should do with Mat's house, and with her life.

After unpacking her groceries, she psyched herself up and headed down to the hall. As she entered, she could feel the excitement charging the atmosphere.

"Hi, Ellie," Troy nodded as he passed her, his hands full of stage props.

She smiled back warmly. "Hi there."

Everyone who wasn't backstage getting their makeup done or doing said makeup came to greet her. Jolie told her they'd missed her. No one looked at her accusingly or made her feel like sheep dung, and some of the coldness in her heart thawed a little.

That is, until she glanced up at the stage, the curtain not yet closed, and saw Flynn's handiwork. The scenery looked amazing. She didn't know how he'd found the time to create something akin to what you'd see on Broadway (well, close enough, considering the materials he had to work with). Even when absent, Flynn was everywhere in Hope Junction. Their golden boy—an all-round nice bloke, hardworking, talented at everything he tried his hand at, gorgeous. He only had one flaw, and that was down to her.

Talk about thoughts to make yourself feel good. Ellie

resolved to focus on the play, not the woeful scenarios replaying in her head. She tracked backstage, where the smiles and enthusiasm of the cast and crew were contagious. She sat on a swivel chair in the midst of the hubbub, and before long she was nattering away, passing hairpins and makeup brushes to the volunteers from Hairlicious, the local salon. It was fun. Relaxing. Ellie had gotten her own hair and makeup done almost every day of her working life, but there wasn't this kind of camaraderie in the dressing rooms she knew. The *Lake Street* cast were friends, but they all wanted to be the best-looking on camera. An unspoken competition wagered between them—who could get noticed on the small screen and make it to Hollywood first. Maybe it was because she didn't harbor any such ambitions that she'd never realized this before. However, she knew that if and when she returned to Sydney, she'd be comparing everything and everyone with how she felt being back in Hope. Even at her lowest, this town was more like home than anywhere else she'd ever lived.

"All right!" Mrs. Ellery came backstage and her voice boomed, silencing the animated chatter. "Five minutes to curtain. Everyone ready?"

An excited chorus of "Yes" answered her. Ellie took her cue to head out to the auditorium, sitting with Sam and Troy, the three of them alone in the hundred chairs set up for next Saturday's opening night. Everyone else was either onstage or backstage, doing their bit to make sure the production went off without a hitch.

At the end of it, Ellie had to say they'd all done a splendid job. They'd come so far since that first day she'd watched them.

"Lucy's really good," Sam said, as the trio stood and applauded.

"You'd say that even if she stank," said Troy on the other side of Ellie.

"Shut up," Sam snapped.

Troy shoved his hands in his pockets and turned to Ellie. "You coming out to celebrate with everyone? I think drinks are at the pub. Ellery said it's the last late night everyone can have until showtime, reckons they all need their beauty sleep."

"Yeah, sounds good." Anything was better than sitting at Mat's place with only her silent phone for company.

The cast and crew cleaned up quickly and everyone piled down to the pub. Ellie's heart sank when she saw Whitney behind the bar and Lauren on a stool, drinking some extravagant, out-of-place cocktail. She braced herself for nastiness, but neither of them lived up to expectation. Although not exactly friendly, Whitney served her without a fuss. Ellie managed to avoid Lauren, and the locals were much friendlier than the last time she'd been here. But despite this, she felt a hundred times worse. What use was the town being kind to her if Flynn wouldn't answer her calls?

As the members of the theatrical society got louder and louder and more inebriated, Ellie slipped out the door.

She kept herself busy for the rest of the week, packing up Matilda's things and sorting them into stuff that she could give to charity and stuff she wanted to keep. She mentally prepared herself for the possibility of putting the cottage on the market. She dropped her calls to Flynn to one a day, not wanting to give up, but not wanting to put her heart through the wringer any more than she already had. She kept odd hours, sleeping much of the day and waking up in the depths of night to pack another box.

With each hour that passed, though, she lost a little more hope and another tiny chunk of her heart.

CHAPTER THIRTY-FIVE

FLYNN TURNED HIS ute into the driveway behind the pub, looking forward to sharing another dinner with Stacey, Sean and their rambunctious boys. He still hadn't come to any conclusions about Ellie. Considering he hadn't a clue what his feelings were, it was hard to work out what to do about them. He loved working with Kyle and Grant on Shamrock Station, but he knew it could never be a long-term thing. A lot had changed since the last time he'd been up here looking for answers.

For one thing, he was an adult now, with more responsibility and life experience than when he'd left Hope Junction at nineteen. He had his dad's legacy to fulfill, and his mom and Lucy to look out for. He couldn't drift forever.

He whistled for Rodger to hobble out of the passenger seat. Sean and Stacey's kids adored Rodg, but as he was getting old, he could only take them in small doses. They wandered up to the house, where Flynn tied the dog to a post. When no one answered his knock, he let himself in.

Squeals of excitement and splashes came from the bathroom. Leaving his boots next to the welcome mat, Flynn headed toward them. The oldest Sean look-alike stood in the middle of the bathroom with a towel wrapped around him. The other three were in the bath, larking about as if they were in the ocean. Stacey was totally drenched.

"Enter at your own risk," she said, the grin on her face telling Flynn she didn't really care about the debacle.

Flynn loved being with these boys. It made him relax and have a laugh, but it didn't make things any clearer in his head. A few times he'd found himself picturing Ellie instead of Stacey, imagining they were *their* sons instead of the Greenways'. He'd shaken it off pretty quickly, though. Even if he did still love Ellie, and even if she really loved him, there were other complications. Things they hadn't yet begun to figure out.

Flynn grinned back. "Anything I can do to help?"

"Yeah, please. You can check on the roast. Should be nearly cooked."

Giving Stacey a cheeky salute and ruffling the eldest boy on the head, Flynn headed for the kitchen. He immediately screwed up his nose at the smell of charcoaled meat. He opened the oven door and flinched at the smoke that hit him in the face. And to think he'd doubted Ellie's cooking skills.

Acting quickly, he switched off the oven, noticing that it was set to five hundred degrees. Then he grabbed a nearby tea towel and dropped the deader-than-dead meat, tray and all, into the sink. The pan of black veggies—at least he thought they were veggies—followed closely behind. Right about the time smoke alarms starting blaring throughout the house.

Stacey came running into the kitchen, her youngest struggling in her arms. She stared at the mess and then glared at the child. "You've been playing with the knobs again, haven't you?" As she let out a guttural groan, Flynn's mobile began to buzz in his pocket. She took another look around the room and sighed. "Aren't you going to answer that?"

He took the phone out of his pocket and glanced at

the screen. Muscles he didn't realize he'd been clenching relaxed when he saw that the caller was Lucy. Until now, his mom had been putting in all the checkup calls—hearing his voice helped her suppress the image of him lying in a gutter somewhere, apparently. He appreciated that this was a mom's prerogative, but her calls always left him edgy. It would be a relief to chat to his sister.

He pressed the button to answer the call. "Hey, Luce."

"Hello, stranger," she said, sounding more grown-up than he remembered. "You could have called," she quipped.

"I've been busy," he said. "Besides, the amount Mom's been badgering me I've got no battery left."

She giggled. "Well, you're lucky I've been busy, too."

"Oh really, what's been keeping you so busy? Study or boys?"

"Flynn." He could almost hear her roll her eyes. Even over the phone, riling her up was fun. "There's only one *man* for me, and you don't need to worry about my exams. I'm making time for them—both NIDA and WAAPA require grades as well as talent."

Flynn thought he could handle it if Lucy went to WAAPA—the Western Australian Academy of Performing Arts—but he couldn't help but feel that the National Institute of Dramatic Art was a couple of states too far for his liking.

Lucy continued. "But please don't tell me you're so stupid as to have forgotten about the play."

The play. He really had forgotten. No doubt Ellie would stay to see the production through, but once it was over, she'd have nothing keeping her in Hope. She'd leave. Despite the pang in his heart, however, he thought this was for the best. Too much had gone between them for it to ever work. He sighed.

"It starts this Saturday," she continued, oblivious to the churnings in his mind. "You'll be back, won't you?"

"Actually, I've been helping out on a mate's station, and they're pretty busy at the moment. I'll see the week out and leave on Saturday morning." With any luck, Ellie would stay for the first performance and then get the hell out.

"So you're going to miss opening night?" She sounded truly distressed.

"Luce, calm down. You don't need me there for that. I'll be back in time for the midweek matinee."

"Fine, Flynn. Be like that. But don't expect me to ever be there for you. Have a nice life."

He jumped slightly as the slam of the homestead phone echoed in his ear. Teenagers. He glanced at Stacey, who was now at the table, sipping a white wine. Her toddler played with cars at her feet.

"Women problems?" she asked over the top of her glass.

"Sister problems. Almost as bad."

She looked wistfully at the kitchen sink. "And now you have dinner problems, too. Are you a fan of beans on toast?"

He shrugged a shoulder and grinned. "When it comes to food, I'm not fussy. But forget about feeding me, I'm going home."

"What?" Stacey looked as surprised as he felt.

"Yeah," he said firmly, trying to get used to the idea, which seemed to have sprung from nowhere. He was always going home at some point, but Lucy's call had put things in perspective. His family meant the world to him, and if his being at the play was so important to his little sister, then staying away would be both cowardly and selfish.

"Right now?"

He nodded and explained the situation to Stacey.

"At least get a good night's sleep before you go," she said, sounding more and more like his mother.

He grinned. "I'll be fine," he said. "I'll get started now while it's not too dark, and when I feel myself getting tired, I'll pull over. I promise. Tomorrow night I'll get a motel."

Stacey stood and held out her arms. "I feel like you haven't been here nearly long enough. You will go say goodbye to Sean before you leave? He's not due back for another hour."

Flynn nodded and returned his friend's embrace. "I'll stop by the pub on my way and tell him to bring home dinner."

"Thanks," Stacey said, picking up her son from the floor. They followed Flynn to the door and waved goodbye.

CHAPTER THIRTY-SIX

"Okay. I'll see you soon, Dwayne."

Ellie hung up and moved to the other end of the veranda. A decision had been made. Her heart should have felt lighter for it, but it didn't, not yet. Right now, she felt as if she was giving up. She gazed down the long street to the cluster of buildings that formed the town half a kilometer away. She knew that wherever she was in the world, she'd be able to close her eyes and conjure up that streetscape, that perfect country vista, and all the noises and smells that went with it.

She loved this town and its people more than anything, being back here had taught her that much. But without Flynn or Mat, she just couldn't see a way to make it home. At least in Sydney, people didn't judge her by her past. At least there she had a reasonable way to make a living. Her flat was there. Her two closest friends...

Ellie wanted to stay to see the play's opening. Only one more day. She felt she owed that much to Matilda, to Lucy and Mrs. Ellery and the theatrical society, all these people that had welcomed her back into Hope life. She wanted to be there to support them, to see their big moment. But she kept thinking about Flynn. About his silence, his absence. What if he was waiting for her to leave? This had been his home, his town, long before it was hers.

Besides, Dwayne had made it pretty clear if she didn't come back to the show immediately, Stella Williams would be leaving *Lake Street* for good. A job might not mean a lot to some people, but it was pretty much all she had left.

She couldn't just hang around in the wings forever, clutching to the vain hope that her love life might fall back into place. Then she really would be Miss Havisham. *The wedding dress*. She cringed at the thought of it scrunched in a ball at the bottom of the wardrobe. The rest of the house was all packed away now—as well as Mat's things, she'd boxed up her teenage years, throwing a lot out, donating some things to the op shop and keeping a few small mementos. But consciously or subconsciously, she'd avoided dealing with the dress.

Even as she realized this, however, she went on to deal with other stuff. She called the bus company and booked herself a ticket to Perth for tomorrow morning. Then she arranged a flight out for the evening. She'd be in Sydney early on Sunday, and back in the studio first thing Monday.

The afternoon was consumed with more such business. The call to the real-estate agent. Organizing to get the boxes she wanted to keep shipped back to Sydney. Making a few quick visits around town. She said goodbye to Jolie and the girls she'd met through the play, and went to the caravan park to let Joyce know what was going on. Finally, she put in a call to Lucy. She would have liked to have seen Flynn's precious sister one last time, but she didn't dare venture to the homestead where Karina would, no doubt, be ready to pounce.

"Ellie, I'm so glad you called." Lucy sounded genuinely so, and that gave Ellie a lift. "I was going to ask if you want to have lunch tomorrow. Before I get done up for the play. I wanna pick your brain for some last-minute tips."

Ellie smiled wistfully—such a lunch would have been nice. "You don't need any tips," she said. "You're a natural actress. Just believe in yourself. I do."

"Thanks, that means a lot. But let's still do lunch. Please say yes."

"I'd love to Lucy, but—" She opened her mouth but nothing more came out. She took a deep breath and tried again. "But I'm leaving tomorrow. I'm really sorry I can't stay, but the show's given me no choice."

Silence. Then, eventually, Lucy said, "But you can't go yet. Flynn's on his way home. He'll be here tomorrow to see the play."

Ellie sagged back against the kitchen bench and shut her eyes. *Flynn*. Would hearing his name always give her goose bumps? Still, Lucy's words confirmed an awful truth. He'd been in contact with his family, and probably Rats and his friends, but he hadn't once called her. Her decision was justified. She had to face facts, however depressing they might be.

She pressed her lips tightly together to stop the rush of emotion. She was now glad this conversation wasn't taking place in person. "That's great," she said, failing to inject enthusiasm into her voice.

"Don't give up." Lucy sounded as distressed as Ellie felt. "You guys are meant to be together, anyone can see that. I'm sure Flynn will realize it sooner rather than later. But if you're not here, he'll think he's making the right choice."

However sweet Lucy's words, however tempting it was to trust in fate, the evidence was still to the contrary. "Has he said anything about me?" she asked.

Another long pause.

"Well?"

"No." Lucy's tone told Ellie she wished she could say differently. Her voice perked up. "Although he knows you haven't left and he's still coming back."

"That's just it, Lucy. He's coming back *in spite* of me, not *because* of me." She couldn't handle this conversation anymore. "I've really got to go and finish packing. I'm sorry I can't be at the play, but I know you'll be a hit. You all will. Thanks for being a great friend." Ellie refrained from asking Lucy to stay in touch. Although she adored the girl, she couldn't put herself or Flynn through that. This was goodbye.

"You, too, Ellie. I wish things could have been different."

"Yeah, me, too." She heard the dial tone and replaced the receiver. "Me, too."

Ellie allowed herself a moment to ponder this thought before she put on her metaphorical big girls' undies and went to finish off her bedroom. A woman on a mission, she flung open the wardrobe door, grabbed the old *Cosmo* and *Cleo* magazines and tossed them into a garbage bag. There. That wasn't hard. All she had to do was the same with the dress and she'd be done, ready to fall on the bed and pray she got better rest than she had the past few nights.

But it was never going to be that easy.

Eyes closed, she thrust a hand into the darkness. She sucked in her breath as she grabbed the dress—but one touch and she was a goner. She let the silky material fall between her fingers and drew the garment up against her cheeks. So soft. It smelled musty from its time in the dank corner of the wardrobe, but still felt good as new.

Knowing it could very well be her undoing, Ellie opened her eyes. She held the dress at arm's length. It didn't look new. It looked crumpled and worn and half of its beautiful pearl buttons were scattered around the room. Whoever bought the cottage would be finding them for years.

Oh, who was she kidding? She couldn't get rid of it. She might be a modern-day Miss Havisham, but now that she'd been reunited with it, she couldn't let it go. She shoved the crumpled mess of lost buttons and crushed satin into her suitcase, piling whatever else she could fit on top. Some of her day-to-day clothes had to be turfed to make way for it, but she didn't care.

Satisfied, she stood up and nodded. Good. She'd think of what the hell to do with it once she was back and settled in Sydney. Right now, it was almost midnight and, exhausted, Ellie fell quickly into a deep sleep.

WHEN JOYCE ARRIVED the next morning, Ellie was a wreck. It took all the energy she had to keep her emotions under control, handing over the keys to the Premier—she'd arranged to have it sent across the country later—and the keys to the house.

"The agent will call on Monday to arrange a time to take some photos." Her voice cracked on the last word. Selling Mat's house seemed more than wrong, but so did renting it, or worse, leaving it unlived in. She'd made the decision to cut her ties with Hope Junction and that meant saying goodbye to the quirky old cottage, as well. Still, no matter how many times she told herself it was only bricks and mortar, it didn't sit right.

"I'll give you a lift to the bus stop." Joyce tucked Mat's keys inside her jacket.

"No, thanks." Ellie shook her head. She'd managed her suitcase and rucksack on her own when she arrived, and she'd manage it now. Anything to avoid another

painful farewell. All it would take was a kind word or a
friendly hug to unlock those uncontrollable sobs again.
Apparently there wasn't a limit on tears. The more you
shed, the more your body made.

Joyce seemed to understand this. Instead of stepping
forward to embrace Ellie, she simply nodded and thrust
a small, white envelope into her hand. "My details," she
informed her. "Email, mobile, Facebook."

Ellie threw her head back and laughed. "I'll friend
you the moment I find some Wi-Fi."

"Good girl." Joyce's eyes were misty. Ellie wanted to
say something but the scratchiness in her throat stopped
her. Joyce went on, "Please, do keep in touch. I'll watch
you on the telly every night, but it won't be the same."

"I will." And she meant it. Joyce felt like her last connection to Matilda. "If you ever visit Sydney, I've a spare
bed with your name on it."

"You might regret saying that, girl."

"I won't."

Oh, to hell with it. If she cried, she cried. Ellie leaned
forward and kissed Joyce on the cheek. "Thanks for everything. This is definitely not goodbye."

Joyce smiled and Ellie turned away. Defeated, she
wrapped her hand around the suitcase handle and started
to walk.

FLYNN HAD WOKEN early in the scungy roadside motel—
earlier than the sun—and decided he might as well start
the last leg of his journey straightaway. The showers in
these places were more like leaking taps, and he couldn't
wait to stand under his own shower, then crawl into his
own bed for a good rest before the evening. Before the
play. Before seeing Ellie, if she was still around. He'd

skipped breakfast, thoughts already spiraling in his head about what he'd say to her.

It felt weird to be arriving back in town on a Saturday morning, two months after that Saturday of Ellie's return. A lot had happened in that time. Felt more like two years.

As he drove down the main street, past the craziness of Saturday-morning shopping, he waved at a few locals. He passed the Co-op, About Coffee Time, the post office, Hairlicious, and when he came out the other side of the tiny business district, he slowed for a stray dog to cross the road. As he did, he saw Ellie sitting at the Transwa bus stop, her suitcase at her feet. Even with her head in her hands, Flynn would know Ellie anywhere. Everything about her had imprinted itself on him.

Distracted, he almost hit the dog, swerving to avoid it at the last moment. His brakes squealed as he slammed his feet, taking a moment to regain control of the ute and moderate his breathing. He drove a little farther and pulled over. Far enough from the bus stop to think, far enough to turn around to take another look. It was definitely her. His chest pounded and his stomach made to heave the breakfast he hadn't had.

The whole time he'd been away, he hadn't come to any conclusions about Ellie. And she hadn't left, not yet anyway. He'd never been one to look for signs, but did this mean something? Did it mean he was becoming superstitious or did it mean his heart had been right, that it was trying to tell him the one thing he'd known all along? That he loved her.

His head throbbed. Rodger started fretting beside him, standing up, placing his paws on the headrest. He looked out the back window and pined. Pined because he saw a bus pulling away. Pulling away and taking the girl they both loved with it.

A rap on the window startled Flynn. Taking his eyes off the bus he saw his mom peering in. Lucy, standing beside her, waved. He wound the window down and stared up at the woman who had dried his tears when he'd broken bones, who'd cooked chocolate brownies whenever he felt down. And right now, he felt lower than ever.

"She's gone, Mom."

Looking close to tears herself, Karina opened the driver's door and knelt down in the red dirt. She leaned forward and pulled Flynn's aching head onto her shoulder. She rubbed his back the way she had when he was sick in bed as a child.

"I know it doesn't feel like it now," she said, "but I promise it'll get better soon. You've been so strong, I'm so proud of you. And I know, my darling son, that one day some extraspecial woman is going to walk into your life and make you forget all the pain Ellie put you through. Make you forget about her."

Flynn froze in his mom's arms. Her words drove home a truth he himself was only just realizing now. That he wouldn't find anyone else. He wouldn't because in ten long years, no other woman had come close to generating the feelings he had for Elenora Hughes. Even her not trusting him, not confiding in him and holding back the truth, it didn't make the love he felt for her lessen. If anything, he reflected, it just made the need stronger. He had to make her see sense, to prove his love, to show her that there wasn't anything he wouldn't do to make her happy and protect her from any more pain.

He pulled back from his mother's embrace. "I'm sorry, Mom, but you're wrong. Ellie's the woman for me. I hope in time you'll let go of the past and see that she's my future, *our* future."

"But, Flynn…" Karina looked perplexed as she pushed herself up and stepped back enough for Flynn to shut the door. Behind her, he could see his little sister smiling.

"I'll explain everything later," he said, starting the car. As he spun it around and back along the main street, she shouted something after him, but he didn't hear what it was. It didn't matter. Nothing mattered now, other than catching up with Ellie and righting his world. And as if he understood, Rodger perked up beside him. He moved his paws from the headrest to the dash, bouncing in his seat like an excited puppy.

"Settle down, boy," Flynn told the dog, "we'll catch that bus easy."

But as they approached the level crossing, the lights began to flash and the bells began to ring. Flynn cursed. He'd forgotten that the train also passed through Hope at this time of day. He resisted the urge to put his foot down, staying on the right side of the law but this side of the tracks.

Rodger barked nonstop as the train passed. It had to be the longest train Flynn had ever seen. Even as a boy, when he'd counted the carriages of every freight train he saw, he never came across one this long. Or this slow.

He glanced at the dashboard clock every few seconds, readying his foot on the accelerator for a speedy takeoff. Even if he broke the speed limit, meeting Ellie at the next town would be touch-and-go. He knew the bus didn't stop for long at Katanning.

"Fuck!" He ran a hand through his hair, still messy from the night before, and wished his ute had wings. Then a thought struck him.

CHAPTER THIRTY-SEVEN

A COUPLE OF people got on at Katanning, but Ellie breathed a sigh of relief when neither of them sat next to her. She leaned her head back against the window, hoping to get some kind of sleep on the journey to Perth. In the distance she could see dark clouds gathering as if to mirror her mood. She didn't want to think about what she was doing, what she was leaving behind. Again. Problem was, every time she shut her eyes, she saw Flynn speeding by the Hope Junction bus stop. She was stupid enough to imagine that he'd seen her and stopped his ute. She swore he'd actually stopped, her heart strumming wildly, dreaming up some stupid fairy-tale ending where he realized he loved her and turned around and came back and stopped her from leaving—all just in the nick of time. But he didn't, and he hadn't. Stupid all right. It could be her middle name.

She heard the doors of the bus close. The driver pulled out of the parking lot and started down the road, but had barely gone a hundred meters when he swung onto the shoulder and stopped again. At the sudden movement and the gasps from the other passengers, Ellie looked up.

The automatic doors peeled back. She expected a late arrival, but instead saw a smiley, redheaded policeman climb onto the bus, pausing to survey the passengers. He pushed his aviator-style sunglasses atop his head and smiled some more.

"Looking for a Ms. Elenora Hughes? Anyone here by that name?"

All the passengers, behind and in front, turned to look at Ellie. Fear washed over her. She'd been through a lot in her twenty-nine years, but never once had a policeman announced he was looking for her. She racked her brain for any misdemeanors she may have committed without realizing it, and slid a little lower in her seat, wishing she had her cap on. She'd definitely paid for her bus ticket—with a credit card, over the phone—and she'd barely driven Mat's car enough the past few days to speed or run a stop sign. As far as she could recall, she'd done nothing warranting police attention.

The policeman turned to the driver. "Know if there's anyone by that name on your bus, sir?"

Grumbling something under his breath, the driver consulted a printout. "Can only tell you if she booked by credit card."

Dammit. Before the driver could expose her, Ellie stood up. "Um, that's me." She waved her hand slightly. She could imagine what everyone was thinking. Hell, if it wasn't her standing there mystified, she'd be picturing wicked crimes, too. Sweat beaded at her brow as the policeman walked slowly up the aisle, his smile growing somewhat creepy. He stopped at her row and gestured to her rucksack.

"Is that all you have?"

Quaking inside, she held her head high and shook it. "I have a suitcase, in the storage compartment."

"I'll get it," said the driver, all too eager to off-load a possible criminal.

"No, wait!" Ellie found the courage to raise her voice. "What is this about? I need to get to Perth, I have a plane to catch."

The policeman held up his hands. "Not my problem, miss. I'm just following orders. If you'll please step this way."

Ellie thought about staging a protest, then took in the gaze of those around her. They wanted her to make a scene, wanted some juicy gossip to tell their friends. But this was already enough to make Dwayne blow a gasket. Gritting frustration between her teeth, Ellie swung her bag over her shoulder, not giving two hoots that she almost hit the officer in the process. She stormed down the aisle and off the bus, and sarcastically thanked the driver, who all but threw her suitcase at her feet. Could this day possibly get any worse?

Her shoulders sagged as she watched the bus pull out onto the seemingly endless country road. She turned to the policeman to demand some answers, but as she opened her mouth to speak, so did he.

"Well, miss, I'll be leaving now. Have a good day."

"What the hell?" She grabbed him by the arm, then, realizing what she was doing, promptly let go. He just looked at her, chuckling. "What do you mean, have a good day? Is this some kind of prank? Are you really even a policeman?" She tried to calm her panicked breathing. A thought struck her. "If you're a journalist, I'll have you for this." Her blood boiled, the bus now a mere speck in the distance. Anger and worry warred within her.

"No prank, miss, and I assure you I am *not* a journalist."

"Then what? A psycho sadist?" She dug her heels into the dirt, looking around for someone who could help her. The bus stop had little to recommend itself, but behind it was a pub—although both were far out of earshot. "Because quite frankly, Constable, I've had a pretty shitty week, and this is the pooey icing on the crap cake."

"I don't mean to make things worse." He shrugged and looked past her, back up the road. "In fact, I hope I'm about to make your day."

With those cryptic words, he swung his keys on his index finger like some sheriff in a Western, and swaggered off to the cop car parked at the edge of the road. And just like that he left her there, in what felt like the middle of nowhere, with nothing but a suitcase and a rucksack. Not to mention she had a plane to catch. If she missed her flight, there was no guarantee she'd get the next one. And if she didn't get back to Sydney soon, she was going to lose her job.

Fuck. She wrapped her arms around herself, trying to tame the shaking. Tears threatened once again. And, dammit, she hadn't packed any tissues.

Wondering if she'd stepped into some kind of alternate reality, Ellie glanced at the pub behind her, contemplating a glass of something potent. Something that would calm her nerves while she worked out what the hell to do next. She could call Joyce, perhaps. Or find out when the next bus was due. But it wasn't like this was city central; there were hours, sometimes days, between scheduled stops. And what cabdriver, she wondered, would come out here to pick her up? Looked like hitchhiking might be her only option. And the clouds were getting closer now, no less, threatening to spill out and strand her further. *Fuck!*

Ellie took hold of her suitcase once again, and began to drag it, and herself, toward the pub. As she made her way across the road, a ute appeared on the horizon. Pathetic maybe, but it sent her thoughts straight to Flynn. Perhaps he'd come to rescue her from Katanning's crazy cop.

Stupid. She let out a near-hysterical cackle. Every second farmer had a ute like Flynn's. She was truly losing the plot.

She plodded on slowly. The ute came to pass her and continued up the road, and soon was gone, just like the bus, the wind whipping around her.

She was fifty meters from the pub when she heard another car approaching, but she didn't bother looking up this time. As it got closer, the driver slowed and did a U-turn. Ellie's heart raced—she could almost hear her pulse thrashing in her ears. She wasn't sure if it was the fear of the driver being another kook, someone looking for a vulnerable female hitchhiker, or the excitement that perhaps it *was* Flynn. No matter how hard she tried, she just couldn't let that fantasy go.

The vehicle pulled up behind her. A little edgy, she carried on, the suitcase feeling heavier and heavier as she wheeled it hurriedly toward the pub.

"Ellie!"

At this shout, her heart slammed in her chest, shuddered and stopped. Her feet froze and the case clattered to the ground at her heels. That voice, she'd recognize anywhere. And it wasn't some loony. It was Flynn Quartermaine.

She wanted to turn around, wanted it more than anything, to face him—one look in his eyes and she'd know why he'd come—but her feet stayed stuck in place. What if he…? What if he didn't…?

The door of the ute slammed, echoing in the wind, and boots slapped the tar as he strode toward her. She waited, agonizing, unable to speak, unable to think.

"He really did it!" Flynn sounded astonished as he

passed her, and then came to a stop right in front of her—so close that he invaded her personal space. She inhaled his unique, delicious scent.

"Who?" she managed. "Did what?"

His lips curled into that famous irresistible smile. Her heart melted at the sight...one she'd feared she'd never see again. "Johno, an old friend of mine. He's the local cop in Katanning and..."

"Your *friend?* But that means..." Ellie's voice trailed off. She fidgeted with the hem of her top and held her breath.

Then warmth touched her icy fingers. She looked down to see that Flynn had taken her hands in his. He nodded. "I asked Johno to stop the bus and get you off. That bloody train held me up and I was scared I'd miss you and—"

"Hold on...rewind a sec." Her head hurt trying to comprehend it all. "What train?"

He laughed a little nervously. "It doesn't matter. I can tell you the whole story later, but right now, there's something more important than anything and you need to know it."

Her tummy fluttered as she looked into his eyes and waited. Hope lifted her heart, but she knew life could be cruel. It had been, so many times already, and so recently too, so she did what she could to suppress it, to manage her expectations. Because whatever she wanted—and desperately at that—she had to be prepared for the worst.

"I love you more than anything, Els. Always have, always will."

That put her over the edge. She felt herself choking up again, but this time she welcomed the tears. Happy tears, tears of absolute glee. Could she possibly let herself believe, if only for one second, that this was really true?

"But…?"

As if reading her mind, reading her doubts, he tightened his grip and brought her hands close to his face. He touched his lips against her knuckles and spoke again. "There are no buts. I've spent ten years trying to get over you, and sure, I could spend another ten trying, but I know it won't do an ounce of good. I'm a lost cause where you're concerned. Let's work out the whole Sydney–Hope Junction thing, because I don't want to live another day without you in my life. That is, if you still love me?"

She blinked, trying to keep the tears at bay at least until she'd said her bit. "Love you? Dammit, Flynn, I don't care about Sydney. I'm only going back because I don't want to ruin your life. I never stopped loving you. I was a stupid, foolish girl who didn't have enough faith. In you, in fate, in myself. But I believe now. I'm so sorry for—"

He pressed his lips against hers and she was silent. Their kiss, which started as a gentle touch, soon became heated and needy. At the same time, it began to rain, likewise starting light but quickly growing into a downpour. But neither of them cared, neither of them noticed as their mouths fed on each other, their tongues entwined in song once again. When Ellie's lips felt bruised and her jacket was sopping, Flynn finally pulled back.

"Don't say sorry to me. We've both made mistakes, done things we regret. I almost made another massive one by letting you go, but from now on, this is all in the past. Let's not waste the next ten years walking on eggshells. You and me, Els, we're real. That doesn't mean this is the end of any heartache and pain—there'll be more disappointment ahead, that's life. But from now on, we're in it together." He tipped her chin up to capture her complete attention. "Are you with me?"

"Yes, Flynn, 100 percent."

FLYNN COULDN'T STOP beaming on the drive back to Hope Junction. He didn't care. He felt as if he'd just won Lotto. He was so stoked he could streak across the oval again. Not bad for the last baby born in Hope Hospital.

Rodger happily migrated to the back tray, but only after taking a good five minutes to lick Ellie all over and revel in the glory as she hugged and kissed him back. This time, however, Flynn wasn't jealous of the dog. He knew he'd get plenty of Ellie's attention as soon as today was over, after the play. In fact, if he played his cards right, he might be able to get a bit of that attention *before* the play, too.

As if reading his mind, Ellie leaned across and whispered into his ear, squeezing his hand suggestively. "Your place or mine?"

"Mine," he replied, taking care not to swerve off the road at the thought. "My bed's bigger. And for everything I've got planned, we'll need all the space we can get."

When they got back to Black Stump, Flynn and Ellie spent the rest of the day in bed. They only came up for air to eat and drink, and once to feed Rodger, who'd spent the afternoon whining, unable to understand why he was suddenly on the wrong side of Flynn's bedroom door.

When six o'clock rolled around, Ellie suggested they migrate to the bathroom and get ready for the evening. Flynn groaned. She punched him playfully in the arm and glared at him. "Yes. Get up. Lucy will be devastated if you're not there. And I want to see the fruits of our labors."

"When you put it like that…" Flynn rolled out of bed and followed Ellie down the hallway, his eyes never leaving the hem of his shirt, which Ellie was wearing. *Only* his shirt.

It hit him then that if he joined her in the shower, they'd never make it to the play. He paused at the bathroom door. "There are fresh towels in the cupboard under the sink. I'll make some coffee and have a cold shower after you."

Ellie grinned and raised her eyebrows.

"Hurry," he said, turning away before he lost all willpower. He sighed happily as he entered the kitchen, pulling two travel mugs out of the cupboard and making their drinks for the drive into town. It wasn't that either of them really needed the coffee—the buzz of getting back together, the buzz of knowing this time it was for good, was more than enough—but he needed something to keep himself occupied, somewhere to funnel his energy. Having Ellie back with him—in his house, in his bed, in his shower—was unreal. And then when he'd asked her if she would…

"It's all yours," she called, breaking his trance.

He jumped in the shower, and by the time he emerged, Ellie was on the couch. Rodger's head was in her lap as she rubbed his ears just the way he liked it.

"Ready?" he asked, unable to stifle a grin at the sight.

"Sure am." Ellie kissed Rodger on the head and then slipped out from under him.

Flynn whistled to Rodger. "Outside, boy, we'll be back in a few hours."

"You can't leave him outside!" Ellie sounded outraged. "It's freezing."

"But…" Rodger looked up at him with pleading eyes.

"Consider yourself lucky, mate. It's two against one now, and it looks like you're coming out in front."

They made sure Rodger's water bowl was full and then stepped out into the early-evening air, ready to show the town they were an item again.

ELLIE FELT A little guilty when she entered the Memorial Hall—with Flynn at her side, his hand possessively holding hers—and immediately saw Whitney and Lauren in the foyer. Flynn was all hers again, but she couldn't blame Lauren for crushing on him—the man was gorgeous inside and out. Ellie was coming back to town, though, planning to get involved in the community, so she hoped Lauren and Whitney might one day soften toward her. With Rats and Flynn as best mates, they'd be seeing a fair bit of each other. Their kids would no doubt play together, they'd serve on school committees together, they'd…

Good God, her imagination was getting ahead of her. But after today's events, it was hard not to get carried away. For the first time in a long time, the future looked rosy.

Flynn stopped at the ticket desk to pay for their seats. Joyce grinned at the sight before her, winked at Ellie and waved them on. Flynn looked confused, money half in and half out of his wallet.

"Don't be ridiculous," Joyce said. "You two have done so much to get this happening, just sit back and enjoy."

"Thanks." Flynn slipped his wallet in his back pocket and Ellie fought the urge to slip her hand in, too, to walk as they'd done in high school, with her nestled under his shoulder, not a care in the world. Instead, she gave his hand a squeeze.

He smiled back and her heart melted for what seemed

like the hundredth time that day. She felt like a bundle of clichés: walking on air, somewhere near cloud nine, a dream come true.

"I'm going to slip backstage and wish everyone luck." She went to remove her hand but Flynn clung on tight.

"I'll come with you."

Not wanting to barge in on anyone semidressed, Ellie knocked on the dressing-room door and waited. The door opened and Mrs. Ellery poked her head through a tiny gap.

"Oh, it's you two," she said, suppressing a smirk. "Come on in."

The actors all looked up as they entered, and Ellie couldn't help but notice their eyes boggle as they realized it was her *and* Flynn. Everyone had no doubt heard about her departure—thank you, grapevine—but no one would have known about her rescue by a knight in a dusty, once-white ute. Luckily they all seemed ecstatic to have her back.

Lucy spoke up first. "Oh. My. God!" She beamed at Flynn and Ellie's joined hands and then met their eyes. "Is this what I think it is?"

"Sure is, little sis." Flynn let go of Ellie's hand long enough to hug Lucy. "Break a leg."

Ellie gave her a quick hug, too. "You're going to be awesome."

"Thanks." Lucy looked to be tearing up. Ellie knew all too well the nerves that came before a production and she didn't want to overwhelm Lucy before her big debut.

"We better go and get our seats. We'll see you after it's finished, okay?"

Lucy nodded.

When Flynn and Ellie made their way back into the auditorium, the seats were filling up fast. It looked like the whole town had turned out, and there was still to-morrow's matinee, and another two shows after that. They scanned the rows for two seats next to each other. They'd almost given up hope when a hand shot up and waved at them.

"It's Mom," said Flynn, sounding relaxed. Which was strange, because Karina waving them over had the opposite effect on Ellie.

She tightened her grip on Flynn's hand, halting him. "I don't know if I can face her yet. What's she going to say?"

The last few conversations with Karina had been like an emotional roller coaster. One minute she'd been loving and ready to welcome Ellie into the family, the next she was warning her off. Ellie could only imagine what Karina would say when Flynn informed her what he'd asked this afternoon.

If she'd marry him. And that she'd said yes. Unconditionally.

This time the wedding would be in Bali, with close family and friends. "You won't be able to escape in another country," Flynn had joked. "I'll be holding on to your passport."

And Ellie never wanted to escape Flynn again. But she thought it would have been safer to have a wedding band on her finger before facing Karina.

"Don't be daft." Flynn tugged at Ellie's hand. "Mom knows I went after you. She knows my heart, and she knows I know it, too. She only wants what's best for both of us. She loves you almost as much as I do, Ellie, she's just scared."

Knowing his words to be the truth, Ellie took a deep breath and ventured forward.

"Evening, Ellie." Karina's voice was neither cold nor

warm as she took her handbag off the seat. Ellie could have shot Flynn when he gestured that she sit first, next to his mother, but her imagination conjured up far worse things than what actually happened: Karina was kind and polite the whole night. Ellie knew she had a long way to go before she regained the woman's trust, but she hoped in time Karina would see that Ellie loved her son more than anything.

Halfway through the performance, Ellie began to relax.

"They're doing so well," she whispered to Flynn as the cast launched into their final scene.

"All thanks to you," Flynn replied.

She shook her head. "They did the hard work themselves."

Silence reigned for a moment, before Flynn leaned close and asked, "Do you wish you were up there?"

She thought for a second, then shook her head. She could say with all honesty, "No. I love it, but I haven't missed acting as much as I thought I would. Teaching and helping produce gave me a buzz. It's something I think I'd like to get into."

"Really?"

Ellie nodded. "Do you think there's room for a drama school in Hope Junction?"

"Are you kidding?" Flynn motioned to the stage, grinning. "Now this lot have the bug, there'll be no stopping them. You'll be run off your feet."

"Good," Ellie said. "I like being busy."

They both turned their attention back to the stage for the finale. Lucy shone as she sang a bittersweet number about unrequited love, while the rest of the cast gathered around her. Ellie thought how perfect the night had been, bar one thing. Mat wasn't here to see her beloved theatrical society come back to life, or to know that she and Flynn were finally going to make a go of happily-ever-after. A tear slipped down her cheek, and she quickly swiped it with the back of her hand, not wanting to divert attention from the action onstage.

The crowd stood and applause erupted as the play came to a close. Ellie breathed a sigh of relief, happy that no one would be looking at her. But, of course, she was wrong. As she tried to join in the clapping, Flynn's arm slipped around her back and drew her into his side. He kissed her cheek.

"She'll be looking down from above, babe," he said. "She'll never leave us."

Ellie leaned into him. Her luck had well and truly changed. This man was a rock and he was all hers. At last.

As Lucy kissed the male lead in the saucy conclusion, making the audience whistle and, no doubt, making Sam's blood boil, Ellie looked up into Flynn's beautiful, dependable eyes and met his lips in the magical kiss that would start it all....

* * * * *

New York Times bestselling author

SUSAN MALLERY

returns with a classic story of destiny, desire and a little holiday magic!

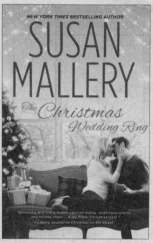

In her youth, Molly Anderson couldn't help crushing on gorgeous bad boy Dylan Black—even though he only had eyes for her older sister. When things didn't work out between them, he said goodbye to Molly as well, vowing they'd have a great adventure when she grew up. Years later, dumped by her fiancé just before Christmas, she's finally ready to take Dylan up on his promise.

A guarded Dylan always had a weakness for Molly, and when she waltzes back into his life—grown-up and gorgeous—he's stunned. So why not whisk her away for some no-strings-attached fun?

Laughter-filled days and late-night kisses are changing Molly's life, for good. The only gift she truly wants now is Dylan's love, but when he discovers the secret she's been keeping, she may lose him again…this time forever.

Available now wherever books are sold!

Be sure to connect with us at:

Harlequin.com/Newsletters

Facebook.com/HarlequinBooks

Twitter.com/HarlequinBooks

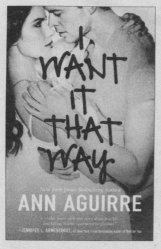

REQUEST YOUR FREE BOOKS!

2 FREE NOVELS
FROM THE ROMANCE COLLECTION
PLUS 2 FREE GIFTS!

YES! Please send me 2 FREE novels from the Romance Collection and my 2 FREE gifts (gifts are worth about $10). After receiving them, if I don't wish to receive any more books, I can return the shipping statement marked "cancel." If I don't cancel, I will receive 4 brand-new novels every month and be billed just $6.24 per book in the U.S. or $6.74 per book in Canada. That's a savings of at least 22% off the cover price. It's quite a bargain! Shipping and handling is just 50¢ per book in the U.S. and 75¢ per book in Canada.* I understand that accepting the 2 free books and gifts places me under no obligation to buy anything. I can always return a shipment and cancel at any time. Even if I never buy another book, the two free books and gifts are mine to keep forever.

194/394 MDN F4XY

Name _____ (PLEASE PRINT) _____

Address _____ Apt. # _____

City _____ State/Prov. _____ Zip/Postal Code _____

Signature (if under 18, a parent or guardian must sign) _____

Mail to the Harlequin® Reader Service:
IN U.S.A.: P.O. Box 1867, Buffalo, NY 14240-1867
IN CANADA: P.O. Box 609, Fort Erie, Ontario L2A 5X3

Want to try two free books from another line?
Call 1-800-873-8635 or visit www.ReaderService.com.

* Terms and prices subject to change without notice. Prices do not include applicable taxes. Sales tax applicable in N.Y. Canadian residents will be charged applicable taxes. Offer not valid in Quebec. This offer is limited to one order per household. Not valid for current subscribers to the Romance Collection or the Romance/Suspense Collection. All orders subject to credit approval. Credit or debit balances in a customer's account(s) may be offset by any other outstanding balance owed by or to the customer. Please allow 4 to 6 weeks for delivery. Offer available while quantities last.

Your Privacy—The Harlequin® Reader Service is committed to protecting your privacy. Our Privacy Policy is available online at www.ReaderService.com or upon request from the Harlequin Reader Service.

We make a portion of our mailing list available to reputable third parties that offer products we believe may interest you. If you prefer that we not exchange your name with third parties, or if you wish to clarify or modify your communication preferences, please visit us at www.ReaderService.com/consumerchoice or write to us at Harlequin Reader Service Preference Service, P.O. Box 9062, Buffalo, NY 14269. Include your complete name and address.

ROM13R

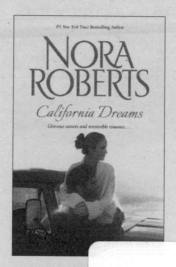